THE MOUNTAINS, THE SEA,
AND THE SPACES IN BETWEEN

SM HYUN

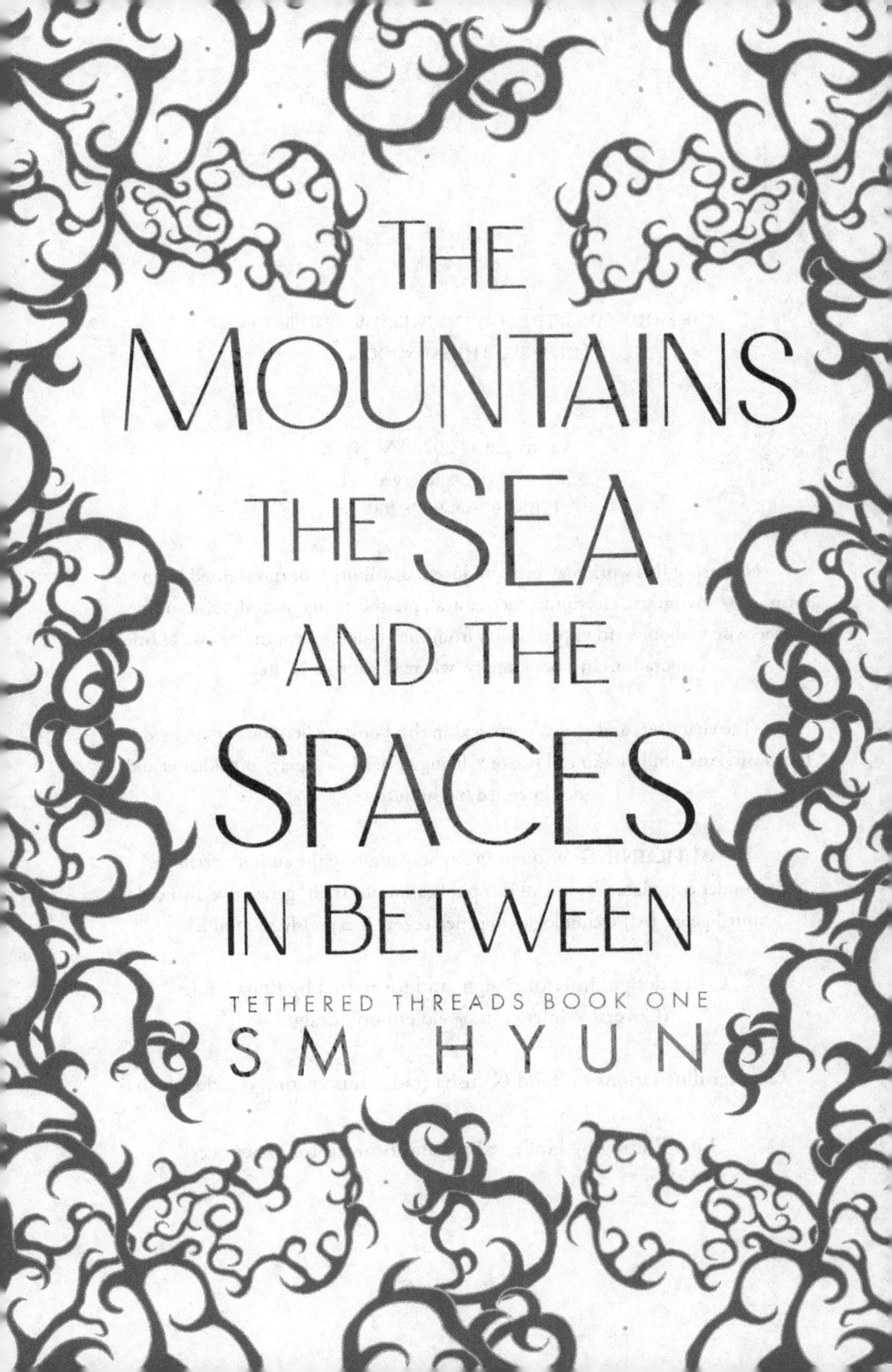

THE MOUNTAINS THE SEA AND THE SPACES IN BETWEEN

TETHERED THREADS BOOK ONE

SM HYUN

THE MOUNTAINS, THE SEA, AND THE SPACES IN BETWEEN
TETHERED THREADS BOOK 1

Cover design, interior design, and formatted by Rena Violet (Coversbyviolet.com, @violet.book.design)

Chapter illustrations by Tadd Galusha (taddgalusha.com, @taddgalusha)

Line Editing by Holly at Bird and Bear Editorial Services

To my husband, the greatest cheerleader of them all.
(Man was convinced this book would be an international bestseller
before he even started reading it.)
May this kind of love find all of you.

HOW THE JELLYFISH
LOST ITS BONES

Once upon a time,
The jellyfish had bones and a shell.

In a land far away from you,
Far from the craggy peaks of the mountaintops,
Beneath the roiling waves of the seas,
There lived a king.
The king had a beautiful daughter, whom he loved very much.

But the princess was sick.
"You must go above the seas and trap a creature,"
Said his advisors.
"To heal your daughter, you require its liver."

So the sea king sent forth his loyal servant, a fish.
The fish went up above the seas and onto the lands,
In search of this strange creature, the monkey.
And a monkey it found! Sitting upon a tree.

"Who are you?" the monkey called.
"What do you want?"
The fish replied, "I have swum the world.
I have seen the finest lands with the most beautiful trees and fruits."

"I want to go!" the monkey exclaimed.
The fish smiled,
And they began to swim.

But the monkey became afraid the further they went,
And soon he changed his mind.
"I must bring you to my king," said the fish.

"Only a monkey's liver can cure my princess."

The sly monkey thought quickly,
"Oh! I wish you had told me.
You see, I keep my liver safe in a jar beneath a tree.
We must go back to get it."

And so, they turned around and swam back to land.
The monkey jumped to his tree and pretended to look around.
"Someone must have stolen it; you must tell the king I am searching for it."

The fish waited for several days,
Until it dawned on the fish that the monkey had escaped,
Deep into the jungle where it could not follow.

The fish returned to the king without the monkey's liver.
The king, enraged, ordered his servant punished.
The fish was beaten until it had no bones and it became jellylike,
And became known as jellyfish forevermore.

CONTENT WARNINGS

- CANNIBALISM

- CREATURES THAT ARE ARACHNID IN NATURE

- TRAUMATIC BIRTH

- CHILD ABUSE AND NEGLECT

- MATTERS RELATING TO MENTAL HEALTH INCLUDING, BUT NOT LIMITED TO:
    DEPRESSION
    PTSD
    SUICIDALITY

PROLOGUE

This would be his final hunt.

The fine hairs on the nape of the male's neck lifted and he felt a pit forming deep in his core as he stood before the sea *kami*. He quelled the desire to shift his weight and remained still, acutely aware of who he stood before.

"My Thread is alive."

The male straightened slightly at this news. Dread leeched into every fiber of his being and he resisted the urge to step back. The throne room was cavernous and empty of life, save for himself and the *kami*. There was nothing that would hide the betrayal of his movement. Nothing that would muffle the sound of a single footfall.

The sea undulated gently against the wards that encapsulated the palace, casting an eerie glow against the walls of opalescent corals. Ghostly shadows of the *habu kurage* danced around them. A silent threat. The deadly viper jellyfish acted as the king's servants and were once a rare sighting in the kingdom. Now the realm was rife with them.

A massive Ulleungdo hemlock tree grew in the center of the expanse, drawing one's eye to the focal piece. It hadn't been there a century past, or so the stories were whispered among those who had been alive in more peaceful times. The hemlock had been grown as a monument to those lost on the night of *Hyakki Yagyō*. The night that marked a before and after of better times long since passed.

"My Thread has been wandering above the waters. I have heard rumors of her consorting with the worst of the *yōkai*. Cavorting even." Power emanating from the *kami* of the seas nearly brought the male to his knees, his leg beginning to jig beneath his silk *hakama* as the sea dragon's eye twitched.

As a child, it had been the male's belief that rulers were composed and stoic.

He was wiser now.

The water began to violently eddy above them as the king's agitation grew, the *habu kurage* swirling in distress, incapable of battling the *kami's* unconscious display of magic. Displays which were becoming more commonplace. Needles from the tree's branches swirled around the male before drifting to carpet the ground.

The male focused his attention on the immense wall behind the *kami* to stymie the heady sense of vertigo brought on by the power. Rows upon rows of carapaces and *saras,* empty bowls which no longer carried life-granting water, covered every spare inch of the space. A testament to two species now gone from the world. Proof of what happened when the *kami* felt he had been betrayed. The male always felt unsettled by the pageantry of the *saras* with their lack of water, as if their continued existence in such a manner was a worse crime against nature than their trophy-like existence.

"This cannot continue," the sea dragon's voice boomed, bringing the male back to the present danger in the room. "She is undermining my rule. She brings imbalance to this place—a sickness to the land. The corals, the schools of fish, the forests of kelp. All are dying. The famines are becoming dire. Civil unrest has been erupting among my people. We are on the verge of a war we cannot afford after we barely avoided one previously."

The *kami* continued to speak, as if unaware anyone else was in the room with him. "I grieved her death after the palace was attacked and my daughters brutally killed. And now I find that she has been alive all this time."

The sea dragon lost his contemplativeness abruptly, his focus narrowing in on the male. The male went rigid, apprehension skittering up his spine. To have the sole focus of the *kami* was no boon. In the past few years especially, the attention of the dragon king was likened to a portent of tempestuous times to come.

"I require my Red Thread to be returned to Ryūgū-jō by any means necessary. This has gone on long enough and she can avoid the palace no longer. This will be your sole duty until it has been accomplished, Sugiyama."

Searing flames blazed against Sugiyama's flesh as the power behind Ryūjin's command was branded into him. Only the slightest tension in his jaw betrayed the amount of pain he endured. Brilliant white flames flared briefly from the bands encircling his forearms. Others told tales of a time when they had free will. Those times had long since passed and had never been an experience he had known. The newly inflamed tattoo of Ryūjin's compulsion was further evidence of that absence.

Only the scorching pain that blazed along his left side prevented him from betraying his shock over what the sea *kami* had just revealed to him. He would be hunting a Thread. A Red Thread connecting two fated souls. The realization filled him with apprehension.

"*Hai.*" The male bowed deeply, accepting what he could not change. "It will be done."

CHAPTER ONE

Ever been woo-wooed at by the saddest pair of doe-brown eyes belonging to the world's soggiest Alaskan malamute? No?

Well, let me enlighten you. Staying strong is a bitch. The power of sad puppy eyes from a malamute is wicked. The power of sad puppy eyes from a drenched, *wooly* malamute is next-level.

"You don't get the hedgehog, Woodrow," I informed the soaked behemoth while trying to swipe water out of my eyes. "Hedgehog time only happens when you find our missing person, not when we lose the scent."

Why did that sound so inappropriate?

Woody grumbled at me, then casually sashayed up the trail a few feet.

I side-eyed my K9. He was up to something. There was far too much sass in those hips. I hadn't given the command to start our search again, so he wasn't quartering for the scent trail yet.

He glanced over his shoulder to see if I was watching. Of course I was. I didn't dare look away. It was like taking your eyes off a toddler—too much chaos could ensue in mere moments. I crossed my arms and glared at him.

"We have a job, Woody. A very important one. A woman is missing. We've been in these woods for four-and-a-half days now. We don't have time for this."

That was technically a lie. I was waiting for my partner to return from shitting in the woods. Still watching my wayward K9 child, I untucked a

7

hand from my crossed arms to snag the radio from my hi-vis jacket and called in to the command post.

"Come in, Command Post. This is Camellia Kimoto."

"Go ahead, Cam. This is Danly."

"We lost the scent again. You want us to continue?"

There was a long pause during which I entertained myself with visions of our illustrious sheriff engaging in some highly invective language.

"Negative. Head on back."

"Copy that."

I cupped my hands over my mouth and hollered. "Lala! We're being called back to staging. Hurry up already."

A groan bounced through the trees. "Shut up and let me concentrate, woman. You try taking a crap in the woods in a torrential downpour. Freaking IBS. My quads are killing me."

I snickered and picked my way over to a moss-covered log, easing my aching body onto it, opting to take a short break before heading back to the staging area. This had been one of the more frustrating deployments I had been on in several years and I wanted to stop and think about the barriers that had been thrown up in our path.

Before I had a chance, a splash hit my face and I found Woody wriggling with joy through a slushy mud puddle. The only parts of him that remained his original color were his deceptively innocent eyes. Even with my ability to see in the darkness of night, he was difficult to make out with the way he now blended into his surroundings.

"You knew that was it for us as soon as you lost the scent," I accused.

He woo-wooed sassily back at me and wriggled onto his back, sliding through the mud with the glee of a five-year-old child that just discovered his first worm.

For the love of all things unholy. I closed my eyes and tilted my face up into the sky faucet, waiting for the world to drown my sorrows away. Or me. The sky faucet could just drown me instead.

Nope. Still alive. Damn.

A mass hysteria of hissing and growling punctured through the sound of pouring rain. One of the saddlebags connected to Woody's harness began to jump wildly, as though possessed by an incensed poltergeist. Almost an accurate description of what he had been hauling around with him on this deployment.

My put-upon sigh immediately evolved into an evil grin.

"You know what. I'm not even mad anymore. You deserve what's coming to you."

A long, thick tail emerged from the pouch before whipping back inside, followed by a small foot, then a white, whiskered snout. That foot with its little opposable hallux viciously latched onto some fur and hauled ass out of its once cozy, now muddy, abode.

Woody scrambled to his feet with a desperate look of regret and immediately backed out of the mud, looking like a swamp monster from a *B*-movie creature feature.

"Nope. Not getting you out of this one, buddy. This is what we call natural consequences."

Because now sitting on Woodrow's head was a tiny, pissed-off demon of a Virginia opossum. Prehensile tail wrapped around his neck for balance as she daintily inspected her one remaining front paw. The malamute was going cross-eyed while assessing the danger of having the devil betwixt his ears, as he well should.

The blast of dry air that whipped through the downpour caused me to stumble, although I had been expecting it. A high-pitched whine emitted from Woody as he braced himself—the gale momentarily creating an arid atmosphere around us. Complete with the feeling of being hit in the face with grit. I was on the outskirts and missed most of the blow. Woodrow, on the other hand, wasn't so fortunate. The malamute was now a massive dirty cotton ball, instead of a wet, muddy mop.

Pea Blossom gave a haughty sniff and a click of admonishment before turning to walk down the length of Woody's back and slither down his haunches. The orange glow that had accompanied the blast of *ki* she had just emitted faded while she lumbered over to me. I bent to pick her up, a smile on my face for the matriarch of the team. Woody sat in the rain that had resumed falling, ears drooped, now looking even more pitiful. I hardened my heart. He was a diva who knew how to milk drama for every drop of attention possible.

"Put the child in his place, did you now?" I asked as I dried her off and zipped her into my coat.

She gave a mild hiss in agreement, then burrowed down in my clothing. In reality, Pea had probably done more to train my K9s than I ever had.

"Do you normally converse with your K9s as if they're toddlers?"

I whipped around, unused to the sensation of being caught off guard. The dry voice had appeared from behind me. The stranger was decked out in midnight blue rain gear, which at least indicated they had common sense. However, it also meant I had no real ability to gauge his traits beyond a deep masculine voice with a slight accent I couldn't place. He looked to be somewhere over six feet in boots, but I couldn't even accurately measure that due to the large hood, which hid most of his facial features.

He had also arrived silently.

For a human assigned to this area, not being able to hear the stranger over this rainstorm might not seem unusual. I wasn't one of those though.

Nor was he wearing any gear declaring him with Search and Rescue.

"I take it you don't have dogs," I said pleasantly, breathing deep into myself, and taking the chance to close my eyes for a touch longer than a normal blink. A warm sense of magic, followed by a faint tinge of nausea and light-headedness washed over me.

When I opened my eyes again, I had a grasp of the molecules that made up his body. I could decide for myself how they conducted themselves. Whether they continued to play nicely, as they were now. Or perhaps... became more excited.

I gazed at the stranger steadily. In the moments I had taken to pull up my power, Woodrow had placed his body in front of mine, his mantle ruffled. He wasn't quite growling, but a low rumble rolled out of his throat in warning.

"Can't say that I ever have."

That was an instant demerit in my book. How could you trust a male who had never owned a dog? Actually, scratch that. I knew I couldn't trust this one. He snuck up on women who were alone in the forest and judged them when they talked to dogs.

Definitely a serial killer.

"That's a crying shame for you. There is nothing in this world more loyal than a dog. You clearly haven't learned their language with your vast experience." I couldn't tell because of the hood, but I got the distinct impression an eyebrow was arched at me.

"Are you trying to tell me your K9s talk back?"

"Are you, someone who has never owned a dog, attempting to tell me they don't?"

Woody barked sharply in response to my statement.

"Case in point." I waved to my stalwart guardian in front of me.

The male inclined his head, allowing me the point and took a step forward.

Woodrow began to growl as I backed up.

"Yeah, that's going to be a hard no. You can stay right there, and I'll stay right here while you introduce yourself and tell me why you're creeping on women in the woods."

"Such little trust, Ms. Kimoto."

My mouth dropped at the absolute audacity of this stranger. When I had control over my words again, I pointed at him.

"I'm going to break this into one- to two-syllable words so you can understand. You, man. Me, woman. Alone. Woods." I made jazz hands. "Rape! Murder! *Baaaad.*"

Males.. My hands fell back down to my sides. "No shit, there's little trust. It's the twenty-first century. Women listen to true crime podcasts and documentaries these days. I work Search and Rescue; I see and hear some horrific stuff on the regular. How the fuck do you know my name anyway?"

He motioned to my jacket where my name was plastered. I had forgotten Lala had insisted on having our names embroidered on the new jackets, tired of everyone thinking we were the same person even though we looked nothing alike. Unfortunately, the name of my agency was also splashed across the back. Which had been facing him before he had startled me. Which meant he had all the means needed to track me down.

Before I could think of a retort, Woody let out a sudden howl and dropped to the ground, ears pricked forward, despite the situation. The thought of taking my eyes off of the stranger, even for a moment, was antithetical to my entire being, but I tore my eyes away from him anyway.

A flash in the woods, off in the distance where Woody was facing, caught my eye. A direction in which Lala and I had already covered extensively with no success.

"Lala!" I whisper-shouted. Stranger be damned, this was the closest we had come in *days*. I began making my way toward the flash of color I had seen. I could hear Lala scrambling in the forest behind me. She wouldn't have a problem catching up; I wasn't worried. She knew this land as well as I did. Besides which, she wasn't fully human after all.

As I approached, the color shifted a bit. I squinted, having difficulty bringing it into focus. What appeared to be an exhausted woman's face leaned against a tree. Scratches marred her cheek and chin, caressed her throat and her arm. But not the type of scratches you would expect from a woman fighting her way through the wilderness. Her jacket, what I could see of it, was torn as if ripped away by claws. Something about the injuries marking her body nudged a faded memory, one just out of reach. Slight imprints were barely visible on her face. As if a hand was covering her mouth from behind, another tipping her chin, and a third cupping a cheek. Hands of different sizes. More importantly, of different species, based on the clawlike indents at her cheek.

"Ma'am," I called out softly, holding my palms up in the universal sign that you meant no harm. "My name is Camellia. This here might look like a monster, but I promise he really is a gentle giant of a dog named Woody." I slowly laid a palm down on Woody's muddy head. "We are with Search and Rescue. May we approach?"

The woman hesitated. Indecisiveness was written clear across her body and her movements. After a few moments she struggled to straighten against the incorporeal grip and attempted to take a step toward me, a hand holding what appeared to be a journal tight to her chest.

That is, until her eyes met something over my shoulder and widened with fright. The woman took off like a doe in the forest. Injuries and exhaustion forgotten. Adrenaline bestowing its favor upon her.

"Shit!" I whipped around to find the stranger had appeared behind me. I didn't have time for his agenda. I didn't know how or why he was following me. All I knew was that he had scared off the only possibility we had been combing this mountain for over the past week.

"Stay the fuck here!" I snarled before Woody and I took off, trudging through the patches of snow and ice as fast as we could. At the very least, the trail was easy to follow this time, the trampled shrubbery a clear path. Pea hissed from inside my jacket, displeased about the bumpy ride, and scrambled up to wrap herself around my neck for a more secure position.

I managed to catch sight of the woman again.

Just in time to see her frantically try to slow herself down.

Just in time to see her go over the edge of a cliff.

I swore viciously and scrambled to the edge where I saw her hit the cliffside before continuing her descent. The fog enveloped her entire body. Then a flare of light blinded me before her body hit the ground.

I blinked several times. And stared.

There was no body below. Our missing person had disappeared yet again.

Woodrow sat by my side and let out a small, mournful howl. Pea climbed down my body and patted him on the paw before crawling back into his muddy harness, providing him with a comforting weight against the loss of his missing person.

A colorful litany of Japanese swearing next to me startled me into slipping on the icy rock, made dangerously slick from the snow and rain. The strong hand on my arm prevented me from also going over the edge.

"Where in Yomi do you keep *coming from*? And why won't you leave me alone?"

"Had I left you alone, you would have gone over the edge."

"Had you left me alone, I wouldn't have been startled into slipping in the first place," I countered. The fall wouldn't have killed me anyway.

I could hear the crunch of forest litter under boots hurrying our way beneath the sound of pounding rain.

He appeared to have heard it too, which was interesting, considering my senses were far from human.

"Dammit, Cam. I might be fast, but can you slow it down a touch to let a girl catch up?" came a voice, followed by a wheeze.

"I'll find you later to finish our riveting discussion, Ms. Kimoto." I was able to make out a small smile that broke out over his face beneath the rain hood. "I look forward to it."

And on that ominous note, he melted back into the woods. Again, without a sound. The grasp I had on his molecular makeup melted away as if I had never had it in the first place.

"Fucking Abstruse," I muttered under my breath, blinking again and releasing the magic I had gathered through my body. Pea popped her head through the pouch of Woody's muddy harness, eyeing the fading trail of his magic, and hissed.

A few moments later, Lala and her hot-pink jacket popped into view, her German shepherd mix by her side. She opened her mouth to say something, saw Woody and me, and whatever words she had fell right out of her gaping mouth unsaid. She pointed at my swamp monster, then me repeatedly, as she propped her night vision goggles on the top of her head.

"I know."

"What. Happened?"

"He's an asshole. You should be able to relate; you named your amazing, loveable cinnamon roll of a dog, *Phallus.*"

Said K9 named for a dick wagged his tail at the sound of his name.

She waved me off. "Why do I sense magic? Was it from the creep I heard you talking to in the woods?"

Lala was a Perigean, which accounted for her heightened senses, though the ability to see in the dark wasn't one of them. Quotidians, affectionately called Quotes, were your ordinary, run-of-the-mill humans who didn't possess any magic or extrasensory skills. As opposed to me, an Abstruse, or Abbie. We included *yōkai,* cryptids, fae, the celestial, and on the list went.

Everyone else fell into the category of Peris. Lala likely had some ancestral Abbies who got busy with some Quotes, but they were so far back that any magic in her lineage was latent. That is, until the Indochina refugee crisis. The trauma her mother underwent while pregnant with her and escaping Laos in the 1970s with her family began to flip that epigenetic switch in Lala. Living in refugee camps, then attempting to assimilate in the United States in the late 1980s firmly turned that switch from *off* to *on.* No one knew why trauma would turn on magic for some but not other Quotes; epigenetics was fun like that. However, that switch could only flip when the initial trauma occurred in the fetal stage. Wars could be traced in history by looking at booms of Perigean emergences. Like the perigean tides, Peris were caught between Quotes and Abbies, not quite as mundane as the first, but not as strong as the second.

"You know how we kept feeling like someone was watching us over the past few days?" I asked.

She wrinkled her nose. "Yeah, but when don't we have that feeling when we have a SAR in the woods? There are so many Abbies who live out here and they're always curious."

She had a point, which is why we had brushed it off and continued on our way. "Except this time, it was this creepy Abbie dude in the woods. Snuck up on me, didn't make a single sound. None of us caught it until he spoke." I motioned to myself, Pea, and Woody.

"Seriously? He snuck up on the most vicious creature in this region?" She frowned.

Woody and I knew better than to think she was referring to us. Pea just preened at the compliment.

"Then just vanished in the woods. And I don't mean walked away and I couldn't see him because a large tree obscured him. He literally *disappeared* from sight."

"Well, that doesn't narrow down the possibilities by much."

I sighed. No, it didn't. There were too many options from shape-shifting and sorcery to potions that could be purchased. There was no point dwelling on it. I turned my attention back to the search at hand, gesturing back to the area we had been working.

"I think we saw her. I think we almost had her."

Lala gawped.

"But we…all over…*hours,* Cam. We spent hours in this area and nothing."

I nodded grimly. "She just appeared out of nowhere. And disappeared. Literally. Into thin air."

While we had a Point Last Seen for our missing subject, her scent kept vanishing for inexplicable reasons then coming back up on an entirely new section of the small mountainside, miles away from the last known position, with no scent trail between the two points. So we had no base to work from. As a result, we had been deployed in several pairs to do a hasty search across the mountainside over the past several days. While Lala and I had been assigned to the actual scent trail, several other teams were working other areas of the mountain in the event we lost this scent, given how the search had gone so far.

However, the difference between the stranger's disappearing act and our missing person's was that he had an obvious magical presence. She, for all rhyme and reason, was a Quote.

Lala groaned. "Are we ever going to catch a break on this one?"

"Pretty sure that was just it. And not much of one at that. C'mon. Let's start hiking back. Scott and Aidan are back at the staging area waiting to relieve us and we're due for our days off. We can let them know what happened and they can pick it up from there."

She and Phally, the K9 of the unfortunate name, fell in next to my unlikely trio and we began to carefully pick our way down the slippery mountainside.

"What do you think the probability of survival is here?" Lala asked softly after we'd been hiking for an hour.

She knew it as well as I did; I made her codirector for a reason. I knew she wanted reassurance, but I couldn't give it to her.

"She fell off that cliff, Lala," I said in a low voice. "I watched her body hit the side of it before she did her disappearing act. And she was already injured to begin with. What do I think her probability of survival is? Low. Very low. I'm amazed there wasn't a body."

Lala nodded and we continued to walk in silence as we contemplated what the implications meant for our missing person. Five days since she was reported lost at the end of April. With the inclement weather, temperatures had been averaging in the mid-to-high forties. Nearly all her gear had been left behind at the campsite. No food—hopefully she knew what was safe to forage in the spring—however, spring meant that hardly anything was growing yet. A fall from a cliff, which meant potential injuries that could range from mild to severe.

The likelihood of the task force finding a live person, if we found anyone at all, was dropping significantly by the hour.

CHAPTER TWO

I attempted to bolt upright in bed, gasping and clawing at my chest. At the incredible *pain* ricocheting through it. My hands grasped at air as if I could take whatever had struck my heart—my soul—and rip it away from me. The agony was unending. My entire body thrashed, trying to escape it, but I was pinned in place, unable to break loose. The haunting echoes of a lullaby faded in my head, outcompeted by the shrieking insistence, the attention-seeking *bitch* in my chest that was shattering my sense of self.

I laid back in my bed, doing my best to breathe through it instead of panicking. Telling myself, reassuring myself, that it wasn't real. I was safe. I was home. I was in my bed. My bed, in my home, in Blue Bear, the tiny little hidden town in Skamania County, Washington. I wasn't in Ryūgū-jō.

I closed my eyes as my breathing slowed and my mind finally, *finally,* realized it wasn't trapped in this dream again. I groaned. We had made it back to staging around ten at night. I had come home after the long drive from the search site and did the bare minimum before falling into bed. Then I had to be woken up by a nightmare?

A gentle whuff blew sweaty strands of blue-black hair into my eyes and I turned toward the sound. A pair of big doe eyes gazed at me soulfully from a gigantic head. Not the deceptively innocent ones; these were genuine.

"Aw, Maxwell. Everything's alright," I murmured to the enormous Saint Bernard propping his head on my bed as I attempted to disentangle myself from the sweat-soaked sheets.

Max snorted at me through his lips, unconvinced. He had been thrilled when we came home late last night. However, he was clearly less thrilled about the return of the nightmare.

"I know, hun, it's been a while since I've had one of those, huh?" I frowned at the sheets, still trapped, and yanked harder without them giving an inch. I shoved a ratty, limp hunk of tangled hair out of my face, only to blow out a frustrated breath when it fell back into place. I needed to go see Kenichi soon and get it all chopped off.

A disgruntled grumble sounded to my left. I looked over and it suddenly all made sense.

"Get your giant ass off this bed so I can get a glass of water already, Woodrow. I'm parched." I shoved at the malamute to no avail.

If I hadn't been so disoriented from the dream, I would have figured it out sooner. Woody hated the nightmares and often tried to wake me in all sorts of manners. Nudging me repeatedly. Rolling me off the bed. Crushing me like a felled sequoia. If a malamute falls in a bed, does it make a sound? You betcha. It sounds like the love child of an old man groaning and an angsty teenage girl sighing. It would probably be hysterical to a bystander, but being trapped in sweaty sheets or waking up on the floor wasn't my cup of tea.

It took several more minutes of swearing, malamute sass, and tug-of-war before I was free. Admittedly, he was also probably getting his revenge on me for giving him a bath last night to ensure he no longer resembled a swamp monster.

"Fucking finally," I muttered, side-eyeing Woody while he huffed at me for ruining his nest. I stood up unsteadily and shook my head wryly as I turned around, took a step, and—

Promptly tripped over a prone body and fell flat on my back, hearing a yelp and the scrabbling of nails on wood mid-flight.

If only I could say it wasn't my circus or my monkeys.

Max's head came into view again as he loomed over me in concern.

I reached up to give him a scritch behind the ears as I called out to my beautiful Heinz-57 of every color. "Victoria! I'm so sorry; come back. I didn't mean to crush you like the great human tower of tumbling Jenga blocks. Come back here, baby."

Vicky came slinking back in, tail between her legs as Max gave her a nudge with his head and nearly knocked her over. It wasn't that she was itty-bitty—she weighed in at a respectable forty-five pounds—Max just didn't always grasp his size. Okay, make that *never*.

With her half-floppy ears, Vicky was my personal Flying Nun and I loved it. However, she was a rescue who had come from an abusive background and an occasional trigger would flare every now and then.

"I'm sorry, girl. That was rough, huh?" I gave her a reassuring hug and felt her body relax with the pressure as her multihued tail gave a small thump on the floor. My own heart rate began to ease as I held her to me.

"Okay, gang, what time is it anyway?" Woody woo-woo-wooed at me and he play-bowed from the bed. "Yeah, I'm not falling for that crap. It's still dark out, there's absolutely no way it's time for your guys' breakfast. My coffee, yes. Your breakfast, no."

I stood up gingerly and clapped my hands, "Alright, who wants to go outside?"

Woody launched his bulk off the bed and a veritable stampede of K9s tore through the house for the back door. Some days I wasn't sure how they didn't crash straight through it.

After releasing the chaos crew to cause further mayhem outdoors, I gave up on the idea of a glass of water and padded to the kitchen where I put a pot of coffee on to percolate. I paused, contemplating the day, and decided to rinse some rice and toss it into the rice cooker before making my way to my bathroom. The soft musical tones of the machine starting up followed me through my home.

Turning on my bathroom light, I smiled and leaned against the doorframe.

"Ah, Pea. I'd been wondering where you were. You know, I bought that towel warming rack for me not you, right?"

She hissed at me from where she lay on the top shelf of the warming rack, then clicked as if to make up for it.

"Yeah yeah, so scary." Turning my back on her, I glanced at myself in the mirror and nearly gave myself a jump scare.

After wrangling Woodrow in the shower last night, I had rinsed myself off briefly, too tired to do the full routine. Big mistake. I looked like I straight up crawled out of the TV and was auditioning for a remake of *The Grudge*.

My gaze caught on the web of scars peeking above my tank top and I absently traced along the silvery lines. I removed my shirt and stared at the sight before me. A shattered pane of glass. That was what the flesh over my heart resembled. Tattooed Japanese red camellias were interwoven between them. The lines extended only a few inches past my breastbone, and I braced myself as I dropped one of my glamours.

Slowly the silvery lines darkened to the blackness of a fathomless abyss. They extended over my entire torso, snaking around my neck, limbs, and feathered along the edge of my jaw. The scars, if you could call them that, varied in size and thickness, leaving gaps, wedges, and holes in my body. The damage had been extensive. The image left behind, unsettling. I resembled a shattered statue that had been painstakingly pieced back together, waiting to be fully repaired. I feathered a touch along a crevice, flinching slightly at the empty space between the fragments that now made up vmy essential self. How my organs continued to function was a mystery, but I chalked it up to *ki*. The life energy that ran through us. Or for the Abstruse, the magic that kept us immortal.

A gentle chatter from Pea snapped me out of it and I shook myself out of the trance, shuddering as I put my glamour back up. It covered everything except for the scarring over my heart. No magic would cover that scar, nor would I want it to.

"A brush isn't going to cut it, Pea. I'm going to have to shower and do the whole nine yards with my hair again aren't I?" I observed, trying to lighten the somber mood as I took another glance at my hair in the mirror.

Pea just waved her tail at me speculatively from her perch and gave me a single click.

"I know. I know. You're right, I need to see Kenichi and get a real haircut for once."

Another click, followed by a regal head nod, and I was dismissed as she closed her eyes, basking in the radiant heat rising from the bars below. I snorted. "One of these days, you're going to forget to turn that back off and you're going to burn this house down."

She flicked her tail at me, Pea's equivalent of giving me the middle finger. Shaking my head, I turned on the shower to magma-level heat. I shed the rest of my clothes and stepped into the shower. Once in, I leaned my forehead against the river rock and let the hot water soothe my demons.

It had been at least six years since I last encountered that dream. Nightmare, really. They used to come more frequently but had thankfully begun tapering off in the past decade. I wasn't sure what triggered the nightmare this time around, but I didn't appreciate it. Nothing about this SAR deployment should have done it. I closed my eyes as the Korean nursery rhyme my mother used to sing to me replayed in my head. The children's folk song had taken on a haunting quality. One that I now dreaded. I traced yet more raised scars that encircled my forearms as the song continued to chant softly in my head.

Let it be known now that children's songs should never, ever be creepy.

I opened my eyes, locating my shampoo bottle, and refocused on the task at hand. I was sure the trigger would reveal itself to me soon. It always did.

I HAD ACHIEVED the bare minimum necessary for my basic hygiene and had an opossum hitching a ride on my shoulder as we headed to the kitchen. Once there, I snagged a mug of coffee, one with an opossum on it declaring itself "Trashy AND Sassy" before heading for the back half of my wraparound deck. On my way through the living room, Pea scurried back down my body and ambled her way into one of the many cozy nests she had assembled both in my home and around the property.

"Yeah, yeah. Just use my body as your locomotive. I see how it is."

I received some vague admonishing clicks and hisses in return. Probably indicating I should expect nothing less, as she was the clear matriarch of this household and I was a mere peon.

I rolled my eyes as I went to grab a blanket off the couch. My hand hovered over my phone charging on the side table. The urge to check for updates was strong. I shook my head, as if I could shake the itch right out of my brain. I could hear the voice of the woman I'd named as my codirector instead, lecturing me on trusting her and my team to do their job and actually rest on my days off. I'd be fully updated when I came in and got the daily debrief. Of course, said woman went by Lala and had named her K9 after a penis, so what did she know?

Instead, I snagged the contemporary romance lying face down next to my phone, spine fully broken, all my favorite angsty scenes dog-eared so I could reread them to my heart's content like the heathen I was. Some people read various forms of fantasy for escapism. I lived it. Contemporary romance was my particular genre of fantasy, sad as that commentary was on my love life.

Book, coffee, and blanket in hand, I ventured out the door, where I wrapped myself up and settled into one of Adirondack chairs. I set my book down on the side table, opting to take a few moments for myself first. It was a cool May morning, the rain having stopped for now, and a light mist still played along the ground. The three dogs were off on the property playing.

Woody was in the water like always, facing off with a juvenile *hanzaki*. I eyed the giant salamander, currently slightly larger than the malamute himself. Woody pounced, splashing a wave of water at the amphibian, and the salamander retaliated by slapping its tail. A giant wave of water washed over the K9, causing him to go wild with joy. Vicky and Max were busy with a game of chase. Vicky, of course, outmaneuvering poor Max who was doing his best to catch her, though he never would.

This was my favorite time of day, the blue hour before dawn, that liminal time before we truly shifted from night to day.

I was locked in a truly gripping *who hurt you* scene with my coffee mug stopped halfway to my lips when I felt the slight shudder in my wards and all three dogs bolted for the front yard. I set down my coffee, the black gold having never reached my lips, irritated at the interruption of my favorite scene in the entire series I was currently rereading. I internally assessed the information the wards were providing, then relaxed. I was cutting through the house when I heard the dogs go wild with joy as a fourth joined them.

I managed to time the opening of my front door with Skamania's finest, Sheriff Jeff Danly, trudging his way up my front steps. "Really, Beauty?" I asked wryly, leaning against my doorframe as I glanced down at an imaginary watch on one of my crossed arms. "It's the ass crack of dawn. Hell, it isn't even dawn yet. You couldn't even go home to your wife first?"

"You know I hate that nickname," he grouched. "Obviously, I went home first. I got Ruby, didn't I? How could I deny her a chance to see her boyfriend? I would never."

"I didn't say she wouldn't get a chance to see Woody, but perhaps a more reasonable hour would have made more sense?"

"Meh." The exhausted man shrugged me off. Standing at a hair under six feet, with thick sandy-colored hair, a strong jaw, lovely green eyes, broad shoulders, and tapered hips, he came packaged together with an affable nature and a dry wit. His wife and close friend of mine, Tisha, had found one of the good ones. "You're the entire reason I'm this exhausted, you know. After your sighting, the search took on a new fervor. Besides, I know how much you hate talking on the phone. I also know you're trying not to check for updates, but it's killing you not to, so I figured I'd stop by in person."

"Mm-hmm. No, you were hoping I'd feed you. Everything you just said?" I circled a finger in the air. "That was bullshit rationalization in an attempt to make this look less *Oliver Twist* and more like official business. Also? You're the biggest enabler in the history of enablers. I'm telling Lala."

He gave me the sad puppy eyes. As if that would work on me. I lived with three actual dogs and an opossum who ruled us all; the sheriff had nothing on them. Besides which, sad puppy eyes were so much more effective when they were brown. Everyone knew that. "You know Tish doesn't get up for hours yet. Take pity on a starving man who has been hiking through the forest for the past twelve hours, existing on nothing but salty nuts and water. Besides, I don't want to get bitten for accidentally waking her at this ungodly hour. And Jesus Christ, don't sic Lala on me. I don't need rabies."

I snickered. One only came between Tish Danly and her sleep if they didn't value their life. Lala was a whole other story. There was a theme regarding the women Jeff knew in his life and that theme was *violence*. "Did you even go home between the time you called me in and showing up at my door?" I asked.

"You radioed in right when I was wrapping up my shift at the command post. I was supposed to go home for a few hours. That chance was shot to hell when you came back. *Noooo*, I got to trek uselessly through the woods on the off chance someone else might spot our missing person. Instead, I got my beauty sleep in the back of my truck for a couple of hours."

"Fine. I should start charging you room and board for the amount of food you eat here. Come on in, update me. Coffee's fresh." I stepped aside and waved him in.

"God, you're the best neighbor in the whole damn county. And you already charge us room and board."

"I'm your only neighbor. And thanks for the reminder. Maybe I'll increase your rent."

"Semantics. You're too big of a softy, anyway." He beelined to the coffeepot, poured himself a cup, and let out a deep sigh of satisfaction after taking the first sip. Then grumbled, "I hate searches with a passion. Why do we have to live in the Pacific Northwest? I look like a newborn baby, wrinkled down to the bone from the damp. Goddamned cheeks are chafed to hell and back. I don't think there's skin left on my ball sack. There's not enough Gold Bond powder in the world. It poured the whole night, up until about two hours ago."

I wrinkled my nose as I began taking ingredients out of the refrigerator. "Ever heard of TMI? I'll take your word for it. Tish can deal with that. So, what's the update?"

Jeff's eyes lit up as he tracked my movements. "Korean breakfast burritos?" Then he registered my question, and I watched that light behind his eyes die. It was like watching a child's balloon deflate. I steeled myself against whatever news was about to come my way.

CHAPTER THREE

Years upon years of doing this work and I still struggled with getting SAR updates during a deployment just as much as Jeff hated giving them. It was one thing doing a search for human remains. You knew what to brace yourself for. But live area searches were brutal, exhausting work, and the longer they went on, the more difficult it was to hold out hope that a live subject would be found in the end. Especially after the first forty-eight hours passed.

I could see all the same thoughts playing out through Jeff's defeated body language. "Five days," he said bleakly. "Going on six. She doesn't have her gear, Cam. You watched her fall off a godforsaken cliff. And not just fall off a cliff, but bounce off a goddamn mountainside. I just don't know how she could still be alive at all, especially in this weather. I had them switch to a live and cadaver search after this morning's shift."

I reached over the counter and gripped Jeff's hand in solidarity. "Hey. I know how much you hated having to make that decision. But that doesn't mean you've given up on her. Tell me what has happened since Lala and I went home."

"Absolutely nothing, Cam. Jack all. None of us have been able to find a new scent to start from again."

I released his hand and checked the rice cooker to see how much longer the rice had left to go. Five minutes. Perfect. I chewed on the information as I went through the motions of frying eggs in one pan, letting the stirred eggs fill the whole pan to fry evenly, while I began assembling the vegetables I wanted for *bibimbap* and let my stoneware *dolsot* pot preheat on another burner.

Nearly every time one of the assigned pairs had lost the scent trail, it was inexplicable. Granted, the conditions weren't ideal; however, air-scent K9s worked well in the rain—the moisture in the air helping to rehydrate scent particles—at least up until the point when the torrential downpour started two days ago. No roads existed in the areas for a vehicle to steal her away where her scent had vanished. Now that I had seen our alleged missing person appear and disappear into literally thin air, it made more sense as to why the scent trail was vanishing.

"We started Cooper and Yumi on negative locations to the east and west of you and Woody," Jeff continued. I removed the eggs and started sautéing my vegetables. Cooper and Yumi were Scott and Aidan's K9s respectively, and damn good ones at that. "Those locations have been eliminated as well. We even called Theo in and brought him to the site of the fall. Nothing." He rubbed his forehead, looking frustrated.

"Twinkle, Twinkle, Little Star" began to play as the rice cooker let everyone in the vicinity know with pride that it had accomplished its due diligence. I scooped my rice into the oiled *dolsot* pot and covered it for a few minutes. The vegetables finished and I removed them from the pan to begin frying the *bulgogi* I had managed to take out of the freezer the previous night, despite being a zombie.

All three of my K9s were cross-trained to be both air-scent and cadaver K9s. As air-scent K9s, they didn't need to be at the place last seen or the subject's prior scent trail to track them. And thank God for that on this search. Woody was able to scent the particles they emitted naturally and follow them to the source, where the scent would be most highly concentrated. The fact that Woody had been unable to track *back* to the last known position when we had found a new scent cone was a first for us.

I could hear the rice begin to crackle and pop in the pot and removed it from the heat and finished up the *bulgogi*. Jeff watched me from the top of his coffee mug. The man was long used to the way I processed information and knew to be silent for a bit. I snagged the pot of coffee and topped him off so he had something to do while I began to mix the ingredients I had prepared for the *bibimbap* in the *dolsot*. I warmed up a few tortillas and laid them down before smearing on a thin layer of *gochujang*, a sweet and spicy chili paste, over the top of them for an extra pop, and layered strips of fried egg over the top of that.

Jeff was overtired right now and wasn't a K9 handler, so I could forgive him his mistake, but even if there had been a cliff or a water source for our subject to drop off into, as air-scent and cadaver K9s, Woody, Cooper, and Yumi still would have been able to pick up a scent. Contrary to popular belief, crossing water does not eliminate someone's scent; however, moving water does disrupt it and carry it elsewhere. Point being though, it still exists.

Pensively, I spread a good layer of the *bibimbap*, rice mixed with various cooked vegetables and *gochujang*, enjoying the crunch from the crisp bottom layer of rice achieved by the *dolsot*.

The most infuriating aspect of this search? The number of times the scent double-backed on us to an area we had previously cleared, only to vanish again.

I threw *bulgogi* in the center before rolling the burritos up tightly as I chewed on my lower lip.

There aren't many ways for a person's scent to just vanish. Not naturally at least. But magically? I needed to go back over the mountain after what I had witnessed. I rolled the third one up in foil for Jeff to take home to Tish later and slid a plate over to him.

He straightened back up, groaning as he held a hand to his lower back, and looked me in the eye with concern before dragging the plate closer to him. "You know we're gonna need Max if we want a chance in hell of finding her alive."

I had been a Search and Rescue trainer and handler for more years than I cared to count. I had created a decently sized operation over time, and I took on small teams for training and certification in search and disaster scenarios. I always got odd looks when I brought in my gang, since neither Max nor Woody fit the typical picture of a K9 SAR. Vicky specialized in disaster operation and recovery. Woody was my wilderness and avalanche go-to. Even Maxwell was certified. Saint Bernards began being bred out of their SAR traits around a hundred years ago and weren't really used for the job anymore. However, Max was unique.

Max could track the *yōkai*. And Jeff knew it.

Many believed the *yōkai* to be endemic to Japan. But as the world's population grew, shipping routes expanded, allowing for migration to become more accessible. Previously, only the seafaring *yōkai* had really been known to immigrate anywhere. But natural disasters occurred, and man-made tragedies happened. Hundreds of thousands of *yōkai* fled after the bombings of Hiroshima and Nagasaki, as well as the Great Tōhoku earthquake and tsunami. Nowadays, a great many *yōkai* can be found along the Ring of Fire.

Which meant a great many missing person cases occurred in the countries *along* the Ring of Fire. There is a reason why Alaska has the highest rate of missing persons cases per capita in the United States. And why California, Washington, and Oregon were in the top ten for highest number of missing person cases. While not all *yōkai* were malicious, many of them were tricksters and weren't necessarily aware that their tricks could ultimately lead humans to their deaths. Nor did they understand why they should care. They simply did not possess the empathy humans did.

The migration of the *yōkai* to the Pacific Northwest was how Max and I ultimately fell into our SAR roles.

Maxwell had been gifted to me as a pup in thanks for a service rendered, and for a long time it had been the three of us—Pea, Max, and myself. He accompanied us on all our treks in the wilderness, Max at my side, Pea riding his back. Until one trek up Mount Hood he became quite anxious, pacing back and forth in a small area and emitting a low half-growl, half-bark I hadn't heard from him before. When I shushed him, I heard the faint cries of a child.

That was the day we had found an *onikuma,* a demon bear—not a *yōkai* that generally bothered itself with Quotes. But just like any other bear, negligent campers and the chance for an easy meal had proved too tempting. Its preferred prey had started out with horses, stranding riders in the backcountry. She had escalated to gorging herself on campers, as she came further and further down the mountainside.

On the day we found the *onikuma,* I had followed Maxwell through a trail of equine carcasses. Three horses and a pony. They hadn't been killed for food, but stealth. A quick slash of claws through the neck before the animals could react and warn the Quotes with their fear. As we continued down the trail of death, the remains of Quotidian adults began to appear. Tents and sleeping bags shredded. Limbs torn apart. Organs strewn on the forest floor, gnawed upon.

At the end of our journey, we had found our *yōkai* tearing between two boulders where a young boy had wedged his body.

I had judged her. Deemed her morality unsalvageable. And devoured her.

The three of us were not quite what we seemed. It turned out the event hadn't been a fluke and Max possessed an extra-sensory ability to track the *yōkai* as well as other magical beings. He wasn't limited to one culture's mythological beings and cryptids.

And Pea Blossom. Well, Pea Blossom was special. She had clearly out-lived the lifespan of a normal Virginia opossum; however, she wasn't really a Virginia opossum at all. I was nearly dead when Pea had found the body of an adolescent opossum to occupy. As I chose not to enslave her to the familiar bond created by the *onmyōji,* she had elected to be my familiar by her own free will and remained loyal to me.

As for me, well I am a unique blend of Japanese and Korean cultures. Japanese on my father's side, Korean through my maternal line, which was where my dominant gene of the *haetae* originated.

I stood against disasters, plagues, and fires. I protected those I con-sidered mine. And I passed judgment upon those who have committed wrongs. Those who cannot be redeemed are consumed.

I had wept for the little boy we had been a touch too late to save for days, his death triggering memories of battles long past. When I had discovered they had no family to find them missing, I had vowed to search for those who have no voice, those with little to no hope of being found for they were trapped by the *yōkai*, which could rarely be seen by humans unless the *yōkai* willed it.

And thus began my accidental career in Search and Rescue. Jeff didn't know all of my history, but he knew of the *yōkai* and how my organization played a role in recovering individuals who went missing because of them. Jeff knew this because he had been tricked by a *kitsune* as a child. I had recovered him with Max. He leaned heavily on my organization whenever a missing person case came up in the county.

I quirked an eyebrow as I slid onto one of my kitchen stools. "I know. I was anticipating this. I need to go back out there and search the Abbie realms. I just hope there wasn't a temporal snare." I took another sip of coffee, then leaned against the low back of the stool and closed my eyes.

We knew the missing woman had set off to summit Mount St. Helens with a friend seven days ago. The friend had told us how excited they had been to obtain the limited permits to do so. When she vanished in the night, her worried friend had contacted the sheriff's department. I wasn't thrilled about the fact she was missing on a mountain.

Mountains were well-known for being one of the favored habitats of many *yōkai* after all.

"When Woody kept losing her scent in the middle of the trails without any rhyme or reason for it, I suspected magic behind it. I don't know if her disappearance is related to the *yōkai,* but I knew I'd need Maxwell."

Jeff nodded and bit into the burrito, letting out a happy little sound of satisfaction as he did so. "Korean-Mexican fusion was the best thing to happen this generation. You know I'll probably have to call the search before you get a chance to come back on, unless we come up with something in the next couple days, right?"

I snagged the candy dish of extra-strength Assorted Berry Tums Chewy Bites I kept especially for Jeff and scooted it toward him. "I figured. It's never stopped me before though. I have the resources to keep going. It's nice when we get a contract and funds to continue the search, but that's the beauty of being independently wealthy. You get to do whatever you want with your money. You're not likely to get as many volunteers to stick around with this SAR either, what with her being an out-of-towner and a single female with no family."

"You're good people, Cam. Never change." He fished out four raspberry Tums and set them by his plate. I eyed the candy dish. He had two raspberry Tums left and then he was going to have to suffer through the remaining flavors before I was going to be willing to buy him a new giant bottle. I wasn't *that* good of a person.

"I wouldn't dare. Who would feed you at five in the morning if I did? Not Tish. And she definitely wouldn't medicate you with Tums; she would simply tell you 'Natural consequences' and cackle in revenge." I grinned evilly while taking a bite out of my own burrito, enjoying the spice and textures.

Jeff flinched, likely remembering the last time he accidentally woke up his wife in the early hours of the morning.

"Speaking of *yōkai*, I was telling Pea it was time for a visit with Ken. Given everything going on, I might as well bump that up to today and see if he's heard anything about our missing person."

Jeff reached over the island and flicked my ratty braid. "Finally doing something about this rat's nest then?"

"I will invite your in-laws onto my land and sic them upon you. I'm sure The Beast will enjoy a visit with her parents and siblings."

The man paled noticeably. "I take back my comment. Please convey our hellos to Ken and tell him Tish has been making noises about needing to head over to his salon soon."

"I'll do that." I smiled in satisfaction as I finished off my burrito.

The screen door slapped open again and a herd of dog paws scrambled over the wood floors with a corgi leading the charge, Woody close to her side.

"Ah, there are the lovebirds." Jeff popped the last bit of his burrito in his mouth and hopped off his stool so he could crouch down with his arms wide to encompass both Ruby and Woody in them as they bowled him over on the floor. Vicky joined the happy dog pile as they rolled around on the floor in a mass of wriggling bodies.

I felt a heavy weight land in my lap and chuff, and I smiled.

"Hey there, buddy," I said affectionately while rubbing Max behind his soft brown ears. "Did you hear us talking about you? What do you say? Shall we see if there's mischief about?"

He butted his head against me in response and collapsed on the floor at my feet, content to observe his siblings roughhouse with Jeff and Ruby. Pea crawled up the stool and curled into a ball in my lap. I would take the chaotic scene for all it was worth. Despite Jeff telling me to take a break, I needed to get Max on the trails. A woman's life was at stake and there were all manners of creatures who preferred the twilight hours, not just the *yōkai*.

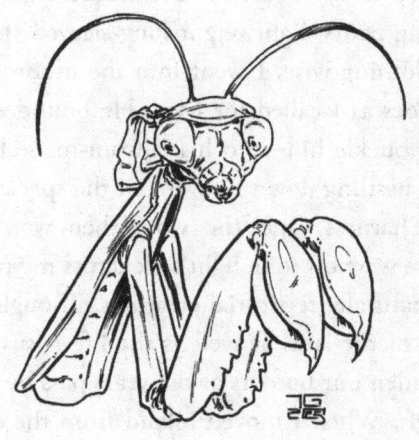

CHAPTER FOUR

I walked Jeff out to his car while he chewed on his Tums, Ruby trotting at his feet. After he got her loaded up in the back, I handed over Tish's burrito. "Give my love to Beastie and thank her for keeping an eye on Vicky and Max while I was deployed, as always. I'll keep you updated once I have something."

He rested his forearm along the top of his car door and paused before getting in. "I know you've been doing these magical SARs far longer than I've been alive, but stay safe, okay? There's only so much support I can give from my end once I have to call the search."

I gave him a shrug, "I always try, Beauty, I always try."

I started walking back to my house as he got into his car, then turned and called out to him, "I might discount your rent this month. But only because I love Tish. Hazard pay for having to tend to your chapped ass cheeks and all!"

Jeff gave me the finger as he shut the door fully and started heading down the driveway. I cackled and gave a woeful Woody a scrub behind the ears. "I know, buddy. Long distance relationships are the worst, aren't they? You and Ruby having to suffer living a whole half mile down the road from each other. I promise, we'll go visit Tish soon so you can see her again."

I headed back to my bedroom and traded my sweats for my typical uniform of hiking pants, lightweight long-sleeved shirt, and socks. Once I was situated clothing-wise, I went into the mudroom and got into my casual hiking shoes as I called for Max. He bounded into the room and I knelt down to buckle him into his custom-made harness. Pea Blossom climbed aboard, nestling down into one of the specially made pouches on either side of the harness. Once the two of them were all set, I whistled for the others and we were off for a light trek across my property.

Haetae are naturally territorial creatures. Though shy, we are instinctively protective of the land as well as the life it sustains, and we have a tendency to broaden our borders as the years pass by to bring them under our *boho*, or aegis. When I moved inland from the coast, the tiny Abbie community of Blue Bear had slowly developed around me. I considered the territory and its inhabitants mine to safeguard against natural disasters, epidemics, and acts of evil. I was not infallible, I was only one *haetae*, the last one that I knew of in this world in fact.

The sea *kami* had begun a campaign against the *haetae* approximately a century ago. Servants of his infiltrated the land above the seas and taught the Japanese about our weaknesses. When Korea's native landscape was destroyed, they harvested the Ulleungdo hemlock trees to turn them into weapons against us. The *onmyōji,* their magic users and diviners, joined them and systematically destroyed our population one by one to harvest our *ki*. I had been fortunate enough to be in America and had escaped the genocide. Which left me as the only *haetae* surviving that I was aware of. And the *kami* knew it.

What was becoming all too apparent was that there were forces at play that were working toward eradicating *all* the guardians who stood against evil, not just the *haetae*. Natural disasters, crime rates, plagues, and wars were on the rise across the globe. I did what I could when I was deployed on international disaster searches, but it was a reactionary response. The disasters had already taken place and I could do nothing to prevent or mitigate them. Every event, every loss, hurt my soul.

On that reminder of the lost, my small group was heading toward a northeast corner of my property and I shook off my melancholy to focus on our surroundings. Max and Woody led the way at a comfortable trot, with Pea's tail looped out the back of the pouch catching the breeze. Their energy was bright and happy, playfully nipping at each other, knowing who they were about to visit and eager to get there. Vicky stuck close to my side like she always did on the trails when she wasn't on the job.

"Oh, you're in for a treat, girl. You haven't met Uncle Kenichi yet."

She looked up at me with her head cocked, and one of her black ears flapped up as her tail wagged. I smiled at the motion. She had come a long way from the emaciated and abused dog I had rescued. We neared our destination and I called Max to heel.

"You know the drill," I told Pea. "You might want to climb out now if you don't want to end up shaken like a martini."

As she climbed out of the harness and plopped down at my feet, I kept my eyes peeled to see if I could spot Kenichi—it was a game of ours I never managed to win. It was a firmly established rule that Max wasn't allowed to interfere. Vicky sat next to me, clearly curious as I slowly spun in a circle staring intensely at my surroundings. Nothing but the usual forest. Lichen-covered trees, moss, leaf litter, and the burbling creek. Oh, and boulders. Can't forget the boulders.

"Alright, Kenichi. You win. I give," I called out after about ten minutes.

A deep echoing noise that was a cross between chittering and hissing filled the air. The equivalent of Kenichi's cackling laugh. A large form, about eight-and-a-half-feet tall, peeled away from one of the old-growth trees to my left, having perfectly blended in just seconds before. Vicky gave a small yelp in surprise while Woody and Max went wild with joy and excitement. She took her cues from the other two and relaxed.

We had once been a quintet of dogs, opossum, and *haetae*. Now, a towering giant of a praying mantis added a sixth to our mix, a *kamikiri* to be exact. His coloration mimicked the bark of the old growth tree he had been attached to, down to the Old Man's Beard lichen hanging off his back in odd places. Unlike a real praying mantis, he could change his camouflage to suit his environment. Also unlike his smaller insect kin, rather than having a tarsus at the end of his forelegs, he had razor-sharp pincers.

I had two reasons for coming out this way. One was vanity and practicality; I needed my damn hair chopped off before my self-esteem took a fatal blow. Kenichi's particular brand of *yōkai* had a fetish for cutting hair. It became an issue when a mischievous spirit went around cutting off somebody's hair without permission. But I found Kenichi when he was a young whippersnapper of a shape-shifting *kamikiri*, cutting off girls' pigtails in elementary school, and brought him onto my property. Nowadays he was a massive adult *kamikiri* and one of the most popular stylists in downtown Portland, allowing him to partake in his species' quirk with consent from his clients. Not that they knew what he was. They just thought he was a gorgeous specimen of a man and threw money at him to cut off their locks.

Sometimes you just need to figure out how to redirect all that mischief.

My second and more important reason was that Kenichi was well-known for being the holder of all *yōkai* gossip in the region. If there was any hint of a whisper regarding the lost hiker being taken by a *yōkai*, he would have likely heard about it by now.

Except the gigantic mantid was currently prancing around on his hind legs between three dogs that were dancing and howling with joy as he pretended to box at them with his forelegs and batted at them gently with his wings. It was an absolute racket.

Not my circus.

Fine, it was 100 percent my circus.

I was about to call out to bring some order to the chaos when I saw Woody dart between Kenichi's legs unexpectedly, and decided against it. The potential fallout was too good of an opportunity to miss.

Kenichi's fore and middle legs flailed dramatically while his wings fluttered, but he didn't have enough time to achieve any lift before he crashed to the ground, K9s scattering everywhere. Vicky had clearly learned her lesson about large falling objects earlier this morning.

Mantid down.

The *kamikiri* did manage to shift before landing and avoided crushing his wings at least, so that was something. Now, in place of the movie-monster-worthy insect, was a man of movie-star-quality looks, in ripped jeans so tight they should've been a crime against nature, and a Man or Astro-man? band shirt. In human form, Kenichi was a svelte Japanese man with insanely high cheekbones, an angular jawbone, and perfectly mussed black locks, who stood at five foot four, just a few inches taller than me. It always amused me that he was over three feet shorter in his human form, but Kenichi had once explained to me that he wearied of looming over everybody as a *kamikiri*, so he enjoyed the novelty of being short as a human male.

"Cam!" Kenichi shouted enthusiastically from the ground. "What are you doing out my way? You haven't swung by for a visit with the doggos in a good bit. They need some love from Uncle Kenichi regularly, you know. And who is this absolutely *adorable* sweetie pie?" He cooed at Vicky while reaching up with both hands to scrub behind her ears as she wiggled her entire body.

My lips twitched. "This here is Miss Victoria. I'm impressed…Vicky doesn't normally take to men right away after her past history with them, but evidently having encountered you first as a ridiculous prancing mantis was enough to convince her you were safe and probably not a man at all."

Kenichi looked conflicted between wanting to go on a murder spree at what I revealed about Vicky's past and wanting to preen in being accepted so quickly. He chose neither, instead sitting up and hugging Vicky to him tightly and proclaimed, "Well, that just means you get all the extra love from Uncle Kenichi now doesn't it."

I snorted. "Good God, the poor girl is going to suffocate in that case then. I did stop by for a couple reasons though, one of them being this." I waved my long thick braid tantalizingly at him.

His eyes glazed over with greed and he stood up as he made grabby hands for it. He undid my braid and ran his hands through my hair, and this time he did indulge in a gasp of horror.

"These split ends, Cam! How did you even let this happen? This is a travesty! Your hair is *furry* it's so split."

"Good God, everyone's a critic today. Well, I'm here to fix it. Chop it all off. It's yours, I trust your judgment. You know me, it just needs to be easy to maintain and stay out of my way."

He humphed. "I don't even know if I want your hair, it's in such bad shape. Leave it down and let it breathe without breakage every once in a while for *kamis'* sake."

"Ah, how I've missed the sweet sound of your lies. I know you want every single strand."

"I really do," he admitted. "Come, come to my throne where all the magic happens."

After taking off my shoes and socks, I was ushered to sit on a log in the middle of a burbling stream. It was May and the water was still ice-cold as it ran over my feet. Woody bounded into the water, splashing everyone within his vicinity. Pea hissed her displeasure from the bank.

Kenichi palmed my face and dunked me backwards into the stream while I shrieked in surprise. He chitter-hissed in his creepy-ass laugh. It was even creepier now, in his human guise.

"You've been coming out to these woods for how many years now to get your hair cut and the dunk still takes you by surprise? If you want the salon experience, you need to actually show up to my salon. Now, spill the tea and tell me why you're truly out here getting your hair done and what information you want out of me. I know better than to think that you just came out for a visit with your ol' pal Ken."

I felt a pang of guilt at his words. "I'm sorry, Ken, I'm a terrible friend. I really do need come out to visit more often without an ulterior motive behind it."

Ken waved me off as he shifted back into his *kamikiri* form and reached high up into a tree above us with a forelimb to retrieve a basket of hair products.

"Don't worry about it. Besides, it's a two-way street. I can't even remember the last time I stopped by the big house. We're equally terrible friends. Pact to do better?"

I smiled as he lightly sprayed my hair with detangler and started cursing as he began trying to comb it out with the spines on his middle limbs.

"It's a pact for sure."

"Now what information did you need from me? Does this have anything to do with that missing hiker I heard about?"

"Yes," I replied, trying not to nod. "Her name is Dr. Misaki Aoki. She's a visiting professor from University of Washington and was in town for the week to do a guest lecture series for Portland State University's Center for Japanese Studies. From her bio online, her focus is in Japanese folklore, specifically the *yōkai*. She's also an avid hiker and after wrapping up her series, she went out to summit Helens with a friend. She vanished overnight. Her friend made it back—Aoki never did. Woody lost her scent a third of the way up the summit. I plan to head back out there with Max as soon as possible, but you can see why I'm concerned."

He patted me on the shoulder with a middle limb before returning to my hair. "Try Oliver. He should know more than I do, I think."

He thought for a moment and continued, "I don't know for sure that it's related to her, but there are rumors about a *bijin,* a beautiful Japanese woman, who appeared in the fog and forests surrounding Helens one day long ago. It was said that she was dazed and mumbling about the *yōkai.* A young *kitsune* approached the *bijin* to see if she needed help and when she did, the woman grasped her and they both vanished. The *kitsune* was never seen again."

"Chi-chi...I *saw* a beautiful woman in the woods. Surrounded by a strange mist. She fell off a cliff but vanished before she hit the ground beneath her."

He snapped his pincers at me absentmindedly for the nickname, more out of habit than anything else. "What do you mean, you saw her, Cam? The story of the *bijin* was an urban myth for us *yōkai* growing up in the PNW. Be careful on foggy mornings, which, let's be honest, when you grow up on a mountainside is *every* morning. If you don't listen to your *okaasan,* the *bijin* would steal you away from your mother and everything you knew."

"Oh, so you mean the *bijin* was to the PNW *yōkai* what every *yōkai* was to Japanese children growing up?" I asked sarcastically.

"Hey now, don't be slandering my good name. I just cut people's hair. I didn't go around stealing children."

"You purposely stuck gum in the hair of six-year-old girls so you could cut off their pigtails, Ken."

"Okay, yeah. So I was a dick as a child. But I didn't steal children."

"She didn't steal anybody when I saw her either."

Ken shifted to human, throwing his arms up in exasperation, then back into mantis, demonstrating exactly how agitated he was. "The *bijin* isn't real, Cam."

"Uh-huh. She isn't real like we aren't real?" I folded my arms across my chest. I couldn't give him a look, since he was behind me. But...

"I can feel the look you're trying to give me, Cam."

"If only you could see it too; it's a good one."

"Getting back on topic, like I said, I'm not sure the *bijin* is directly related to Dr. Aoki in regard to her being missing; however, I do know she was looking into the story of the *bijin* as part of her research, given it's unusual in that it's a Japanese folktale which originates in the PNW. So if her disappearance does happen to be *yōkai*-related, I think Olly is going to be your best starting point for information there." He shifted back to human and passed me a hand mirror with a flourish.

"I gave you an inverted lob. Translation: your stick straight hair is in a long bob that should be long enough for a ponytail, but for my sake, please leave it down every once in a while. Since your hair can't hold a curl for the life of it, this shouldn't require any management on your part. It will look fine messy, and I thinned it out so, even with your wildly thick hair, your head won't resemble the head of a penis when it drizzles. You know, only at least three-quarters of the year."

I grinned while admiring the cut in the mirror. "You rock, Ken. Thank you for the tip on the *bijin* and Oliver. I'll pass your love to Murry and I promise to bring the pups by to play more often. Speaking of, Beauty and The Beastie send their love." I turned to give him a kiss on the cheek.

"Yes, yes. I know I'm prodigious. And tell Tish to get her ass in my chair already. I shudder to think what her dye job looks like at this point." He reciprocated the kiss and bent to give all the dogs some love, then picked up Pea to give her a cuddle before placing her on my shoulders. His face turned somber as he tucked her tail around my neck. "Be careful. I'm serious, Cam. I have a bad feeling about all of this. I probably wouldn't be around if it wasn't for you. There's a lot of us who wouldn't be. We need you to stick around. Not because you keep us safe, but because we love you."

I smiled softly, a bit damp behind the eyes, before hugging him tightly. "I love all of you too. You all saved me in return and made me who I am today."

Pea gave a firm click, a reassurance to Kenichi that she would be my backup and protector, as she had been all of these years we had been together. And then a three-legged opossum-*shikigami*, a lonely *haetae*, and their gang of K9s were back off on their path in the woods.

CHAPTER FIVE

I was nearly back to the house when my pocket vibrated.

"What's up? Didn't you just leave my house?" I asked Jeff.

"I can feel the love. I wanted to give you a heads-up. A relative reached out to me this morning. I gave him your card, since it's likely I'm going to have to call this search soon. Told him about your organization and that you'd been contracted out for cold cases and to continue other SARs in the past. Also told him about your track record for finding and closing searches where others have failed."

"You know that's fine, but a relative? I don't remember seeing a relative in Dr. Aoki's file."

"Said he was related through a previous marriage, grew up with her in Japan. Didn't find out she was missing 'til day before yesterday, then caught the first flight he could."

"What's his name?"

There was some rustling of paper in the background, then the sheriff's voice came back on the phone, "Rafael Sugiyama."

I went silent at the name and its implications for me.

"Hey, Cam?"

"Yeah?"

"I don't think I have to tell you, but this guy's fishy. He's too slick. I know you have discretion regarding the cases you take on, being a fancy pants private agency, so you take care, okay? 'Sides, I already know you plan on doing this search regardless."

"You know me way too well."

"When you get rescued a time or ten by a person, you tend to get to know them."

"Well, if you would have quit getting kidnapped and giving your parents heart attacks as a toddler, it would have done them and me a world of good."

"Ah, but how would I ever have met the love of my life?" he teased.

"Straight facts. Now go get some sleep. You sound like shit."

"I'd take offense to that remark, but I know it's only the truth," he grumbled. I laughed as we disconnected. I headed into the house with the K9s and turned on the news as I idly went through the mail from the past few days.

"Our latest updates from the Oregon Coast: Officials have shut down beaches from Del Rey clear down to Beverly Beach following the deaths of three adults and one child due to injuries related to swarms, or what marine biologists call smacks, *of jellyfish washing up onshore. Four more patients were rushed to the hospital late last night and are reported to be in critical condition. Marine biologists are at a loss regarding this bizarre incident. We have Dr. Sylvia Amato from the Hatfield Marine Science Center with us today. Can you tell us more about the deadly marine phenomenon that has been hitting our shores?"*

"Thank you. At first glance, the jellyfish appear to be Chironex yamaguchii, a particularly dangerous species of cubozoa. However, they are typically found in the Indo-Pacific region. These waters are not their usual habitat and we are speculating as to why they have been migrating to our coasts. These creatures are considered to be quite lethal to begin with and yet the jellyfish that have washed up on our shores seem to have some distinct differences in the venom contained in their nematocysts. This factor quite possibly makes them even deadlier than their close relative, the Chironex fleckeri, otherwise known as the Australian box jellyfish. The Australian box jellyfish is commonly believed to be the deadliest marine animal known to man. We're not sure if we have a new species on our hands yet or not. We cannot stress enough that it is in everyone's best interest to steer clear of the water and the beaches until these smacks have stopped."

"Shit, shit, shit, shit," I chanted under my breath. At various points in history, Abstruse lived openly among Quotidians. We were not currently in one of those eras. The fact that the sea *kami* was risking discovery of Abstruse was an ominous one. He was risking not only the potential backlash of Quotidian response, but the wrath of the other Abstruse factions as well.

"What can be done in the event of a sting, Dr. Amato?"

"Absolutely fucking nothing," I muttered. I was honestly shocked four had even made it to the hospital. My guess was the patients who had been hospitalized were Abstruse in human form or under a human glamour and not Quotidian at all. Someone would need to get them out of the hospital before they were found out. I turned off the TV as they were talking about vinegar, tweezers, and antivenom; all useless when it came to the magical *habu kurage*. There was no treatment in the world that was going to save you. Straight up—if you were a Quote and you were stung, Death was coming for you in minutes, if not seconds. I rang Jeff back up as the TV went black.

"Didn't we just hang up, like, not even fifteen minutes ago?" Jeff answered.

"The four people from the Oregon Coast who were hospitalized today. What hospital are they in?"

"I know you generally suck at phone etiquette, but we typically start out phone calls with phrases like, 'Hi, Jeff, how are you?'"

"*You* started the call with '*Didn't we just hang up, like, not even fifteen minutes ago?*'" I parroted back at him sarcastically. "I don't have time for niceties. I think the four who were hospitalized could be Abstruse. I'm assuming they've been transferred to one of the Portland or Salem hospitals by this point. Not all of the hospitals along the coast have Abbies in place to take care of records or labs that get collected."

"Ah, *fuckmewithadamnedlog*," he spat out as if it was all one word and promptly hung up on me. I snorted. This is why I loved Beauty. He spoke my language. I knew without any further comment from him that I'd be getting a call back within the next hour or two with more information, if any information was to be had.

I tapped my stress out on the kitchen counter, worrying about what communities of Abstruse might now be caught up in this pointless hunt of the *kami's*. Why now? Not for the first time, I wished I could just pick up the phone and call Murry to find out what was going on. Especially after Ken's vague comments earlier. A small head rested on my foot. I smiled and reached down to give Vicky's ears some love.

"You never fail to realize when I'm internally freaking out, do you, sweetie?" I said affectionately, leaning my head into hers.

She gave a little yip and licked my cheek.

"I get it, I get it. I need to stop worrying about things outside of my control. How do *you* know it's outside of my control though. Hmm?"

Max gave a grumbling woof from the living room, where he and Woody were curled up with one another. "I'm not listening to your two cents. Y'all are not the bosses of me!"

Woody woo-wooed at that. "Shut up. I know. At least give me some semblance of control in this household, guys."

There was a chorus of indignant canine noises at that comment. And they say dogs don't understand us. That's a bald-faced lie if I've ever heard one. Of course, the K9s in my company might be slightly…*different* than the typical dog after the types of magic they had been exposed to all these years. I settled on the couch with my laptop in hand to begin writing my report. Being productive was the least I could do while I waited for Jeff.

The phone rang again two hours later and as soon as I picked it up, Jeff began talking. And he tried to lecture me about phone etiquette? Ha.

"Family of four visiting Lincoln City. Last name Morlo. They were stabilized at Samaritan North Lincoln, then medevacked to OHSU."

I nodded absently, although Jeff couldn't see me. I knew that Samaritan North was a critical access hospital, being located in a rural setting, and would have focused on stabilization. It was also one of the few hospitals Abstruse avoided when possible because we didn't have anyone on staff there.

"Thanks a ton, Jeff. I'll get on it. Now get some sleep."

"You sure? I'm not gonna get a call in ten more minutes?"

"No. I'm going to go pick on other people now, you dick."

"You take care, Cam. Get some sleep yourself today. You sound tired too."

As soon as he disconnected, I was asking my phone to dial up Kenichi.

"Gum Drop Salon, this is Kenichi speaking," he answered.

"Hey, Ken, the last name Morlo strike any bells for you among the Abs?"

"Morlo, Morlo, Morlo..." he hummed as *snicks* filled the background. I couldn't wait to hear how he would avoid discussing Abbie business around a Quotidian. "Oh! I remember now. They were this selkie family in some urban fantasy series I read way back when. I think it was set in Salem. The family played some side characters who lived out on the coast but were pretty important to the story."

Shit. "Do you have the number for the Shifter council leader?"

"The author of the book?" He hummed for a bit as he thought. "You trying to set up a date? I know he's hot and all, but don't you think that'll make you look like a stalker?"

"It's a good thing you've amassed as much hair as you have, otherwise I'm pretty sure you'd have died so many times by now."

"It's not my hair, it's my charming personality."

The woman in his chair and I both scoffed at the same time.

"Utter arrogance is not charming, Ken."

"Ah, but confidence is. You just don't know the difference, sweet cheeks."

I recoiled in my seat. "Please don't ever call me that ever again."

"Yeah, that left a foul taste in my mouth as it came out too. Is that all you needed?"

"For now. I think I have all the other information I need."

"Give me a second, I'll go look it up." I could hear his shoes ringing against the floor as he made his way through his salon. They stopped and after a few moments he texted the number to me."

"Mmmkay, bye now. Gotta get back to this gorgeous head of hair." I could hear the woman start to ask him questions about the fantasy series, wanting to know what the title of the first book was and the name of the author. I laughed to myself about the hole he had dug himself as I hung up to call the Northwest Regional Shifter council head. I needed to notify them of the circumstances surrounding the Morlos so the necessary precautions could be taken to keep their faction hidden. I desperately wanted to rib him about their choice of name, but it wasn't the appropriate time nor place. Additional phone calls would need to be made to the community leaders up and down the Oregon Coast to warn them of what was to come. I sighed, drawing a legal pad to me to take notes on, as I asked my phone to dial the council leader and braced myself for the onslaught of phone calls.

I FINALLY PULLED into my training facility in Skamania, completely drained from the third degree I'd undergone, and had just let everyone out of the car and into the building when I felt it. The slight shudder in the wards surrounding the property. Since the building was in the Quotidian dimension, these wards only served to alert me when people were on their way—and whether they had magic or not. This intruder had paused near the entrance of the property. A regular car by the feel of it. But not a regular inhabitant within it. They were heading to the building without invitation or notification, the ultimate sin to an introvert like myself. I was not amused. My organization's address was not advertised publicly and we were by appointment only.

I made my way to the entrance and leaned against the frame, arms crossed, one hiking boot hooked around the other at the ankle in a closed off and unwelcoming position. Resting bitch face firmly intact. Magic in place. My default go-to mode.

After a few minutes, the vehicle got started again and a white rental car came up the drive and parked next to my 4Runner. The car idled for a few moments, then shut off and the equivalent of hot honey on a maple bacon waffle stepped out of the car. I really needed to go into Portland to get my fix already. Of waffles. Not men.

The stranger looked to be of mixed Asian descent. Hair that was a deep black with nutty undertones. It was thick and just long enough to have a slight wave to it. His skin tone a few shades darker than mine—a beautiful rich brown. I'd place him just a touch over six foot, based off where he stood in comparison to my SUV, so he'd tower over me. He was clearly fit under his beautifully tailored clothes.

As he began approaching me, it became clear his eyes were even darker than mine. Nearly black, a color that gave nothing away. He had strong facial features with high cheekbones and a chiseled, square jaw. And a nose to die for; one with a bridge that wouldn't let a pair of sunglasses slide down it every five seconds.

Pretty little lies.

The flavor of his magic screamed at me. The *umami* of it, and the delicious subtle undertones. This was the stranger from the mountain. The one that had slipped under my notice and whispered away silently into the woods.

I wondered what he looked like under the masks. We all wore glamours to hide our true selves. I could barely remember the last time I had been my own self for more than a few moments at a time.

I surveyed the stranger with a raised eyebrow. "What's a male like you doing out here in Sasquatch country? 'Cause you sure as hell don't look like your everyday bigfoot hunter."

The man saw my eyebrow and raised both in return. "Racism first thing in the morning? Lovely." He had a slight accent that I had a difficult time placing.

"Oh, definitely not. I'm all for equal opportunity Sasquatch hunting." I really was. Dalton was a jerk of the highest order and deserved to be caught. I motioned up and down. "Has more to do with your outfit than anything else. You won't find too many people out here squatchin' in a dress shirt, vest, slacks, and Oxfords."

Before he could reply, there was a skittering sound across the tile floor, then a sudden screech rent the air.

"What the hell was that?" the male asked, rocking back on his heels just a touch. There was no change in his expression though.

I sighed internally. Would a circus want my monkeys?

Violent hissing noises ensued. Followed by more screeches. Massaging my left temple with one hand, I reached down and scooped up the menace between my legs with the other.

"Pea Blossom, meet..." I looked at the man expectantly.

"Rafael. Rafael Sugiyama. And I will repeat. What the hell is that?"

He didn't pronounce Rafael the way Danly had. The way Americans traditionally did. His accent changed with his names, code switching as one does with languages. Rafael rolled off his tongue as *Rra-fuh-el*. It vaguely reminded me of the Portuguese I had encountered in Japan, but with a different lilt to it. Sugiyama fell out of his mouth the way I would expect a native Japanese speaker to pronounce it.

I let all of that information rattle around in my brain as I covered Pea's ears. "Let's be careful and not insult the lady if you value your life. Pea here is a classy Virginia opossum who doubles as my guard dog from the depths of Hell."

I tracked my memory back to yesterday evening. She had been hidden in my jacket, or in Woody's pouch, every time he had been around and had apparently managed to escape his notice. I wish I could have said the same.

"Mmm." He side-eyed Pea and me with a clear *this-lady-is-nuts* vibe, then attempted to pass me a card, deftly avoiding the snapping Jaws of Death. Little did he know, everything I said was true.

My eyebrow raised, almost as if on its own volition, and I left the familiar card in his hand. "I don't know where you come from but, generally speaking, around here when we offer people business cards they aren't for the receiver's own business."

He pinched the unfairly perfect bridge of his nose in a clear attempt for patience. Point to Cam. "Did Sheriff Danly not tell you about me?"

"Oh, he did. However, Jeff Danly is also incredibly respectful of my time and my organization. He knows how we operate. Therefore, I also know he would have informed you that you would have needed to call ahead to schedule an appointment."

"I would think you would be more compassionate toward a relative of a missing person."

"Oh, I am incredibly compassionate toward relatives and friends of those who are missing. But I think we both know Dr. Aoki had no known relatives. So cut the bullshit. What are you doing on my property? Why are you stalking me?" I asked sharply.

"My, we have a really big opinion of ourselves, don't we? You are not the one I'm interested in. I am looking for Dr. Aoki. Your goals just happen to align with mine."

"And for what purpose?" I hadn't relaxed my stance to allow him admittance into the building yet.

He stared at me, face blank, all previous façade falling from his expression and posture. "Ms. Kimoto. You were seen talking to a rather large *kamikiri* a few months back. I hear you and this *kamikiri*, Kenichi I believe his name is, are quite close."

"What are you trying to imply?" My tone dropped, becoming a near growl.

"Merely an observation of something I had overheard. It seems you must not fall into the ranks of the Quotes if you have befriended a *kamikiri* in his natural form. Perhaps that explains your success rate. I am sure if he too went missing, you would go above and beyond to find him."

"Is that a threat?" I asked sweetly.

"Oh, Ms. Kimoto. I do not play in the sandbox of threats."

"Then we should get along just fine because neither do I, Mr. Sugiyama.

"Excellent. Now that we've established neither of us are children," he said and gestured toward the lobby beyond me, "shall we move past this doorway?"

Of all the smug, arrogant, entitled, little—

"Stop sputtering in your mind and listing off a bunch of unfavorable adjectives. We have work to do." He took me by the shoulders and neatly set me to the side as if I weighed nothing, then brushed past me and into the building, narrowly missing being torn to shreds by Pea's snapping jaw.

My jaw dropped at his absolute gall and I stood there fuming.

"Any day, Ms. Kimoto," he called. "Or should I call you *Tsubaki* since we seem to have dropped the formalities? And no, I cannot read your mind. You were forming your words with those lovely lips of yours."

"My name is Cam," I gritted out, finding the opposite problem with my jaw now. It felt like a steel trap that had closed on air.

"Mmm," he mused. "Perhaps *Baki* would be better suited. Yes. Baki. Like the sound of a snapping branch. Much like the sound of your protests."

I could feel a tic forming under my right eye as I gripped an irate Pea closer to me and followed Rafael into the building. I was grateful we didn't have any current deployments and none of my usual employees were present. Yuriko, my coordinator and an exceptional SAR handler herself, would have shattered him where he stood before he could take another step. Not for the first time, I grieved the changes in my life that prevented me from making additional moves as I watched him make his way into one of the conference rooms. I swept past it, not bothering to say anything. As if I would cater to a male's needs like that. I may not hold the power I once did, but I could still manipulate the situation in other ways. If he wanted to talk, we would do it in a room of my choosing, not his.

I walked right past the room he entered and into our break room, stepping over the prone body of Woody who was lounging in the doorway of the room, for all intents and purposes looking as though he had not been closely watching the interaction between me and Rafael.

Vicky's tail thumped from her usual spot under a table as I began working the espresso machine to make myself another cup of coffee. I pulled out some food from the refrigerator as the espresso machine occupied itself with my shots and began to assemble a lunch for myself. Far be it from me to waste time while Sugiyama decided to play games with me. I had better things to do, like eat.

CHAPTER SIX

Right about the time I finished making my sandwich, I heard a stirring in the other room and I smiled to myself. Two points to Cam. After a few moments, footsteps neared the break room. Woody shifted, lifting his head to assess the stranger encroaching on his territory. I leaned back in my chair to see how this would go. Woody was protective and territorial; not over property, but over his chosen family. He wouldn't attack, but would use his body to block and intimidate if he sensed a threat unless I recalled him.

Rafael came within a few feet of the door when Woody stood to his full height, hackles raised. He was a good thirty-six inches at the shoulder, without the extra fluff, which took many by surprise. Rafael stopped in his tracks, more leery of the large guardian in the doorway than he had been of the four-pound opossum.

"Sorry, Pea," I whispered quietly, giving said creature a scratch under her chin. "Just demonstrates what a flaming idiot this man is. Won't that be a fun surprise for him?"

We had the eccentric opossum lady role down to an art. Who needed cats when you had a sassy magic-wielding *shikigami* possessing the body of a dead opossum? I had unlocked the most forbidden of the cats.

Rafael attempted to edge closer to the door but abstained from this when Woodrow's head dropped and turned to face him, increasing the threat in his stance. Taking pity on the male, I called Woody to me. His demeanor immediately changed and he bounced into the break room, tail curled up and wagging. He sat by my side, taking me for my word that Rafael wasn't a threat to us for now, though he had clearly been unconvinced by the encounter he had witnessed at the front door.

I gestured toward the refrigerator. "Stay by the fridge for now. I have a dog under this table next to me with a traumatic history due to men. She'll be fine after being exposed to you for half an hour or so, but she needs to get used to being around you first."

Rafael's expression darkened for a fleeting moment then cleared so quickly I wondered if I had imagined it. He cocked his head to the side by an infinitesimal degree, "How does that work when you're on a deployment with other men?"

Much as this male might rankle me, I was always willing to talk about my K9s and how they operated. "That's a great question. It took us a good bit to get to this point, and for a long while I wasn't sure if she'd made it through the training or if it was fair to her to continue. But when she has her vest on, she knows she's on the job and focuses on the task ahead of her rather than the fear from her past, and she absolutely loves her job. When she doesn't have her vest on, she doesn't have a specific task distracting her from those triggers. However, she's come a long way. For instance, she's calmly lying at my feet despite you being in the doorway, approximately six feet away, with nary a tremble."

"May I ask what happened to her?"

I reached under the table to rub Vicky in her favorite spot behind her ears to give myself a moment before relaying her story.

"The boys," I motioned to Woody, "Woodrow and my Saint Bernard, and I had been in Laurelhurst Park wrapping up a training one evening when I was suddenly unable to divert Woody from a specific path. He ultimately guided me to a home, and as it turned out, Vicky was being used as leverage against her owner. Both had significant injuries when I came across them. The perpetrator was found guilty of assault in the first degree and was sentenced to ten years. Vicky's original owner begged me to keep her, afraid of a repeat situation in the future should he ever find her again once he was out."

He wouldn't. I'd make sure of that.

Her owner was now safely situated several states away. I'd made arrangements with contacts of mine, as her abuser had isolated her from all of her resources. I frequently sent her updates and photos of Vicky. Time with Pea had healed Vicky's physical wounds and time with all of us was slowly healing her emotional ones. Giving her a job had helped to refocus the anxiety and trauma that had accumulated from the situation, and her natural agility allowed her to excel in disaster scenarios.

"Mmm. It would have been better if you had killed him." I didn't disagree, but alas, Quotes had a different sense of justice. Sugiyama frowned at the fluffy malamute staring at him with a tongue lolling out the side of his mouth.

"Isn't that much of an independent streak somewhat undesirable in search dogs though?"

I heaved a sigh and side-eyed Woody. "It can be. However, independence to a degree is what we look for in our SAR K9s. This one makes it work. When we're on a search he buckles down and does his job. But only when he's actually searching. This one's intelligent enough to know the difference between training and searches."

"So that night on Helens..."

"We were on a break due to having lost the scent and had just been recalled. He wasn't working. And you admit you were the creeper in the woods."

"What can I do to make her more comfortable with me around?" Sugiyama changed the subject rather than addressing my statement. However, the sincerity behind his question took me aback again and I noticed he had remained in the door, despite calling off Woody. He clenched his left fist as he rubbed at his forearm with his right hand.

That question went a long way toward softening me, as did the way he respected Vicky's space. It didn't make me trust him, all things considered, but it provided a small window into the make-up of what made this male tick. And the sliver I could see from this small glance was thus far better than Creeper In The Woods. Although, there was a real possibility he was just asking so he could avoid a mauling by my K9s.

"Move calmly and softly. Don't speak harshly around her at this point, or ever if you can help it. Don't approach her—she's a naturally curious dog and she's gotten to the point where she will approach you on her own for the sake of her curiosity. Just ignore her and allow her to seek you out, then reward her with some good loving behind her ears when she does. Once she does, you're in, unless you do something to revoke that status."

He followed my guidance, moving into the break room at a relaxed pace, dropping all arrogance from earlier, and sat down at the seat I had indicated. Interesting. In the fifteen minutes since meeting this man, he had worn three different masks on top of Creeper. Business Suave. Dead-Inside Arrogant Asshole, and Considerate Toward Animals. I was going to get whiplash at this rate. I wondered which one was the real Rafael Sugiyama.

"Thank you. Regardless of everything else, I appreciate your consideration for Vicky's needs." I took a bite of my sandwich and regarded him. Swallowing, I continued. "Now, why are you looking for Dr. Aoki? You need to understand, I don't just search for a missing person on behalf of an unknown party. There could be a number of reasons an individual goes missing, including an attempt to escape a dangerous situation, and I'm not about to release information to someone who could place that person in harm's way. Well-intentioned or not. And to be quite frank, I have major doubts about your intentions from the little interaction I've had with you thus far."

Rafael appraised me from across the table for several moments with a serious gaze. I could practically see his internal scales weighing what information to dole out to me and what information to hold back behind those rich brown eyes. Woody leaned his body against me and rested his head on the break room table, gazing back at Rafael.

I raised an eyebrow in a *get on with it* signal.

"We have reason to believe Dr. Aoki is not a Quotidian, but instead a citizen of the Ryūgū-jō of rather high importance."

"And what makes you think she would like to return to the Undersea Kingdom? Perhaps there was a good reason she left," I questioned, unimpressed. "Several of our *yōkai* immigrants are originally from Ryūgū-jō. Some are even of noble rank. That is no reason for me to risk her safety on your behalf."

"I would personally be delighted to allow her to stay here, if she so chose. It would make my own life so much easier. However, it would seem her absence is the cause of the famines and the unrest that is plaguing the kingdom."

"Ahhh, yes. Breathe in the fresh smell of misogyny in the morning. So like the sea *kami* to blame it all on a woman and not his ability to control the tides and the ocean's harvests," I sneered. "What, is she a *yamauba* or an *oni baba* that cursed his domain? They don't even live in the sea. But wait, you said a citizen of high importance, and a mountain crone or demon hag would never hold positions of high importance in any of our kingdoms despite their power." It was the reason why so many of them had flocked to the mountain ranges found in the Ring of Fire.

"I am afraid I am unable to say what her position was. I only know what I've been told and what I have seen," he responded stoically.

"I am also afraid I have yet to see reason to work with you to find her, *kariudo*." I eyed him with a steady gaze.

Rafael stiffened at the use of his title.

I nodded. "You're not the only one holding cards here. I am aware of who you are and what you represent. Do you see why I would hesitate to collaborate on a SAR with the huntsman of the sea *kami*? Your reputation precedes you."

"My reputation may precede me, Ms. Kimoto," Rafael began quietly, "but the deaths of innocent children and families overtake my reputation by far. May I?" He held up a small drive.

I got up and motioned for him to follow me. Woody and Vicky fell in between us as I entered the third conference room to the right of the break room. As Sugiyama settled in, I accessed the system's guest account and passed him the keyboard silently as my assent. He pulled out the drive and plugged it into the hub. After a few clicks, a slideshow of horrors began to play across the entire wall.

Dead infants and children laid out with their parents kneeling over them, keening with grief. Others too mired in trauma to weep and staring with eyes with no life left within them instead, as if their souls fled the moment their children's souls left this realm. All malnourished. The parents just moments from their own deaths. A video played as a female died, a wailing infant in the distance. Her spirit rose, visible only to me and few others. She would be a *kosodate yūrei* now. Cursed to try to find her child in her death.

Adult bodies laid out, gaunt and showing signs of malnutrition. Mass graves. Forests laid barren where kelp should be thriving. Massive red algae blooms suffocating growth. Then the next slide clicked over.

These families lay dead of mortal wounds. Not of starvation.

"What happened here?" I whispered. Yet I knew. It was the same event which repeated itself over and over again in history.

"With the famines, some citizens have resorted to slaughtering one another for their neighbor's food stores. Riots have been breaking out."

"Why hasn't the *kami* done anything to stop this?" Rage leaked into my voice as my words came out clipped and raised.

Rafael hesitated. "Ryujin's powers are...not what they once were, according to the immortals who have known him the longest. His powers are unstable. Unreliable at best. He has been unable to stop the famines or put a stop to the riots at all." He winced minutely, as if in pain, rotating his wrist just ever so slightly against the table. Had I not been watching him so intently, I would have missed it.

There was a hollowness in Rafael's eyes after what he had showed me. A quiet whine sounded in the room. He glanced down and a touch of the despair left his gaze. His hand left the keyboard as he reached down to scratch Vicky behind her ears, and the thumping of her tail echoed in the room as she tried to fill his void and comfort him.

I closed my eyes and my own nightmares flashed before me. I silently calculated to myself what the toll of working with this male would be. The trauma I would relive over and over again.

But then, it was never any question at all, was it? When weighing the personal cost to myself as compared to the cost of the lives already lost, I had no choice.

"We will work with you." *Kamis* damn us all.

CHAPTER SEVEN

When my eyes reopened, it was to a fleeting look of immense relief and gratitude across the table. I was getting glimpses of who I thought might be the genuine person underneath it all. Which reminded me…

"If we are going to work together, I'm going to have stipulations. First and foremost is that you will leave that arrogant asshole suit packed away in the closet. I understand if you need to pull it on in public around others. But around me and my team, it will be left at the door. Are we understood?" I intoned.

"We are understood," he assured me.

"Second, you will tell me as much as you are able. I understand you have your own stipulations on what you can say, but my team and I will be hamstrung if you withhold information from us."

"The same goes for you."

"Only if I feel that it is in the best interest of Dr. Aoki's safety. I will not risk her life in any way. If I feel divulging her information to you at any point on this search will risk harm to her being, information *will* be held. Bar none."

Rafael's right eye tightened just a touch in response, but he nodded. I would need to watch him carefully to learn him; he barely gave away any of his body language.

"Now, on that topic, when you said you are unable to tell me Dr. Aoki's position, do you mean you *won't* or you *can't.*" I asked, backtracking to our earlier topic of conversation.

"Ah. I cannot."

Those three words told me quite a bit in terms of the nature of his servitude to the *kami.* I shot a quick glance at the wrist he had been rubbing moments before. His wrists were covered by the button-up he wore, but I had my suspicions. His form rippled at my glance, minute movements betraying the discomfort he felt.

"What *can* you tell me about her then? It will make this less tedious if I'm not repeating information you already know."

He nodded, relaxing as my focus shifted. "If she is the one I seek, she was one of the many who went missing during the infamous *Hyakki Yagyō* when Ryūgū-jō was attacked. Sometime during the chaos of the Night Procession, she vanished despite the guards who were assigned to watch her. Initially she had been presumed dead, but no body was recovered. Recently, information came to the attention of the *kami* that she was seen in the Pacific Northwest, associating with the *yōkai* living in this region."

"That goes with the information I just collected. Have you heard the tales of the *bijin*?" I asked, bringing up another keyboard in order to access my own account.

"A beautiful woman? I mean, I have met my fair share and have heard tales of many. But I have a feeling that's not what you mean."

I snorted. "I am sure you have. No—I learned in the past few days, the local *yōkai* developed their own bogeyman tale up here in the Pacific Northwest."

"And of course their bogeyman would be a gorgeous woman?"

"It tracks, doesn't it?"

"Sadly yes. What of this tale you speak of?"

"Supposedly, many moons ago, a beautiful disoriented Japanese woman appeared in the misty woods of the Gifford Pinchot National Forest, on Mount St. Helens, mumbling about the *yōkai.* Sound like it could be our gal?"

He stared at me.

"What?" I looked down at myself and at Pea. Was I drooling? I tried to wipe my chin surreptitiously.

"Why are you still here if you have this information?"

"What do you think I was doing when you showed up? I was going to start prepping for another trip to Helens to meet up with a contact I have up there who should have more information."

"When do we leave?"

"Well, *Rafe*." If he wanted to bastardize my name, I would do the same to his. As I suspected, there was that barest tightening to his eye when I did so. I leaned way back in my chair and Pea gave a low hiss, disgruntled with my movement, and scrambled for the tabletop. "We certainly aren't leaving today. First, you are by no means prepared to go hiking in your current getup. Given you are the *kariudo*, I am going to assume you are prepared for all manner of scenarios and can handle the trek, and you either have, or can obtain, the appropriate gear. So, you would need to go off and get yourself situated and then return. And second, it's midafternoon. Helens is another three-and-a-half hours away. I just got in from a four-day deployment late yesterday evening. I need a real night in my bed. We'll spend a few more hours comparing notes and planning and then meet here at the crack of dawn to leave for the mountain tomorrow."

He sighed and agreed, clearly having done a similar routine in his position many times before. The urge to immediately act on new information was strong, but being impulsive could result in someone getting injured or killed.

We spent another hour comparing notes before we started planning our trip.

"Oliver is...eccentric," I warned. "You will need to be incredibly respectful. He has been through a lot over the years and has no kin left. His family didn't have a good history with the previous *kariudo*. You will not harm him in *any* way, or this partnership is off."

"I understand," Rafael said solemnly.

"I don't think you do. He is deeply paranoid. And rightfully so. You'll need to earn his trust and you'll be working with a bank balance that's heavy in the red when it comes to him."

My warning had lit a spark of curiosity under Rafael, but I wouldn't be revealing Oliver's species to him beforehand. The last *kariudo* had decimated them on the *kami's* order and his kind were all but extinct.

"In that case, how would you recommend I start garnering his trust?" he queried.

I shook my head. "No. Your trust with him will have to be entirely gained on your own grounds without any prior aid on my part for it to be genuine, otherwise it will be immediately suspect. What I've already told you has gone far enough."

I stood from the table and motioned to the hall. "Come on, I'll give you a brief tour of the facility and then you should go get prepped for tomorrow."

I led him out of the conference room, Vicky and Woody happily trailing me, while Pea settled back into the chair I had been in, seemingly okay with Rafael's presence for now.

"As you can see, we have six conference rooms. Each one serves as a base of operations for a deployment, as we may have multiple deployments going at any given time. The one we were just in is the one we are using for Dr. Aoki, so consider it your home for now." I spoke as we walked through the grounds.

I had walked him through the break room, equipment room, and was in the process of showing him the gym when I heard the heavy slap of the dog door on the back entrance and the subsequent thuds of Maxwell's lope. Max typically liked to stay outdoors so he could sleep in the rubble of a disaster simulation whenever we were at the training facility, ironically making it nearly impossible to spot him. I took a couple strides back from Rafael, curious how this would play out. He glanced at me quizzically, clearly confused as to why I was backing away from him.

With Max's ability to track magic, he typically reacted to the owner of the magic in one of three ways: hostility, indifference, or intrigue.

The beast in question came thundering around the corner at a speed too fast for him to control and he smashed into the opposite wall as per his usual. If dogs could roll their eyes, I could practically feel Vicky doing the canine version of it next to me. He scrambled to regain his balance, then spotted Rafael and, to my utter shock, did not react in one of the three ways.

The mad dog launched his entire bulk on the man, toppling them both over, sending me, Woody, and Vicky scattering, and absolutely slobbered all over Rafael's face while wriggling with joy and making frantic whimpering noises. I had no idea what to make of it and stood there sniggering.

Rafael sputtered, trying to get his hands up to protect his face, but they were pinned to his sides. "What is even happening? A little assistance here?"

"Mmm, nah. I'm kinda enjoying this."

He glared at me from the floor. "You planned this, didn't you." A long slurping tongue traveled from his chin to past his hairline, leaving him with one hell of a cowlick.

I leaned a shoulder against the gym wall and grinned wickedly. "I really didn't. All of the credit goes to Max. But I wish I *could* claim credit."

Having mercy on the male, I called Max to heel and he bounded away, using Rafael as a springboard. The male folded in half with the involuntary exhale. He took a few moments to recover his breath before he stood. Taking a good look at him, I started laughing outright. Living in the land of weather mood swings, Max had, of course, found at least one mud puddle, and Rafael's beautifully tailored French blue button-up now had several paw prints decorating it. His carefully styled coif was…well, you could say it was styled. Just maybe not carefully.

Trying to hold in my cackles, I offered, "Let me know where you're staying and I'll cover the dry cleaning. It's the least I can do since I imagine you don't want to set a new fashion trend in Ryūgū-jō."

"No need," he said before muttering something under his breath.

"I'm sorry, what was that?"

"I said I can't imagine The Hairy Inn has anything remotely resembling dry cleaning services to begin with."

My eyes widened. "Oh God. What possessed you to make a reservation at *The Hairy Inn*? Don't you read reviews before making reservations? I'm beginning to rethink this whole idea of working together if you can't do a simple thing like read a review."

"Yes, well, I was going for proximity over luxury and thought it couldn't possibly be as bad as the few reviews made it out to be. Joke's on me."

I shook my head. "I have a few studio apartments nearby for staff to use when we have deployments going. You're welcome to use one when we get back in town. No one should be subjected to the crotchety moods of ol' man Dalton."

It wasn't an offer I had initially planned on making; however, I was pleading the case of keeping my enemies closer. Besides, as I eyed Max, his tail thumping happily as he stared adoringly up at Rafael, my K9s' judgments went a long way for me.

Rafael's shoulders went limp with relief. "You have no idea how much I appreciate the offer. Thank you."

I waved off the thanks and our procession continued out the door Max had just barged through. The facility sat on slightly over a hundred acres, and over the years, my team and I had built up different areas, each devoted to a different disaster scenario. Underwater, urban bombing, various natural disasters, etc. The only one we didn't have was a mudslide. None of us wanted to mimic those conditions here. It had taken thousands of hours of manpower, and not a little bit of magic, but the effect was impressive.

Judging by the look on Rafael's face, he thought so too. "I can see why so many people come to your facility for their training."

I shrugged. "Anybody can have a fancy facility if they're bucks up or if they have an investor who is. It's about being able to partner handlers with a dog who will be the right fit for this job. And training the handler to listen to their K9, to understand what their needs are, not to let their K9s burn out and to give them the right amount of engagement. And how not to become burnt out or depressed themselves. This is not an easy job. That's not about the facility; that's about the instructors. Luckily, I have some amazing ones who've stayed on." I gestured to the property beyond us. "This was just fun for us. Basically Legos, but if you got to blow shit up, in the case of the urban bombing scenario. The training and the searches are where our passions lie."

"I have an immense amount of respect for that, Tsubaki," Rafael said with a smile, though it seemed to be touched by sadness. "On that note—I'll head back to the inn so I can get prepped to head out and pack so I can check out of that godforsaken place."

I smiled in return, then circled my index finger around in the vicinity of his hair. "Uh, before you, um, go out into any public spaces, you might want to…fix your hair."

His hand flew up to gingerly pat his hair, now stiff with Saint Bernard drool. He groaned while I cackled madly. In the end, the scoreboard went entirely to Max today.

CHAPTER EIGHT

Rafael wearily inserted the key card in the door, which blinked red in defiance. He cursed in Japanese and tried again to no avail. Irritated, he pulled the card out and counted to thirty in Portuguese in his head before trying again and this time he was finally able to enter his room at The Hairy Inn. A hot shower was all he had wanted for the past week, but the Abstruse lodge was owned by a cantankerous Sasquatch and getting the hot water fixed in his room had been an exercise in patience. Far be it from him to understand why someone with such a nature would be in a position of hospitality.

He threw the key card on the rickety table, letting the door automatically slam shut behind him, and caught a glimpse of himself in the cloudy mirror hanging over the table that failed to hide the peeling wallpaper behind it. He quickly looked away, never enjoying what he saw in his reflection.

He held the name Rafael Sugiyama. But like everything else, it was yet another façade, a role, a mask he wore. He was *tabula rasa* under it all, a blank slate, never quite certain who or what he really was anymore after the many decades he had spent bound to the sea dragon. His name felt like an ill-fitting pair of shoes that left your feet bleeding and raw in the end. It had only set him further apart from his peers, accentuating the difference in his lineage as compared to theirs.

Rafe. He rolled the nickname around on his tongue, tasting it. He'd never been bestowed one before. His father, enraged that he had not been given a traditional Japanese name, never bothered to call him anything but "the boy," the words imbued with contempt. The sea *kami* had no use for such worthless, useless things such as nicknames. The only other name he was called was *kariudo* and that was said with trembling fear, for those he hunted knew the wrath of the sea *kami* was behind the hunt. He wondered how Rafe would end up fitting in the end.

He was startled by how much he had enjoyed the hours he had spent in Camellia Kimoto's company. Her sharp mind and wit kept him on his toes, and he found himself having to catch himself before responding reactively. It had been the most alive he had felt since childhood. He also couldn't remember the last time he had been taken down so quickly. Let alone by something as mundane as a dog. He cringed as he touched his crunchy hair. A hot shower. Was that too much to ask for? He shook his head as he began unbuttoning his shirt, revealing his skin marred with images of violence.

In all honesty, he was tired. Physically, emotionally, and mentally exhausted. He dropped his shirt on the bed and headed to the bathroom, removing the thick leather cuffs he wore around his wrists as he went. Next came the glamour that fell away like a woman's slip, delicately and gently, which only served to heighten the harshness of what it revealed on his forearms. Rafael let out a heavy sigh of relief and shuddered as the glamour dissipated. He turned the shower on, as hot as it would go, though he knew the effort was futile—the filth he felt was internal and not so easily removed—and turned his attention to the remainder of his clothes. He absentmindedly rubbed his wrists when he was done. Every day the effort of keeping up with the masks, his missions for the sea *kami*, missions which ate away at his soul, wore him down. He could feel it in his bones. He was caring less and less about the details and the importance of maintaining a persona. He would find it a relief when his end finally came.

But it apparently wouldn't be on this mission. His interest had been piqued and he was too intrigued to see where this would go.

The game had started. The players on the board had been set. He hadn't anticipated the SAR woman wouldn't fall for the distant relative story. After all, the sheriff had. He'd had enough social media and paperwork to back it up. The wonders of technology, photo editing, and the Undersea

Kingdom's magic users. All of the background information and character profiles he had amassed over the past week had led him to believe she was a kind, compassionate woman. The fiery and fierce protector he was met with today had taken him by surprise. But he would read her cues and adapt his own façade. It was why he excelled in his position.

It was why he no longer knew who Rafael Sugiyama was.

CHAPTER NINE

Before I called it and went to bed, the gang and I had made another trek out to see Kenichi so I could warn him of Rafael's implied threat and update him on everything. To say that I didn't think my eardrums would ever recover from the mantid's admonishing screeches would be putting it lightly.

"He did what?" Ken seethed, looming over me threateningly. "You bet your bottom dollar this eight-and-a-half-foot mant-*ass* ain't going anywhere it doesn't want to. He can just fucking try to disappear me. He's not going to succeed. You know damn well cockroaches have nothing on *kamikiris* when it comes to immortality. Especially the males. Decapitate us all you want. It'll grow back. With the amount of hair you've given me over the years? On top of the hair I've collected from my salon? There's no way he's finding all of my hidden stores and burning them."

"I'm sorry. Rewind. You need to back up several sentences. What did you call yourself again? An eight-and-a-half-foot *what*?" I slow-blinked at my friend.

He clacked his pincers at me. "Focus!"

"Oh, no. I'm not ever letting you live this down. From here on out, you shall be dubbed Mant-Ass-*sama*."

He groaned and four of his limbs flew into the air in exasperation. "Cam! There is a *kamis*-damned *kariudo* in town. You are clearly being hunted. And this! This is what you focus on?"

"Mm-hmm. Can you blame me? Who would want to focus on all that crap when you are dangling something as juicy as *mant-ass* right in front of me?"

"Yes! I am blaming you right now! Did your mother drop you off a cliff onto a pile of rocks as a child?"

"Most likely yes. Or beat me with one. I mean…Korean here. *Maemmae* sticks weren't necessarily sticks, just whatever happened to be handy at the time I needed to be disciplined."

Ken facepalmed. That had to hurt with pincers.

"Look. I promise I'm not just going into this willy-nilly with no plan whatsoever."

"You offered him an apartment, *Cam*."

"Okay, first of all, breathe, *Ken*. Second, haven't you ever heard the saying, 'Keep your friends close, but your enemies closer'? That's the principle I'm applying here. And third, for the love of God, breathe. Don't forget what happened to the last *kariudo.*"

Kenichi just glared at me. An eight-and-a-half-foot mant-ass glaring at you was exactly as intimidating as it sounded.

I sighed. "I swear to all that is unholy. The last thing I am trying to do is get captured or killed. I'm being careful. What I came out here to do was warn you and to ask you to look over this territory while I'm gone. I'm not sure how long this search is going to take. You're the one I trust most in Skamania."

His gaze immediately softened. "Cam, of course I will, but—"

I shook my head. "There can't be any buts for something this important, Ken. No qualifiers. Either you're all in or not."

"It's not that I'm not all in. It's that I need to know you're coming back. We all need to know you're coming back."

My shoulders fell. "You know I would never willingly leave you without notice, right? But I can't promise anything beyond telling you I'll do everything in my power to return."

"That's all I'm asking for." He laid a midlimb gently on my shoulder. "And for you to stop fucking with my nonexistent heart like this."

"That, you'll have to take up with the *kami.*"

I JUST FINISHED brewing myself a quad-shot latte when I felt the shudder in the facility's wards notifying me Rafael was on his way. I had dragged myself and the gang to the office after being abruptly woken up by another nightmare in the wee hours of the morning and failing to see any point in trying to go back to sleep. Might as well use the time to get some work done, and the time had been well spent finishing up my report for Jeff and reviewing last month's financials.

I hauled the pack I had prepped yesterday, and the K9s' harnesses, onto a worktable and settled back to take a sip from my travel mug. Pea eyed me speculatively from the table.

"Not you too."

She gave me a series of admonishing clicks followed by a long hiss.

"I don't trust him either. He changes personas too quickly for me to get a grasp on him. But his concern for the dying citizens seemed genuine. And I'm pretty sure he's unwillingly bound to the *kami*. You saw him rubbing his wrists, right?"

A shorter hiss.

"Besides, he has information on Dr. Aoki that we don't. I'm hoping we get to her first and ultimately keep her out of the sea *kami's* grasp."

Pea cocked her head and clicked in surprise.

"Gee, thanks. You seriously thought we were just going to find her and hand her over? Come on, you've been with me for how long now?" I shook my head and took another sip of my coffee as I heard the front door open. Max scrambled to go say hello and I called him back to heel so we wouldn't have a repeat of yesterday. I wondered what it was about Rafael's magic that appealed to Max so much.

I lifted my travel mug in greeting as he appeared in the doorway.

"Coffee?" I gestured to the espresso machine with the mug.

"Dear gods, yes," he groaned. "Of course there isn't any at Satan's Inn."

I snickered. Ah, Dalton. I wasn't sure how the furry guy stayed in business. I wasn't sure he even wanted to stay in business. Hell, I wasn't sure *why* he was still in business.

"How do you take yours?"

"What are you drinking?"

"This morning it's a quad-shot latte."

"That sounds like bliss. Absolute bliss."

I got to work and handed him his own latte in a travel mug soon after. He closed his eyes as he took his first sip and I'm pretty sure the male traveled to the Otherworld of Heaven in that instant.

"You, Baki, you are a goddess among immortals."

I snorted. "How much gear do we need to transfer over to my vehicle?"

"Just my pack and what's on me." He stepped out from behind the island he'd been leaning on and spread out an arm to gesture toward himself.

Oh. Hello there.

The man had looked good in a tailored shirt and slacks, but I'm not shy about having a type and knowing my type was a nice rugged, outdoorsy guy. He was in a snug, thermal long-sleeved top that clung to his torso and biceps. The fact that it covered his wrists didn't go unnoticed by me. His pants were waterproof trekking pants that somehow absolutely hugged his ass in all the right ways and tapered off at his boots at just the right length. Was there a company out there that tailored trekking pants? If so, I was sending them all my money. He had a tactical knife strapped to each thigh. Both of which had magical enhancements I could sense.

"My eyes are up here."

My gaze snapped up to said eyes, one of which had a brow quirked in amusement. I cleared my throat, "What magical enhancements are on those blades?"

The eyebrow raised slightly higher, going from amusement to inquiry. "So you weren't admiring my ass? Ah, I'm so disappointed."

I began coughing as my coffee chose to commit the ultimate betrayal and leapt into the wrong pipe. My lungs weren't even connected to my trachea anymore. How was that even fair?

"You wish," I sputtered, trying my best to deny that I had, in fact, been checking out his body. "It's the sharps I'm interested in. Not the curves."

"Yes, well, we'll bypass that obvious lie for now, for the intriguing fact that you can sense magical enhancements? What an interesting trick you have up your sleeve. You're certainly no Quote. I think I shall enjoy trying to figure you out. Two are maintenance spells. One keeps the blades sharp, the other is a self-cleaning spell."

"Ah. So you're lazy."

"Mmm. I prefer to think of it as efficient."

"You said two, which implies at least one other."

"The last is a spell which prevents any wound caused by one of these blades from healing."

Pea growled while I stared at him aghast.

"Do you know what that would do to an immortal?" I demanded.

"Of course I do," Rafael responded disdainfully, as if I were a small child. "A festering wound which would never, during the eternity of an immortal's lifespan, heal. Only the *kami* holds the antidote. Never forget my position, Baki."

"Those blades are not coming with us."

"I'm afraid they are, Ms. Kimoto."

"You don't understand. If Oliver sees these blades and senses those enhancements, he will never speak with us. Our chances of getting any information whatsoever will be nixed. Hand them over and I'll put them in the safe."

He surveyed me skeptically for a few moments before he sighed and unbuckled the sheaths from his thighs and handed the weapons to me. I gingerly carried them to one of the safes which only I had the combination to and placed them inside. He had capitulated so easily, I suspected he had other weapons on him, but at least these were the ones that would have been easily visible to Oliver.

"While we are on the topic of your ability to sense magical enhancement, what are you, Baki?"

I turned around and smiled sweetly, feigning ignorance. "American."

He bared his teeth in return, a semblance of a smile. "You know what I mean. What are you?"

"Korean and Japanese."

He didn't make the grimace or commentary I typically received when I revealed my heritage. *Huh.* Maybe the sea *kami* had started to offer sensitivity training. And maybe they had started offering ice water in hell.

"No questions about how I came to be? Comments about how those two nationalities usually hate one another?" So sue me if I was a little defensive. A lifetime of discrimination for just existing would do that to you.

Rafael gestured toward himself. "Brazilian and Japanese here. As another *hafu* who has always been looked down upon for not being one or the other, I can hardly talk."

He continued in a reasonable tone of voice, "If we are going to be working together, it would behoove me to know what you are in the event we run into trouble. It would allow me to better utilize my own resources. Thus far, I obviously know you're Abstruse. You can perceive the *yōkai*, you can sense magical enhancements. But your…" He appeared bewildered as he gestured all around me. "Your soul. It looks…fragmented. As if—it looks shattered. Like shattered glass. I've never seen anything like it."

I froze, feeling the blood draining from my face. Blackness began to infiltrate my vision, creeping in from the edges.

The sea is all around me.

I feel like I am drowning.

An immense pressure closes on my heart.

I run. Looking for him.

I hear a snap.

And my whole world shatters.

"Baki? Baki!"

The sound of Rafael's voice startled me back to the present. His presence was all-encompassing, a warm heat close to my front, a hand against my bicep. Warm, concerned eyes looking into mine, far too close to my own.

I turned back to the safe and slammed it shut, the force of it reverberating through the room.

"Tsubaki. Where did you go?"

"Never speak of my soul again," I snarled, barely holding back a shift, a shift that would be devastating under these circumstances.

He held up both hands in surrender as I swept past him, heading out to my vehicle, grabbing my gear and pack from the table. Pea scurried down the table, hissing at him as she went by.

As soon as the front door swung shut behind me, I dropped the gear and folded over, bracing myself against my knees. Deep inhales of crisp morning air filled my lungs while I desperately tried to regulate my emotions again. I could feel beads of sweat trickling down the back of my neck and forehead. Pea's tail curled around my ankle and she butted her head against my leg. I slid against the wall of the building and sat next to her, concentrating on the feel of her individual strands of fur as I stroked her, grounding myself in the here and now. Vicky, the most sensitive of my K9s, came around the corner of the building and pressed her body to mine. I hugged the two of them to me tightly. I had wondered what the omen behind my nightmares would be. I had my answer. The dead and the dying in Ryūgū-jō. The unexpected ties the famines would have with my SAR. Rafael.

The front door began to creak open and I scrambled back to my feet. A silence fell over us, though not uncomfortable in nature, and Rafael surveyed me while holding both mugs of coffee in his hands.

"I know how it is to have your soul shredded into unrecognizable pieces," he began in a formal tone. "Torn to such small pieces, you are unable to put them back together again. Not knowing who is staring at you in the mirror. Or which way is up or which way is down. It was thoughtless of me to ask that question. I had only been thinking in terms of how to work as a well-oiled team. I was careless. I sometimes become blinded by my goals and forget to see others and I should be cognizant of that. I hope you're able to forgive me."

I stared at him in silence for a few more moments, unsure of how to respond. Of all the things I had been expecting to come out of his mouth, this hadn't been it. I eyed him warily while he gazed at me with respect in his expression. His words had been genuine, but I was unable to get a read on the slot machine of personalities he seemed to have. As soon as I felt like I had a grip on one, it would slip my grasp and another would slide to take its place. But, reflecting on his words, it seemed this was the outcome of the shredding of his own soul. The inability to hold down any one personality for longer than fifteen minutes at a time. It made it difficult to trust him. Not that I wanted to trust him.

I gave him a slight head tilt to acknowledge his words, feeling uncertain of my ability to form my own in this moment. Instead, I opted for my favorite party trick and chose avoidance by picking my gear back up and heading to the *furin* wind chimes hanging from the eave. After I chose one of them, I pinched the *tanzaku* at the end of the paper and began delicately ringing it. Within seconds, a cacophony ensued, stemming from the lineup of vehicles in the parking lot. Rafael took a step back at the noise and reached behind his back. Well, that at least confirmed my belief about his weapons. I waved him off, waiting as hood after hood of our fleet of vehicles popped up, using the time to gather my emotions and shove them back into place. I squinted and counted the number of vehicles currently occupied.

I sighed. "I thought we discussed this. We need to have at least two vehicles in rotation at all times. You've left us one."

There were about three to five gremlins occupying all but one of our company vehicles. They all started chattering and banging their tools at me until I raised my hand. "I know we have shitty vehicles. The work you do on them is priceless, but if we have multiple teams who have to take off, what are they supposed to do if all the other vehicles are being worked on?"

The oversized ears on the small creatures drooped and their eyes grew round and sad. I rubbed my forehead. "Which one can be ready to go in the next six hours if you guys focus your attention on the basics and not the extras? I'm taking one now, and we absolutely cannot have just one working vehicle on the premises."

A small, high-pitched voice spoke up. Approximately eight inches tall, blue-skinned, with ears about half the size of their body and eyes overtaking their face, they climbed to the front of the SUV and balanced on the grill. They were wearing a combination of metal washers strung together as a top and what appeared to be rubber tubing as a skirt. Their hair was slicked back with motor oil. They raised a pierced eyebrow. "Do you know how shitty the SUVs you bought were? They would have broken down before you got out of driveway regardless of whether we were in them or not."

I snorted. "You're not wrong. I'm sorry, I should be more grateful. The past few days have been fucked, but that's no excuse."

A moment passed before they nodded, deciding to accept my apology, then pointed to two of the vehicles at the end of the lineup. "Those two should be drivable by the end of the day. Customizations will happen after we work on these here."

I sagged with relief. "Thank you, Aether. Love you lots." They turned around and began barking orders and using the wrench in their hand to point out various vehicles with their instructions.

A mass exodus of gremlins began leaving the vehicles and congregating into the two indicated instead. A small green body shimmied out from under the axle system of a truck and scampered my way. Their stout little body wore a dress made out of car seat leather which squeaked as they climbed up my body. I smiled when Gale stood on my shoulder and gave me a kiss on the cheek, chattering excitedly in my ear about the work they had done, before they gave Pea a hug and raced off to join the others.

I headed to the 4Runner that had been vacant of gremlins from the start, tossing my pack onto the roof of the rig, and began strapping things down as I stewed in silence. Vicky sat leaning against my legs, keeping me grounded, and waited patiently for me to load up. I wasn't sure what Rafael was, but I had never encountered a *kami, yōkai,* or *onmyōji* who could see the souls of living beings. It had to be a trait from his Brazilian heritage.

"This isn't the vehicle you typically drive," Rafael observed after he retrieved his own gear from his rental car. He took a sip from his latte while Vicky nosed at a fifty-liter pack sitting at his feet. I snagged his pack and tossed it on the roof to join mine.

"No, you stalker," I said shortly. "Oliver doesn't live in the Quotidian realm. Where we're heading, the road isn't maintained. My other 4Runner, much as I love it, wouldn't be able to make it. Well…it probably could. But I don't want to put it through that hell. This is my original baby." She was a 1984 Toyota 4Runner, a First Gen, with a number of modifications. Including the necessary hybrid of magic and gas for fuel, considering the current economy. I dropped the tailgate and whistled for the rest of my K9s who came sprinting from the back and leapt into the cargo area. Vicky jumped in after the behemoths made themselves comfortable and settled in between them. Rafael made his way to the passenger door.

Having secured everything, I opened the driver's side and bent to pick Pea up, placing her on the front seat. From there, she climbed into the hammock hanging between the two front seats.

"Really? The opossum comes too?"

I leaned my forehead against the frame of my rig and closed my eyes, not sure if this partnership was worth it. Apparently, the man was going to eviscerate my memories, nearly force me into a PTSD-induced shift, and question my genetic make-up, while making me want to pull my brain through my nostrils with a crotchet hook, all before six a.m.

I opened my eyes and pointed at him through the doorframe. "Suck on your coffee. Give me blessed peace for at least three hours. Don't touch shit in this car. And maybe you'll survive the trip to Helens without me killing you."

"As if you could," he smirked.

Oh, if he only knew. Pride always goeth before the fall.

CHAPTER TEN

Stepping up onto my running board, I hauled myself into the driver's seat. Rafael passed me the travel mug I kept forgetting about.

"Thanks," I said in surprise, taking a sip before placing it in the cupholder.

He inclined his head toward the facility. "Do we need to lock up or anything?"

"It's covered." The gremlins lived on-site and would lock up until day shift got here.

"Pea, music me, please."

I got the truck started while Pea rummaged behind me. A cassette tape dropped into my lap.

Rafael considered me. "Have I gone back in time? I don't remember when I last saw one of those. Should I pull out a No. 2 pencil just in case? Is shotgun in charge of winding the tapes back up with a pencil when they become unspooled? Also, did the opossum just pull out a cassette tape for you on command?"

"*You.* The deal was 'blessed peace for three hours.' Shut your gob. Also, her name is Pea." I opened the case and popped the tape in. I felt my nerves begin to settle as Michael Kiwanuka's vocals came over the speakers. Pea knew what she was doing. I shifted my baby into drive and we were on our way, just as the first rays of dawn were starting to break.

"I have to hand it to the furry critter. She has good taste. I didn't think Michael Kiwanuka put his hits on cassette tapes though," Rafael spoke after we'd been on the road for about fifteen minutes.

Apparently, this man was entirely unable to follow directions.

"I have no idea if he did or not. I doubt it. But I never upgraded the stereo in this vehicle, so I just buy cassette tapes and make mixed tapes the old-fashioned way," I explained shrugging. "Besides, it's good nostalgic fun."

"Mmm, I'll have to take your word for it. I never had that luxury."

Well that was a potential minefield of trauma I wasn't about to walk across. I side-eyed his countenance and observed him staring pensively out the window, watching the scenery whip past us.

"So. Gremlins. They're real. They weren't just World War II propaganda/morale booster bullshit."

I snorted at his choice of subject changes.

"They were. But they became tulpas by the end of the war. With so many people believing in their mythos, they were imagined into reality. Then the war ended and we had these gremlins who had no purpose anymore."

"And you let them work on your vehicles?" Rafael's tone had an air of disbelief to it. "They sabotaged countless aircraft during the last World War."

I waved a hand at him. "They weren't actually trying to maliciously damage anything. They were trying to fix and upgrade machinery. It's a compulsion for them. But you have a mix of Quotes who have no idea they have gremlins because they can't see them, gremlins in the middle of a project, and a partially disassembled engine, and well…shit is going to go wrong in the air. That's why we have the system we do and we check which vehicles we're taking out first."

I could feel holes being bored into the side of my skull and I glanced over to find Rafael squinting at me. "I'm pretty sure you're simplifying it by several degrees."

"Listen, a lot of the problems we have in the world aren't due to ill intent but a mismatch of needs, timing, and/or communication. Identify what the issue is, redirect it in a way that satisfies everyone's needs, and a lot of problems are resolved or don't come to pass. Is that an oversimplification? Of course it is. But it's also the truth."

He hummed under his breath and returned to looking out the window. Silence fell over us at last.

The rest of the three-hour drive was fairly peaceful as Rafael took the opportunity to take a nap after asking me a few more questions about climbing Helens. I felt myself relax significantly once he was out and the truck was only filled with the sounds of heavy breathing from the dogs, the soft crooning of the new cassette I had popped in, and the pelting of rain.

When we neared our destination, I finally spoke up, waking Rafael. "Oliver lives in the Spirit Lake of the Abstruse realm. In the Quotidian world, the only trail access after the eruption is off of Forest Road 99 and is a relatively short hike to the northeastern shore. However, Oliver's trailhead is trickier and hidden. Not only that, but since it's still early May, we won't be able to access it by vehicle. It'll still be blocked by snow, so it'll be a much further hike than normal. I hope you have some spikes in the pack."

Rafael nodded. "I have them covered. Temporal snares?"

I tapped my head. "Got them memorized. Follow my path and you'll be fine. Or the K9s."

You would think with landmarks being largely the same between the Quotidian and paranormal realms it would be as simple as just switching realms, but it wasn't. If you didn't start off from the right access point, you could lose days, decades, even centuries off your travel times due to temporal snares. Accidentally stumble into a temporal snare, such as a fairy ring, and suddenly you've lost centuries in what feels like a blink of an eye. Being a guide was a lucrative career in the Abstruse realms, though one that was typically associated with a short lifespan. Animals naturally avoided the snares, but unless you followed their exact path, it was still easy to become distracted and fall into one. Spatial snares altered the distance between two points, but they were far rarer.

"So, Oliver's an aquatic *yōkai* then?"

"You'll meet him when you meet him. You have rain gear and extra layers, yes?"

"Yes, I've summitted other peaks so I just went with my usual."

I nodded. He should be fairly well-set then. I had everything else we would need.

Soon enough we reached our destination and I switched between realms. The ride instantly became more jarring while I navigated ruts, avoided potholes and fallen trees, branches slapping the sides of the vehicle.

"Baki?" Rafael's questioning voice filled the air. "Um, Baki. Baki!" Each iteration of his nickname for me grew more alarmed. He scrambled upright and grabbed the *oh-shit* handle as we appeared to drive right into a copse of trees without switching realms.

I smiled with satisfaction as we came out on the shitty road on the other side of the trees. Max woofed happily, knowing we would be getting out soon and set his head on Rafael's shoulder. Traitor.

I stopped on the road shortly afterward, where the snow began. I didn't worry about blocking any other vehicles. I was one of the select few who used it.

"We're here," I announced, putting the rig in park and setting the emergency brake.

"My heart attack and I gathered," Rafael grumbled, climbing out the passenger side and groaning as he stretched out his back.

I went around the back and dropped the tailgate to allow the K9s to roam free and stretch their legs while Rafael unstrapped our gear and pulled our packs down. The rain that had started on our drive turned into sleet as I pulled out my heavier jacket, spikes, and gaiters and started strapping them on over my rain gear, then whistled for the K9s to start getting them into their harnesses. Although I didn't expect for them to pick up Dr. Aoki's scent—we were far from where she had initially vanished—it wouldn't hurt for them to be on the job while we were in the area. I gave them some material of hers to scent before resealing the bag. Pea climbed into her harness on Max and settled in with a short hiss at the weather.

"Visibility's going to suck monkey balls in this weather," I warned as the wind began picking up and I pulled my goggles on to protect my eyes. "Stay close." I heaved on my pack and picked up my trekking poles, then began heading up the path once Rafael was situated.

"This is my first trip to the US. It's rained every day thus far. I can see why everyone always comments on the beauty of the Pacific Northwest when you can only see ten feet in any direction and you spend every day feeling soggy unless you spend it indoors," Rafael commented sardonically from behind me.

"Haven't you heard? If you don't like the weather, wait five minutes," I called over my shoulder as I ducked my head and leaned into the biting wind. I had hoped for calm weather but knew that chances were 50/50 this time of the year. However, this was a little extreme and turned a relatively mild hike into a brutal one.

"Somehow I doubt I'm going to like the weather in five minutes."

The man had an excellent point.

FIVE LONG, BEDRAGGLED hours later, we stumbled to the snowy shore of Spirit Lake. Rafael had predicted the weather correctly and the sleet had soon turned into whiteout conditions. Max and Woody were the only creatures currently happy with the situation. The rest of us were cold, wet, and exhausted.

"Ah, here we are. Rafael, meet Oliver. Oliver, meet Rafael," I waved a tired hand in the air to gesture between Rafael and what could be seen of the empty shoreline. I brushed off the snow before sitting on a nearby log that had washed up.

He gave me a look, clearly questioning my sanity. I wondered how many times he had done that since meeting me yesterday.

After a brief moment, the sounds of cracking ice could be heard above the gusts of wind and Oliver emerged from the log-ridden Spirit Lake. Standing at about four feet tall, he was a deep olive green with touches of brown, and he had a sparse ring of black hair dripping water down his head. In the center of that ring was a *sara*, a bowl filled with water from Spirit Lake. He had a thick, razor-sharp beak and a carapace on his back, both of which were patterned in a dark brown and ivory, though it was hard to tell under the forest of algae growing on them.

Rafael startled slightly at the sight of him, sending me a quick, eyebrow-raised glance before saying, "Good morning, Oliver-*san*."

And proceeded to reflexively bow his head in greeting.

Oliver shot him a suspicious scowl.

I stifled a snort. Good manners died hard.

Holding back my grin, I called out, "Don't be too offended by the attempt to kill you, Oliver. Rafael here is just afraid you'll rip out his *shirikodama*."

I hadn't thought it was possible, but Oliver managed to look even more offended and huffed. "I'm sorry, but misinformation is not only hurtful, but harmful. My soul, your soul, *no one's soul* exists as a ball inside one's anus. And for another, why in bloody hell would I want to stick my hand up someone's anus? To rip out an alleged ball organ? To *eat*? That's just disgusting." He shuddered into his shell. My words had the intended effect and Oliver was more focused on his disgust than suspicion. For now.

I cackled. Rafael's jaw was working overtime while he tried to keep it from dropping. I wasn't sure if it was the unexpected British accent, the realization of his absolute fucked-up *faux pas*, or the revelation of the *shirikodama* tidbit. That made-up factoid was always one of my favorites.

"Please accept my sincerest apologies, Oliver-*san*. Ms. Kimoto—" Rafael aimed a filthy glare in my direction. "Ms. Kimoto told me we would be meeting a friend of hers to see if they could help with our task. I wanted to pay my respects as it is of the utmost importance; however, I was clearly flustered and as such, the correct manner for greeting a *kappa* fled my mind. There was no ill intent behind my greeting. I had not been aware there were any *kappas* remaining."

I nodded and looked to Olly in question. He eyed the *kariudo* but waved a webbed hand at me in permission to tell his story, his trust in me bringing strangers to his territory evident, and not something I took lightly. I loosened the top of the pack before I got started and removed my haul. Oliver's entire countenance brightened and he clapped his webbed hands. Rafael looked absolutely befuddled. I took joy in his current state.

He enunciated his words carefully. "This entire hike. Knowing the forecasted weather. *Experiencing* the forecasted weather. This whole time you've been packing along cucumbers, eggplants, and *melons*? I thought you were hiking in backpacking supplies. You know, in the event we needed to overnight it?"

"Nah." Olly snagged a melon and dug into the it with relish. I wasn't worried.

"Huh." The single word was filled with judgment.

I ignored it. "Before Oliver was born, his parents lived in the Urakami River. Then the US bombed Nagasaki on August 9, 1945. The radiation bled through the realms and their home was destroyed. The river itself was not only contaminated with radiation but filled with bodies of the dead and dying. Quote bodies entered our realm, first by the force of the bomb, then through Death. His mother told me the cries of the dying begging for water while in the river haunted them for the rest of their lives. His mother had just laid her clutch of eggs a few days prior, and they fled the country with the help of their *gameshirō* cousins in the ocean, settling in the UK, where Oliver was born as the sole survivor of the clutch. Due to the radiation poisoning, his parents were unable to conceive again."

I took a deep breath. Oliver took up his story in my pause. "And then that bloody maggot of a sea dragon set a decree that the *kappas* and *gameshirōs* were enemies to Ryūgū-jō for helping the *haetae* evade him. He set his assassins and his *kariudo* out to eradicate us. I was twenty when the *kariudo* came for my family. My father died to give my mother and I a chance to escape and we fled to the States.

I kept quiet as a wave of guilt overwhelmed me. The sea *kami* had made the decree after discovering that a family of *gameshirō* had aided in my escape. The *kappas* were caught in the genocide by their relation to the *gameshirō*.

He nodded to me. "We had heard of a territory where we would have protection and stowed away on a boat that took us to this land."

Shit. I needed him to stop before he revealed more. Rafael's eyes were already gleaming with curiosity and the chance to gather more information about me.

"Protecti—," he began to ask.

"His mother wanted a location that was less populated and resettled in Spirit Lake," I cut in before he could finish. "Sadly, she perished when St. Helen's erupted in 1980, but Oliver was able to burrow deep enough to escape the worst of it."

"My mother perished due to wounds from the *kariudo* finding us again. Not because of St. Helens erupting." Oliver clarified. I attempted to interrupt again, but he forged on, determined to tell the story. "My mother told me to hide, which is why I was so deeply burrowed when Helens blew, and Cam got here in time to kill the *kariudo* before he could get to me."

His eyes flashed in warning to the *kariudo*. A subtle threat toward the male.

Fucking hell.

Rafael's head whipped to me. "*That's* what happened to the last *kariudo*? If Oliver had to burrow so deeply to survive the eruption, how did you survive?"

I bypassed his question and attempted to change the subject. "Due to the decree, Oliver is now one of few remaining *kappas* in the world that we know of and the only male. I've tried to make his location as difficult to track as possible." Turning to Rafael, I said in a serious tone, "Do you understand why I am so hesitant to go on this SAR with you? To return a person to this *kami*? A *kami* who does not hesitate to commit genocide?"

Oliver set down the piece of melon he had been about to eat and looked between the two of us. "What is this about? You're here on Ryujin's behalf." His voice rose and he stood to return to the lake. "I trusted you, Cam."

"Olly, stop. Please. You know me. I would *never* put your safety at risk."

He paused briefly. I watched as his carapace sagged in defeat. Oliver's entire life had been ripped away by the sea *kami*. I was asking too much of him. I knew this. And yet, I needed him to wait. My missing person needed him to wait. Her life depended on him. So many lives depended on him. My heart ached at what I was putting my friend through.

I took a deep breath and began to explain the situation in Ryūgū-jō. He slowly sat back down as he listened. Rafael filled in the gaps where I was lacking.

Oliver stared him down for a long moment once we were done, assessing him. "You are the *kariudo*."

"I am." Rafael nodded respectfully.

"You have done evil acts."

"I have."

"So why is this important if life has such little meaning to you?"

"I make no excuses for my past. I have committed atrocities and I cannot take them back. But my people are dying. Despite what my past may insinuate, I love my people."

Oliver scoffed. "You say you love your people. Yet how many of your people have you killed who were innocent and undeserving of your judgment? I loved my people. I loved my mother and father. My cousins. And now none of them remain. And in the future, all of our kind will be erased. Because of *kariudo* like you."

Rafael bowed his head and said nothing.

"Rafael," I said as softly as I could, my voice barely heard over the winds. "Show him your forearms."

Rafael jerked his head back up and looked at me with wild eyes, his body rigid with tension. It was the biggest reaction I had seen from him yet. I gestured toward Oliver. "Show him," I repeated carefully.

He shook his head fiercely. Like a feral animal backed into a corner.

I slowly withdrew my hands from my gloves. I removed my coat, feeling the brisk wind cut through my layers. I rolled up the sleeves of my shirts, instantly beginning to shiver in the cold. Finally, I removed the glamour I had not dispelled since first placing it an eternity ago.

"Look," I said gently. I cautiously reached my hand out toward him, mindful of not touching him in this state. I knew the painful experience of dissociation triggered from touch firsthand.

At first nothing happened. Then Rafael slowly turned. The outstretched forearm which revealed the brutal scars which circled my arm from elbow to wrist now in his view.

"You're not the only one who has been bound against your will. We're all broken here. You made that clear when you offered your words of solace to me this morning. If nothing else, your pain is safe with us."

Oliver was forgotten as Rafael's lips parted, forming a silent *how?* on a soft exhale. A brief flicker of hope flared in his eyes before it guttered out. The remains of my soul wept at the sight. Rafael removed a glove and reached out, gingerly touching the scars. There were five. Another five still hidden on my other arm. I was unable to feel his touch through the thick keloid tissue, but I could see the gentleness of his caress. His fingertips were calloused, his touch tender and featherlight as if I were a doe ready to bolt with the slightest movement. After a few moments, he pulled his hand back in and removed his other glove. His coat. His layers. Under his layers, a pair of supple leather cuffs.

Finally, he dropped his own glamour, allowing the enchanted obsidian bands that were deeply embedded in the skin of his forearms to be revealed, confirming what I had suspected. The rubbing of his wrist, the minute winces; someone else might not understand, but I knew from my own experience.

The circlets could barely be seen they were so obscured by decades of scar tissue. A violent shudder wracked his body as they came into sight. I winced, remembering the agony of my own experience. He stretched his own forearm out, comparing his obsidian bands to the white, raised marks along my arm. I faced Oliver.

"Unlike the last *kariudo*, Rafael isn't committing these atrocities because he enjoys them. He is compelled to do them against his will." I nodded at our outstretched arms. "He has been enslaved by the *kami* and has no choice in the matter. That is the other reason why I have chosen to work with him."

Oliver's eyes were wide as they bounced between the two of us. "I—"

Before he could finish, I heard the sharp half-bark, half-growl from Max that signified magic nearby. I stood abruptly, whistling for the dogs and Pea.

Near simultaneously, the winds picked up to gale force speeds, the trees bending with the strength of the currents. The snow turned into pelting ice and the temperature dropped suddenly. I cursed loudly. I should have seen the signs on our way in, but I had thought it was our typical unpredictable spring weather.

"Olly!" I shouted desperately, no longer able to see either of them. "We need to find Yuriko."

CHAPTER ELEVEN

Before I could say anything else, a crushing pressure enveloped my ribs and I was snatched away into the howling winds and ice. In the space of time it took for me to attempt a breath beneath the vice, I was smashed against the volcanic rocks, shattering them with the force of the blow. Dazed, I struggled to free myself, shoving the pain into the back of my mind. Olly or I had to get to Yuriko before Rafael. The weather had been a warning to us, not a threat, but Rafael wouldn't see it that way. I could hear the dogs going wild and the sounds of another fight in the distance. How far had I been taken?

Whatever had me in its grip lifted me into the air, ten feet, twenty feet up. As I fought against my bindings, a laughing face appeared before me. A Japanese woman with long flowing hair and madness in her eyes. A face once beautiful, now gaunt with starvation. Her head began to serpentine from side to side, attached to a neck that elongated further and further with each movement as she cackled with me in her grip.

Fucking *rokurokubi*. At least I knew what was wrapped around my body now. If she was here, I could assume at least one of her deadlier counterparts, the *nukekubi,* was also here. Unlike the *rokurokubi,* the *nukekubis'* heads completely detached from their bodies. And they enjoyed draining the lifeblood out of any living being. The sea *kami* had clearly found me and dispatched his servants to collect me. The *rokurokubi* to restrain me and the *nukekubi* to dispose of anyone in the way. I wondered if that would include Rafael or not.

Rafael complicated this situation tenfold. While I knew he wasn't a willing huntsman, he was still under the sea *kami's* compulsion. I couldn't afford for him to know my heritage, if he didn't already. I couldn't rely on any of my usual tactics.

Forcing my *ki* as a temporary fix to block pain from my shattered ribs and other various broken parts, I centered myself and focused on the bond between myself and Pea and began to pull, hoping we wouldn't have too many injuries among our group. Utilizing the bond between us, rather than my own *ki*, I grasped the cells that made up the *rokurokubi's* neck that coiled around me.

And lit them on fire.

Abruptly the laughter cut off and changed to shrieks of pain.

The *rokurokubi's* neck contracted tighter around my torso as she began to whip wildly in an instinctual response to flee from the source of the pain, causing us to crash into the surrounding landscape. The obvious starvation also lent her an additional weapon; as her vertebrae protruded, the spinous processes of each bone mercilessly stabbed into my flesh. If I could only move my damn arms I could get to the blades I had strapped to my thighs before starting on this *kamis'*-forsaken adventure.

I heard the sounds of snarling coming closer and suddenly Woodrow launched himself out of the blinding whiteness. He latched onto the length of her neck, sending both of us crashing back down.

A piercing sensation shot through my chest as we landed. It had only been a matter of time before something pierced a lung. Another pang shot through my right ankle as it bent in an unnatural position. Thankfully, the coils loosened around me as we landed and I took advantage of the moment to snatch a blade, unsnapping the sheath and struggling to draw my arm up until I was free from the coils of the *rokurokubi's* neck. I didn't like to kill without judgment and without opportunity for atonement, but the complications of the *kami* and Rafael had left me no choice. I began to saw at her neck while Woodrow tried to keep her pinned down, snapping at her face and neck whenever it came within reach of his jaw. It was like trying to ride the most fucked up bull ride in existence. Tactical blades were not meant for this task, but decapitation and keeping her head away from her body was the only way to successfully kill the *rokurokubi*.

At last, the muscles in the neck gave up the last of their contractions, loosening in death, and I was able to pull myself out of their grip, wheezing as I did so. The length of her neck began to recoil, returning back to its body, leaving a trail of blood behind. Burning the head later would ensure she stayed dead. I stumbled over to Woodrow and knelt down to his bloodstained head, leaning my forehead to his.

"Who is the bestest boy?" I gasped. "Thank you for saving me." I wrapped my arms around his neck, taking comfort from his wooly body as he leaned against me. I rose stiffly, guiding more magic toward my numerous injuries. Grimly, I limped over to the *rokurokubi*, and bent to lift her head by her hair before Woodrow and I began the slow walk back to the lake. I siphoned a thread of Pea's power as we went to better block the pain.

The deeply unpleasant process of jagged pieces of bone working themselves out of my lung had begun. Although I had blocked the pain, I couldn't help squirming against the sensation of somebody drawing dulled instruments through my inner organs as the natural healing process of the Abstruse focused on the worst of the injuries. It would ignore the scrapes and cuts, leaving those to heal naturally, only caring about injuries that could be incapacitating.

The *rokurokubi* had dragged me at least half a mile. By the time I got back, I found a downed Rafael, Oliver fending off a *nukekubi*, and a disemboweled *futakuchi-onna*. It was like a Japanese freak show version of *Charlie's Angels* had been sent to collect me.

Never mind.

The longer I took in the scene, the more bashed-in, disembodied female heads I could count. The unlikely pair of *kariudo* and *kappa* had evidently figured out how to work together in the name of survival. Vicky and Max were guarding Rafael's body, leaping and snapping at the *nukekubi's* head whenever it came near. He was pale—nearly blue—from blood loss.

"I have this," Oliver shouted, batting the head away with a clawed hand. "Yuriko needs you." There was a note of desperation in his yell.

The winds had died down to barely a breeze and the lightest flurries. Normally I would be thankful for the change in weather; however, this change concerned me.

This change meant Yuri's *ki* was faltering. Time was running out before we would be able to save her at all.

Hurriedly, I threw the *rokurokubi's* head to join her companions where it bounced a few times, then rolled, coming to a rest forehead to forehead with one of her sisters in death. I called Max and Vicky to me before I laid my hand against Woody's withers, cringing as I felt shattered rib fragments continue to shift and right themselves within me. "Guard Oliver and Rafael." The situation required using each and everyone's strengths to the utmost of their ability.

He wooed quietly at me before bolting down the path where Rafael's body lay prone, taking up the position left vacant by his siblings.

Once Max and Vicky were at my side, Pea clambered out of her harness, and climbed up my left side, settling around my neck. A pink glow settled over the two of us, taking away the rest of my pain. I stroked her head affectionately. "Thank you, friend. Save your powers though. I have I feeling we'll need them more urgently soon." A punctured lung wouldn't kill me. Very few things would; the pain would only hamper my progress.

Bending down to Max, I looked him in the eyes and gave him the command to seek out Yuriko's trail of magic. I had no marker for him to work from, but Yuriko was a good friend and handler, and he was trained to seek all of our handlers' magical signatures as a safety precaution. Everyone at Blue Bear SAR worked with Max at least once a month to ensure he remained familiar with their *ki*.

Max immediately settled into his role, and I knew he would have no problem finding the trail with as much power as she had put out to warn us. I only wish I had picked up on the warning sooner. He took off heading northwest and we followed through the brush. I cursed my ankle and lung for the slowness of our pace.

We had traveled for about four miles before he alerted and I signaled for him and Vicky to stay. I silently crept forward to assess the situation before I went in. Horror ripped through my body at the sight.

Yuriko was a powerful *yuki onna* in her own right, a snow witch who commanded the colder elements, but nine against one was not a fair fight. While most of them had left to take on our small group, one had remained behind to keep her bound.

A *futakuchi onna* sat upon Yuriko's bare back. From the front, she looked like a normal woman. From the back, her hair formed eight snake-like whips which lashed at Yuriko's flesh, tearing off strips and bringing them to a gruesome mouth embedded in the back of her head. Her hair eagerly fed her ravenous mouth, as though its appetite could not be satiated. A small sparrow flitted past, seeking to flee the danger lurking in the woods, and one of the whip-like cords lashed out, extending far beyond what appeared to be its reach, capturing the small bird within its grasp and bringing it to the maw on the back of its head.

Nausea tore through me as I beheld what was in front of me. The *futakuchi onna*, though violent, had never displayed cannibalistic behaviors in the past. Had the famines in Ryūgū-jō brought them to this level of depravity? The irony in this situation, considering how I rendered judgment, was not lost on me; however, I never tortured those who fell under my judgment.

I weighed the circumstances and decided they were worth the risk of shifting. I set Pea on the ground and quietly spoke. "You know what to do as soon as I have her distracted."

Pea gave me a soft hiss of concern followed by a click.

"I remember. But we don't have another choice. Not with Yuri's life on the line."

Her tail twitched in acknowledgment before she began to scurry along the edge of the clearing.

Seeking the flame of magic within myself, I closed my eyes briefly and began to shift. My body dropped from a bipedal position to that of a quadruped. I flexed and retracted my claws while my perspective changed as I grew taller. The world changed from the gray overcast day to a rainbow of warm reds, oranges, and yellows, with hints of blue-whites in small areas. I shook out my body—fur, scales, and feathers murmuring in a symphony of whispers—and I reveled in the feeling of finally being in my true form for the first time in what felt like an eternity, straining to hold on to the sensation for as long as I could before the crash.

All too soon, the inevitable clash of competing magics splintered within me, as the flames were suffocated by a strange translucence. In the blink of an eye, all but the barest spark of my *ki* remained in my field of vision. Vertigo became the overwhelming sensation and I fell to the ground as the feeling overtook me. It was like riding a Gravitron but trapped on the outside. There was no safety, no thrill, just sheer terror, swirling lights, and spinning. The fragments of my body and soul were being torn a little farther apart each time I shifted and I could feel every shred of pain.

I had not allowed myself to fully shift in decades for this reason. My magic was fighting a foreign entity that was trying to consume it, and I didn't know how many chances I had left before it killed me.

CHAPTER TWELVE

After several moments passed, I fought back the foreign magic and allowed my natural power to once again take control. Shaking my large head, I climbed back to my feet, muscles trembling. Unfortunately for Yuri, the *futakuchi onna* was so preoccupied with her hunger that she hadn't noticed the commotion behind her.

I turned my gaze upon the *futakuchi onna's* heart, where her morality lay.

I was unable to see souls. Many believed evil stained the soul. But it wasn't a stain. It couldn't be something so innocuous as that. Evil was something residing within each and every one of us, whether we were aware of it or not. It was a living being that inhabited our hearts from the moment we were conceived and held a symbiotic relationship with us, one parasitic in nature. When we gave in to our desirous natures without care for the harm it would bring to others, we fed the parasite—allowing it to multiply. If we continued, it infected our hearts, to the point we no longer cared about the harm toward others and reveled in the harm instead. When the infection overcame the host, the heart would wither and die, evil taking its place with a wild and unnatural beat. The parasite then spreads throughout the entire body, overtaking the entire vascular and arterial network. What was truly terrifying about the parasite was its insidious nature, how it crept in over years and decades, how it glamoured itself under the appearance of a false heart and beat, so no one but the *haetae* could sense its presence. Not even the infected individual.

As I beheld the *futakuchi onna's* chest in my true form, I saw no heart. Instead, a squirming mass, sickly green in color, pulsated erratically where the heart should be. Rather than capillaries, veins, and arteries, her body appeared to have a vast roadway of maggots wriggling frantically, desperately seeking the void where the heart once lay. There was nothing remaining in her body to restore. No atonement could bring her organ back to life. Only judgment remained.

I stepped forward from the brush, no longer trying to conceal myself. The *futakuchi onna* whipped around and shrieked when she saw me. She eagerly stepped forth, using six cords of hair to propel herself forward, her own human legs hovering above the ground. She left Yuriko's body behind, in anticipation of larger prey, a greater meal that would provide more satiety. Two cords of hair flailed before her, plunging toward me, one lashing at my chest in search of sustenance. However, the cord of hair gained no flesh as it struck my armored jade thorax. Like the *rokurokubi*, there was only the kind of madness caused by hunger left in her eyes as she charged toward me.

Before she could lash at me again, I leapt forward to meet her, my jaws cleaving her torso from her pelvis, my spaded tail divesting the *futakuchi onna* of the two cords of hair reaching for me. She howled in rage, only faltering for a split second, before continuing her advance on me, four of her remaining lashes of hair propelling her forward as her body soaked the forest floor in blood, entrails dragging beneath her. Her only thought was to consume.

Until the dull thud of her hair landing against the soft snow registered to her ears.

The *futakuchi-onna's* eyes widened as her own momentum worked against her and she sagged forward. A small gasp echoed through the clearing as her human mouth formed a small *o* of shock. The impact of our two bodies colliding felt as though it should have had a more cataclysmic sound than the slight exhalation of air from one's lungs. It felt wrong somehow, as if the sound did not do the act justice, the act which left the *futakuchi-onna's* body impaled against the lethal horn upon my head.

I closed my eyes and shuddered as images flew past my mind's eye as my horn slowly siphoned the evil from her body.

A small girl lays in the fetal position in a corner of a cold and damp room, the strong odor of mildew pervading the surroundings. As she shivers violently, her thin, worn clothing clings to various parts of her body, revealing hands and forearms that are mere skin and bones under the rags she wears. She gazes longingly out the doorway where a woman and another girl, healthy and maybe one or two years older, sit on their cushions around the chabudai, *eating from several dishes. A loud rumble emits from her stomach and the girl cringes like a dog expecting to be hit. The woman spares a brief glance at the girl before turning back to her daughter. She shakes her head, as if disappointed. "Sachi still has not learned discipline. She will have to go without yet another day." The daughter's lip curls up in a smirk over her cup of hot tea. Sachi curls into a tighter ball as the parasite within her heart wakes and begins to feed on something called hope. She's unfamiliar with this feeling and doesn't understand what is happening.*

Scenes flash by in dizzying speed before they stop on skeletal hands. It's the same girl, only older, perhaps late teens, early twenties. Her growth has been stunted, she is far smaller than she should be for someone her age. She is dressed in rags, in someone's home she has broken into, with a knife in one hand, standing over a dead body. She feels shock and repulsion for what she has just done, but it is immediately overridden by her hunger and she falls to her knees to the meal she had just killed a man for. The parasite feeds on more emotions, beginning to eat away at remorse, guilt, and shame.

A flash. The young woman has resorted to prostitution. Another flash. The young woman has worked her way up to being a rich man's mistress, but he is stingy with her, commenting on her weight constantly, withholding food from her. Until she begins to believe the comments he makes about her weight. A flood of images shows Sachi gaining access to her lover's wife's perfume and magically dosing her with an appetite suppressant, slowly starving her to death, allowing Sachi to step from the shadows as his mistress and into the light as his wife.

The scene slows down again as Sachi believes this is where she will finally find fulfillment. But instead, she finds herself deeply unhappy as her husband continues to criticize her weight. She no longer requires him to withhold her food for she does so herself. She falls into periods of weakness and binges and feels nothing but self-hatred and loathing for everything around her. The parasite consumes the last of her hope as her husband leaves for a business trip. The cycle of abuse continues when Sachi strikes her stepdaughter across the face as she accuses her of stealing rice from the pantry and locks her away without food for several days. At the moment in which her stepdaughter's heart stops, the back of Sachi's skull splits open into a second grotesque mouth and Sachi will never know what it is to feel her hunger satiated.

I stumbled back a few steps as I'm abruptly pulled out of Sachi's memories. Every immoral act in her life was revealed as her body was rid of the parasite, and I saw the tipping point in which the famine and hunger drove her past the brink of recovery. I mourned that I had been unable to reach her before the sea *kami* had unleashed his influence upon her and driven her to this final point of depravity.

I saw her human life, before she became a *futakuchi onna,* and saw the same sad story repeated. A life of food scarcity, neglect, and abuse as a child. Grief, loneliness, and depression evolving into greed, jealousy, and envy until she learned to savor the acts of cruelty she engaged in, shedding all sense of guilt and shame. Soon thereafter she fell into the curse that turned her into one of the *futakuchi onna* and prevented her from ever leaving the vicious cycle she knew as a child.

As the last of the evil was drained from the empty space and I withdrew my horn, the madness left the *futakuchi onna's* eyes and peace settled over her body.

"Thank you," she whispered as her eyes closed.

I nodded and stepped back silently, the feathers on my leonine legs ruffling in the remnants of the barest breeze, which indicated that Yuriko was still hanging on. There were no more words to say. My jaw unhinged and I began to draw in the air around me. Sachi's body began to slowly dematerialize as I consumed her body and soul to allow her to pass through to the next stage in life. A brilliant smile took over her face, one encompassing the definition of joy and bliss, this female finally fitting with the true meaning of her name, before she was gone from this realm forever.

I bowed my head and said a silent prayer for Sachi's soul before taking a look at my surroundings. Pea was sitting on Yuriko, a warm pink glow encompassing them both as she worked earnestly trying to heal her. I could see new skin forming over the flayed wounds already. Worry began to niggle in the back of my brain that Yuri had not yet stirred, considering the length of time Pea had spent healing her, but she had been through a horrific trauma. Max and Vicky had joined them once I had disabled Sachi, each one stalwartly standing guard to either side of their friends. There was something missing from this scene, but fatigue and pain kept me from identifying what it was.

Surrounding us were six headless bodies of the *nukekubi* that had attacked Oliver and Rafael, as well as the body of the *rokurokubi*. Although I wanted to relish the freedom of being back in my shifted form, I knew I couldn't afford to stay in it any longer. I could feel the drain on my power as the foreign magic ate away at it. I could take care of these bodies easily enough in my human form.

Shifting back, I took a moment as I grasped a nearby branch to steady myself until the vertigo passed. I strode over to the bodies, cringing a little. The way they had congregated made the pile appear disturbingly like a mass grave. The fact they had no heads made the scene that much more macabre. After I had removed the head of the *rokurokubi,* her neck had recoiled back to her body, leaving a serpentine trail of blackened blood in the snow. Now approximately two feet of it lay limply on the ground, attached to her body. I removed the threadbare coat of one of the *nukekubi,* to confirm my suspicions. They had all been starved like Sachi and the *rokurokubi* I had encountered. Her clothing clung to her skeletal frame, and her ribs protruded from beneath her shirt, appearing malformed in shape. Her back was grotesquely skewed out of place. Had she been standing upright, she likely would have appeared at least six inches shorter than her actual height as a result. Their severity of their malnourishment explained the delirium I had seen in their eyes and the reason why each fight had taken so little time. I could feel my internal temperature rising as my rage grew from seeing the state of the bodies before me.

Each of the *yōkai* sent for me was an immortal. For those of us that fell under the category, we could only meet Death if our source of magic was destroyed. I was one of the few beings in the realms with the universal power to kill an immortal without knowledge of their source, so long as I am shifted as a *haetae*. Starvation would not kill us. It would simply send us deeper and deeper into madness, and the lack of nutrients our bodies require would force our bodies to feed upon themselves as well as our magic stores, causing them to become contorted, twisted in nature, and irreversibly warped. If one was lucky, they may come out of the delirium once provided with sustenance, but they would never again know their former selves or a life without physical pain. After so long, our minds and bodies become so distorted, we become unrecognizable as the being we once were. Most of us would choose death over an eternity living like this; however, by the time we reached this point, we no longer had the capacity to realize it.

I gathered my magic and unleashed my *ki* on the bodies, igniting them with flames to ensure they wouldn't be able to reconnect with their heads and attack us again in the future. I kept the fire carefully contained and burned through the bodies in a matter of moments. Ashes gently flitted in the light breeze, bouncing from one zephyr to the next, swirling and dancing in a sunbeam as if their souls were celebrating their newfound freedom from the struggles in life. Max, always keen to the presence of magic, solemnly watched the display until the ashes slowly began to dissipate on the wind until they disappeared altogether.

Surveying the clearing, I gathered my power again and this time released it in a burst of ambient warmth to melt the snow around us and remove all evidence of my shifted prints in the snow.

Exhausted, heartsick, and in pain, I limped back to the group and knelt by Yuriko's side. The last of her wounds were sealing over and the pink glow was fading as Pea crawled over to me. I carefully rolled Yuriko over to her back and cupped her cheek.

"I'm sorry I didn't understand your warning for what it was until it was far too late," I said quietly.

A sigh whispered from her lips as her fingers contracted as if she were reaching for something.

"Willa." My head whipped up as the name was breathed from her lips.

"Willa was with you?" I swore under my breath. Willa was her entire life and had seen her through her worst trials.

"Made...run. Didn't...want to." No. No, Willa wouldn't want to. She was one of the most steadfastly loyal K9s I had ever met.

I gazed around the clearing and lit upon a scrap of fabric snagged on the trunk of a tree, about eighteen inches off the ground. A piece of handkerchief that Willa loved to wear when she wasn't on the job.

Squeezing Yuriko's hand in reassurance, I leaned down to comfort her. "Pea and Max will stay here to guard you; Vicky and I will go track Willa." Her hand went limp in response and Pea placed her own paw in it to replace mine.

Standing, I gave Max the command to guard and called Vicky over to the tree where I had spotted the handkerchief. I caught it and held the fabric out to her for Willa's scent.

Despite the number of scents in the clearing, Victoria had no challenges picking up the trail and immediately began to track. We headed into the woods again. I was hopeful. Given Willa's loyalty, I didn't think she would run far, and my hope panned out. We found the small Labrador mix trembling, tangled up in thorny blackberry bushes not a quarter mile away from the clearing. The blackberry plant had become even more invasive in the Abstruse realm than the Quotidian world, growing like wildfire on the mountain in this domain thanks to the influence of the earth-natured creatures that lived here.

"Oh, sweetie." I dropped down to my knees and carefully reached out to her, not wanting to spook her. "It's me. You know me."

Her doe-brown eyes looked up at me as she cautiously bumped her nose to my hand and gave me a hesitant lick.

"That's right. I'm your momma's friend. You've met me and Vicky bunches of times. You've been through one heck of a scary time, huh? And now you're all caught up in these thorns and you don't know where your mom is. Give me one second to get you loose and we'll take you to her."

I pulled my blade out in case it was needed and kept my voice down in a soothing, calm tone, despite the curses that wanted to roll off my tongue.

"If you want to remain on these lands and not find yourself severed from another host, you will release this beast *now*," I relayed to the *kodama* of this particular shrub while keeping my tone sweet, as if I were still talking to Willa.

The brambles around Willa loosened slightly, as if contemplating my saccharine threats and not finding them worthy.

"While I may make you bleed sap, this being belongs to Yuriko, the *yuki-onna* of this mountain. You may heal and regrow from the cuts I make from my blade, but she will wither your soul with frost and shatter your branches from the cold if she finds that harm has come to her Willa," I snarled, no longer attempting to keep my voice low and soothing.

The branches immediately began receding upon this pronouncement, allowing enough room to maneuver at last.

"There we go, girl. Easy does it, come on out of there now."

Willa inched her way back out of the brambles slowly and bumped me again with her head in thanks once she was free. I ran my hands over her body looking for any injuries but thankfully found nothing more serious than superficial scrapes and cuts that could be easily taken care of. The *kodama* had not yet begun to feed from her. At least one thing had gone right today.

"Alright, sweetie." I stood up, brushing off my pants and sheathing my blade again. "Let's get you back to your mom. C'mon, girls." Both K9s' tails wagged eagerly and Vicky led the way as we headed back down the trail. As soon as we came within sight of the clearing, Willa raced to Yuri's side and dropped to her belly, frantically licking her face, letting out soft whimpers when Yuriko didn't respond.

I felt a stinging behind my eyes as I reached the two of them and watched Willa nudge at Yuriko's limp hand and worked her body underneath it. I paused at their side and whispered, "She's here, Yuri. She's safe. But you know that, I know you know that, otherwise you wouldn't be resting now. You keep healing your mind. Olly and I will keep your body and Willa safe."

Blinking furiously, I bent down to snag Pea, placing her in my hood. I tested my ankle. It and my ribs had knitted back together, but they were by no means finished healing. I groaned quietly. "This is going to be a monumentally bad decision."

Before I could change my mind, I bent down and scooped up Yuriko in a bridal carry, my ribs shrieking and staggering slightly as I stood. Pea hissed at me in concern.

"Don't give me sass right now. Either heal me or don't. You have a better gauge on your power. But from the way things looked when we left, you're going to have to do some healing when we get back on someone you've never worked on before. I'm not going to die from this. It'll just *feel* like I'm dying. Slowly. Like someone is carving out my lungs with a spoon."

Pea bit my ear.

"Ow! What the fuck! So you hurt me more?" I shook my head as I got started on the path back to the lake, my K9s behind me, Willa trotting with her nose touching Yuri's boots. I smiled with exhaustion. It was going to be a long walk back, but I was going to be doing it in the best company around.

CHAPTER THIRTEEN

We arrived back at the Spirit Lake right as the sun began dipping back down in the sky. Olly had a bucket with him and was walking back and forth between the lake and different patches of the shore, for all intents and purposes appearing like he was trying to rinse the blood out of the dirt and snow. *Well, that seems like an exercise in utter futility.*

Rafael was still down for the count, but he lay off to the side now, near a copse of trees, with Woodrow standing guard over him. When he saw us, his tail began to wag, but he remained with Rafael like the good boy he was. Max and Vicky bolted over to join him, while Willa remained glued to her owner.

"What in the ever-loving hell are you doing?" I called out to Oliver once we got within shouting distance.

The *kappa* whipped around, still hypervigilant after their recent battle. He relaxed when he saw us, although his shoulders hiked up in concern after seeing Yuriko in my arms.

"I don't like to shit where I eat. I'm trying to clean this mess up. This is my home. I don't need blood, intestines, and general gore rotting around my front yard." If a beak could wrinkle, his would have. He gazed at the fruit I had brought for him and his head nearly disappeared into his carapace in disappointment.

"What a bloody waste," his voice echoed through his shell.

"If you had just waited for me to get back, I could have saved you a lot of work. Let's get Yuri situated first and I'll take care of the mess out here."

"I needed to stay busy, otherwise I would've gone out of my mind with worry. It's not like I could have gone after you. I have no idea how to track and had no clue where you had gone." Oliver gestured to Yuri before making his way to his home. "I'm not going to ask if she's okay, because she's clearly not. What happened?"

How to answer his question? I hesitated, knowing how special a relationship Olly and Yuri had.

"*Futakuchi onna.*" The simple answer was all I could think to say.

He shook his head, knowing I was hiding much under my reply, and turned back around, making his way to the door cleverly hidden in a little-known lava tube that had developed after the eruption. "I hope you incinerated the bitch."

I bent down to clear the door, straightening immediately in the immense expanse that opened thereafter. Olly wandered from wall to wall, turning on lights fueled by magic. A soft bluish-green glow illuminated the living space and kitchen. It was a homey area with a well-worn *chabudai* in the living room and piles of cushions for seating scattered throughout. The table had been lovingly hand-carved by his mother after they had immigrated to Europe, though the cushions were newer. Only one was frequently used, though there was a second that looked like it had been reliably visited.

"Come, we'll put her in my bedroom for now. It'll be the most comfortable for her." He waved me down one of the lava tubes that branched away from the main space and opened into a smaller cave. The room featured a small futon nestled off to the far side, a large *tatami* mat in forest hues that took up the majority of the room, a desk and chair to my right, and a pile of cushions next to the desk. Olly pulled back the bedspread as I carefully skirted the mat, having committed the cardinal sin of not removing my boots, and laid Yuri on the futon. Willa gently crawled onto the bed and laid down next to her, snuggling her head under Yuri's arm. Oliver pulled the heavy mink blanket back over the two of them and brought a cushion next to the futon to settle down on.

"Go ahead and take care of the *kariudo*." He nodded to the bed, "I'll watch over these two."

I hesitated, feeling guilty for my brief answer and I traced the plush synthetic fibers of the flower covering Willa's body. "Olly. I know I can be a terrible friend, and I'm so sorry for that, but thank you for being my family and being there when I needed you."

"Love. You are not a terrible friend. You are brash, you are blunt, you push people away, you don't let others in. You yell at us and make fun of us."

I let out a bitter laugh. "You're not doing much to argue the terrible friend point."

"You didn't let me finish. But you are always there for us. You celebrate us for our differences. You give us chance after chance. You provide us with a refuge when others would strike us down. You would burn down the world for us. And that is where you struggle. You don't know how to balance your guilt around the gray. It always has to be black-and-white for you. Especially when it comes to your own struggles. You don't have to tell your story to me…but you need to share it with someone."

"No one would believe me," I whispered.

He tapped his claws along the hard volcanic rock that made up the cavern of his bedroom. "You live among the fairy tales and folkloric beings passed along by generations of Quotidians. You are one yourself. And you think one of your trusted family members wouldn't be able to suspend their belief on your behalf? Just think on it. For me, okay?"

I nodded and stood. "I will consider it. For you, Olly."

He sighed in exasperation. "Not for me. For *you*, Cam; only for you. Now shoo." He waved his hand dismissively at me. "Go collect your *kariudo* and resurrect him so we can discuss what was so rudely interrupted earlier."

I headed back toward the lava tube that would lead to the hidden door, stopping once to glance back on the unlikely trio, seeing the *kappa* tenderly clasp the *yuki onna's* limp hand between his own two and a tear roll down his face. I quickly turned back around and headed out the door, feeling as though I had invaded a deeply private moment.

RAFAEL WAS STILL prone, sheltered on one side by a large boulder. Drag marks clearly depicted a story of Olly dragging the man's body over here once the battle was over. Pea was circling his form and slubbing occasionally on various parts of his body to better assess his injuries. Something she hadn't had to do with Yuriko, since she was well acquainted with her.

There was a vulnerability to Rafael as he lay there—one that wasn't present when he was awake—that had nothing to do with his injuries. A sense of lost innocence, or rather, the man he could have been if his life had gone down a different road. The thought gave me a vague sense of discomfort. There was no sense in becoming caught up in the quagmire of *what-could-have-beens*. I shook off my thoughts. Max's feathered tail wagged happily as I approached.

"Who's the bestest boy?" I cooed, bending down to ruffle his ears. Woodrow wooed in protest from atop the boulder where he and Vicky were holding court. "Yes yes, you are tied for bestest boy as well. Only Vicky is uncontested for bestest girl."

Pea snapped her head from her assessment and growled at me.

"Oh, for fuck's sake. I'm talking about the K9s, Pea. You know no one beats you."

After a moment of side-eye, she clambered on top of Rafael, clearly exhausted after doing what she could to stabilize Yuriko. Clambering on top of his prone body, she opened her jaws wide, sharp teeth glinting in the newly cleared skies, and clamped down on the most easily accessible piece of flesh there was.

His nose.

Rafael bolted upright, which only flung Pea's body wide and made her teeth tear into his flesh, "*Que caralho!*"

I winced, holding my own nose in sympathy. "Welcome back to Earth." Pea was trying to gain purchase back up his chest, but the movements were causing more tears in his nose.

Rafael grabbed my small furry friend by her waist and tried to pry her off his proboscis, but she only clamped down harder.

"Ah, maybe just support her weight and let her do her thing?"

The infuriated male glared at me then glared at the opossum hanging off his nose. "*Sua puta,*" he seethed at her in a nasally tone, while he swayed from evident blood loss. Could you even call it blood loss? Exsanguination was probably the more appropriate term. I doubted he had a drop of blood left in him. Magic was the only reason he was conscious right now.

"And why, pray tell, should I leave five pounds of rodent better suited for roadkill hanging off…my *fucking* nose." Rafael inquired ever so delicately.

I raised a finger, "First off, she's four pounds, not five. She's very sensitive about her weight. Second off, she's a marsupial not a rodent. And finally, saying she's better suited for roadkill is just offensive when she's healing you. You might not want to offend her when she's doing you a boon *and* she has her teeth embedded in your nose."

His body stiffened nearly imperceptibly. "I may not be familiar with the habits and mannerisms of opossums, but *that* is not normal opossum behavior," he declared, nonplussed.

"Nope," I replied with a straight face.

"She is a *shikigami?*

"Mmmm," I responded noncommittally.

"Please tell me she's bound."

Pea hissed at him around the bulk of his nose in her mouth.

"You seriously might want to stop insulting her. You have scores upon scores of wounds from the *nukekubi* and I would bet you probably lost most, if not all, of your lifeblood. Immortal, I take it?"

He grumbled something under his breath I couldn't hear. Then again, it was probably just something unsavory in Portuguese again.

That was apparently the final straw for Pea. She detached from his nose, violently hissed at him and stalked over Max, where she curled up and turned her back to us. Apparently, I was included in the snubbing even though I had been defending her.

Rafael groaned and laid back down in the snow. "To be fair, all I knew at the time was that a large rodent-like creature was biting the shit out of my nose and had no idea she was healing me. Now that she's no longer clamped down…yeah, there's a definite difference. Please accept my apologies, Pea," he called over to her from his prone position on the ground.

"Oh, no. You're going to have to do so much more groveling than that, Rafe. You called her a rodent. You said she was better suited for roadkill. You didn't appreciate her efforts to heal you despite the fact she doesn't even really like you to begin with, and, if my rusty memory of Portuguese serves me well, you called her a bitch. But above all, you asked if she was bound."

"She's a *shikigami*. All *shikigami* need to be bound as a familiar, otherwise they risk mass destruction with their malevolent ways. History has shown evidence of this time and time again."

I could feel my temper rising as my magic began to overtake my vision.

"Have you…" I snarled balefully, choking on the words. I took a deep breath and tried again. "Have you ever, for once in your life, as someone who is also bound, considered the other side of those stories?"

I could tell I had caught his attention, but I was too pissed to care. "History, as the saying goes, is written by the victors. And *shikigami* have never been the victors. They easily could be, but they'd rather be left alone."

He opened his mouth to challenge my last statement, but I didn't give him the chance, "The only reason why the *kamis* have not destroyed their species, like they have the *kappas* and so many others, is because they use them. Without their consent. They have the *onmyōji* bind the *shikigami* to them to boost their powers. The more they have, the stronger they are. And they pull on the powers constantly, leaving the *shikigami* weakened.

"Those moments in history you refer to? Those are when a *kami* has decided a *shikigami* is no longer useful to them as a familiar. They abandon them in a location with a spell that disorients them, then sever the binding. The rebound of all the magic causes the destruction. Very few *shikigami* survive the severing. The few that do often swear revenge, understandably so. The ones that don't seek revenge fall into a deep depression they are unable to recover from due to the rebound. The *kamis* could humanely release the binding, but they don't because they don't want another *kami* to capture the *shikigami* and seize their power, so they destroy them instead, ignoring the consequences of their actions.

"I will never bind Pea," I said fiercely. "She chose me freely and she will always have the choice to stay or go. I will never do to another what has been done to us." I felt something wrap around my calf and felt hot stinging in my eyes as a warm lilac glow washed over me in Pea's manner of giving me a hug.

I picked her up and held her close to me. In moments like this, I wished more than ever that the exchange of magic was reciprocal so I could refill her well in kind after healing three of us.

Rafael looked deeply unsettled. "I never knew about this. About what the *kamis* did to the *shikigami.*" He struggled to raise himself up, supporting himself by the elbows, which put him at eye level with Pea, then lowered his head. "I am truly sorry for my words. I know I cannot ask for forgiveness yet. I'll work to earn it through my actions, and I will. I promise you this."

Pea regarded him for a moment, then twitched her tail at him and clicked once from my arms, accepting his words. I wasn't sure I could yet.

Olly laid a hand on my shoulder. I startled at the touch, not knowing when he showed up. "He may be a wanker, but at least he's demonstrated he's willing to learn and be humbled, yeah? I just wanted to let you know—Yuri woke briefly and went to sleep. It seems lighter, not a comatose state like previously."

I sagged in relief, both physically and emotionally done. I covered his hand with my own in support and gratitude. "Thank you for letting me know. We'll be there soon."

He nodded and eyed Rafael briefly before heading back to his home.

"It would, perhaps, behoove you to remember that there is far more that goes on behind every being's existence than what meets the eye." I waved at Rafael's forearms, hiding his obsidian bands beneath both glamour and leather cuffs. "You should know. You hide behind a glamour just as much as the rest of us."

I sighed before continuing my lesson in not judging others. "Let me guess. You never saw any *shikigami* around the sea *kami*?"

Rafael shook his head weakly as he collapsed. I could practically feel Pea internally roll her eyes as she scrambled out of my arms and back up his body.

He eyed her warily as she settled on his chest.

"Don't worry. She only needs to bite you to heal you the first time, in order to establish a connection through her saliva in your bloodstream. After that she only needs to maintain physical contact, unless you have a familiar link."

Rafael's tension ebbed as Pea alleviated his pain once again, then went back to work repairing his body. His injuries began to seep as blood flow slowly returned to his body. Wounds required blood to heal, so the sight of him bleeding was a welcome one.

"You didn't see any *shikigami*, because they are an open secret among the *kamis*. To parade their familiars would be to demonstrate that they are weak. To parade many would indicate that they require several to hold their seat of power. So they keep their *shikigami* hidden. They remain shunned and shoved away in a space not suited for the living."

His brow furrowed as he regarded me. "You are *onmyōji*." He said this as a statement of fact, not a question. That solved one major problem.

I inclined my head as an affirmative; he didn't need to know the rest. Leaning back on my hands, I allowed my eyes to close and my *ki* to rise, then sent it out along the banks of blood and gore, seeking every molecule of death that lay on the shores and shallows.

Once I was certain I had them all within my grasp, I plucked a molecule, sending the entire order of them into chaos, lighting them up.

"Well, that was entirely unsettling," came the voice beside me.

I opened my eyes to find Rafael was upright once again, a little more steady than before. I knew what he would have seen. Every blood stain, every rope of intestine, every sightless head, would have suddenly glowed like an ember, before blackening, then dissipating into nothing on a nonexistent breeze. Not even ash would remain. Olly's shores were pristine once again. I had ashed his produce out of existence as well, knowing he wouldn't want to touch them now.

I rose from my position before he could continue this line of thought. "If you're strong enough to sit up without collapsing again, let's get you inside already. We've wasted enough time and we haven't even touched on the reason why we came out here to begin with." I shoved my shoulder under his armpit and heaved him upright.

"Such bedside manner, Baki." He grinned weakly, as he took a few faltering steps at my side. The dogs bounded alongside us, Pea following far more sedately. "You have my heart all aflutter."

"Shut up. I will leave you here to rot."

"Can't. You need me."

"Um…last I checked, you're the one who sought me out. Came to my doorstep. Begged for my help."

"Who took out five *nukekubi* and saved your friend from being a blood bag while he was trying to take out a *futakuchi onna?*"

"Don't let it go to your head. I was busy with a *rokurokubi* and my very own *futakuchi onna*. For all I know, you led them here."

Rafael stilled at my statement, bringing our slow progress to a halt. "There were more?"

"Come on, lover boy. Let's get you inside and I'll tell you my tales of woe."

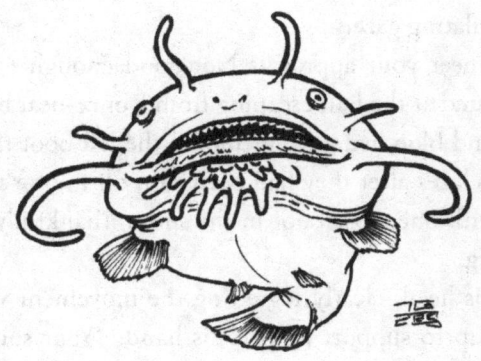

CHAPTER FOURTEEN

Rafael stood in awe in Oliver's living room, taking in the massive cavern and the pieces of art that Olly had created that made this place into a home. While Rafael's face was filled with wonder, all I felt was sorrow for all that Olly and his family had lost—first in Nagasaki, then when they fled Europe from the last *kariudo,* and a third time in the eruption. Olly now only engaged in art that he viewed as temporary. Replaceable. There were several *ikebanas* scattered throughout the space. The beautiful minimalist floral arrangements were backlit by the magic that brightened the cavern.

"Sit first. Stare second," I directed, leading him to a stool. Eyeing his grayish-blue skin, I made a judgment call and knelt by his feet to start untying his boots.

"Hey," he protested, feebly trying to pull his feet away. "I can do that myself."

I stood and stared him down, raising an eyebrow. "Bend over, touch your boot, and sit back up without falling off that stool and I'll believe you. But I'm leaving you on the floor if you fall off."

I could see the war going on in his mind between his pride and the need to prove me wrong. Evidently the risk of injuring his ego and being laid out on the floor won out, because his jaw clenched and he nodded.

Males were idiots. Shaking my head, I went back to my task. I could feel him watching me intently as I did, and when I glanced up at him, his brow was furrowed while he looked me over fully. I felt my irritability rise beneath his calculating gaze.

"Do I not meet your approval? Not good enough to take home to Mother?" I gestured at the hair escaping from a once-neat braid all the way down my torn and bloodied gear, including the left boot that was missing a solid half of its laces after they had been torn off in one of the fights. It's a bitch hiking with one loose boot in the snow. Thankfully, it hadn't been on the injured leg.

He shook his head, clearly regretting the movement when he immediately reached up to support it with his hand. "Your soul…" His voice trailed off as his eyes darkened in concern.

A weight settled over my shoulders. I didn't regret the choice I had made to shift when I did. When I left this world, it would be with the knowledge I had lived a life most would never get to see. But I still had unfinished business.

I closed my eyes and took a deep breath then let it out slowly. I avoided asking the question that was on my mind. I could check to see how much farther my body had split the next time I was alone in front of a mirror. Instead, I asked curiously, "How are you able to see my soul anyway?"

"Ah. Trade secret." His smile held a brittle edge to it. "We'll call it genetics for now."

Call me a cat, because my curiosity was further piqued now. I didn't know any *yōkai* who could see souls. Auras, yes, but souls were a different story. I opened my mouth to ask more questions, but before I could get out a sound, he shushed me, holding a finger up in the air.

"You get to keep your cryptic mysterious airs about you, I get to keep mine. Fair's fair. When you decide to share, I'll share."

I shut my mouth. The man had a point. I glared at him. "Did you just shush me?"

He grinned cockily. "I did. What are you going to do about it? Kick a man while he's down and recently bled out? That's hardly sportsmanlike."

"What on God's green earth makes you think I'd be sports*man*like? If I want to punch you in yours for identifying too hard with your genitalia and acting like a dick, I will. Sorry. Can't help dick-punching you if your entire self is a dick. It's a little hard to miss." I motioned my hand in the air to encompass his body to make my point.

He burst out laughing. "Anyone ever tell you you're a little intense? And maybe a little violent?"

"Cam considers all insults regarding how violent she is compliments," Olly commented, wandering out into the kitchen and throwing a couple of water bottles our way.

I caught mine and raised it to him in a toast. "I'll take *a little intense and a little violent*,—although, let's be real, it's a *lot* violent—over *dick*."

"I thought we had established that *dick* was an identity and not an adjective, hmm?" Rafael stated with a twinkle in his eye.

"This is very true." I opened my bottle of water and chugged half of it. "However, *dick* is one of those incredibly versatile words, much like *fuck*. It can be a noun, such as *your dick*," I motioned to said body part, admiring it as I went. "It can also be an adjective, like when you're being *dickish*. Which is 80 percent of your personality thus far. By the way, excellent job toning it down. When I first met you, I thought for sure it was going to be 100 percent."

Rafael had just started drinking his own water when I started my tangent and he choked at this proclamation, spraying water all over the ground. I grinned wickedly.

"I didn't take you for one who liked to be choked, *Sugs*."

The coughing just intensified. *Oops*.

Oliver clacked his claws against his counter, "Brain out of the gutter, Cam. We have matters to discuss." He began pulling items out of his refrigerator.

I clapped my hands. "You're cooking?"

He paused his ministrations to look at me as if I were an idiot. "You," he pointed a knife at me, "and him," the knife swung to the *kariudo*, "are stuck here for the night. Did you think I wasn't going to feed you?"

"I mean, I didn't want to assume you were going to feed your hated enemy, especially since I dropped him on your doorstep and all. We have provisions."

"You have supplies here?" Rafael asked.

"You didn't honestly think I'd hike up a mountain with only an assortment of fruits and vegetables, did you?"

"I'll be honest, I did seriously question your judgment and mental capacity until the *nukekubi* attacked. Now my brain is too muddled by blood loss to be capable of questioning it."

"Well, you're in for a treat. Olly's food is way better than any supplies we brought. Speaking of which, I'll be right back. I'm going to go snag our packs. Don't kill each other until I get back."

Olly muttered to himself as he started slicing and salting some eggplant. I laughed and darted out the door, snagged the packs which hadn't moved from their original position from hours ago, and came back inside. My ankle only throbbed with each step now, and my breath was raspy rather than feeling like I needed an inhaler with every gasp. Figured, now that we were safe indoors.

I finally took my boots off at the door and sighed in relief. I removed my sodden socks and laid them over the top of my boots, cringing at the green and yellow hues of my foot. The other was white and pruney. I dug into my pack and stuffed my feet into a pair of dry socks, activated a pair of foot warmers, and shoved them in my socks too, moaning with joy as I did so.

"Do you and your feet need a room?" Olly asked dryly.

Rafael was snickering over his water bottle. "I feel like I should have recorded that. You probably could have made a fortune from that video on OniFans."

I threw his hefty pack at him, which he managed to duck, barely. "I was going to toss you a pair of socks but here's your pack instead, just for that comment."

He dug through it, finding a change of clothes, and came back up. "I'll just change real quick and we can get started."

Oliver pointed a spatula toward a lava tube. "Hot spring that way. You can wash the blood off."

Rafael set off in the direction indicated, slightly off-kilter but miles better than he had been a few minutes before. Blood loss, even complete exsanguination, was significantly easier to recuperate from than bones or organs reknitting. I was jealous.

I joined Olly in the kitchen and we settled into the comfortable silence of two friends, long used to the company of one another as I helped him prepare our meal.

We were just dishing up the bowls of *donburi* when Rafael reappeared, hair wet and slicked back, highlighting his chiseled jaw. His skin was starting to regain its color, returning to its dark, healthy hue, no longer a bluish-gray. The dark green henley he had thrown on clung to his damp skin, highlighting the muscles of his core. He lifted up the bottom hem of his shirt to wipe the water droplets collecting from his forehead. I caught sight of a colorful tattoo taking up his entire left side. From across the room, it looked like a Japanese sea dragon entwined with a beast. Olly cleared his throat and elbowed me in the ribs.

"Fucking *ow*. Those were shattered not that long ago," I complained, rubbing my side.

"Eh. You've had worse."

Rafael looked amused. "How can I help?"

Olly pointed to various drawers. "The goods for place settings can be found in those drawers. You can do the honors. And the dishes when we're done."

"Deal."

A few short minutes later we were settling down around the *chabudai* to eat, bowls and chopsticks in hand.

Raising an eyebrow, Rafael commented on my bowl, "No fish for you, just eggplant?"

"To quote Bruce, 'Fish are friends, not food.' I don't do fish or seafood. Crabs on the other hand are the pricks of the sea. I'll eat those."

"Yeah, well, you should have made an exception for this one," Olly muttered. He stabbed his chopsticks toward the catfish heading to Rafael's mouth. "That was a juvenile *namazu* who had somehow made its way under the lake. It was starting to cause magnitude 4.0–5.0 quakes. Ike was worried so he had me take care of it. You're reaping the benefits. I, however, am going to be stuck eating variations of *namazu* for the better part of a year now, and that's after foisting off half the carcass on Ike. If the reason why you won't eat fish is because they're friends not wankers, well, this one was the absolute definition of a wanker."

The chopsticks had paused their journey during the recounting of the tale as Rafael paled and studied the catfish. I could tell the thought of eating a fellow *yōkai* didn't sit well with him—giant, non-sentient, quake-causing catfish or not—and his character continued to build in my eyes.

"You don't have to eat it," I assured him. "Olly won't be offended." Said *kappa's* ring of hair raised above one eye, as if it were an eyebrow. I amended my statement. "Well, he will be, but it won't be because you've offended his sensibilities. It'll be because you've left him with that much more *namazu* to eat on his own, since he won't waste it even if he's generally a vegetarian. We can easily solve that issue with the dogs."

I shoved a small plate his way to put the pieces of fried *yōkai* on to give to the K9s later and Rafael set to work picking the pieces of flaky fish out of his bowl with great relief.

I turned to Olly, "Now, *a million years later*, we can get down to the reason why we came up here in the first place. The *bijin*. Do you know of her?"

I could sense the shift in Rafael's focus, from eliminating the fish in his bowl to me, with my last statement.

"Misaki? Sure. She used to drop by from time to time to pick my brain for information about the *yōkai* for whatever her latest research project was on."

I slow-blinked at Olly, then turned to Rafael and blinked at him before looking back at the information-dropping *kappa* and blinked some more.

"Is there something in your eye? They have drops for that you know," the smart-ass said as he shoveled eggplant, *namazu*, and rice into his beak.

I opened my mouth, but nothing came out.

Rafael picked up my chopsticks and put a small portion of *donburi* in my gaping hole. I began chewing automatically.

"I think," he began diplomatically, "Camellia is trying to process what seemed like a simple statement to you, but what was a week's worth of manpower and worry for her."

"Well, why didn't you just come to me in the first place and save yourself the work?" Olly said matter-of-factly.

Why, that short little—

Rafael snagged me as I started lunging up off my cushion and sat me back down.

"Now, now. No strangling the bearer of information," he said mildly. "Dr. Aoki is missing. Camellia has been deployed on a search for her. It's only just recently come to her attention that Aoki might be the *bijin* as well as the same being of interest that I am looking for."

Oliver's gaze sharpened at the news. "Misaki is missing, Yuriko is essentially held hostage, and the three of us are attacked? This isn't a coincidence, *kariudo*. What is going on?"

I surveyed Olly and Rafe as a thought occurred to me. Before Rafe could answer, I interjected, "The two of you seem to be getting on much better. I know we discussed slave bands and all that jazz, but what gives? Before the attack, you were still incredibly mistrustful, Olly."

His carapace rose in his version of a shrug. "One," he held up one finger. I knew it was awkward to do with a webbed hand. "The sea *kami's* minions targeted all of us. They didn't spare him. In fact, he very well may have borne the brunt of the attack."

Not gonna lie, in my mind that just made him more suspicious, but whatever worked.

"Two," he went on, freeing a second finger. "The *kariudo* saved my life. There's absolutely no way I could have survived the melee on my own. That carries weight with me."

It would. I would grant the huntsman that and thank him for it, since Oliver was an important presence in my life.

Rafael straightened at my side. I could practically feel the surprise oozing out of his pores. He gave Olly a respectful nod. "I could hardly let one of Cam's friends die now, could I?"

Oliver snorted. "Oh, I think the previous *kariudo* would have had quite an easy time letting a *kappa* die. It doesn't mean you're off the hook, or that I like you, but I'm willing to work with you. Now, Cam, stop avoiding the subject."

I hesitated for a moment, debating whether to provide the additional information regarding the attacks in Neskowin, as that line of questioning had potential for uncovering what I was; however, my friend instantly saw my pause.

"Don't you dare hold back information now, Cam." He stabbed his chopsticks at me. "Remember the conversation we just had? My closest friends are in danger. You were there for me back when I needed you in 1980 and every time I needed you thereafter. Don't deny me the chance to be there for you now."

"The *habu karuge* have been swarming along the Oregon Coast. There have already been fatalities among the Quotes and critical injuries among the Abbies." I just wasn't sure what was related to the sea *kami* learning of my whereabouts and what was related to Aoki's disappearance. Rafael, nor Oliver, could ever know about that aspect of my heritage.

Rafael swore viciously.

Oliver regarded his reaction carefully. The *kariudo* carried the news like a physical burden, his shoulders weighed down, the light in his eyes dimmed. Vicky rose from her spot near the door and lay next to him, nosing her head into his lap, offering comfort to another damaged soul.

"You didn't know about this facet of the *kami's* plans," Oliver stated, rather than inquired.

"I did not." Rafael lifted a hand to stroke Vicky's head. "I would have tried to find some way to warn the community."

Olly made a sound of disbelief. "And we are supposed to believe this?"

He looked back up, some of the fire flickering back in his gaze. "You just spoke about being willing to work with me. Much as you may like to put me in the same camp as my predecessors, I am not in my position because I enjoy it. I am in it because I was never given a choice."

Vicky whined a little, her tail thumping against the cavern floor, and Rafael returned to stroking her head, murmuring reassurances to the smallest of my K9s.

I sighed. I knew this wasn't going to be an easy relationship to navigate. "Back to Misaki. I brought up the *habu kurage* attacks because the timing of everything can't be coincidental, not so we could bicker like children. Misaki went missing on April twenty-seventh. Her friend didn't make it back down the mountain until late the following day. Search and Rescue began their operation on the twenty-ninth. The first *habu kurage* sightings began the following day. Hunter Boy here showed up on my doorstep yesterday, but I suspect he's been in the background for a few days longer than that."

"I've been here since the thirtieth," Rafael said quietly.

I nodded, not surprised, storing that bit of information in my head for later. "What was Aoki researching this time?"

"She wanted to know about the tide jewels and what became of them."

Rafael's movements stilled. "The tide jewels?"

"Yes, she said her next paper was to be on the Quotidian mythology of Toyotama-hime and Hoori. She wanted to know what had happened to *shiohiru-tama* and *shiomitsu-tama* after as nothing has been heard of the ebb and flow gems in about a hundred years."

A deep grief swept through me at the mention of Toyotama. The loss of the princess had cut through my already ravaged soul. The night we lost her, we had lost so many in the chaos of *Hyakki Yagyō*.

"Olly," I spoke quietly. "We told you briefly what has been happening in Ryūgū-jō before the attack, but we didn't get to all of it. What have you heard from below?"

His gaze shifted to me. "I try to avoid news of the Undersea Kingdom whenever possible. A throne room that holds the carapaces of my deceased relatives isn't a place I like to hear word from; you understand, yes?"

"I do. More than anything, I understand. But listen to Rafael regarding this next bit."

I tuned out as the *kariudo* filled the *kappa* in about the famines and civil unrest happening in Ryūgū-jō in far more detail than he had during their initial meeting. The tide jewels had gone missing the same terrible night when the Night Parade went so wrong. It was one of the worst-kept secrets, with rumors abounding about their whereabouts. But the death of the princesses and the loss of the tide jewels were tied together. If Misaki Aoki was related to the jewels in *any* way, her level of importance in this melodrama had just skyrocketed.

CHAPTER FIFTEEN

After Oliver grilled Rafael on what he knew, I switched gears to interrogating my friend for the knowledge he had of Dr. Aoki's movements.

I'm sorry. Not *interrogating*. We don't interrogate friends. We ask *politely*. Patiently, even.

"When was the last time you saw her?" I questioned.

He finished chewing thoughtfully and swallowed. "I believe it was a little over two weeks ago. I told her I unfortunately didn't have any information regarding the tide jewels. I knew any of the ones in the shrines in the past few hundred years weren't the true jewels and told her as much."

"And where did she go from there?"

"I believe she went to Ike's place to ask around, but she stopped back here before heading back down the mountain, so I know she didn't have any success there."

"Do you know why she would have tried to summit the mountain?" Rafael asked.

It was Olly's turn to swear. "That's where she went missing?"

I rearranged my legs under the short table and confirmed.

"Bloody idiot. She must have gone to see if Reika had any information."

I stiffened. Reika's involvement couldn't be a good omen.

"We know the hag isn't the reason why Aoki is missing," Rafael said calmly. "You said yourself her scent went completely cold without explanation several times. There would have at least been signs of a struggle if the *yamauba* had been involved. Did any of the trails get close to the *yamauba's* home?"

I let out a breath, trying to release the tension in my neck and shoulders. This was just one more thing I would have to take care of and with due haste.

"Why would she have assumed the *yamauba* had any information about the tide jewels in the first place? They're mountain witches, not sea witches."

Olly's neck and half his head retracted into his carapace and he mumbled something under his breath. I side-eyed the *kappa*, bracing myself for more bad news.

"What was that again? I couldn't quite hear you,"

"I try to avoid Reika whenever possible," he said in a hurry. "I might be neighbors with her, but not willingly."

I opened my mouth to ask the obvious question when a hesitant voice cut in.

"Oliver?"

We all turned to find a diminished Yuriko carefully balancing herself in the entrance of a tunnel, one hand along a wall, the other using Willa as a touchstone. Her usually immaculate hair fell like an unruly waterfall to her waste, and her skin glowed an unearthly, yet ethereal, blue under the lights. She gave the impression of fragility, of a thin sheet of ice just one small movement away from breaking. It disturbed me to no end. Olly leapt to his feet and hurried over to assist her to the table and began to serve her a heaping bowl of *donburi*.

Since I had just been about to ask Rafael a question, I didn't miss the brief flutter that passed over his gaze. It could have been a myriad of emotions, ranging from calculation, shock, wonder, confusion; all I knew was the moment had passed too quickly for me to be sure, and I didn't like that at all, especially with a team member so vulnerable at the moment. However, I knew Yuri and she fought her own battles, so I held my tongue as she settled herself and waited patiently.

She ate a few bites of food while she evaluated Rafael. He wisely held himself still beneath her gaze and assessed her with his own, waiting for her to pronounce him worthy or not.

"Name?" she asked around a bite of *namazu*.

"Rafael Sugiyama. You?" he responded politely.

"Yuriko." She had a last name, but it was a manufactured one for the benefit of the Quotes and their government. Granted, the moniker of Yuriko was manufactured as well, but it was a name she had chosen to adopt to replace her past life, and it had a great deal of meaning to her. Her last name had none. We had come from an era when surnames hadn't existed.

She swallowed delicately and regarded him for a long moment. Olly and I held our breaths.

"You are the *kariudo*."

Bulgae fire. Olly and I exchanged another glance, this one wide-eyed, each of us bracing ourselves for shit to go down.

Rafael merely nodded.

"And your plans?"

He just grimaced, then shrugged.

She surveyed him as she took another bite and chewed thoughtfully. Took another bite. Chewed some more. Swallowed. Took a brutally long sip of tea. I was dying inside. Yuri may not go by the name of Fuyuhime, or Winter Princess, anymore, but fuck was it apt. Diminished by the attack on her or not, she carried herself with an elegance that one was both born with and cultivated over thousands of years of practice, and it was utterly demoralizing to have it aimed in your direction. I didn't know how Rafael was holding up so well under her regard.

She finished draining her tea and set it down while Rafael looked on, amused.

"You'll do. For now."

"Thank you, Fuyuhime."

I kept my jaw from dropping. Barely. Her past life was information that precious few were privy to. She wore her current glamour flawlessly.

"Yuriko. Never Fuyuhime."

He tipped his own cup of tea to her then drained it. "To new partnerships and overcoming tyrannies."

Before he could finish his proclamation, the porcelain cup fell from his grasp, shattering on the floor, and he doubled over in pain, as the bands enslaving him delivered swift punishment for daring to speak against the sea *kami*. Faster than any of us could react, he held up a hand, indicating that he was fine. Several moments passed as he caught his breath.

"Worth…it," he gasped.

There was a long pause as he coughed into a napkin for several minutes. He tried to hide the evidence discreetly, but we all saw the speck of bright red dotting the napkin before he crumpled it into the ball,

I didn't know if I could trust him. But hell if I wouldn't give him the benefit of the doubt in the meantime, until he proved me otherwise. Because everyone should always be given the opportunity for second chances in life. It was the motto I had always lived my life by.

Olly silently rose from the table to retrieve a new teacup. Yuri and I both waited until Olly had freshened a new pot of tea and I carefully poured everyone a new cup. Then we all toasted to his willingness to defy a corrupt king.

"To new allies."

ONCE YURI WAS fully updated, and we had all savored the notes in our tea, we asked Yuriko what she knew.

"Reika," she said simply. I resisted the urge to sigh. Yuriko's tendency toward one- to three-word sentences was great when you needed quick and dirty reports in the field. Not so great when you actually needed information.

"What did Reika do?" Olly encouraged gently. "In full detail, if you can."

She sipped her tea. "I can't say. I've been placed under a geas."

"Did you know Misaki Aoki as well? If you did, do you know if she specifically sought out Reika?" I asked, trying to find a loophole around the magical binding preventing her from speaking about this subject.

"Misaki?" Yuri looked surprised.

"We think she might have gone to Reika to see if she had any new information about the tide jewels. She's the missing person Cam is looking for." Rafael explained as he shifted to look at me. "I can't speak for her for certain, but the tide jewels have been all that Ryūgū-jō has been concerned with for decades, since the famines have become dire. I can't imagine that Reika knew anything of significance."

This male didn't know Reika like I did.

Yuri shook her head. "I met with Misaki several times and she often talked about her theories about the tide jewels. She was…different about the tide jewels than she was about her other research regarding us last time I saw her. Almost obsessive, like a dog with a bone. I saw her just a few weeks ago. I didn't know what changed for her.

I sighed, then got up and walked my dishes over to the sink and rinsed them off before placing them in the whirlpool that acted as a dishwasher in the cavern. "I didn't get a sense of magic at any of the locations where Woody got her scent, but there has to be magic involved. Yuri, Olly, she is for sure a Quote and not an Abbie?"

They exchanged a loaded glance, then nodded.

Max plodded over to me and laid down behind me. He knew I was done eating and he might score some scraps of *namazu*. The other three K9s made their way over for their shares of scraps too, as I scraped the other dish of catfish into even portions for them.

"See, here's the thing." I leaned against the counter. "Initially, we thought that Dr. Aoki was up here researching the *bijin*, then Olly here casually confirms that she is, in fact, the *bijin*, someone who is generally older than most human lifetimes and certainly doesn't look like a Japanese woman in her early forties, let alone in her hundreds. And the *bijin* can allegedly teleport. So why are we all saying she is human?"

Oliver hesitated before responding. "Because, just like you haven't found any magical signatures at any of the sites, there isn't a trace of magic around her when she comes to visit. Not even like a Perigean. She's just pure Quote."

This search was going to be the death of me. Hopefully not the death of Dr. Aoki. "I'm relying on you, buddy," I informed Max. "I've got absolutely nothing. We've never had to search for the absence of a magic trail. But if anyone can do it, you can."

The plume of his tail waved in the air enthusiastically. A woman's life was in the paws of a K9 whose nose was currently stuffed in fried quake-causing catfish. I wasn't holding my breath. This was going to take the entire team as soon as we got down off this mountain.

Yuri looked grim. "In all our years together, I've never had to be on a SAR for a friend before. For others we're acquainted with and people we know, sure. But not a friend."

As much as it would pain me to take Yuriko off the ground search, there was no way I would have put her on it after everything she had gone through today, let alone knowing that Dr. Aoki was a personal friend of hers.

I shook my head, mentally mapping out my team. "You won't be. I'll need you to liaise with the crew up in Seattle for information. Olly, I know you hate coming off the mountain, but I'm not leaving you up here by yourself with these attacks. Can you help fill in the holes about Dr. Aoki? Maybe corroborate with Kenichi and fact-check what gossip he's collected?"

Oliver groaned. "I knew this was coming. Yeah, I'll head down with you guys. I'm going to go head off into the lake now, since who knows how long it'll be before I'll be back in it. You guys can figure out your own sleeping arrangements. You both know where everything is. Sleep with one eye open with the *kariudo* around, allied or not."

Rafael casually flipped him the middle finger, which shocked me, then I grinned.

Maybe this team would work out after all.

CHAPTER SIXTEEN

Aidan was at reception, muddy boots propped up on the desk, leaning back in his chair and tossing a ball across the room for his lab mix, Yumi, when our bedraggled crew stumbled through the door the following day, having hiked for an interminable amount of time in the pouring rain. This time the weather was Nature's gift, as opposed to Yuriko's. We had made a detour on the mountain that was ultimately unsuccessful, which didn't improve anyone's mood. The hours-long ride home with four cranky *yōkai*, four wet dogs, and an angry, soaked Pea had been less than fun. The vehicle had been cramped, reeked of wet critters, and was—worst of all—humid. Aidan's eyes widened and he straightened at the sight of us.

"What the hell did the *jorōgumo* drag in?" he asked as Yumi brought the soggy ball back to him and dropped it in his lap.

I glared at him and my hand went straight for the side pocket of my pack, drawing out a sock, now stiff with mud, sweat, blood, and remnants of what may have been intestines? Some type of organ at least. Good enough for my purpose. Which was to hurl it straight for his head.

"What the fuck, Cam!"

"That! That was for hanging out with your great uncles *without showering* first," I hissed at him.

"Oh."

127

"Oh? That's all you have to say? Do you know how much grief they put me through?" I groaned, striding over behind him and dumping him out of the chair so I could fall into it.

Rafe remained near the entryway, a twinkle in his eyes. Yuri and Olly, being familiar with the facility and our antics, ignored us and headed for the locker rooms to freshen up. The K9s followed them.

Aidan's handsome face peered up at me from the ground. "To be fair, I didn't have time to take a shower. You know that. They called me with a so-called emergency while we were in bed. You and I both agreed it was best if I went, since they were my uncles. I dragged my pants on, grabbed my keys, and ran out the door. How was I supposed to know the emergency was to settle a feud with the local raccoons. One they could have easily handled on their own?"

"It was probably to settle a bet among themselves about whether we were sleeping together," I muttered. "Do you know what I went through, Aidan? Do you?"

He snickered. "They're my uncles and *tanukis*. So I have a pretty good guess, yeah."

"They gave me advice on sex positions for us. And proceeded to *demonstrate*. My eyes and ears will never recover."

He howled with laughter and a low chuckle emitted from Rafael as he settled on one of the couches near us and began working off his hiking boots.

I slumped down in the big leather swivel chair and gazed up the ceiling as if it could give me salvation from males. "Why did I sleep with you again?"

"For my great sexual prowess."

"Oh. Right." I sighed. He wasn't wrong. His genetic make-up made for a master in bed, but a disaster at commitment, which was perfect for me. Except when he didn't have a chance to shower before rushing to his uncles' supposed rescue.

"So," Rafael said, gesturing to us, "the two of you are together?"

Aidan and I looked at each other with matching looks of horror. Me from his formerly occupied chair, him from where he had made himself comfortable on the floor, wrestling with Yumi.

"Absolutely not," we said in unison.

"We just like to fuck," Aidan added.

"You dick," I kicked him in the side.

"I can't be with a woman who abuses men," he said solemnly, entwining his hands to lay over his chest. "I'm holding out for a woman who has more respect for a relationship than that."

He glanced at me, tried to keep a straight face. Failed abysmally.

"Aidan is the quintessential stereotype of a playboy afraid to commit." I nudged him affectionately with my foot as he nodded in agreement.

"More like my DNA would never allow me to commit," he put in cheerfully. "I'm a *tanuki* and gean-cannagh cross."

"And he likes pain, don't let him fool you."

Rafael raised an intrigued eyebrow as he perused Aidan. I couldn't tell if the intrigue was about the comment regarding his genetic make-up or about the pain, and that was kind of hot.

"Is he checking me out?" The love-talker and shape-shifting raccoon dog whispered to me as he sat up.

"I can't tell," I whispered back.

"I can hear you."

Aidan blushed bright pink, complimenting his deep auburn hair. I snorted. "Okay, enough fun; is the gang all here?"

He nodded. "Yeah, they're in Aoki's conference room...at least everyone who isn't on a call-out. We got a new one last night. We've just been waiting for you guys to get here."

"Great, I'm just going to hop in the shower real quick. Rafe, you know where the locker rooms are from your tour. There should be some extra sets of pants and shirts in the cubbies, so feel free to find something in your size if you don't have anything dry in your pack. I'm going to go get rid of this mud for once and for all." I waved them off and made my way to seek out blessedly warm water.

Yuriko had freshened up with her usual brisk efficiency, so I had the locker room to myself by the time I finished showering. The thought of looking at myself in the mirror without my glamour was horrifying. A pit formed in my stomach as I dragged my hand across the mirror, clearing away the fog. I stared at my appearance, bracing my hands against the sink.

And dropped the mask mocking me in the reflection.

I felt my knees wobble beneath me as if they belonged to another body while the damage I had done to myself with one shift glared at me like floodlights. The fragments of my body had drifted even further apart. In some cases, smaller pieces had shifted so they were no longer positioned correctly. I winced as I prodded where my ribs had shattered. Evidently, healing while also shifting had lent itself to coming back together *wrong* this time. My mind wandered back to Rafael's comment about my soul after I had shifted and I wondered what he had seen. And yet...

I didn't want to know. There was no good that would come of knowing.

I turned my back on my broken self and threw my glamour up, focusing on one task at a time. *Dry my right leg. Then my left. Focus. Clothes, Cam. You need to leave the locker room with clothes on. The small things first. Socks. You can manage socks.*

When I wandered back into the designated conference room with a towel wrapped around my hair and fully dressed, everything seemed perfectly normal. Which meant it wasn't. Seeing as how it was my circus. A vociferous argument was taking place, one in which Lala was clearly losing.

Steeling myself against social interaction for the next few hours, I dropped into the empty chair next to Rafe and unwrapped the towel from my head. "What are they arguing about now?"

"From what I've been able to gather, James Michener and a book club? The one who was in the woods with you seems pretty passionate about the topic," he answered with a slight smile.

"For one, that's creepy. Stop referencing watching Lala and I in the woods. Normal people don't do that. For two, Lala's heart and soul belong to Michener. He was probably her Thread, but he was a Quote and died before she could meet him and profess her undying love and go delulu over him."

He squinted at me. "I understood you up until the last part of that sentence. I'm pretty sure that wasn't English."

"Some people have K-pop. Some have *Lord of the Rings*. Lala has James Michener. It's better if you don't ask." I called out to the room, "Hey! Stop debating next month's book club. We've got a missing person."

The room was descending into shouting. Mostly everyone against Lala, who had climbed onto the table in her combat boots to make her points with more emphasis. I threw my wet towel in her face. "You! Get off my damn table and eat your Red Vines. We have a guest, for the love of all things unholy."

After a few mutters and shoves, everyone settled into their usual spots. Olly, although not a typical member of the team, was comfortable enough with everyone, given how often we conducted SARs on Mount St. Helens, and settled onto a stool someone had brought in for him to accommodate his carapace.

"Everyone, this is Rafael Sugiyama. He's invested in the search for Misaki Aoki and will be helping us out for the foreseeable future. Rafe, you've met Olly, Yuriko, and Aidan. Do you band of reckless idiots want to introduce yourselves to him?"

Lala waved her licorice as she kicked her boots up on the table and hung the towel off the arm of her chair. "I'm Areola. You can call me Lala. My K9 is Phallus, also known as Phally. You'll understand his name when you see him sleeping separate from the dog pile sometime. I'm the codirector."

Rafe blinked for half a second at her introduction before he inclined his head in greeting. It was commendable, really.

Hideki knocked her feet off the table. "I'm Hideki. I'm one of the Search and Rescue gang. My K9's not here right now; she's at home with my partner. My pup was injured during our last deployment so she's recovering and we're grounded for now." The stout Japanese-American member of my team had been devastated when his girl had been hurt during an urban SAR. While Pea had healed her physical wounds, she was still recovering from her emotional ones and regaining her confidence.

Emma waved shyly from across the table. "I'm Emma. I'm not SAR, I'm Research. I work with Whiz looking into the backgrounds of our missing persons to see if we can piece together a case that might help our SAR team, particularly with cold cases."

Theo threw an arm around Emma affectionately. "And I'm Theo. I'm half-SAR and half-Med. I used to work rural emergency medicine, so I come in handy every now and then when one of these guys fuck up and get hurt."

"And when Theo's the one getting hurt, I'm the one stepping up. I'm Leilani. I'm both SAR and Med as well. I stabilize 'em until Theo can get there. The splotchy one over there is my K9. Roxy is her name. Best guess is she's some sort of German shepherd and cattle dog mix."

"And that covers everyone present in the room right now. Thanks, all. Now, what's the update since we've been up on Helens?" I directed my question to Lala, who was chewing on her Red Vine contemplatively.

"Danly called the search yesterday. He couldn't justify the financial drain of resources on his department anymore. He did his best to extend it for as long as possible, but with as screwed up as this SAR has been, there just was no way, especially with the missing child case that just came up. We've got four of our guys out on that call-out."

I nodded. I had been expecting it, which is why we had talked it over before I had gone up to see Oliver. I directed my next question to Rafael.

"That means the ball is technically in your court, as you would be the one now contracting our services for the search. Would you like us to resume the search for Dr. Misaki Aoki, officially missing since April twenty-eighth, whereabouts unknown for nine days?"

"I would."

"Excellent, after this meeting, we will go over contracts. But before we do so, let's cover the information we have, so you can make a fully informed decision before committing. Whiz? Do you have a summary of everyone's reports from the past two days?"

"Is that an insult?" an offended voice emitted from the display on the wall, shortly before a gremlin leapt out of it. Rafael started slightly, his right hand twitching for a blade that wasn't there. I stilled his hand, shaking my head.

I gestured to the gremlin with his ass in the air as he searched for the clicker on the table. "Why do you disrespectful peons always mess with my stuff?" he shouted.

"Whiz is one of our gremlins," I whispered. "He never connected with machinery, but one day in the early nineties he discovered a computer, and it was all over from there. He usually lives in a data cloud somewhere—I have no idea where—but he does all our technology."

Whiz had a miniature flash drive sticking out of his mouth like a cigar. He had warped a floppy disk into a poncho, but given that old-school floppy disks weren't *that* floppy, those of us facing his back could see everything as he bent over. He whooped with victory when he found his clicker and straightened back up.

"I can say one thing for sure, Baki. You have introduced me to a one-of-a-kind experience with the *yōkai* since I've met you," Rafe muttered out of the side of his mouth.

CHAPTER SEVENTEEN

I smothered a grin in response to Rafe's proclamation. Whiz marched over to the conference phone, unplugged it, tossed aside the headset, and settled into the depression where the headset had rested as if it was an armchair. The floppy disk garment rose as he did so. Which Whiz, as per his usual, gave zero shits about. He aimed the clicker at the board, and it switched from a simple projection into a 4D projection of St. Helens. Complete with trails, pins, even 3D replicas of ourselves and our K9s. Whiz bent his forearm, aiming the clicker at the opposite wall and a similar projection came up. This one was projecting recordings of the encounters we'd had with the *rokurokubi, nukekubi,* and *futakuchi onna.* Notably missing though, was my brush with Sachi and rescue of Yuriko. I knew enough about how Whiz's technology worked and had shut all that down before I went to track Yuri down.

I felt Rafe straighten beside me as he took in the projection of Helens. His head whipped to the bored gremlin. "You were recording us the entire time?"

Lala interrupted him before he could berate Whiz, who was giving him a deadpan stare while gnawing on the flash drive. "It's procedure. Take a closer look at the projection—you'll see your vitals running constantly. Oh look. There. You just got taken out."

"Wait. Replay that again, please. From the beginning of the attack this time, as opposed to when his vitals dropped." I wanted to verify I had indeed seen what I thought I saw.

My body was whisked away into the trees. It had happened faster than I thought, which at least made me feel a little better about my reaction time. Everyone in the room flinched as my body slammed into the rocks before it disappeared into the whiteout. I could feel an echo of pain through the misplaced fragments of my body as I watched the scene play out again.

While everyone was distracted by my sudden disappearance, six disembodied heads materialized from the snow. The Oliver and Rafael of the past were unaware at first of their silent arrival. The Oliver and Rafael of the present were rigid, knowing exactly what would come next.

Before the heads could fully descend upon them, Rafael tensed and whipped around, a pair of tactical *tanto* blades appearing in his grip. The motion was so smooth, I wasn't sure exactly how or when it had occurred. I watched carefully and saw the widening of his eyes as he took in the *nukekubi* surrounding them and processed who would have sent them in a moment's time. We observed as he shouted to warn Oliver and leapt to ward off the *nukekubi* targeting my friend, sacrificing his flesh for the deed as one managed to tear into his side.

"I can't imagine how starved they must be," Emma murmured in empathy. "To go for the flank? The opportunity to access arterial blood flow in the torso is nearly impossible with incisors. And that's before you factor in clothing. She's grasping at straws, desperate for any sustenance." Emma's own head detached from her body, almost as though she had forgotten she had one to begin with, and she floated closer to the screen. Rafe shifted in his seat next to me, perhaps disconcerted by Emma's objective analysis of the accessibility of his lifeblood.

The tape continued to roll and the *nukekubi* focused on Rafael as both the greater threat and the easier target for blood, not having a carapace to get through. He had managed to rip the one off his side and incapacitated her, his blade slipping through her skull like a heated blade through snow. The amount of force needed to do so would have to be astounding. A collective inhale sounded around the room at the brutality of it.

I frowned. There was something strange that occurred in the moment of the *nukekubi's* death, like the slightest glitch in the system, but I couldn't put my finger on it. I blinked and a swell of magic filled my head, bringing on a rush and a headache as an aftereffect. But I could see magic now.

Another *nukekubi* latched onto Rafe's upper arm, trying to gain access to his brachial artery, severely limiting his ability to fight. Oliver was doing his best to lend a hand but was hindered by his shorter stature. They took out a second and third *nukekubi* when my sight caught on to the strangeness I had perceived. At the time of each death, the parasitic evil within him swelled. The muddy, yellowish green mass within him grew exponentially, but before I could become concerned, a flash of light occurred, and the parasite receded back to its original size.

I had never seen anything like it before.

Before I could ponder on this some more, cords of hair began to lash wildly through the snow and Oliver yelped in pain on the screen as one cracked against his limbs, ridding it of a strip of flesh.

The *futakuchi onna* came fully into view, rising on her six cords of hair and hovering over the fallen *nukekubi*. Slower to arrive than her companions, who could ride the currents of air, she was late to the party. The strands of hair that had carved the flesh from my friend eagerly presented it to their master, like a small child showing their parent a new piece of art. It bounced with joy and slowly lowered the strip of flesh to the gaping maw on the back of her head. It whipped back as soon as they dropped their treat, careful not to become food themselves. The *futakuchi onna* wasn't as starved as the one I had encountered, which explained why she had been willing to leave Yuriko at all.

Everyone in the conference room swore quietly at the sight. Except for Yuri. The room's temperature dropped, and a slight frost built along the edges of the windows. I had no doubt that if her power had returned fully, we would be experiencing much more discomfort. But her eyes. Her eyes were dead at the sight of the *futakuchi onna*.

Oliver leaned over, placing a gentle hand on her shoulder, and whispered in her ear. The room warmed slightly and the frost melted. I glanced down at his limbs, now seeing the newly healed skin he had managed to hide before. Sneaky little *kappa*.

The *futakuchi onna*, now having a taste of Oliver's flesh, had gone mad with bloodlust and dropped to scrambling on four cords of hair, allowing the other four to whip at his flesh. Rafael abandoned the *nukekubi*, only taking the time to tear the one from his bicep, allowing blood to gush from his arm. He would only have a matter of minutes at this point. Longer than a Quote, but magic could only sustain an Abstruse for so long without blood.

Rafael became a whirlwind of blades, his short swords slicing into the hair supporting the *futakuchi onna's* body, avoiding each flailing ribbon of death with savage grace. She shrieked as she dropped to her human knees in pain and shock. Oliver used the opportunity to pounce on her and used his vicious claws to disembowel her as her four remaining cords thrashed in distress overhead. He dug into her body, ripping out her intestines with claws and beak, flinging them as far as he could down the banks of the lake.

The hair dropped, limp at last, and Oliver violently twisted the *futakuchi onna's* neck. As the snap rang clear, he used his claws to slash across the cursed mouth that now faced the sky. The magic that sustained the *futakuchi onna* faded with the destruction of her digestive system and the insatiable maw on the back of her head. He looked up then, for Rafael, and the dismay on his face was clear as Rafael attempted to rid himself of the three remaining *nukekubi* now attached to his body. Oliver leapt up and wrested them off Rafe's body, arterial blood spraying, then slowing to a trickle. Oliver smashed the first head savagely into a boulder next to him, only to be dived upon by the other two. He batted another one into a tree. Only one *nukekubi* remained when I reappeared on the screen and he shouted for me to find Yuri.

And with each death, regardless of whether it was dealt by himself or Olly, that swell of evil, then the brilliant light occurred.

Silence reigned around the table for a few moments as everyone digested the violence they had just witnessed in their own way. None of us were a stranger to it, but we all carried our own histories. I needed to take time to wrap my head around the way this male had sacrificed himself for the safety of my friend, whom he had only just met, and what that might mean. I swallowed hard against the lump in my throat, the burning in my chest where my heart used to beat, and met Oliver's gaze in the corner of the room.

He inclined his head to the *kariudo* who was busy adjusting his cuffs. *That's why*, he mouthed. I agreed. That was why Rafael had gained Oliver's trust so fast indeed.

Lala broke the bubble of silence and pointed at Rafael's vitals as they flatlined at last. "You see how they dropped? If Cam and Pea hadn't been with you, or, if Cam and Pea's vitals had also dropped, it would have triggered an alarm for Theo and Lani to haul ass to your location. Since you *did* have Cam and Pea with you, and they were reasonably hale and hearty, no alarms were sounded and all was good. And *that* is why we record always and forever. Not to mention it makes paperwork a hell of a lot easier when you can reference back to exactly what happened."

Rafael remained stiff, but he nodded to accept her reasoning. "When exactly did you pass a tracking device off on me?" he questioned me.

"It was in your coffee that morning. Whiz's tech. You chugged that espresso like you had been on a three-week bender and it was the first drop of black gold you'd had in the entire duration." I shrugged. I wasn't going to make any apologies for it.

I could feel Theo's hard glare on my face. I met his with my own steady gaze. Theo tilted his head to Yuriko with a raised eyebrow. Letting me know he hadn't missed her diminished power and what it meant. How the clips playing out on St. Helens weren't quite matching up to the full story. Yet another time when his director had gone off script. We would be having words later.

Aidan, who was asking Rafael for his written report about what happened with the *nukekubi*, glanced across the table at Theo and noticed the tension between us. He whistled softly between his teeth with a wince while Whiz quietly turned off the display. A beat of awkward silence followed before the team began filling the void, discussing and discarding theories.

We watched our conversation in Olly's home regarding the tide jewels but cut it off before revealing Rafael's damning statements. I could see his shoulders sag slightly, the air around him become lighter.

Max's head popped up from the giant puppy pile in the corner and he growled softly. I raised an eyebrow. The wards hadn't notified me of anyone passing them, so that meant it could only be one person.

The door slammed open, startling everyone except for me. Lala, who had her damn feet on the table again, toppled over completely. She popped back up, coughing and slamming her fist against her chest. I shook my head. She was a Peri; she wouldn't die due to Red Vine asphyxiation. I swiveled in my chair to face our newcomer.

I snorted when I saw her appearance. "Woman. Where the fuck have you been?"

CHAPTER EIGHTEEN

The tiny, ancient Japanese woman who looked as frail as a cobweb gave me a sharp glance and waved her cane at me, looking like she would fall over without it.

I gestured to Olly, Yuri, Rafe, and myself. "Do you know how far out of the way we had to hike to try to find you? Answer your phone once in a while so we know you're not home before we try to track you down."

"Camellia Kimoto. Only psychopaths and telemarketers *call* people anymore. Text me for Quotes' sake. Why would I answer my phone?"

I rolled my eyes. "Find a seat. We need your information."

Before she entered the room, she scanned it, her gaze settling on the one person unfamiliar to her. "And who are you?"

"Rafael Sugiyama." He bowed to her.

She paled significantly and stumbled back a step, but then seemed to give herself a mental pep talk, firming up her stance. She gave him a bow in return and responded, "Reika. *Yamauba* of Mount St. Helens. *Oni baba* of the Pacific Northwest."

Then her glamour fell away.

The hideous lavender jumpsuit fell away, as if it never existed. In the place of an old woman was a statuesque beauty. Reika stood tall, her hair falling into a sleek, glossy black sheet down to her waist. Unlike myself and Rafe, her skin was bone-white, contrasting sharply with her black hair and blood-red lips, as if she had never been touched by the sun. Her eyes were a deep dark reddish-brown, similar to the color of coagulated blood. Having that color of eye turn malicious was disconcerting at best. Her cane transformed into a wickedly sharp *deba* knife. She tucked it into a sheath along her thigh. While it may look like a simple kitchen knife to many, it was far from ordinary and made from stone harvested from whichever mountain she derived her power from at the time. Reika glided over to the chair at the head of the table and settled into it.

"You will not find Misaki in the mountains. Not anymore," she said with a grim conviction before we could even address the topic of our conversation. I bit my tongue, wanting—*needing*—so many answers.

"She managed to get to me before her magic malfunctioned and caused her to vanish again. I told her to head to the coast. So that's where she will be going next," she continued, as if it was no big deal to drop all this information in our laps.

"Wait," Aidan held up a hand. "So she does have magic? How?" His hand descended and gestured to Olly and Yuriko. "They're both friends with our missing person and they've never detected magic on her. They've sat down with her and had conversations with her for hours. And zip, zilch, nada. No magic. Not even a Peri. Cam even watched her vanish and detected no magic when it happened."

Everyone zeroed in on Reika expectantly. She sighed. "Her magic was bound long ago. But that binding has started to erode. Which is why she is blinking in and out of existence. I would think it obvious that she wasn't a Quote. You call her a *bijin*, she's obviously lived beyond the lifetime of most humans *without aging*, so why on earth would you think she doesn't have magic? Use your common sense. Are you all idiots?"

"To be fair, all but two of us in the room thought she was in her forties up until very recently," I said wryly. "Excuse our brains for taking time to process. Accuse Yuri and Olly of being stupid; the rest of us just got info-dumped. Oh, and Ken. You can accuse Ken of being stupid. But you do that all the time anyway. He's used to it. Now, what exactly do you mean by 'blinking in and out of *existence*?'"

Not gonna lie...that statement horrified me.

Reika waved me off while muttering under her breath. Probably something about our stupidity. "That isn't important. She comes back. What I need you to focus on is where she went." Before she could say more, or even look at Whiz, he brought up a projection of the Oregon coastline. She smiled. Reika should never smile. Her lips exposed rows of needle-sharp fangs with a set of four tusks that extended whenever her teeth were bared. I restrained the need to shudder. "At least one of you here is brilliant." Whiz preened at the compliment.

She pointed to a specific area of the map and the projection responded to her magic, zooming in. My gut dropped and I felt a pit in my chest as I watched the pins from the *habu kurage* attacks grow in size with every moment. Beginning to focus in on one area in particular with every passing second.

Neskowin, Oregon.

Theo's attention sharpened. "The *habu kurage* attacks. Do you think they were there for *her*? For Dr. Aoki?"

Reika shrugged, avoiding the question neatly, I noticed.

Theo pivoted and pointed in my face, "You are *not* going to Neskowin without me and Lani. Not with *habu kurage* swarming the beaches. I don't care about any excuses you come up with. You need us there. That hospital has no Abbies and no idea what they're dealing with." Lani nodded emphatically from where she sat.

I batted his finger away. "I'm not sure what you or Lani can do either. I'm not fool enough to turn down the offer though, Theo. But Lani, I can't take both Meds with the rest of the crew on a call-out. You need to stay." She opened her mouth to protest but shut it before she could say anything, seeing the reasoning behind my statement.

"Lala and Emma. I'm leaving you two in charge here. It'll be me, Rafe, Aidan, and Theo at the coast. The rest of you hold down the fort."

Emma frowned. "Why me? Normally it's Yuriko."

Everyone turned in their chair to look at Yuri as if they were synchronized. I knew how much she was hating the attention right now. She didn't bother to speak; all she did was hold out a hand and form a small cluster of cherry blossoms made of ice in the palm of her hand. Everyone in the room paled.

Impressive, perhaps, to others.

Pathetic for the Winter Princess.

"Exactly how bad were your injuries that your magic has only recovered to this point?" Theo asked tightly.

"Bad." She shrugged.

He groaned and pinched the bridge of his nose. "You and Cam are going to be the death of me. You're on light duty while you're here. And *you*."

I raised an eyebrow as he turned to glare at me. "Yes?"

"How much damage did your *ki* take?"

The audacity of the males in my life. I ignored the question from this particular one and bent across the table so I could knock Lala's boots back off the table. Hideki yelped as they landed in his lap, and I stole a few of her Red Vines amid the mild chaos. All the while staring Theo down, enjoying the increasing level of sweat dripping down his face, soaking his shirt, and drenching his skin.

Why the hell was Lala addicted to this shit? It was like chewing on plastic, faintly poisoned with something that allegedly tasted like cherries.

"You've made your point," the doctor conceded through gritted teeth. I tongued my own, trying to rid them of the red gunk now wedged between them, and stoked Theo's temperature a touch higher to prove my point before allowing his body to drop back to its natural baseline.

"I'm so glad. May I, the director of this agency, be given permission to go on this deployment now?" I asked sweetly.

"You made me medical director for a reason, Cam. You could stand to listen once in a while; it just may save your life one day." Heat flashed through Theo's eyes as he surveyed me.

The tension rose in the room again. Rafe shifted slightly, unsure of the cause, I'm sure. My smile shifted from saccharinity to bitterness. The *habu kurage* couldn't kill me. Only a very specific substance could. And whatever was happening to my body now.

"On that wonderful note of existential crisis, can we get to the actual point of this meeting?" Reika interrupted.

A few relieved sighs were heard as our eye contact broke and we refocused on Reika. She gestured to the map. "Based on what I know from Misaki and the attacks, you'll want to target Neskowin, despite the report of swarms up and down the coastlines. The only actual casualties have occurred there." She gave me a hard stare once she began talking about Neskowin and everything within me stilled.

She couldn't know…could she?

"Cam, you'll need to call in your contacts. Murry, in particular."

I swore under my breath. I already knew I needed to get ahold of him, but the male would be furious. And no one enjoyed an angry Murry.

The team turned to tackling assignments and planning the division of labor for the rest of our time. Contracts were signed, maps were reviewed. As the meeting wrapped up, I reached behind my back and stretched, groaning as the aches within my body attempted to resolve. Unfortunately, I didn't think stretching would realign the fragments back into their original positions.

"Emma, please take Rafe to one of the unoccupied apartments," I instructed wearily, too tired to deal with the errand myself. "While there, the two of you review the footage of Ryūgū-jō that Rafael has with him and see if you can identify any new information for your investigation. Rafe, Aidan, and Theo, meet me here at 0500 tomorrow morning. Let's see what we can do to beat Portland rush hour. I'm going home. I'm fucking beat. Yuri and Olly, you're welcome to accompany me as usual."

Everyone began packing up their belongings and the dogs sleepily began untangling themselves from their pile. Yuriko, Oliver, and I headed to my newer 4Runner. Yuri and Olly would stay in the forest, as was their preference, and I would finally get some peace in my home for one night.

Reika grabbed my elbow and pulled me aside before I made it halfway across the parking lot. My friends gave me curious looks, but I shook my head at them.

The *yamauba* and I had a score to settle.

"What is going on, Reika?" I asked, crossing my arms tightly, as if they could protect me against whatever she had to say.

She ripped a fingernail off and threw it over her shoulder, surrounding us with a barrier of silence. Even Pea was isolated from us. Our connection vanished abruptly, and I was utterly bereft in a way I had not been for over a hundred years. I watched as she threw herself against the barrier, hissing and screeching.

"Was that necessary?" my voice dead of feeling. There was no way to express the pain of watching my Pea struggle to reach me, knowing her past. I knelt and touched my hand to the barrier and she lifted a paw to mine. Only then did she begin to calm. I glared at the *yamauba*.

"Do not question my choices, little girl."

The words whispered around me, as if she hadn't spoken them, but placed them on a breeze to be carried to me. They bounced and echoed, as though they had no escape from this place and ricocheted off the shields put into place. Her eyes glowed in anger.

"There are more things at stake than you know. A far larger picture than you could possibly be aware of. One that the sea *kami* has been fighting for millennia."

I scoffed as I stood. "And what has the sea king done for his people besides brutalize, murder, and starve them in this past century? Commit vast acts of genocide. Allow his atrocities to bleed over and above the seas and infect the world of Quotes. Tell me why I should *care* beyond helping the people?"

Her teeth flashed as she spoke, "You will never truly understand what the *kami* has given up for his people."

I hid the flinch that came with her statement and stared her down, biting back the words I wanted—no, *needed*—to say. "Then make me understand. Tell me what I need to know, Reika. Stop with these vague statements for Quotes' sake. Because all I see is Death. And the spread of evil and hate. And far too few guardians to prevent it from advancing further."

"Then you begin to see, girl, but you do not *understand*. All is not as it seems. You must look within. Don't trust your eyes; trust the heart. You must continue to give them a reason to fight."

The exhaustion within me grew exponentially. I was already tired, but now my body felt leaden, weighed down by the burdens I already carried, only to be given even more to place upon my shoulders.

"Who, Reika. Who are these beings I must give a reason to fight?"

"You won't know until the right time, then all will become clear."

I resisted the urge to scream and simply nodded curtly. "May I go now?"

She eyed me to consider whether I was worthy of being freed from her grasp or not. I was debating whether it was worth a shift, revealing myself to whoever was left in sight, and potentially ending my existence to end hers, before she nodded and spat on the ground to drop the shield.

The link between myself and Pea rose immediately, and I sighed in relief as she scrambled to my side. I leaned down to lift her into my arms as she began crawling up my leg, spitting and growling at the *yamauba* as she went.

"Good night, Reika. Please do text if any other information comes your way, since you clearly do not like talking on the phone," I said politely as I made my way to my 4Runner, where Yuri and Olly waited patiently with the four K9s. Pea hissed at her over my shoulder.

We settled in the vehicle, and I watched as Reika grew smaller in the rearview mirror. Not only due to the lengthening distance, but as she placed her glamour back on and became a deceptively small *obaasan*.

"Problem?" Yuri asked delicately.

"Nothing that a bottle of wine, a hot bath, and a steamy book won't cure," I gritted out through my clenched jaw. "You two set for the night?"

"We should be good. I'm looking forward to catching up with Ken, and we've got our usual haunts by the creek. You don't need to worry about us," Olly patted me on the shoulder.

Thank goodness for forest-loving *yōkai* because this introvert wasn't up for more peopling tonight, good friends or not.

CHAPTER NINETEEN

Rafael stood beneath the underhanging of the facility and observed Cam as she headed out to her vehicle with Yuriko and Oliver. He wasn't sure what he felt, but something pulled within him at the fact he wasn't joining them. Sometime, somewhere along the way, a sense of... *something*...had begun to build. Partnership? Community?

It couldn't be family.

Whatever this feeling was, he was unused to it, having never experienced it before. He had worked with partners and teams in the past, when necessary, but always as an outsider looking in. And standing here, now, on the doorstep of this facility, he felt like an outsider once more.

He didn't like it.

He shifted his weight and began to take a step in their direction. He wasn't quite sure what he would say yet; all he knew was that perhaps he was beginning to learn who *he* was when he was with them, and he didn't want to give the feeling up.

"You have a minute, Huntsman?" A large hand snagging him by the shoulder halted his momentum. Rafe had sensed its owner's presence coming up behind him. Yet he hadn't done anything to evade its owner or stop its progression.

Maybe, subconsciously, he was still afraid to find out who he really was.

He shoved his internal turmoil into a box in the back of his mind to inspect later and acknowledged the owner of the hand. Theo, he recalled. The male was close to his height. Korean American. He exuded magic like pixies sweated dust, but he wasn't sure what type of Abstruse the male was.

"What did you need?" he asked pleasantly, shrugging the hand off his shoulder. He had never cared for the invasion of his personal space. These were Cam's people, and he didn't want to make waves, but he had his limits. He had made a deal to keep the arrogant asshole persona in the closet, he recalled with some amusement. Those limits hadn't extended to Cam though. The memory of her touch on his body following the attack ghosted over him, as though her hands were trailing over his now. He resisted the urge to fidget under the other male's gaze.

"Cam trusts you. I don't know if I do yet. Emma's going to be taking you to the apartments," Theo motioned to the petite, anxiety-ridden *nukekubi* as he eyed Rafe skeptically. "Take care with her. If I hear from her that you made any aspect of tonight difficult, I will make your life hell."

Rafe raised an eyebrow. "I have no intention to do so. But how exactly would you? I thought a doctor's oath was to do no harm."

A sadistic smile spread across Theo's face as his magic flickered, revealing the *dokkaebi* underneath his current guise. Rafael swore internally at the sight. "While I may do no harm as a doctor, I can do plenty of harm as my true self. And you, Huntsman, have quite the karmic balance coming due. I may not act now, because Cam requires us to work with you, but in the future, I'd be watching my back if I were you." The goblin's face spun through a dizzying array of faces—male, female, non-binary, non-*human*—in the span of seconds, before settling back onto their current chosen skin.

Rafe knew the *dokkaebi* wasn't demonstrating their skill in glamour. No, the goblins didn't simply change their outward appearance. They changed their complete genetic make-up to suit their current circumstances. Which was to balance karma. Some chose to specialize in negative, some positive, some both. And if Theo chose to focus on the negative karma he had accumulated during his time as the *kariudo*, Rafael would be fucked.

He tipped his head. "Duly noted. Emma is safe with me tonight."

Rafe offered nothing beyond tonight or assurances for the safety of anyone else, because life held no guarantees. And he didn't want to break promises. Not when he was bound as he was.

He observed, with interest, as Theo's shoulders crept up and a crease furrowed across the bridge of his nose. As he turned to see what had caught the *dokkaebi's* interest, a flash of magic flared in the peripheral of his vision, instantly increasing his tension.

"Don't," Theo said tightly. "It's Reika. If she's put up a sound barrier, it's not to harm, but to impart information she didn't want to share with the rest of the class. There isn't a single one of us here, not even you, *kariudo*, who could go up against a *yamauba* as old as her. She willingly chose to give up Mount Fuji as her seat of power in Japan. She only lowers herself to Mount St. Helens to be near the ones she cares about."

Everything in Rafael wanted to go to Camellia. If not to Camellia, then to the damned *shikigami* that had tried to bite off his nose to heal him, if only to hold her the way he had seen Baki do to relieve her distress. He could feel waves of it pouring off the opossum as she repeatedly threw herself against the barrier, screaming. These protective instincts were new to him and he didn't know what to do with them. Especially because he couldn't *act* on them. Even if Theo hadn't advised against it.

He watched as Baki held out a hand to Pea and they both calmed. He watched as she talked with the *yamauba*, the fatigue evident in her eyes. Not only fatigue, but defeat. Depression. He watched as the barrier dropped. And as she finally got into the vehicle with her friends and family and drove away.

And through it all, he just stood by, futilely, silently hating himself and his role.

CHAPTER TWENTY

The trip to Neskowin, Oregon, should theoretically only take three hours. But alas, it required driving through Portland and the city's population had exploded in the past ten years. I swore, it didn't matter what time of day it was, it was always rush hour. On the bright side, I lived east of the Bonneville Dam and could take the Bridge of the Gods rather than deal with the Glenn Jackson or the I-5 Interstate bridges. I'd happily pay the minor toll any day of the week than be caught dead on either one of those bridges when there was traffic or—God forbid—an accident.

After a sleepless night, riddled with anxious thoughts and nightmares, my capacity for patience was at an all-time low. Which was why my annoyance with the three posturing males in front of me was at an all-time high. We would never get on the road before rush hour at this rate.

Something had clearly gone down between Theo and Rafe while I wasn't looking given the tension between them. They weren't necessarily talking to each other, but the air was thick as they packed the vehicle. Aidan was his normal golden retriever self. However, he couldn't resist prodding the *kariudo* and the *dokkaebi,* throwing his arms around the two of them good-naturedly.

"So. Who gets shotgun? Because I'm obviously driving," he said cheerfully, plucking the keys of the multicolored Jeep out of Theo's hand before he had a chance to react. He skittered off, dodging the goblin's reach. I shook my head as I threw the last of my gear into my SUV. It was a good thing he couldn't shift. I couldn't imagine the hell he would raise if he could.

I caught Rafe staring at me, giving me a look. Was that a look of plea?

"Absolutely not. After yesterday's drive back from Helens, I am driving to Neskowin in my nice, clean, well-ventilated car in *silence.*" I got into the driver's seat and shut my door with purpose.

"But—" he started, through my open window.

"Sugs, you have beef with one of my team members. Anybody with a functioning brain can feel it in the air. You get to work it out with him during the hours between here and there. I don't want to deal with it. We have a person to find; I'm not interested in the drama. Now, did you and Emma find anything last night?"

He sighed as he ran his fingers through his hair. "No. But I have quite a bit more material than what I brought here. I had Whiz copy it and sent her home with it. Handy, that one."

I smiled affectionately. "That he is."

"How does he work exactly? He just…sort of appeared out of thin air when she said his name."

Ironic question for a male who just vanishes into thin air.

"When nanotechnology began to appear on the frontier of engineering, Whiz grabbed onto it for all he was worth and made it his own. As a tulpa, his magic is very different than yours or mine. It's grounded in belief and thought. After a lot of trial and error, he fused his magic into his own brand of nanotech, which, really, for all intents and purposes, is himself. Because the nanotech is part of us now, we just have to think of him with intent and he's able to project himself to wherever we're located. It's far more dependable than a cell or satellite phone."

Rafael leaned against my 4Runner. "And when I go back to Ryūgū-jō?"

I shrugged. "That's your choice. But the nanos are part of Whiz. So if you decide you don't want to be part of the network, or we deem that it's unsafe, Whiz self-destructs the nanos, much like dead skin cells sloughing off a person's body. Now, off you get to your own vehicle. And it looks like you lost the chance for shotgun by the way."

"Why do they keep talking about weapons?" I heard him mutter to himself as he walked back over to the Jeep. I snickered, a tiny bit of good mood restored as I started our drive. The K9s had long since fallen asleep in the back while waiting for us to get rolling, and Pea was hanging out of her hammock, pawing through a selection of cassettes for me.

Despite meeting at 0500, we weren't able to get on the road for another hour and a half due to the posturing among the males. I arrived in the small coastal town just under four hours—several swear words and at least three brain implosions later. That's what happens when you don't leave until after 0600. Thank you, Portland rush hour. Who knew when the rest of the crew would arrive. They had gotten caught at a red light behind me and it was all over from there.

I drove along one of the residential streets until it appeared to come to an end and kept driving straight into the dense trees. Anyone watching in the Quotidian realm would have received a strong mental inclination to believe they had seen me turn around once realizing I hit a dead end. The older beach homes faded in my rearview and were replaced by another neighborhood. Some homes looked similar to the beach homes we had left behind. Others were built into old growth trees, some in enormous toad-stools, others under massive ferns. A few were multiple stories of seashells. One was a particularly impressive sandcastle. To this day, I was not sure how it withstood the weather, but that was magic for you.

I slowed to a stop where the coastal shore pines and the forest under-growth were replaced by an ominous display of transplanted *Citrus trifoliata* which grew far beyond their natural size, branches entwining closely with one another, towering into the sky, preventing easy passage for most. The interwoven Flying Dragons were home to the *kodama* that had fled Japan, now cursed after their trees had been destroyed in the aftermath of the bombings in World War II. Their vicious thorns curved anywhere from three to six inches, and some glistened scarlet in the sun, dripping blood onto the leaf litter below. The color contrasted vividly with the purity of their white blooms. I squinted at the fluid suspiciously and scanned the ground looking for signs of what they had fed on. A few moments later I spied the corpse of a *jorōgumo* that had been plaguing the community for the past several months. Satisfied that they hadn't been decimating the wildlife population, I turned my attention back to the guardians of my territory.

With my regard back on them, the *kodama* took notice of us, thorns attentively turning in our direction. They began to part, revealing another path in front of us, albeit overgrown and washed out, erosion having taken its toll. I bowed my head respectfully, thanking them for their service in protecting my gates and allowing us entrance

Returning to my vehicle, I shifted back into Drive. A prickly feeling of static electricity washed over me while I carefully picked my way through the potholes. It wasn't a pleasant feeling, but it gave me a sense of comfort to know the ward was in place. The flora wavered as the shore pines shot up into the sky, their colors far more vibrant, their size far more massive in this realm, occupied by other *kodama* with lesser curses.

I wound my way up the long driveway, enormous ferns creating a canopy over the path, and let out a deep sigh at the sight of my first home in America. I had since torn down the original structure and replaced it with a larger, cedar-shingled home with modern features. This land had been my refuge when I first arrived in the US and would forever be my first love. The entryway to the boxy home with its large, black-framed windows was bordered by an immense red camellia tree which flowered eternally. Its offspring also stood sentry on either side of my front porch at my Skamania home, but they didn't hold the same presence as their progenitor.

Letting everyone out of the SUV, I hauled out my gear and walked up the pathway to the camellia. I kissed my fingertips and pressed them gently to the trunk.

"I've missed you," I whispered, blinking back tears, my heart aching. The nightmares always left my equilibrium reeling, prone to vulnerabilities and unexpected upheavals. Pea placed a gentle paw against my leg in recognition of the moment and curled her tail around my ankle. The branches rustled gently in the sea breeze and a red petal drifted down, caressing my cheek like a lover's touch welcoming me home. I closed my eyes and took in a breath, steeling myself as I struggled to reel my emotions back in.

Wiping a knuckle under my eyes to catch my tears, I keyed in the code and opened the door. I took another three deep breaths, shaking off the rest of my melancholy, then obnoxiously coughed three times. A loud shriek sounded from the back of my home and a whirlwind of long black hair, bright colors, and petite Korean outhouse goddess came bursting into the foyer and slammed into my chest.

I'm not a tall woman by any means, but Cheuksin was four foot ten if I was feeling generous.

"You're here! You didn't tell me you were coming! Why didn't you tell me you were coming? You always accuse other people about not calling ahead!" she scolded me.

"Well, for one, this is my house last I checked. And two, isn't that what the coughing is for? So I don't startle you into choking me out with your hair and giving me the plague?" I teased.

She punched my shoulder in mock outrage. "*Aish, kijibae!* Don't tease me with a good time."

"I kid, I kid. That being said, we do have three incoming guests. You're not allowed to sic the plague on them. Yet. We could change our minds about that later though. Especially if they're being *shitty.*"

"I hate you. No warning about your impending arrival. No warning about impending guests. And toilet jokes on top of it all."

"You love me."

"I really do. I don't know why. But I do." The literal goddess of out-houses let out the most dramatic sigh I had ever heard.

"I think our guests might be on the way. Heads up—when I last saw them, the testosterone levels were at toxic levels," I informed my friend as the wards sent an alert through both of us.

"As if I am not equally, if not *more*, attuned to our wards than you, yourself." Cheuky's eyebrows lifted as the Flying Dragons rose ominously into the sky. "Is there something I should know about your guests, Cam? Beyond their testosterone levels?"

I snickered. "Sure. We've got Theo's charming and demanding self coming."

"Uh-huh," her body did a quarter turn toward me while her wary gaze remained focused on the angry *kodamas.*

"Aidan too. You know whenever I come to the coast I try to bring him so he can see his uncles."

"Hmmm."

"His K9."

"Camellia."

"And the *kariudo.*"

"I'm sorry, *what?*" Her attention whipped fully to me. "Did you at least warn the *kodamas* that the *kariudo* was coming? Why in Sinhwa would you bring the *kariudo* onto this property anyway?

"Think of it as a test. Of our security system and my trust in him. He won't hurt them if my trust is warranted. And the security system just proved itself." I gestured over our heads to the dome of thorns now encircling the entire property.

"Has he attempted to harm you?" I called out.

The lethal thorns turned toward me. All of them cocked slightly to the right as one, as if considering my question, then wavered side to side, mimicking someone shaking their head *no*.

"Excellent. Thank you for your help. You may let them pass." I bowed to the Flying Dragons and they rapidly receded and disappeared past the flora.

"I've lived here for how many decades? And I will still never get over how creepy that is," Cheuksin muttered under her breath. "Even when it's me talking to them."

After a couple more minutes, which Cheuky and I used to catch up, the battered Jeep pulled up and the three men plus Yumi all but fell out of the vehicle. Stoically, of course. But clearly anxious to get the fuck away from each other.

Well. Except for Aidan. Aidan never gave two shits about what other people thought about him. He bounded up the short walkway and snagged Cheuky in a hug, ignoring all personal boundaries, and whirled her around in a circle. Life would be so much easier if we were all like Aidan. Alas, we were not.

"Cheuky! How's my favorite shrimpy shrimp? Uncles have been telling me you've been keeping them stocked in some good smut," he grinned as she sputtered, insisting that he put her down.

I groaned internally. Maybe not. *Tanukis.*

Rafael appeared to be no worse for wear, beyond his fatigue, so I assumed he passed the test. I motioned to him, "The only stranger here, Rafael, *kariudo.* Meet Cheuksin, Outhouse Goddess. Fuck with her and she'll give you syphilis." I introduced the two to one another, breezing past them into my house so I could get to the kitchen.

"I'm sorry—" Rafael muttered as Cheuksin chased after me, scolding me with every step.

"Cam!" She swatted the back of my head as I dug through the pantry. Aidan cackled from behind her, while I heard Theo *tsk* to himself in despair, clearly wondering how he ended up in my circus.

"I said fuck *with* her and she'll give you a VD, not *fuck* her," I clarified with an evil grin as I emerged from the pantry with a mouthful of a protein bar. "You have to listen to *all* my words, Rafe. Not just the words you want to hear."

"I'm going to give *you* syphilis," she threatened. Except she knew she couldn't. I smiled indulgently. She sighed and settled for ripping the protein bar out of my mouth.

"I only let you keep these disgusting things in the house for when you have searches. You're not on a SAR. You're in this house. Sit down, shut your mouth unless you're telling me what you all are doing here, and let me make you guys some real food. Not this cardboard." She threw it over her shoulder and wiped her hands in disgust as it disappeared into thin air.

"We are, in fact, on a deployment. Reika told me I needed to come down to talk to Murry in relation to said deployment, which Rafael has contracted us out for. So, here we are," I replied, as we settled onto stools. The four K9s had already made themselves comfortable in various locations of the house. Some in a small pile. Woody, loyally by his favorite being besides Danly's dog Ruby. I was a distant third on that list, despite having rescued the traitor from abandonment in the woods.

I heaved my bag up onto the granite counter with relief, it having sat on my shoulder this entire time. Cheuksin waved a hand and a slew of Tupperware and Ziploc bags appeared on the counter from the refrigerator. She made an admonishing clucking sound at me and shooed my bag away from her space. Well, technically it was my space. But we were in her domain now. Duly rebuked, I set my bag back on the floor. She began pulling out a stack of tiny dishes from the cabinet.

"Really, Cheuksin. You don't need to cook," Theo protested. "You definitely don't need to set up *banchan* for lunch."

She bared her teeth at him and smacked his hands with a spoon. "You're in my kitchen. You'll eat what I put in front of you, and you will like it."

It was a lot more frightening when Reika bared her teeth, given the shape of hers, but Cheuksin was only marginally less scary, despite her diminutive size. She waved our protests away with a hand over her shoulder as she got out a tabletop butane burner and set it up on the counter, maneuvering around Woody in a well-practiced dance, before scooping out some rice from the rice cooker for each of us. "It's no bother. I already had some *daeji bulgogi* prepared. It won't take long at all for me to cook for five as opposed to one." She shifted topics. "Murry's going to bellow at you for an eternity in that deep voice of his. Probably cause a tsunami or a landslide or something."

I started prepping the tiny *banchan* dishes and breaking off lettuce leaves, while Cheuksin fried the *daeji bulgogi* on the burner between us, filling the kitchen with the scent of Korean spices. The men attempted to move into the kitchen to help but were whacked with a spoon for their efforts until they gave up. It wasn't about sexism. It was about having too many cooks in Cheuky's domain for her comfort.

She frowned, considering, as she moved the cooked spicy pork to the cooler edges of the burner to make room for more meat. She continued, contemplatively, "Murry hasn't mentioned anything to me. But I'm not plugged into that particular stream of information. My realm is with the Korean deities, and well, you know my history with them. I prefer to be a loner after everything. The information gateway coming from the undersea kingdoms are usually beyond my surface knowledge. And Murry is a like a steel trap with that information—unless you absolutely need to know, you won't know a thing about it."

I nodded, snagging a lettuce leaf. "That's about what I expected." I added *ssamjang* to my lettuce, piled on some rice and *daeji bulgogi,* and folded it into a neat package before biting into it, groaning in appreciation.

The lettuce was going fast, as hands kept grabbing for more. "I'm going to have to meet with Murry on my own first," I warned Rafael. "Unlike Oliver, there is absolutely no way he will meet with you without warning first."

The male paused with a *ssam* en route to his mouth. He set it back down, though he held onto the neat little package of lettuce to prevent it from falling apart. "I am not so arrogant that I'd believe you can just spring me on everyone without a problem, Baki," he said carefully.

"So long as we are on the same page. The three of you okay formulating a plan tonight while I go out to see the big guy?"

Theo and Rafe looked pained, but Aidan was fully agreeable as always, simply nodding as he continued to attack the food as though he hadn't been fed in a week.

Cheuksin smiled with pleasure at his obvious enjoyment while she picked at the variety of *banchan* dishes. She pointed her chopsticks at him and me, "You might have a chat with the *tanukis*. When they're not taunting the local raccoons, they've been out carousing the town."

"*Why?*" I grumbled to the ceiling. "Why me? You go, Adie. You're their nephew."

"You need to get it over with sometime, Cam. C'mon, I'll go with you," Aidan managed to get out between his laughter.

I sighed heavily. "I hate you. I hate you both so much right now."

"My job here is done." She gave me a wide smile before stuffing her face with the lettuce-wrapped *daeji bulgogi*.

I shook my head and sat back to enjoy my meal with my friend before returning to a life of responsibilities and burdens.

AFTER LUNCH WE all climbed the stairs to settle into our respective rooms. I tossed my duffle in my room and laid on the comfortable mattress for a few minutes, trying to ease the pain from the muscle guarding that worked to keep me together. When no relief was to be had, I dragged myself back up and left the room in search of Rafael.

I found him in the room next to mine, looking somewhat out of place as he sat on the bed, gazing out the window.

I knocked on the wall to alert him to my presence.

"I'm aware you're there, Baki," he said in reply, amused and not bothering to face me.

"Duly noted." I dropped down onto the bed next to him. "Did you and Theo figure your shit out along the way? Things still seemed tense when you arrived."

Rafe snorted. "I don't think there will be any 'figuring things out' with that goblin, Baki. I am the *kariudo* and that is all there is to it. My karmic scales are too badly unbalanced for them to trust me."

"Him," I said absently. "He prefers to utilize the pronoun of his current shape. He uses they/them when he is in his true form. It prevents potential slip ups when he is balancing scales." Then my attention focused in on what he said, and I frowned.

"You don't think there is a way to balance them, do you."

There was no particular physical tell I could witness, yet I could still sense the change that came over him. It was like a cloud covering the sun. A slow suffocation as all oxygen was removed from a room. The claustrophobia of being contained in a small space.

"I deserve all the karmic backlash I receive," was his heavy response.

He didn't. No matter what he thought he had earned, I had seen his heart during his fight alongside Olly. Despite being under the sea *kami's* service, he had been fighting against the *kami* for just as long. His heart remained more good than evil. I had no way of telling him that though.

"C'mon, Sugs. No more of pity party for you today. Time for you to witness mine. Let's go meet up with some gross old males." I held out a hand and pulled him up off the bed. "You ready for this?"

"Perverted old Japanese males? Every day of the week. What do you take me for? A coward?"

I shook my head as we entered the living area and I hollered, "Aidan! Time to head out; we need you to corral the Uncles for us!"

His auburn head popped out of the pantry, a bag full of snacks in one hand, and a bag full of smut in the other. "I'm armed and ready. Let's roll."

Rafael didn't comment on the ammunition, which was a solid indicator of his wisdom. We tromped into the woods. About fifteen minutes later, shouting was clearly heard. Aidan let out a long-suffering sigh and hung his head. The slump of a child about to deal with recalcitrant parental figures.

"*Oi! Oi, oi!!!*" The sounds of smacking followed the shouts. "What did I tell you about making *shishi* around the den! You do that on the territory! Not the den itself!"

"Eeeeeeeeeh. You know my prostate isn't what it used to be! It was late. These old bones weren't going to make it to the territory line."

Smack, smack.

"Eat ketchup!" *Smack.* "I keep this den clean for the two of us and you just go and piss all over it?!"

It was slow at first. It started as a tremble in his shoulders. Then a full-on shake. A few moments later Rafe was laughing. A deep, rolling, belly laugh. It was hoarse, as if he hadn't used it in a while. But it was beautiful. I couldn't help but stare at him for a moment just to take in the sight.

"Uncles! We have *guests*!" Aidan hissed, ditching his bags to hurry over to the scene of the crime.

"Aidan!"

"Nephew!" came the delighted cries.

Then.

"You came empty-handed? What is this? You do not love your uncles? You do not respect us anymore?"

Shaking my head, I handed the bag of smut to Rafe. I wasn't going to be the one to bear that load. I picked up the bag of snacks for myself. "Best we go save the nephew now."

As we came into the clearing beneath a massive shore pine, a small, dapper Japanese man, with an enviable head full of beautiful salt-and-pepper hair and a well-groomed beard turned to us. Meanwhile, a large, barrel-chested bald man with a wild unkempt beard still black as night was crushing Aidan in a hug, still holding a broom overhead in one hand like a weapon. The first uncle lit up at the sight of us. Once upon a time they may have had first names. But as such things tend to happen in our cultures, names get forgotten in familial relationships over time. Or they're never acknowledged to begin with. Thus, they were only known to us as the Uncles. Usually as a unit. It was rare that someone ever referred to one without the other. It seemed confusing to outsiders, but it made sense to us.

"Uncle! Here is our offering." The shorter of the two nudged the one breaking Aidan's ribs.

"I knew you wouldn't let us down, Nephew. You're our favorite after all," Uncle Crusher of Ribs' voice boomed.

"I'm your only." Aidan then muttered to me, rubbing his ribs, "Thank God you showed up."

If I had thought they had considered the bags the offering, I was sorely mistaken.

"So, Tsubaki! Our Nephew! Is he not a wondrous lover? Have you chosen him as your mate? You would make beautiful babies together. They wouldn't have the great scrotal power of the *tanukis* unfortunately, that line is too diluted now, but! That is no reason to not consider our Nephew a great steed! We would be honored to drum for you at your nuptials."

Jesus, take the wheel; Izanami, open a portal to Yomi and kill me now. Or perhaps, Yeomra had already taken me and I was in the Hell of Mirrors of Retribution at this very moment. *Why for Quotes' sake did I agree to this?* I could swear Uncle's voice was still echoing his proclamation through the forest. My panicked gaze caught Rafe who was standing behind the Uncles, now howling with laughter, not even bothering to hide his reaction with any grace. Aidan was no better.

I will end you, my eyes communicated. At least they would have communicated it if I didn't have to smile at the *tanukis* between us and them.

"Ah. While I, um, *appreciate*…your Nephew's…*wondrous* talents, I have no plans to mate. Perhaps there may be another occasion where you may demonstrate your—" I started coughing.

"Drumming?" Rafe suggested.

"Yes. Drumming," I wheezed.

Aidan was frantically shaking his head *no* behind me and slashing his hand across his neck, but it was too late, the damage was done. The Uncles beamed.

"Tonight then! We will go to the Shore Inn and serenade you!"

"Yay?" I said with pain.

"Uncles, we came here for a reason." Aidan changed the subject diplomatically, stepping forward to form a circle. "We are looking for a woman."

They gasped with intrigue. "A woman? Nephew. Tsubaki? Is she one of your missings?" The Uncles asked, delighted. The petite one rubbed his hands in glee. It reminded me of the raccoon gif, but I would never in a million years tell him that if I wanted to enjoy the rest of my days, however numbered they may be.

"Do we get to be part of a search?"

Rafe hesitated, knowing better than to answer that question, then called, "Whiz?"

The gremlin popped out into the center of the circle. This time he was wearing overalls made of keys from a keyboard. Gremlin magic. Their fashion choices wouldn't be the slightest bit comfortable for anyone else.

"What?" Whiz asked with his usual attitude as the Uncles oohed and aahed. Whiz just eyed them with suspicion, already knowing them, of course, from Aidan's files.

"Can you bring up a model of Dr. Aoki for the Uncles?"

"Mmm." A moment later a full-scale 4D rendering of Dr. Aoki was projected into the clearing. My thoughts raced as I thought back to that day in the woods. Something didn't quite match up. Maybe it hadn't been her we had seen? I didn't know who else it could have been though. Maybe I was making it up in my head, it had been so fast and at a distance. My eyes met Rafael's and he gave me a slight nod. He saw the difference too.

"Oh yes! We have seen this woman!" All our heads shot back to the Uncles at the shout they made in unison.

At last. A break.

CHAPTER TWENTY-ONE

"What was that look?" Aidan demanded as we started walking back to the house.

Rafe and I exchanged glances.

"*That* look," Aidan pointed between the two of us. "Don't think I didn't notice it while we were at the Uncles'."

I took a deep breath. "Remember the last day I was on the search? When I actually caught sight of our missing person? And she *fell off a fucking cliff?*"

"How could I forget a report like that, Cam?" Aidan replied dryly. He gestured widely with his hands. "Missing person appears out of thin air. Falls off cliff. Disappears before hitting the ground. No body to be found. Oh yeah, and mysterious invisible hands seemingly covering her face. I'm not likely to forget anything about that."

"Well. This is Creepy Abby Guy from the report." I jerked a thumb at Rafe.

Aidan pulled back to glare at Rafe. "Bro. Patently uncool. You don't stalk women in the woods. It's the twenty-first century. Not the twentieth. Males are supposed to evolve."

Rafe chuckled. "I got the lecture already, thanks. I've learned the error of my ways."

"Anyway, he saw her too. Who I saw doesn't quite match up with the rendering from the photos."

He shook his head. "Agreed. There's something in the eyes, I think. And skin."

I sighed. "It was so fast though. And at a distance, so who knows."

I got a raised eyebrow for my comment. "It might have been at a distance, but neither of us are human. We have better than average eyesight and you know it. For both of us to think the same thing is not insignificant."

Aidan shrugged. "Regardless, we're meeting the Uncles tonight where they saw her. We have a Point Last Seen to start from."

"You guys and Theo will be meeting them," I corrected, feeling an overwhelming gratitude that I had a legitimate reason to miss out on the drumming session. "I need to catch up with Murry. Theo's just as good at detecting magic as Max, so you'll be in good hands."

Rafael's brow furrowed. "I noticed he didn't have a K9."

"He doesn't need one," Aidan explained. "So long as he can grasp an aspect of a person's life, he can follow their karmic balance. Dr. Aoki's has been particularly challenging. He described hers as being like a cobweb that has several potential directions he could follow, but someone has torn gaping holes through it. Large gaping holes that make it nearly impossible for him to follow a path."

We reached home as he finished talking, and I bid them farewell after asking Aidan to catch Theo up on the plan. I found Cheuky on the wrap-around porch in the back. The late afternoon sun formed a halo of light over her hair and her diminutive size was emphasized by the cushions she surrounded herself with for comfort. Bright and colorful, unlike the soiled white linens she had been cursed to wear for centuries until she escaped the outhouses she had been subjected to. She sipped on her tea and simply enjoyed nature as it was intended. Something all too many took for granted and something she never did again.

I padded over, dropping into the chair next to her and groaned, stretching out the kinks in my neck, but there was only so far a comfortable chair could take you for pain relief. I poured myself a cup of tea and we sat together in nature, watching as the sun set over the coast. At some point I heard the males and Yumi leave the home, setting out to begin their search. And still we sat in peace.

The silent companionship and understanding of a true friendship was something else one should never take for granted.

When I raised my head, I found Cheuksin regarding me solemnly.

She motioned her head toward the door. "Go. Confer with Murry. I've got the dogs. I have the sense there is more to this story than what you are willing to say to the others. And I know the two of you have shared a long life together."

I got up and gave her a hug. "Thank you. For all that you do. The food, the wisdom, the levity."

"Psh, that comes free of charge. Now, shoo. Air out your grievances. Go rant and rave in the water."

Once I started passing through my home, Pea got up to follow me. I eyed her. "Are you sure you want to follow me? I'm going to be talking about *that night* with Murry."

She froze midstep. Pea was the only one who may have been as traumatized—if not more—as I had been that night. She was a familiar who had lost her bonded master whom she had been with for tens of thousands of years.

I nodded. "I saw some *goguma* in the kitchen. Go pester Cheuky for some of the sweet potato before the dogs get all her attention. I'm sure she'll heat it up for you. I'll be safe with Murry; you don't have to do this with me."

She looked up at me with pleading eyes, torn. I gave her a sad smile and scooped her up, cuddling her close to me. "I know—it hurts so much. But I promise, I'll be okay and you will too. Spend time with Cheuksin and the family. They need you to keep them safe as well. I'll come back to you this time, I swear it."

Pea placed her remaining front paw on my chin and I obediently brought my face down so she could better look me in the eyes. She gave a formal nod before squirming to be let down. After she made her way to Cheuky, I headed out to my vehicle and drove down to the beach. It was late enough that most of the beachcombers had packed it in for the night, the spring chill and brisk wind sending them to their hotel rooms and vacation rentals for warmth.

The sunset was fading to the cooler tones of blues and purples as I picked my way down to the shoreline and the Neskowin Ghost Forest. Tide was going out, revealing more and more of the barnacle-encrusted remnants of the Sitka spruce forest from years long since passed.

I set out for the far side, allowing the fading light to swallow me up until I wasn't able to see anyone. Only then did I allow myself to begin wading into the water, ignoring the way it seeped into my clothing.

Once I was waist deep, I took a breath and dove, allowing the waves to swallow me down, straight into the sandbar. I wasn't risking staying in the Quotidian realm for this encounter. I swam through what felt like miles of sand, until I came up on the other side.

Brilliant, crystal clear water greeted me. The magic once gifted to me allowed me to take a deep breath of air. Homes dotted the ocean floor beneath me. I smiled at the water-faring *yōkai* making their way through the day, some of them stopping to wave at me. I waved back and swam toward the surface where a dinghy always remained anchored for my meetings with Murry. I hauled my body over the side and laid out on the bottom of the small craft, completely dry, and waited.

"What the fuck are you doing here, Camellia?" a deep voice boomed over the still water.

I SAT BACK up to the brilliant bluish-green glow of bioluminescence illuminating the sea. The skeletons of fish jumped out of the water near our skiff. One nearly landed in the boat until a giant skeletal fin rose to bat it away, bones scattering everywhere, reforming a moment before hitting the sea. Birds the likes of which Quotidians had never seen flew serenely nearby, before settling upon the massive skeleton of a baleen whale. The bioluminescence outlined the shape he would have held in life. An orb of black fire sparked from his eye socket and emphasized exactly how angry he was with me as he eyed me from the side.

"Camellia Kimoto, I'll not ask again. What are you doing here?" he threatened in a low voice.

I smiled, not feeling threatened in the least, knowing my oldest and most cherished friend would never harm me. "Reika," I said simply. There was more to the story, of course, but her name would suit well enough.

The *bakekujira* swore descriptively in Japanese. "That hag. She knew I didn't want you down here. And you used magic on this shore, not once, but twice! You know they can track you by your magic."

I scoffed. "They would need to know my magic signature first. How else was I supposed to get out to you? Would you prefer I shifted completely and come to you that way? She demanded I come down here and talk to you, Murry. What the hell is going on?"

He sighed, in as much a skeleton of a whale can sigh, a sad plume of water ejecting from his twin blowholes. "I believe everything we've feared is finally coming to a head."

I pretended to be shocked. "What? No! Murry, say it isn't so!"

I was pissed. Absolutely enraged. And it all stemmed from this big bastard and his ideas about how to *handle the situation*.

A short burst of water erupted from his spiracles, a show of his frustration with me. I suddenly found myself in the water as he smacked one end of the boat with his flukes, sending me flying.

Whatever. I didn't need the dinghy to stay afloat.

The magic bestowed to me once upon a time kept me buoyant as I shoved a finger toward the maddening whale.

"You *sent me away*, Murry. You sent me away from my home. My friends. My support. *You*. This place kept me together during the worst time of my life. And. You. Made. Me. Leave It. This place holds my last memories of *him*." My voice was near hysterical by the end.

"Yes, I did. And I would do it a million times over, Tsubaki, if it keeps my friend alive," he bellowed, causing enormous rolling waves to crash down over the boat and us. His birds took flight, despite their non-corporeal state, instinct riding them hard.

"How alive am I going to be when the *kariudo* is in my home, when there are *nukekubi futakuchi onna*, and *rokurokubi* in my backyard attacking me and those close to me? Tell me that, Murry. How alive am I going to be when I'm separated from my best wards, my best people, and *he comes for me anyway?*"

Murry dipped beneath the water for a moment before rising again, his fluke giving a light flick, belying his anxiety over the situation. "You were willing to accept the plan when we came up with it decades ago."

"My *ki* wasn't nearly gone thirty years ago. I don't know how many more shifts I have left in me. Less than ten, maybe even less than five. This isn't sustainable. I will die anyway, but I will die in hiding. A coward.

Never having done *anything* to help his people and mine. That is what I cannot accept."

Murry rolled slightly to the side, all the better view to judge me from, the black fire in his eyes dimming a bit.

"The *kariudo* truly came? Just how I predicted?"

"Yes, Murry. Exactly like you predicted. Although the missing person aspect was unanticipated." I rolled my eyes and swam over to the dinghy to haul myself back in. I was tired of being wet.

"What is he like?"

I hesitated, uncertain how to describe the huntsman and all his disguises.

"He is…a good man underneath all his layers, I believe. No, I know he is. I've seen his heart. But he is unaware of it and that makes him dangerous. I don't know that he's ever had a role model of 'good' in his past, so he has no comparison, which clouds his judgment. He also has no free will due to the bands, which is another risk factor to consider."

"Tsubaki," Murry's tone urged caution.

"I know. I'm not trusting him, don't worry. I live over a hundred years in peace and quiet, then suddenly I'm attacked once he shows up in my life? I'd say I trust him as far as I can throw him, but I've been living in the Quote realm too long, and that doesn't work for the Abbies. I trust him for about as long as an *akaname* can go without licking a bathroom."

I was shot in the face with seawater as Murry snorted at that. Gross.

"Now. What the hell is going on down here? Why did Reika want me to see you?"

The sparks in his fiery black eye went out abruptly, indicating his sorrow. "The mated *umibōzu* pair lost three of their children. The other two are critically injured and not expected to survive. The youngest had been playing along the Siletz Reef while the two eldest watched over them."

"What aren't you telling me?" The mated pair had migrated here, seeking a place to live where tales of their ancestors' destruction wouldn't haunt their children. They had hoped to raise them without discrimination. To hear they could lose their entire brood was devastating.

"Camellia. There is nothing you could have done. There is no way you could have predicted or prevented this."

"*Stop* trying to protect me and tell me."

Murry's bioluminescence dimmed. "The two eldest showed evidence of torture. The vein of torture preferred by the *habu kurage*."

Only the knowledge that fully shifting would reveal my presence and cause more harm to those under my protection prevented me from doing so in rage. I could give zero fucks if it was my last shift. Despite that, my four fangs still lengthened as I snarled.

"I am *failing* him, Murry," I growled, my voice deepened from the partial shift. I shoved the vertigo down. It was easier to do with the fire burning deep within my body at what had been done to a family under my protection. "I am failing our people. This ends now."

"Tsubaki, he wouldn't have wanted this for you. You know you're different," Murry said gently, but with urgency. "You also somehow inherited your father's *onmyōji* powers despite the *haetae* gene being dominant. Not only that, but the night we never speak of, you know the impossible happened and—"

I held up my hand. "My differences are not the issue here. The fact that the *kami* is using them as an excuse to hurt others again is," I hissed. "I can't even go out to sea to offer my respects because of him."

"We *cannot* allow him to attempt to devour your power." His voice boomed over the ocean with his distress, causing the gentle waves to swell and crash. "You are the *last*, Tsubaki. The destruction he could cause if he gained the power you have? And above all of this, you are my friend and I will not allow you to—"

"Funny that, Murry. I love you, but I am no child to be told what I am allowed and not allowed to do. The last time someone was *allowed* to tell me to do anything was the day I broke my slave bands.

"I may be the last *haetae*. But I am dying anyway. You and I both know this. I have been dying since *Hyakki Yagyō*. I will not go knowing that our people, children no less, are dying in my place. Tortured. You say he wouldn't want this for me, Murry? You know nothing of what he wanted for me. Why else would he have broken me like this," I hissed, drawing up the foreign translucent magic. The urge to buckle over was nearly overwhelming as my natural *ki* fought the intruder.

"Tsubaki, stop. Please," Murry pleaded. "You're right. Compared to the connection the two of you shared, I couldn't know."

I collapsed back into the skiff and retched over the side. A shard of guilt worked its way through me for emotionally manipulating my friend, but was it any worse than how he had been manipulating me by withholding information as he saw fit and moving me like a pawn on a chessboard? It was partly my own fault for never setting those boundaries. But I had been wallowing in my grief for those first few years and he'd taken over. He'd forgotten what our past relationship had looked like when we were on equal footing.

"You never mention *Hyakki Yagyō*," he said hesitantly once I recovered.

I sighed, wishing more than anything for some fresh water to rinse out my mouth. My nightmares were going to be awful tonight.

"I never talk about it because of the horrific PTSD that comes along with it," I said wryly. "However, it's relevant now. The *kariudo* believes our missing person is actually a citizen of Ryūgū-jō who went missing that night."

The fire in the eye facing me flamed high in alarm. "Does he know?"

"That I was also there for the infamous parade?" My body sagged into the boat, exhausted. "He does not."

"*Tsubaki.*"

"I know, Murry. I know. However, I caught a glimpse of our missing person. We both did. And I don't think he's wrong. There is something familiar about her. Something off. I haven't been able to put my finger on it yet."

I described what I had seen that night in the woods to my friend and we did our best to scan our memories, both before that night and during, but nothing came up for either Dr. Aoki, or the type of magic I'd seen. I shoved the other memories back as best as I could, yet visions of my slaughtered friends still rose to the forefront of my mind and I found myself hanging over the side of the dinghy again. The pain I lived with daily dialed up in volume, demanding to be heard, and I wanted to curl into the fetal position, as if that could possibly reduce the cacophony ringing through me.

The fracturing of my body.

The splintering of my soul.

The loss of my heart.

The death of *him.*

I sighed, weighed down by heartaches of the present and the past. "It has been a long week. What are we doing to protect the marine *yōkai* in the area?"

Murry rolled partway to aim a bony pectoral fin at the skeletal fish jumping around us. "The *habu kurage* can't kill what is already dead. My fish are keeping an eye out for them and warning the *yōkai* to leave immediately if there is a sighting. So far, the habu kurage have only been seen individually or up to groups of three. Depending on which of my fish are scouting, they'll devour them. If they are close enough to the surface, my birds snatch them up." This time he rolled to indicate some phantom species of prehistoric-looking pelican.

I grimaced. "They may have only been sighted up to groups of three here, but they have been swarming the Oregon Coast in the Quote realm, Murry. Whole smacks have been washing ashore for close to a week now. Humans are dead. Scientists have taken in some of the servants as specimens to study. What was the sea *kami* thinking, risking exposure like that?"

"You know the Quotes will quantify any magical discovery as an evolutionary quirk, a new species. They are narcissists, Tsubaki; they cannot possibly conceive of any other sentient beings co-existing in these realms besides themselves."

I snorted. "Let's not be speciesist, Murry. Not all of them. Why else would they be so interested in aliens? And hunting down poor Dalton who just wants to be left the hell alone? While their tendency to lean toward the evolutionary argument might save us this time, we can't keep relying on it. We need to wrap up this situation before it spirals any further out of control and more beings die."

He sighed. "I'll accompany you to the Quote realm so we can do what we can to mitigate the *habu kurage*. You will have to ward me though, lest a pandemic or natural disaster befalls Oregon upon my arrival."

The nonchalant way he addressed his curse was another stab to my conscience. Another way in which I had failed those I had sworn to protect. Unlike Cheuksin who was able to target the individuals she infected with incurable diseases, Murry eliminated all life-forms he approached with extreme prejudice, though it was not by choice. No, the *yamauba* who had first killed him, then damned him for the petty reason of wanting to cause me pain, had ensured all in his vicinity would fall, whether by epidemic or natural disaster. For someone with as kind a heart as Murry, it was crushing and prevented him from leaving the area I had warded for his benefit. And it was a lonely existence for a creature who had migrated such great distances with his family when he was alive. It was another layer of guilt blanketed on my shoulders.

"Hey." He nudged the skiff carefully. "You know there is nothing to forgive. Then or now."

"Sure. Anyway." I smiled weakly, desperate for a change in subject. "You accompanying me works out well. The *kariudo*, Rafael, would like to meet with you."

My undead cetacean friend eyed me carefully. "Rafael, hmm?"

I glared at him. "That is his name. What would you have me call him? Harbinger of Evil?"

"I made no judgment. Just an observation. I will be curious to meet this young man to see if he is how you describe him to be. How is Aidan?"

"Oh, don't you even start. I already had to deal with the Uncles to-night." I eased my body back into the water; I don't even know why I bothered with a watercraft at the rate I got wet when I met with Murry. "Now get your bones over here so we can get you warded."

He tsked me for being lazy as I snagged one of his birds and used its talon to open a vein down my wrist. I'd shift and use my own, but I needed to spare my *ki* where I could.

"You can make the sacrifice of swimming a few feet closer to me if I have to swim laps around you while bleeding onto your bones to ensure all of Oregon doesn't succumb to some plague," I said evenly, beginning the process of pulling Pea's power and mixing it with my own to strengthen the ward. My blood began to well sluggishly, dripping a brilliant jade with a golden sheen running through it like fire. Where it used to flow easily, it now had challenges circulating through my body, no doubt due to the damage my body suffered. I still wasn't sure how it was possible when my heart was no longer whole, nor in working order. But alas, as long as I could still get the job done, I wasn't going to ask questions.

I dipped my fingers into the wound I had made, treading water to keep myself in place, and began smearing it onto Murry's bones in *hanja* characters. His body shivered as I worked.

"*Kuso*. Shit, that tickles," he muttered. "What makes you so confident it's Dr. Aoki he's hunting?"

I shivered, thinking of the tattoo I had caught sight of. I snagged another bird who squawked indignantly and reopened my injury. "Who said I was?"

Murry's fluke hit the water in distress. "You must find out what the *kariudo's* orders were, Tsubaki. Your life and Aoki's may depend on it."

CHAPTER TWENTY-TWO

Three small figures stood on the shore when I rose above the waves in the Quote realm, causing me to stiffen.

"Stay below for now," I murmured to Murry, who remained an ominous blue glow just below the water's surface.

"Do you take me for an idiot?" was the irritated response I received. Though it was garbled through the water.

A small fourth figure came into focus as I drew closer and my tension bled out of me as confusion took its place. It was three males and a *tanuki* in his raccoon dog form on the shore. Based on his svelte shape, I could easily tell which Uncle it was. I was close enough to see their expressions, which were grim, and they were gathered around one spot. I whistled to let Murry know it was safe enough to beach himself as I waded to shore.

"Olly? What are you doing here?" I asked, averting my eyes as Uncle shifted his scrotum into an armchair so he could curl up comfortably as he listened to us, instead of laying down in the sand.

"Reika sent me. She needed me to help them find that." The *kappa* pointed a clawed finger to the object Rafe was holding gingerly by a corner as Theo was rummaging through his pack. I presumed he was looking for an evidence bag.

My anxiety rose. "Reika sent a *kappa* to the coast. A people that has essentially gone extinct due to genocide because of the *kami's* orders? While the coastline is being swarmed by *habu kurage*? Oliver. What was she thinking?"

His head sank into his carapace. "That she has it out for me? I don't know, Cam. It's Reika. She does her scary eye-glow, teeth-baring thing, and I just follow her orders. It's easier to die than to say no."

I face-palmed to avoid a complete panic attack right as an explosion of sand and water announced Murry's arrival just to our left, which Oliver took the brunt of. Uncle whistled and yelped excitedly and leaped up from his scrotal couch, which shifted back to its normal shape so he could dance around the whale. Thankfully Theo had finished sealing the evidence bag, given that it appeared to be a journal.

"Melon Boy! What are you doing here! Do you want to die?"

"Already covered that. Thanks, Murry. I like to think I'm a little hardier than the melons I eat and can maybe survive a little longer," Olly said. Based on the way he was picking bits of seaweed off himself, it was safe to say he wasn't amused. I scooped an upset sand flea out of his *sara* and placed it on the ground where it started to burrow back into the sand.

"Tell me that was *not* in my bloody *sara* and contaminating my *ki*, Cam," the poor harried male shrieked, batting at the rest of his body and dancing around to try to rid himself of anything else clinging to him.

"Mmkay. I won't." A *kimengani* that had washed up with Murry's great splash dug up the partially buried sand flea with its pincer claw and stuffed it into the maw of the face upon its shell. I ignored the demon crab and turned back to Rafe "This is Murry. Murry, the *kariudo,* Rafael Sugiyama."

"Murry. Is. The. Fucking. *Bakekujira?*" He took a giant step back. As if that would have helped if I hadn't warded the undead cetacean from causing a sea of death.

"Yep. He's warded, so you're not going to die of some horrible plague. Just…maybe don't kill a whale. What's up with this book?"

Theo took over. "We started off at the PLS that the Uncles told us about. I was able to pick up a karmic trail and Yumi picked up a scent trail as well, but as this has been the most unpredictable SAR in the history of SARs, we opted to split up. Aidan, Yumi, and Uncle headed into the

Siuslaw to see if they might pick up anything there. I followed the karmic pathway which ended abruptly here. Where we ran into *him*."

Olly wiggled his claws at me. "Reika knew where the journal was going to be. Apparently, it was part of a larger prophetic vision an *onna uo* once told her. She recalled this bit of the vision and sent me on my merry way to dig up this creepy book made up of dead prophetic fish-women skin."

I frowned. "I think I recognize it. Vaguely. It's what the woman we saw on St. Helens was holding that night, isn't it?"

Everyone focused on the book.

"Are your lives always this exciting?" Uncle's voice startled me, given that he had been in animal form moments ago.

Theo snorted. "If you only knew."

Murry blew water in commiseration. "What is so important about this journal that is causing people to go missing, *kariudo*?"

Four of us exchanged glances.

"*Shiohiru-tama* and *Shiomitsu-tama*," I said softly.

Uncle inhaled sharply.

"Oh, fuck no, Camellia Kimoto. You drop this search. You drop this search right now before all of you end up missing and killed. Those jewels are a *curse*." I could tell there was more Murry wanted to say to me, but even though he had no tongue, it was still bound due to the presence of others.

"I am not dropping a search when there are lives at risk. You, of all beings, know me better than that."

His bioluminescence flared bright in anger, blinding us all for a moment.

"Throw your childish tantrum, whale. It's not going to change matters. Reika sent both Oliver and me down here for a reason. We cannot turn back now. Now tell us why she would send me to *you* about this."

As he slammed his fluke against the sand in frustration, I felt a canyon yawning between us that hadn't existed before he sent me away. His fear for my life was beginning to create a gap I was afraid we would be unable to bridge. I understood his worries, but I couldn't live my life like this anymore. I had allowed him to dictate it out of necessity, out of grief, for far too long, and while that was my own fault, I couldn't let it persist any longer.

"Murry," Uncle said quietly. "Although I call Cam *Niece* out of affection, you and she are far older than I. So I mean no disrespect when I say this—if the jewels are involved, the situation has gone far beyond personal biases and fears. I have talked to the refugees as they have arrived onto our lands regarding the conditions in Ryūgū-jō and they are unacceptable. I have talked further with my nephew, the *dokkaebi*, and the *kariudo* tonight and I believe this matter goes beyond any one of our lives. Even Kimoto-*sama*."

I stiffened slightly at his use of *sama*, but forced myself to relax before anyone could notice. Right now, everyone's focus was on Uncle. Except, I noticed, Rafael. His eyes tracked me closely, an emotion on the verge of conveying...concern? His body leaned in my direction ever so slightly, closer to me than anyone else. I forced my hands to unclench and gave him a slight smile. He nodded and turned back to the arguing Abbies.

"Why are you so dead set against this search?" Theo asked reasonably.

Murry's light dimmed. "Because..." He sighed. "Because the jewels aren't located where everyone has searched. They've never been lost."

Everyone started yelling at once.

Except Rafael.

The *kariudo* became deadly quiet and focused on Murry.

"You've known?" His voice somehow managed to cut across everyone else's, despite, or perhaps *because of*, its quiet tone. "You have known this entire time where the tide jewels were?"

"I have." My friend met his gaze steadily. I felt ill.

"I have endured and committed atrocities at the behest of the *kami*. I have executed, extorted, coerced, and engaged in horrific acts of genocide that I will never be able to wash from my hands. But through it all, I have *never* stood by if I could, and allowed millions of people to starve, die, and kill one another because I was *afraid*. I am afraid every moment of my existence, Murry-*san*," Rafael spat out the honorific like it was a slur. "And yet, despite the bands that bind me to the *kami*, I still manage to find a way to help when I can."

Before Murry or anyone else could respond, the *kariudo* straightened and walked away without a backwards glance.

I shot Murry a look and shook my head.

"Tsubaki..."

"Murry." I hesitated. Photos of the devastation from the famines rose to my mind. "I need time. That's all I have right now. I can't talk about this right now. I'll meet the three of you back at the property."

With that, I took off after the shrinking figure in the mist, catching up to him after a few moments. I had no words to offer, simply falling into step next to him and providing him companionship.

Sometimes, it's enough. To know you aren't alone in the world.

I felt a pinky brush tentatively against mine and smiled into the brisk ocean breeze as it whisked away my tears. I grasped his hand firmly in my own. Reassuringly. And leaned into him. We continued to walk along the shoreline, ignoring the path to the parking lot, and just supported one another in silence as the sun rose.

Yes. It was enough.

CHAPTER TWENTY-THREE

About an hour later, everyone from the beach had gathered back in my home. Aidan and his Uncle were still out on their search. Woody, Max, and Vicky bounded toward us as we settled in the dining room. Pea was already sleeping in the middle of the table, atop a place mat. Theo pulled the book out of the backpack he had been carrying and sat, taking the evidence bag and easing the damaged book out.

"It's damp." He grimaced, doing his best to open the book with care. "It looks like a journal of some sort."

"It is," Rafael said softly, looking at the pages from Theo's shoulder. "I recognize it. The cover—it was made from the skin of an *onna uo*."

Everyone fell quiet at Rafael's words and looked at the journal in horror. Theo lifted his hands from it, his face contorted with disgust.

"The journal is an accounting of possibilities for where the tide jewels may be. The sea *kami's* theories. It's his writing. Someone stole this journal from him." Pain washed over his face with the realization.

Without doubt, Rafael would be sent to kill whoever had stolen the book.

I sat opposite of Theo and pulled the book toward me. He practically pushed the foul pages at me, except he clearly didn't want to touch it. Pea extended her tail and lightly touched the journal. Orange flared over it briefly before dissipating, the pages now dry. I smiled at her in appreciation and opened the journal.

It was a mess. Scribbles in no coherent order filled the pages, written in every possible direction. Sketches interrupted the sea *kami's* musing here and there. One drawing in particular stood out, taking up a full page, repeated throughout the book.

A sea dragon. Not an actual animal; the sketches made it appear as if it was carved into a wall, its eye a glaring black orb.

Yamauba, palace, and *America* were scribbled across the pages repeatedly. TOYOTAMA was written boldly on nearly every page and underlined. Every time I saw it, my heart cracked a little further.

"There is no rhyme or reason to these words," Cheuksin grumbled. "And he basically drew himself or a relative over and over again. How does Reika expect us to figure this out?"

Reika always expects the impossible. I sighed tiredly. "Someone get the whiteboard out."

It was time to try to sort out a sea *kami's* twisted thoughts.

"This is going to take hours," Theo said grimly as Cheuky materialized a whiteboard into the room.

"Nothing worth it was ever easy, right?" My smile was weak.

WE POURED OVER the journal for hours before I had cried uncle. For mercy, not for the *tanuki*. It was the early hours of the morning, before dawn, and I hadn't slept in over twenty-four hours due to my sleepless night and early start before coming here. I went into my bedroom and drew the curtains, but after attempting and failing to fall asleep for several hours, I gave up. Nightmare after nightmare pursued me and my mind couldn't take more. I threw the tangled covers off and swept my legs over to the side of bed, glancing out the window. The branches of the camellia tree swayed gently in the breeze. My heart ached as I looked at the flowers in eternal bloom.

"Why did you have to leave me, you bastard," I whispered, getting out of bed.

I put on a robe and slid my feet into a pair of slippers. My home was eerily quiet. Max gave a soft woof that rumbled through his lips as he looked at me with concerned eyes. He didn't get up though. He was used to this routine. Woody and Victoria didn't stir. I made my way through halls, wraith-like, absently running my fingers along the walls as my mind left the present and faded into the past.

His eyes. Staring into mine. Feeling like I was home again. Secure. In his arms, everything felt safe.

Being ripped away from all of it. Losing it all. Unable to move on. Seeing the last of him fade away before me in my arms.

I faltered in front of my door, my knees going weak at the memory. A sob catching in my throat; the nightmares had made the memories that much stronger. My magic sensed Cheuksin at the end of the hall as she monitored my path but let me be. I closed my eyes, took a breath, and grasped the doorknob. Turned it. And moved past the threshold.

Chirping greeted me before the tree. Pea's tail dropped down to my shoulder and caressed it knowingly. I reached up into the branch she was perched on and stroked her back.

"Hello, you son of a bitch," I said to the air, sliding down with my back against the trunk, ignoring the scratches being left on my body. Those would be the least of the injuries incurred by him. "I still hate you. You left things a fucking mess. *I'm* a mess. Why? Why would you leave the way you did?"

Airing my grievances didn't help. They never would. He wasn't here. He would never return. He had left me in the most permanent way possible. His soul had been obliterated—I wouldn't even be reunited with him in Yomi. And for that, I would *never* forgive him. All I had was this fucking tree.

I sighed. There was no point to my anger. It would always exist. I was broken. My heart, my soul, my body—none of it could be repaired. Dwelling on it would do me no favors. I moved on, placing my hand on one of the roots rising from the earth.

"I'm sorry I haven't been back in decades. It hasn't been safe. It isn't safe now. I wish you were here to help me through this. But then, if you were here, I wouldn't be in this mess, would I?"

And so I told him my story as I did every time I came back home. My heart broke a little more each time though, because I had lost the person who *listened*. My Thread who had been made for me was gone.

Rafael watched Baki from the window while sipping a cup of coffee that had been freshly brewed despite the early hour. She was sitting by the massive camellia tree. Head bowed, hair hiding most of her face, though a sliver of it was still visible in the moonlight. He could see her talking; however, it was quiet enough that he wasn't able to pick up her words with his attuned senses.

Her soul though. Her soul was darker than it had ever appeared in the time he had spent with her thus far. Darkening to the deep stormy grays of the skies and the seas. Not only that, but each fragment was roiling as if there were actual waves and clouds within them. He felt distinctly uncomfortable, more so than if he had seen her physical body bare of any article of clothing. She had given him an immeasurable level of peace the prior evening on the beach. He wished he could go to her and offer her the same now, but he had the feeling it wouldn't be received in kind.

He heard padding footsteps behind him. Cheuksin stood a few feet to his left, holding a steaming cup of tea. The stalwart malamute sat at her side. Victoria bypassed both of them and came to sit next to him, nudging his hand. The Saint Bernard sat on his feet. The goddess looked out to see what he had been watching.

"This is her way of decompressing," she said softly, taking a sip of her tea. "Cam hasn't been able to come home in some time; I imagine she has quite a bit to get off her chest. Come, we should give her privacy."

Somehow feeling more harshly rebuked with three sentences barely spoken over a whisper than some of his worst punishments, he glanced once more out the window, where the opossum had crawled into Baki's lap, and noticed the tears streaming down her face. He quickly looked away and followed the household goddess to her kitchen, knowing he had observed something intensely personal. A burning sense of resolve settled deep within his soul. An urge to ensure she would never feel those emotions again. Rafe shrugged the feeling off. He knew it was impossible.

Cheuksin waved him to a stool and motioned to one of the small *dolsots* sitting on the bar top. "*Gyeran jin.* I don't know how you like your steamed eggs, but it's pretty standard fare. I wasn't feeling too creative this morning."

Rafe shook his head. "I'm not picky. Thank you for making breakfast in general. And the coffee, I'm assuming."

"Eh. The coffee is Cam. She sets it on a timer when she's here. I don't touch that shit." She made a face as she buried her face back into her steaming cup of tea. "Update me. What do I need to expect? I'm the guardian of these lands when Cam isn't here."

He quirked an eyebrow. "Why do you trust me?" Not that he minded. It was a novel experience for the *kariudo*. But he was curious.

"Cam brought you to her home. The Flying Dragons let you pass the gates. Both are solid enough tests of trust for me. If either of them didn't think you passed muster, you'd be dead before you set foot in this particular house. Especially the *kodamas* who possess the Flying Dragons."

"That's reassuring."

"It is for the refugees who live on this land. Every being who resides here has lived through unspeakable trauma."

He nodded. "I understand."

"I thought you might. Now, you are the *kariudo*. What do we need to prepare for?"

Rafael grimaced and ran his right hand over his wrist. He was going to have to watch the newfound habit when he returned. But the longer he spent around these Abstruse, the longer the shackles itched at his soul.

"Ryūjin has been sending his servants out to test defenses and to hunt. I was lucky that his orders to me were just vague enough that I have room to breathe and work around them. I have been under his control for long enough that I have his confidence. That's his mistake." He flinched at the stab of pain that shot through his nerves at the criticism he made of the *kami*.

"The others are either in his camp or not fortunate enough to have his undeserved trust. They will come, they will test your borders, and they will test hard. Your people will need to be ready. Those who cannot take a stand need to be prepared to evacuate. It's going to be traumatic for them. They have already been refugees once. They will become refugees again."

Cheuksin stared him steadily in the eye. Rafe knew better than to underestimate women in small packages. They were often the most terrifying. He met her gaze without backing down. "And what, pray tell, does he want on our lands, that he would go to such efforts against our defenses?"

"I honestly couldn't tell you. That wasn't my mission." As much as he wanted to divulge what his actual mission was, he could not speak it and had yet to find a way around it.

"And what does your mission pertain to?" Cheuksin had yet to blink. It was unsettling and inhuman, and yet, they *were* inhuman, were they not?

Rafael carefully evaluated his words. Examined each one and set them aside if he felt they could not be used, if they would bind his tongue and mind.

"My orders pertain to…Fate, matters of the heart, and a long ago history," he finally chose to say.

"Ah." Those dark eyes continued to peruse him. "Ryūjin wasn't mated. He was threaded. As far as anyone knew, his Thread was lost during the infamous *Hyakki Yagyō*, along with his daughters. At least that's what I have been told by the refugees who were alive during that period, as well as Murry. Cam never speaks of that time."

Cheuksin nodded at the expression of shock that Rafael was unable to withhold. "From what everyone who has come overland has said—no one has been allowed to speak of his Thread since *Hyakki Yagyō*. Anyone who lived in his domain and the neighboring domains who spoke her name after the event immediately died. Not killed, *died*. It wasn't long before the curse was noticed and her name was forgotten to history. Most are still wary about speaking of it, even though the curse has faded with time and distance, so getting others to talk of it is challenging. I'm not of your culture, so I have further immunity."

Things were beginning to become even more complicated. He hated complications. "So what exactly would lend him to believe that his Thread was still alive? Who was she?"

"I would suggest starting by asking Pea. She was his personal *shikigami*, before the night parade. However, she chose an opossum as her avatar in this next phase of life, which makes communication a bit difficult. I imagine there was a reason for this decision. Murry would be the next best bet. But Murry would rather die his final death than reveal his secrets."

As she spoke, Rafe heard the front door close gently. Stemming his shock, he held his breath as he listened to the footsteps wandering throughout the house heading in their direction. His heart stuttered for a beat and his breath let out in a soft sigh as Baki entered the kitchen, somehow seeming shrunken from her usual confident persona. Magic infused with something that seemed off pulsed from her and her jade eyes were red and swollen from crying. Every fiber of his being called out, wanting to comfort her. A corner of her mouth pulled up as she gave a wry smile.

"What are the two of you doing in the kitchen? Planning world domination? Or merely a coup d'état of my territory. You've already taken it over, Cheuky."

"*Aish, kijibae*. You love me for it. Now eat. You look half-starved." The diminutive deity chose to ignore all evidence of tears and shoved the other earthenware pot over to the spot next to him. Cam plopped down on the stool and opened the lid, groaning.

"You're right. I do love you. I'm starving. Hand over the chili oil." After liberally dousing her eggs, she shoveled a massive spoonful in her mouth.

"You're old. Do you remember anything about Ryūjin's thread?" Rafe asked casually, turning on his stool to await her reaction. He wasn't disappointed.

Baki's eyes bulged as she swallowed wrong, and eggs sprayed out everywhere. Pea hissed in distress and clambered off of Cam and away from the chaos. Cam began coughing and looking for water frantically, while Cheuksin shook her head. She clapped her hands and the kitchen was spotless once more, a glass of water in front of her friend.

"Told you she doesn't like this topic. Also, *'You're old?'* Do you get many ladies, *kariudo*?"

"Why is that?" he inquired ignoring the Outhouse Goddess. His lack of dating life wasn't any of her business.

"I'm ancient. I'm not offended by facts. I don't talk about that period because *trauma*, you assholes. And I'm not about to start now."

"So you do know something."

"Absolutely not. I am not talking about this."

"So who should I talk to about this?" he insisted. "This relates to my actual mission. You are aware of how these shackles work. I have some room for interpretation, but incomplete missions eventually lead to my death."

"No one will talk to you about it," she whispered, looking haunted. "The curse is too ingrained in those of us old enough to remember. We've lost too much. There has been too much death and destruction." Fury began to rise in those jade eyes of hers, which he far preferred over the despair.

"You should know. You understand the loss. How could you possibly ask this of any of us? I thought your mission was to find Dr. Aoki. Or was that just a front?"

He stood from his stool, the *gyeran jin* still untouched. "Because, Camellia, consider for one moment—if I die because of an incomplete mission, what does that mean for the citizens living under Ryūjin when he obtains a new *kariudo*? One who believes in his duty wholeheartedly. One who *relishes* his job. Who lives for torture and murder? What happens then?"

Rafael turned then and left the two women, making his way out the door. The *shikigami* gave an inquisitive chirp from an Adirondack chair she had escaped to, but he ignored it and headed into the dark woods filled with refugees. He needed space. He couldn't spend any more time in that kitchen without considering the unfathomable.

Giving up.

FUCK. FUCK! I buried my face in my hands and screamed silently.

This was the last thing I needed after the night I had. This was the impossible situation. I couldn't see any way out. I continued to scream internally while Cheuky watched, without saying a word.

"Cheuk. I quit. I'm done with this. I'm going to go open my *tamatebako* and let Death take me now."

"Stop being dramatic."

I knew she didn't know the underlying details, but the disbelief that riddled my body was still real. I bit my tongue to hold my retort.

"He can't ask you directly, but his fishing for information was essentially telling you what his orders were. He is looking for the sea *kami's* Thread," she continued calmly.

I had gathered all of that. I wasn't a complete waste of a brain cell. But I needed the exact wording to know how much room I could play with and I had no idea how I might go about finding out. So I told her exactly that.

"Wording is going to be important, Cheuksin. You know those slave bands. Your family is the one who first developed them; the Undersea Realm just stole them. The specific wording is going to matter a lot here."

Because if he was asked to bring home Ryūjin's Thread, then we were well and truly fucked. If the sea *kami* had asked him to bring home his wife, then that was another matter entirely, and one we could work with.

Because Ryūjin wasn't sitting on that throne. A pretender was.

Ryūjin had destroyed everything that night of *Hyakki Yagyō* when chaos reigned. Above all, he had destroyed me.

Because Ryūjin was dead.

CHAPTER TWENTY-FOUR

took the liberty of taking a shower and getting dressed before girding my loins and going after the *kariudo*. I knew we needed time and space after the heated emotions of the past day and night. But this wasn't a topic I could avoid.

It was easier to find him than I had anticipated. I stepped out the back door about to head into the woods when I found him in one of the chairs. Wherever he had gone to cool off couldn't have been far for him to be back on my porch. Pea was curled around his neck, Vicky wrapped in a tight ball in his lap as he stroked her fur, Max flopped out at his feet. Woody, I suspected, was in the kitchen with Cheuksin. The image was one of contentedness. Hard-won peace. A moment of still waters in the eye of the storm.

And I was going to be the one to disturb the waters again.

I grabbed one of the pillows and carefully chose to sit in the chair next to him so I wouldn't have to look him in the eye during this conversation. I hugged the pillow in front of me like a shield. As if it could do anything to protect me from the onslaught to come.

"I'm sorry for my outburst this morning." I ran my hand across the texture of the pillow, concentrating on the feel of the different fibers. The pillows were new; Cheuksin had redecorated since I'd been gone. The one I had in my hands was threaded with reds, golds, and oranges in a brilliant depiction of the sunrise and beautiful birds in flight. Rafael's cushion, I knew, would be woven with blues, greens, and silvers in a rendition of the sea.

I took a deep breath. "There was a lot I was triggered by, but it was still no excuse. You're right. Without you around to mediate the *kami's* orders, we would return to what it was like before you. And it was much harder to get refugees out before your…"

I faded out. There was no good way to phrase a period of enslavement. Your term? Your stint? Your tenure?

His lip quirked up in a wry smile as he shifted to look at me directly. Vicky grumbled at the maneuver. "We can call it what it is. What's a little bluntness among slave and former slave, eh? My *bondage*."

Pea whacked him on the head with her tail for forgetting her. "I'm sorry, I forgot you as another fellow bondaged being."

"Yes, well she started out unwilling, but they grew to appreciate one another," I said softly, remembering. I cleared my throat. "Pea, can you put up a sound barrier? And you may want to leave for this."

He looked at me curiously. "Why would she want to leave?"

"Because we're about to have story time. And this particular story time is especially traumatic for Pea."

She scrambled off Rafe and entwined herself around my neck instead, "I need to breathe to speak, Suītopī," I rasped gently as I tugged at the tail constricting my neck. She hissed, chirped, and growled at me as Rafe looked on in fascination.

"If that's your choice. You can stay. But if your magic gets unruly…" She shook her head frantically. I sighed. "You need to move to my lap though; I can't have you squeezing my neck. You're going to have to settle for an emotional support arm or leg."

After she resituated herself, a dome not dissimilar from Reika's went over the five of us. However, unlike Reika, it didn't require the sacrifice of body parts. I could feel my anxiety rise as it sealed us off.

"You asked about Ryūjin's Red Thread," I spoke tonelessly.

"How are you able to talk about her?" he asked curiously. "Cheuksin said there was a curse upon her name."

"I never said I was going to say her name." I began to pick at the threads in the pillow. I had unconsciously found a red thread and started the process of unraveling it. I don't know what that said about my frame of mind. "Please, this will be easier for me if you don't interrupt."

He nodded, understanding that at the very least.

I closed my eyes. Exhaled. And threw my mind back into the past. On purpose for once. Into the memories I had avoided for over a century now.

"Where are you going, love?" I asked. For weeks, I had felt the thrums of disturbance through our thread. There had been no specific emotion that I could pinpoint, but there was enough to tell me something was off.

"Nothing," Ryūjin answered distractedly, looking out the floor-to-ceiling windows that encompassed our suite, clearly not listening given the way he had answered my question. I eyed his muscled back, enjoying the view.

"Why don't you come back to bed then; it's early yet. We have time before we need to get back to our duties."

He shook his head. "I have something I need to get done before our night gets started."

I sat up, holding the sheet over my breasts. "The onmyōji *all predicted that the Night Parade would go smoothly. The Night wouldn't influence the* oni *to too much chaos. We have spent weeks preparing for this* Hyakki Yagyō, *what more could you possibly need to do?" I asked frustrated. He had spent most of his time away in recent months, leaving me to handle matters over the realm.*

I recalled how biases had run deep in Ryūgū-jō and nobody wanted a hybrid Abstruse as a ruler, let alone a hybrid of two cultures. As a result, I hid my true self under a glamour, masking myself to appear fully Japanese. There, I had only allowed one half of myself to shine through to avoid trouble. Only those closest to me new my true self. And even fewer knew me now.

"I don't have a choice. I must go." He turned and started getting dressed.

"Maybe you shouldn't have a choice about leaving your Thread behind for yet another night and in charge of your Quotes-damned realm," I snarled. "What kind of ruler and Thread are you to leave me behind again. And the night of Hyakki Yagyō *no less?"*

Ryūjin slipped through door, "The type of ruler and Thread who loves you and his realm."

"That was the last time I saw him whole."

The diviners had lied. I had always regretted not divining the outcome of that night myself, but my strengths did not lie in my *onmyōji* powers due to the matriarchal dominance of the *haetae* gene. I thought I could rely on the *onmyōji* to be loyal to their ruler. Turned out, I was wrong.

I kept my eyes closed tightly, tears beginning to leak from them, unwilling to see what Rafael's reaction might be. Pea's tail wrapped around my arm, light tremors vibrating through her small body as she anticipated what came next. I began to narrate what I saw that night.

Screams shuddered through the air all around me, as I ran through the night. I was surrounded by oni *on all sides, attacking our citizens everywhere I looked. Throats torn out, limbs ripped off.* Kanobōs *mutilating helpless bodies beneath them. The worst were the children, their eyes vacantly staring, one last unanswered plea for help in them. I knew those stares would haunt me for my remaining immortal life. More than anything, I wished I could stop to help them, but there was something wrong with my thread. I could feel it pulling taut. It grew tighter and tighter, to the point where it felt as though it was in danger of snapping, which was impossible. I ran faster, trying to find Ryūjin. I couldn't accept what was happening before me. The number of* oni *was overwhelming and far more than should ever be present at a Night Parade.*

I began to shake as the next images passed over my mind. I shoved my fist in my mouth as I sobbed. Keened. I rocked back and forth with Pea in my lap, her tail now a vice on the arm gripped around the pillow. A heavy weight draped around my shoulders, a cold nose shoved into my neck in comfort, another in my other hand. Though I knew it was happening from a distance, I couldn't feel any of it anymore. I had retreated fully into that small corner of my being that allowed me to protect myself from these memories.

I slammed to a stop in horror, finding Toyotama-hime and Tamayori-hime's bodies limp, torn to shreds. Toyotama shifted into her crocodile form, draped over Tamayori, protecting her younger sister to her last breath. I was unable to catch a breath, unable to comprehend how I would tell Ryūjin that his daughters were dead. My best friend, Toyotama, the one I had found on the shore that fated morning, being attacked by boys in her turtle form, the one who had led me Undersea to my Thread. She was gone.

An ushi oni *speared a piece of Tamayori's body with one of its claws at the end of an arachnid leg, placing the flesh in its oxen head. The thread pulsed and pulled tighter again. I winced and turned my eyes away from the horror, ducking under another* oni's *kanobō. I continued my run in the direction the thread demanded, running, dodging, and killing* oni *as needed. Finally, at the edge of the wards of the realm, I found what remained of my Thread, his* shikigami *huddled pitifully at his side, sorrowful eyes gazing up at me, communicating to me what I already knew,*

His wounds were fatal. Only another kami *could have done this. He smiled weakly at me and lifted his hand to touch my leg.*

"My beautiful Thread. How I love you."

I dropped to my knees. "What have you done, *Ryūjin?"*

"What needs must."

"What does that mean?"

"One day you will see." He coughed and blood ran in a thin line from the corner of his mouth. He wiped it with his hand and slid the hand under my clothing, covering my heart with it. His other hand covered his own heart. Connecting us from thread to thread.

"What are you doing, Ryū?"

"What I have to. I will miss you. Take care of her always, Suītopī."

Before I could comprehend what he was doing, there was a snap, a ricochet. A blinding force slammed into me and our thread. Our bodies were sheared from each other and as my body filled with a strange magic, my heart and soul shattered.

Then everything went black.

"That is all I remember until I woke up in Murry's mouth with Pea's apparition and Ryūjin's body, with just the faintest pulse and breath left in his body as we fled Ryūgū-jō. His soul had—" I choked on a sob and retched, dry heaving.

"His soul was already gone. Murry had already been called by Ryū some hours earlier. His body made it until we made it to the shore of Neskowin, a place completely foreign to the three of us. But safe. The magic that had kept Murry corporeal enough to get us here finally dissipated and it was months before he could check on us again. By then, Pea and I had made our way inland, where Ryū took his last breath and faded completely."

Pea began making a strange cry I had never heard from her before. I wasn't sure if it was one an opossum could make. I dropped the pillow, and held her tightly to my nonbeating heart, resting my face against hers.

I hadn't added how Pea contained the immense backlash that was the severing of her connection with Ryūjin by focusing it on the sole task of keeping the shattered pieces of my body together. How she had painstakingly collected each and every piece she could find and used her *ki* to keep them from falling apart. How she blamed herself for the gaps in my body that were missing, for the fragments she hadn't been able to find in the chaos of that night. I hugged her tighter, trying my best to communicate that no forgiveness was needed, because none was ever warranted in the first place.

I tried to catch my breath.

"He destroyed our thread. Something I hadn't known was possible. In doing so, he had destroyed both of our souls. He no longer exists in any of our realms. There is no afterlife for him in Yomi. I will never see him again."

For that, I could never forgive him.

"So." I opened my eyes for the first time to look at Rafael fully. I tried to give him a watery smile. "You asked who Ryūjin's Red Thread was?" He remained still, only a small furrow between his brow forming with equal parts dread and anticipation.

"You are looking at her."

I COULDN'T CATALOGUE all of the emotions that passed through Rafael's eyes fast enough. Horror, understanding, *grief.* But above all of these. Betrayal.

Rafael had been forced into the mold of an abomination for a false god.

"You were able to tell me who his Thread was..." he began slowly, clearly shutting down his emotions, just as I had.

"Because I *am* his Thread," I used present tense. Just because the thread no longer existed didn't mean anything. I would forever be Ryū's Red Thread, and he, mine. Fate had bound us together. Fuck Fate if she was such a weak bitch that a *kami* could snap a supposedly unbreakable bond. "I don't need to use my name to tell my own story."

"And Pea...Cheuksin said, but—"

"Pea truly was his *shikigami.* Perhaps an opossum seems a little undignified for a *kami,* but she wasn't always one." She was curled into the tightest ball possible in my lap. I sighed. This was why I hadn't wanted her to stay. But this was her choice to make and I would never take away her

THE MOUNTAINS, THE SEA, AND THE SPACES IN BETWEEN

power to choose. I ran a soothing hand down her trembling back. She edged her nose under my arm and hid her face in return.

"She chose a broken animal for her avatar with her freedom, as both a self-imposed punishment for being unable to save Ryū and because Pea simply never wanted to speak again. The trauma was too much for her. It was too much for me." I sagged in my seat, bringing Pea to my chest so I could drag my legs up in an imitation of the fetal position. A mockery of protecting a heart that no longer needed protection. Emotions were starting to filter back in and I didn't want them. I preferred the cold, dark cave of dissociation. If only I could remain there.

"Baki? You still here?" a gentle voice nudged my consciousness.

I shifted just enough to look at the voice interrupting my melancholy. "The tattoo on your side. Tell me about it."

CHAPTER TWENTY-FIVE

Rafe's hand began to rise slightly to his right, as if to brush along the tattoo, but halted before it could give anything away. I could sense his frustration beginning to rise with my change in subjects, then it eased into acceptance and understanding. The tacit knowledge that I needed an escape from the memories before I went under forever was something that only another survivor of trauma could truly understand.

"There is a stylized Japanese dragon entwined with another creature inked into your side from what I glimpsed at St. Helens. Judging by the size of the tattoo, the command was no small order given."

He swallowed hard. Pain glimmered in his eyes as he opened his mouth to answer my question. Instead, he removed his shirt to show me the tattoo in full.

The ink was still in color, indicating the mission had not yet been fulfilled. Faded gray tattoos littered his torso. One other color tattoo was evident on his pectoral muscle, but I would look at that next. This one was enormous, taking up his entire side, wrapping from the center of his torso to his spine, and dipping under his waistband, indicating the priority of this task. It overlapped several older faded tats.

"How far does it go?" I asked quietly.

"Down the thigh, clear to my knee." He grimaced.

I traced the stylized creature with a finger, not quite grazing Rafe's skin. He shivered below me as though he could feel my touch despite my care in not doing so. A sea dragon battled a beast with the head and body of a lion. Feathered legs. A dragon's tail. And a single horn upon its lion head. Primarily white in color, with jade features and an occasional flash of red.

A *haetae*. But one much younger than myself who had evolved over generations to appear as this one did on Rafe's body. My fingers brushed down the path of its battle. I glanced up as I heard a quiet gasp as though he had to force himself to breathe under another's touch. Except it wasn't past nightmares I saw when I found myself in his gaze.

My own breath caught at the flash of desire in the depths of his eyes before he shuttered it away and I questioned what I saw. I gave a small shake of my head and looked back down at the tattoo and the vibrant flames bursting from where the guardian's liver would be. Branches of the Ulleungdo hemlock tree dotted the negative space between the battling creatures.

On its own, it was a beautiful tattoo. But the meaning behind it was sinister. It was a command that had been branded on the last two *kariudo*. A chill wracked my body at the sight of it and I blinked away the burning behind my eyes. This ink would be my damnation, for as long as it still existed in color, it confirmed there was still at least one *haetae* in existence. Rafe would have no tattoo for Oliver, for the last *kariudo* died believing he had eradicated the two races.

"Have you ever?" I asked quietly.

He held my stare without pause. He had no need for me to clarify the question. I waited for his answer, unsure how I would respond if he answered in the affirmative.

"I have never had the need." I watched as his body convulsed. Payment. The cost for answering my question against the parameters set by his master.

My fractured soul keened at his answer and I resisted the urge to double over in pain. He had never harvested the liver of a *haetae*. Simply because there were no other *haetae* remaining for him to find. I couldn't allow him to question why this had such a significant impact on me.

I was the last. And I had goals I needed to achieve before our race no longer existed.

I cleared my throat, then stood and went back into my home. When I returned, cold water bottle in hand, Woody padded behind me silently. I placed a hand on Woodrow and the two of us were allowed re-entrance into the sound barrier. After removing the cap from the water bottle I had retrieved, Rafael accepted the small token in silence and took a sip. A small trail of blood ran from his left ear and right eye, signs of exactly how high the cost had been. Before I could mention anything, he swiped at it, smearing the blood across his face and into his hair, absently, as if this was a common enough occurrence that it was to be expected. He coughed weakly a few times and waved at me to say whatever I needed to say.

Sighing, I gathered whatever fortitude I had left—which wasn't much—to continue. But if this man could go through this level of pain to answer my question, the least I could do was touch upon my trauma yet again for him. Woody huffed and collapsed to the deck next to Max, laying his head on my chair, eyeing the *kariudo* with suspicion.

"The rumor from all the refugees is that the sea *kami* has slowly been succumbing to madness over the past century." Rafael nodded to confirm. "He orchestrated the genocide of the *haetae*, believing their livers may heal his madness."

Rafe frowned. "How did he make that leap?"

Rather than answer his question, my hand lifted to his left pectoral muscle, over his heart, and trailed over the exquisitely illustrated tattoo there. The back of a beautiful woman with blue-black hair, surrounded by shadows and entwined in a ribbon of crimson. My hand stilled at the sight.

Fuck.

"If you had a child you loved unconditionally and they were ill, what lengths would you go to in order to heal them?" I asked instead.

Rafe paused as he considered my question.

"That's not something I've had experience with," he answered carefully. "But I'd like to imagine I would do whatever I could, go to the ends of the world to find a cure for them. At the same time, I'd not want to miss a moment of time with them, should the cure not work. It's not an easy question to answer. I'm not sure how this relates."

My hand dropped to rest against his tattoo. I felt the warmth of his skin. The slight gasp he made as I did so. I noted the skip, then the reassuring strength of his heartbeat as it resumed.

"Are you familiar with how the jellyfish lost their skeletons?"

"That old legend?" His flesh broke out in goosebumps beneath mine as his breaths came in shorter intervals.

"Hmmm. Are *onis, kappas, tanukis,* and such not legends themselves?" I mused, just as I had with Kenichi about the *bijin* a few days ago. Had it only been a few days? It felt like an eternity. "There are many different versions of this tale. Some involve a wife, some only Ryūjin, and some his daughter, but I digress. Let's get back to how the jellyfish lost their skeletons."

"Once upon a time, a long, long time ago, long before you or I were born." A quiet skeptical scoff blew out from the lips next to me. I felt how the difference in his breath altered the beat of his heart. "In a land far, far away, a powerful sea *kami,* Ryūjin, of the Undersea Kingdom, grew lonely and he created two daughters using the power of his *ki* to keep himself company, Toyotama and Tamayori. Tamayori was beauty, grace, and perfection. Unlike Toyotama. When Toyo was first created, Ryūjin believed he had achieved flawlessness. And then he began to perceive the darkness within her and believed this to be an ailment, rather than simply one of the ways her *ki* manifested. Ryūjin was nothing, if not prideful," I recalled sadly.

"Determined to achieve perfection, Ryūjin had heard from the *oni-babas* serving his court that the liver of a monkey may serve to heal the darkness within his daughter. He sent his loyal servants, the jellyfish, across the seas and onto the lands to try to obtain a liver from such a creature for his daughter to heal her, for no such animals existed in Ryūgū-jō. At the time, the jellyfish had bones and shells, allowing them to travel on land to a degree. Finally, a smack came back triumphant, with a monkey in tow. Alas, in the end they were outsmarted, and the primate escaped, liver intact. And Ryūjin took his anger out on the jellyfish by taking their bones."

It had been far more cruel than that. He had brutalized them. Beaten them so badly, their bones could never be restored by any healer.

"Dark," Rafael remarked, his hand reaching up and lacing with mine, pulling my hand to the side and away from his heart. "And what does this have to do with us now?"

I took a deep breath of the coastal air around me. Held it in for a moment. Then blew it out as slowly as possible. I didn't question how my body worked anymore, fragmented as it was. The first few years, I would stare in the mirror, unglamoured, and watch myself eat and drink, wondering how liquids and solids made their way down without slipping through the cracks. I didn't know why my body bothered to breath when my heart wouldn't beat. In a sense, Ryūjin had done the same to me as he had to the jellyfish.

"What do you know about the *haetae*?"

"There's not much on record, beyond how the various applications of Ulleungdo hemlock can be utilized to hunt them. I assume that's because they're essentially extinct now."

I did my best not to flinch at his clinical tone as he spoke of the assassination of my people. My mother. My family. The matter-of-fact way in which he spoke about us—as if we weren't *people* deserving of life, deserving of an existence free of fear of being hunted for simply *being*—made me hesitate in sharing this next bit of information.

"The *haetae* filter their *ki* through their liver. Which means these organs contain the purest form of their magic. The monkey had tricked Ryūjin. He never did attempt to cure Toyotama's ailment due to his rage at being outsmarted, so it is technically unknown whether it could have worked. As a result, the false *kami* holds the belief that the liver of a *haetae* could cure his madness because of the unadulterated nature of the *ki* found within them. Every *kariudo* was automatically branded with the command to hunt them down once the *kami* perceived himself to fall ill. However, to my knowledge, they have been unsuccessful harvesting the liver with the *ki* intact."

I squeezed Rafael's hand. "I need to know, Rafael. Why are you looking for Misaki Aoki? Do you suspect her to be a *haetae*?" Tension wracked my body—for what I was hiding, for the subtle deceit in my wording, for Dr. Aoki. For what this answer would take from him.

"I do not." This answer cost nothing, as it wasn't in direct relation to his command. It also, however, did nothing to reassure me. He took a deep breath and steeled himself against the pain. My heart froze and everything in me begged him to stop, while the other half of me *needed* him to answer. Before I could stop him, he continued, "I suspect Aoki to be the *kami's* Thr—"

This time the convulsions threw him out of the patio chair and onto the unforgiving deck. Pea dropped the sound barrier as I scrambled to place my hands under his head to support it and shouted for Theo. I grabbed the pillow from his chair and attempted to get it under him without success. Blood started draining from his eyes, nose, and ears. It began pouring from his mouth as he bit through his tongue, nearly severing it. The oceanic landscape of the pillow turned into a mix of muddied brown and shades of a deep bruise, as his blood soaked deep into the fabric.

"You fucking idiot," I murmured, swallowing around the pieces of my heart that had shifted in my throat. Nails scrambling across wood and boots running through the house joined the discord of sounds ringing through my ears.

Theo. Thank the Quotes.

Pea dropped to my side first and immediately a pink glow settled over him to no avail, his body going into tonic-clonic contractions. She chittered at me with a worried look on her face. "I know, girl. I know. This is magical, I don't think there is anything we can do except heal his physical wounds."

The door to the patio slammed open and Theo arrived, his medical bag in hand, knowing whenever I shouted for him in that tone, an emergency was likely. I glanced up at him, no longer trying to hold back the tears in my eyes.

"What—what the hell, Cam?" He immediately began clearing the furniture away. "Turn him on his side if you can," he instructed. "How long has it been since this started?"

How long? It felt like it had been an eternity and an instant at the same time. "I have no idea, Theo. I don't have a stopwatch to time everyone around me when they drop into a seizure." My terror turned me snappish as I attempted to roll Rafael onto his side.

I expect them to know better than to trigger a goddamn grand mal seizure.

Theo shook his head in annoyance as he dropped to his knees and threw his watch at me, the timer already running, before assisting me in rolling Rafe to his side. He did his best to ensure that his mouth faced downward, allowing the blood to begin to flow out. Shame ran through me that I hadn't thought to do so. The blood quickly began to slow, the physical injury healed by Pea.

"Does he have a history of tonic-clonic seizures?" Theo asked.

"I just met the man a couple days before you did, Theo. We haven't exactly run down our medical histories." The thought of disclosing Rafael's slave bands felt wrong. With the exception of needing to gain Oliver's trust, that was Rafael's story to tell.

Theo removed the cap of a needle with his teeth as he prepared an injection. I held back my doubts, given Pea's lack of success. He did his best to stabilize an arm and quickly stabbed the syringe into it, depressing the plunger, releasing the contents into Rafe. Minutes, hours, an eon later, Rafael's muscles relaxed as the convulsions slowed, before stopping altogether. He didn't regain consciousness.

"Time?"

I'd forgotten about timing. Again. I glanced down at the watch, stopping the timer. "Eleven minutes and thirty-eight seconds." Theo nodded grimly.

"Add another minute, give or take, before we started tracking it. It's going to take time for him to recover magically from this."

His tone dropped then as his expression grew even more serious. "Cam...I don't know if he has enough positive karma for me to shift the scales in his favor. He has done too much harm in the sea *kami's* name."

I couldn't speak, simply nodding, unable to resist the urge to reach out and take one of Rafael's hands in my grasp. Needing to tether him to something in this world.

"What did you give him?" I asked to distract myself. "Pea couldn't stop it."

His lip quirked up at the corner. "Maybe Pea on her own couldn't stop it, but she and I have been cooking up some special remedies in the lab during our off-hours." He patted his medical bag. "We've come up with some things here for the team for lifesaving measures given her uniqueness and the way she twists the *ki* of those who spend enough time around her."

Pea chittered at him and wrapped her tail around my wrist. She nudged Rafael's limp arm then looked up at Theo expectantly. He sighed. "Yes, I'll also be the packhorse." He gathered Rafael in a bridal carry and his hand fell out of my grip. Theo nodded at the door that had slammed back shut behind him. "If you could grab the door, I'll carry the patient to his bed and monitor him."

I stood, my body taking time to shift its fragments into the correct positions, and waited for the two to enter the house. Vicky scrambled to her feet and followed the unlikely pair, her nose keeping in contact with Rafael's limp hand through the house. I remained outside, needing fresh air to clear my mind and recover from the adrenaline rush, and sat heavily in one of the chairs. Max set his heavy head in my lap, offering what comfort he could. A soft woo-woo drew my attention to my feet where Woodrow settled himself. I absently rubbed his soft ears for a moment, the motion calming my nerves.

"Why, Pea. Why would he risk himself like that? His first answer was sufficient and posed no risk at all to himself. *He didn't need to keep going.*" I buried my head in my hands.

"Perhaps he wanted to," a quiet voice interjected. The light scent of jasmine and toasted rice wafted toward me and I lifted my head to find a cup of tea in my field of vision. Cheuksin was solemn as she continued on, "Perhaps, underneath everything, he is a good male, trying to find himself and trying to prove his worth to those around him. And this is his way of doing so."

"By attempting suicide, Cheuky? What does that prove? Where does that get us?"

She held her silence for several moments, allowing it to weigh down on me, before speaking. "Are his actions any different from your own, Camellia Kimoto? Don't answer me. I simply want you to think about my question. And whether you may be mirrors of one another."

I balked. The desire to run far away from her question was strong.

"Don't let his actions be in vain. Where does his answer place you now?"

I dropped my head backwards and stared up at the sky. The sun was just beginning to peek over the horizon. I wondered if Dr. Aoki was looking at the same sky somewhere out there. Perhaps she was in another realm and looking at a different one. Or perhaps she was imprisoned. We still had no idea.

"He believes that Dr. Aoki may be the *kami's* Thread is my understanding."

"Hmmm."

I lifted my head. "What does *hmmm* mean?"

"Are you willing to return a Thread to the *kami*? Given the reports you've heard about his state?"

My body sagged, releasing the tension it had held from the last half hour. "Absolutely not."

Before I could contemplate all the possible implications of everything that had just been revealed, my body shuddered from the roots of my hair down to the heels of my feet. My teeth chattered. My lungs seized. Warmth flooded my body and the Flying Dragons shot up in the air. I whipped to Cheuksin who had received the same signal I had and was rigid with tension. I mentally went through roll call in my head and my world slammed to a halt.

"Cheuk," I said urgently. "Aidan. He didn't come home. I assumed he spent it with his Uncles, like he normally does. *Did he check in with you?*"

CHAPTER TWENTY-SIX

t was a major oversight on my part. I might have been distracted by Murry's news, having to recall the night of Ryu's death, and Rafael's seizure, but we were still on a deployment. *I had failed my team member.*

Please, for the love of all things unholy, Cheuksin, tell me he checked in. I needed a break. A chance to recover from the turmoil of the morning. This was too much. I felt selfish for the thoughts even passing through my mind.

He's just in his Uncles' den catching up.

She shook her head tightly, draining my hope. "I received no word from either Aidan or Uncle after the four of you returned."

The guilt threatened to drown me. I shoved my way back up to the surface, I couldn't afford to go under now.

"*Whiz.*"

The gremlin popped in front of us instantly, likely noting the undertone of panic in my voice and the change in my vitals.

"What do you need, Cammy-Cam?"

"Aidan. What's his current location? His status?"

"Hold one moment." Whiz turned inward as he concentrated on obtaining the data. I focused on his outfit of the day. He was dressed in all black, having created a suit out of old film cannisters and electrical tape. I hoped it wasn't an omen.

He shook his head, his large ears swaying with the motion. "He's not online, Cam. I can't even access his emergency backup beacon. His nanos may have been purged."

I sucked in a breath. "What's the last data you have on him?"

A projection of the Shore Inn came up against the side of my home. The three of us watched quietly as Aidan, Rafe, Theo, and the Uncles made their plans to split up in the parking lot. Aidan, Yumi, and his boisterous Uncle climbed into one vehicle. Along the drive, white noise overtook the projection, then black wiped the screen, Aidan's vitals going blank.

"I have no explanation for what could have caused this, other than a purge of my nanos. Or..." Whiz's voice trailed off, unwilling to say what we all feared as the *kodamas* lashed over our heads.

"You're fine, Whiz. Thank you so much for your help. We'll call you again if we need you." I tried my best to convey gratitude, but my voice was toneless as dread continued to creep over me.

He nodded and popped back out. I turned to Cheuksin.

"You'll gather the refugees? I'm going after Aidan and Uncle."

"I'll gather everyone," she confirmed. "Not all of them will be willing to leave."

"Don't force anyone; it's their choice to evacuate. We've never been about taking away choices. If they want to fight, let them fight for their homes." I was already heading into the house as I shouted over my shoulder, "Max!" I needed Pea. I needed Max. I could do anything, find anyone, with the two of them by my side. Woody would help protect Cheuksin and I knew Vicky wouldn't want to leave Rafe. I knew deep inside I was losing her heart to his. Their souls were too similar.

I skidded into Rafe's room, breathless. He was already sitting up in bed. Still pale, but much steadier than I anticipated. Who was I kidding? I had expected him to still be unconscious. Blood smeared across his chest, where he had attempted to clean it off. The crimson obscured the cursed tattoos. Vicky scrambled to her feet at our arrival.

"Pea." My voice came out in a gasp. It wasn't due to the exertion. It was fear. Yuriko's attack on Mount Saint Helens was one thing. She was the *kamis*-damned Winter Princess. She could handle herself. Aidan? He was an exceptional SAR handler. An amazing friend. The most loyal one you could ask for. But he was gean cannagh and *tanuki*. And his *tanuki* blood wasn't strong enough to lend him the power to shift. Was he going to seduce his attackers if he was in danger? No. Because Aidan was the biggest believer in consent.

Aidan would rather give himself up than use his powers to take away someone's will. I could only hope he was still with Uncle.

Theo stood quickly from where he had been checking Rafe's vitals. "Are you okay? What's going on?"

I shook my head as I scooped up Pea, who had shimmied off the bed and scurried to me. "No time. Aidan never came back. Ask Cheuksin for more details." I felt a tugging in my chest. I rubbed at it as I secured her in my jacket.

"Baki, wait." Rafe ripped off the blood pressure cuff and rose. "You shouldn't go alone."

I couldn't deal with this right now, as I rushed out the door with Max at my side. "It's your funeral. You know your limits."

Theo kept pace with us, Rafael not far behind. Both staggered to a stop when they saw the shadows cast by the Flying Dragons through the bay windows.

Theo shook off the image. "I can help."

"I need you here. If anyone is hurt, they'll need you."

He nodded with grim purpose. "Slow down for five minutes. Take the time you need to prepare for a search. You won't do Aidan any favors going into this half-cocked."

I gritted my teeth but nodded, gathering our gear and harnessing up the K9s. Before we could get out the back door, Oliver burst into the living room. My level of frustration rose. *Why couldn't I just* leave *already?*

"The journal is missing," he spat out. "I just went to secure it and it's gone."

Theo and I exchanged glances from where he stood on the other side of the room. I shook my head.

"The journal is lowest on my priority list right now. Stay safe. I can't lose you too." I stared Olly hard in the eyes. He gulped and nodded.

With that, we took off running, Max keeping pace at my left side, Rafe and Vicky on my right, despite the ordeal he had recently gone through. Frantic *yōkai* streamed past us in droves. None of us stopped to acknowledge one another.

We didn't stop until we reached the Uncles' den.

"Aidan! Uncles!" I called out. No one answered. The door hung open, off-kilter, as if someone had burst through it. I swallowed hard as fear gained higher ground and forced myself to pass through the entryway, Max leaning hard into my side as we crossed the threshold.

Rafael and Vicky stood guard in the doorway while I searched the home, desperate to find answers. Though he didn't make a single motion, I could feel Rafe tracking my every move, assessing my state of mind, while also looking out for everything around us.

Signs that Uncle had made it home after we left the beach were apparent. The jacket he had worn hung neatly on the coat rack. What was out of place though, was the sand tracked all over the den. Despite their argument earlier, both Uncles were fairly fastidious and swept obsessively to keep sand out of their den. The infamous broom was left toppled over, like a fallen soldier, from its usual station in the corner. There was no indication that Aidan or his other Uncle had returned.

Uncle had either left in a hurry, or someone else had entered the home since he had left. Whatever it was, no one was home and I didn't have the luxury of time to investigate while we were under attack. I snagged items that belonged to each of the family members, just in case. I didn't know if we would need to extend our search to either of the Uncles as well.

I stepped out of their den into a horror show. The mass of thorns above us writhed and convulsed with pleasure and pain as the *kodamas* took part in a bloodbath. I doubted they had taken part in one since the last World War. Fires raged throughout the dome encapsulating us, wailing all around—the sound of *kodamas* dying.

No. Pea placed her paw against one of the camellias curling around a crevice in my chest. Flashes of fire from a long-ago night and screams of the dying echoed through my thoughts. *Never again.* Power flooded through me as Pea fed *ki* through our link.

The world around me faded, the people, the animals, the flora ceasing to have structure or meaning. Instead, everything broke into molecules. It had taken me so long to understand the world in this form—as a hybrid, it hadn't come instinctually. There were just so many possible compositions of fire.

I sought the *ki* deep within myself and pulled it forth, putting my millennia of education and experience to use and focused on twisting the compounds before me. The living ceased to be a concept to me. Instead, all were simply infinitesimal specks in this universe, there for me to manipulate. I starved the flames of their fuel, silently praying whoever was impacted would be able to heal. The inferno itself, I claimed as my own, absorbing the atoms into my being. A wild sense of exhilaration and sheer *power* filled me as it hadn't in countless years.

I reveled in the feeling. It had been too long. The sensation was like warm sunshine on your face after a bleak winter. It was the first hit of heroin, that first high that could never be found again. The utter stillness in your mind when everything…is…just…*right*. When all the noise in your brain suddenly shuts off and you experience actual silence for the first time in your life.

I wanted to stay in this moment forever. I reveled in the feeling, allowing the power to continue funneling into me.

Fires smothered throughout my territory, and I consumed the inferno with intensifying greed, I lost control. The flames were dead, but I was thrown out of the atomic world and back into the living as one of the Flying Dragons imploded, showering the land with crimson and black flecks of ice—its *kodama* lost to this plane. Guilt competed with vertigo as I bore witness to another death on my conscience.

As the air cleared of the glimmering motes, I staggered, panting from the power raging in my body. My vision shifted to the small bodies I saw flailing in the mass of briars. Some in the form of small girls with the jointed legs of arachnids protruding from their backs. Others with the anatomy of a spider and faces of deceptively innocent girls upon their grotesque forms.

My mind flashed back to the *jorōgumo* carcass I had seen upon my return to Neskowin. She hadn't been just a feral *jorōgumo* wandering the forest. She was yet another thing I had missed. Another servant sent by the *kami* who had been laying a silk sac of eggs to prepare a veritable legion against us.

She had been killed too late and her children had been well-advised of what to do in the event of her demise.

"Camellia." A firm voice and a tiny paw hitting my cheek interrupted my self-flagellation.

I came back out of my thoughts to find Rafael looking at me with concern and Pea in my face hissing at me.

"Aidan," he said carefully.

I nodded, struggling to surface from the dual effect of overwhelming *ki* and the emotions that kept dragging me down. I anchored myself in Rafael's steadiness, grateful for his presence. A dragging sensation in my core grounded me further.

"The entrance to the Siuslaw National Forest, the one Aidan would have likely taken, isn't far. It would take longer to backtrack to my car," I said, steeling my voice.

Rafael nodded and we picked through the forest toward the entrance, I evaluated the companion at my side. Assessing him, as he did me.

Rafael remained shirtless, as he didn't have a chance to grab a top after our conversation in all the chaos. He hadn't had a chance to grab any of his weapons, and yet…based on what I had witnessed in the playback of the attack on St. Helens, I believed his weapons were never far from him, regardless of whether they were on his body or not. His *ki* wouldn't be restored yet either, due to the extent of seizure he experienced. I wouldn't be able to rely on him for magical backup.

I wondered how many times he had manipulated his way out of the *kami's* demands and saved people over his years as the huntsman. He was right. To lose him as the *kariudo* would be a tragedy. But to leave him as a slave was another gross injustice which couldn't stand.

"Well it seems the *kami* has learned of the missing journal," I said grimly as we reached the border of my territory. The sounds of shrieking girls and screaming *kodamas* rang through my ears. Flashes of other sight-less children ran through my mind. I squared my shoulders and locked my psyche tight for the battle to come. I hated the *jorōgumo* and the mindfuck that came with exterminating them. "You ready?"

"Do I have a choice?"

"Sure you do. You could have stayed back with Theo, Olly, and Cheuksin."

"And let you have all the fun slaughtering soulless spiders? Spiders that wear the faces of young girls to make men hesitate so they can feast on them? Never."

I scoffed. "Pea, you got Max and Vicky?"

She had eased her way off my body and was seated on Max's accommodating back, fur gripped tight with her three paws and tail. A brilliant blue shield dropped over them. They'd be safer than anybody else in this region behind that.

When I glanced back at Rafe, he had his *tanto* blades in his hands.

I stabbed a finger at him. "One of these days, you're going to tell me where those come from."

His blades shrugged with his shoulders. "And perhaps one day you'll explain to me the immense prowess you have over fire."

I ignored him, shoving down the flare of guilt his words brought forth, and tapped on a thorn to request passage through the mass of brambles that had formed at my boundary. Several of the lethal barbs—dripping in the crimson of blood and black of ichor—came down to caress me, my hair, my face, my body. I made a concerted effort not to shudder. I knew they were trying to convey their gratitude. I didn't feel worthy of it after killing one of their own. A small passageway opened up, still hidden within the Flying Dragons. They were keeping us protected from the *jorōgumo* for as long as they could.

I sliced my wrist open along a barb as we ran through the tunnel and dripped my own blood among the flora. My own sacrifice—payment—for what they had given today. It was hardly adequate. The spirits shivered in delight over the blood offering, an eerie clacking echoing all around us.

We burst out into the day. Into the brilliantly sunny day. The only one since this accursed search had started. It felt like a slap in the face with all that had happened since I had given up on sleep and crawled out of bed this morning. Rather than the sound of birds singing, the wails of prepubescent girls met us instead.

Rafael spun in front of me, his blades moving in that beautiful dance of his, keeping my body protected.

Maxwell, Victoria, and Pea were a blue dot dancing among a sea of jointed legs.

I took a breath.

A chance.

I closed my eyes, trusting in Rafe to keep me safe. Refusing to add the twisted faces of childlike girls to my nightmares with my next deed.

The flames I had so recently claimed roared free from my being, rolling across the skittering swarm before me, harmlessly skirting Rafe, Pea and the K9s.

The world burst into molecules again as I expended my power. I used the fuel from the screaming, burning *jorōgumo* to find every creature with a similar structure in my territory and commanded my flames to *consume* them.

And then I fed the fires with every ounce of *ki* I had.

I'm sorry, Aidan, I whispered in my mind.

He would understand. If I found him and was unable to save him because I had no well of *ki* to draw upon, he would forgive me. I, however, would never forgive myself.

The fires burned fast and bright. A flash fire too fast to catch anything other than what I had instructed it to. The flames were *mine* and would obey only my *ki*. They quickly began to die, screams dying in the wind. It would have to be enough for now. I knew this was only the first assault. The foreign translucent *ki* began to creep over my vision in the absence of my natural magic, causing a nauseating haze to form over all I could see as I switched back to the living.

The stakes were too high, I pleaded with Aidan in my mind. *The refugees. I had to protect the refugees.*

I dropped to the ground as ashes fell like snow drifting from the sky.

CHAPTER TWENTY-SEVEN

"Cam," Rafael breathed.

I looked up into his faces, seeing double. A tortured expression pulled at his brows. Pea sat on his shoulder alternating between hissing and clicking in concern. She knew there was nothing she could do for me when I burned out my magic.

"I have you," he murmured, wrapping my arms around his neck as he scooped me into his arms. I swallowed hard, fighting against the vertigo as my center of balance shifted and the rocking motion aggravated the feeling of being on a small vessel during a wild storm. I shut my eyes tightly.

"Just until we reach the entrance," Rafe admonished before I could protest. "Let yourself catch your breath until then."

Max whined by his side. "I have her, ol' boy. She's okay. Don't worry."

"To think, when we first met, you made fun of me for talking to my Woody. Look at how far you've come," I joked weakly.

"I have stood corrected on many things since meeting you, Baki."

Vicky just stared at me accusingly from ten feet away.

"I'm sorry, baby girl. I promise that wasn't risky for me. That was just a little burnout."

"A little burnout, my ass," the gore-covered chest under me muttered. "I didn't realize dogs could give side-eye."

"You still have many things to learn, young grasshopper."

"You know, I'm over a century old. I'm not that young."

I untangled my hand from behind his neck and felt for his face with my eyes closed, brushing ashes from his hair, then patted his bloody head. "You're just a baby. It's okay."

I allowed myself to rest against his warmth, listening to the reassuring beat of his heart as he continued to grumble. Although I'd never admit it, I was thankful he had come along. Thankful for the distraction he was providing from the dark turn my thoughts were taking.

For better or worse, like Vicky, I could feel the remnants of my battered heart becoming lost to his. In my mind, I knew it was for the worse.

Rafael carefully lowered me to my feet once we reached the trailhead I had specified and held my arms until he was sure I was steady. Once he let go, I knelt down and pulled Aidan's shirt from the evidence bag I had stuffed in my coat pocket for Max.

"I know you know Aidan's *ki* like your own tail, buddy. But take an extra long look just for me this time, okay?" I whispered. "This one is really important. The three of us are going to do our absolute best."

Max settled a paw on my bent knee and rumbled. Rafe stood a few feet away and Vicky sat by his side, head cocked. She had only seen Max's routine a few times. Rafe's hand rubbed one of her half-mast ears. I massaged my chest, as if the motion would rid me of the tug that had taken up residence since Aidan's disappearance.

I gently set Aidan's shirt on a nearby rock so my *ki* wouldn't interfere with Aidan's signature and let him take his time. My heart dog, my incredibly special, ninety-eight-year-old Saint Bernard gazed at the piece of cloth intently, walking around it, viewing it from different angles. He sat and inhaled deeply before pawing at it, changing up the magic particles and drawing them in at different intervals, absorbing Aidan's *ki* into himself. Finally, he lifted it with his mouth and chewed thoughtfully, tasting the magic interwoven in the cotton.

He set it back on the ground and gave a low woof to let me know he was ready. My Pea, Suītopī, tapped me with her one front paw, letting me know she was also ready. I rested my hand on her back, silently conveying my gratitude for Pea and the quirk of her *ki* that twisted the DNA and extended the lifespan of the animals she healed. Thanking Pea for giving Aidan this chance because of it.

Next, Vicky stepped up and took a long sniff of the shirt, gathering the scent, allowing her to join this search as an air-scent K9.

When I straightened, I had settled back into the cold, logical place I needed to be in yet again. I gathered the cloth, carefully sealing it away and placing it in my pocket. Victoria and Max watched me attentively. Waiting for the command they knew was coming.

And with that, we began our search.

THINGS COULD NEVER be easy. Aidan and his Uncle hadn't started off at the trailhead. It took us just shy of two hours for Max to find Aidan's *ki*. Vicky confirmed the scent around half an hour after. Since then, we had been making our way through the forest for hours.

The longer we spent in the forest, the harder it was to retain my hold on the cold place. Rafael, on the other hand, appeared to have become more withdrawn the further into the Siuslaw we went. The sun beat down on us wherever the tree line broke, giving us a clear day to work with.

I sighed to myself as we broke from the trees yet again, and shaded my eyes with a hand, wishing I had thought to grab a hat or sunglasses on my way out to shield me from the midday sun. There was no particular trail that Aidan had followed, which had made the search that much more difficult when trying to pick through the dense overgrowth of a forest floor that was also spurred on by the magic of arboreal spirits. Every now and then we popped back into the Quotidian realm to verify we were on the right track, but Max was insistent. Aidan had never left the Abstruse realm.

We had gained elevation and were now in the thick of Cascade Head, overlooking the Pacific Ocean, when a sharp bark that strangled off into a growl had me sprinting from the overlook. A short series of quick yips followed Max's alert. Rafael was a silent presence behind me as the two K9s bounded up to us and then dashed forward excitedly down the trail they had found. A sense of déjà vu ran through me, sending an ominous chill trickling down my spine.

I crashed through the underbrush to meet Maxwell and Vicky, the two of them lying down, ears pricked to indicate their success. Before I allowed myself to be caught up in the scene, I immediately pulled out their toys to reward them. I played a quick, gentle game of tug-of-war with Max's old well-worn security blanket, while I threw Victoria's favorite duck keychain with my other hands, quacks sailing into the trees. She immediately pounced on the poor duck with feral joy while Max whipped his blanky around his blocky head.

Pea was already crouched on Uncle's large, prone form, working on healing him. A second pool of blood lay not far from to him, and my breath stuttered at the sight. Rafael still had not yet approached the scene, giving me my space and allowing me to do my job. I winced as I knelt down next to Uncle, taking in his wounds. As a *tanuki*, he would heal from these. He hadn't been castrated, but a section of his spine had been torn out and he appeared to have suffered a severe head injury. The head injury must have been the more serious of the two; it had mostly healed before we arrived and Pea was focused on his spine. Her one remaining forepaw and tail were painstakingly putting vertebrae back into place to make her job easier, her whiskers vibrating furiously as she concentrated on her task.

I left her to it and zeroed in on our surroundings. Avoiding what I had seen in that darkening pool of crimson next to Uncle. Putting off the pain for now. I couldn't do anything to help Pea and there wasn't anything I could change about the past. Until Uncle regained consciousness, all I had was the evidence around us.

And there was an abundance of evidence.

To someone unfamiliar with Uncle's nature, it might have seemed as though several different creatures had fought in a battle in the space around us. Limbs splintered from their trees at various heights, clearly due to the impact from a body. Fur of different coarseness, types, and lengths littered the branches. Claw marks ripped into the ground, tore the bark off trees, left gouges in the boulders, with a few ripped out claws remaining behind. Iridescent scales were scattered on the ground. The giveaway, though, was Uncle's distinctive coloring in all of these scenes. Bald he might be, but his beard and his *tanuki* shared the same coloration: a unique oil-slick gleam to the fibers. It was what had caught his Thread's eye all those years ago, Uncle liked to boast.

Uncle had waged a war against someone, or some*thing*. He had shifted into all manner of creatures to fight off their opponent and protect his nephew. A harness lay clutched in his left hand. One of the items I had tried to avoid looking at. One of the thoughts I had to try to suppress.

Vicky lay down by the harness and let out a small mournful howl.

I held back the intense feeling of terror swirling in me. I refused to give up hope.

But I faced my fears and the congealing pool. The congealing pool that held *pieces* of Aidan. Pieces of him that were still alive with *ki*. He was alive. Suffering. But the drying liquid in front of me wasn't just made up of Aidan's blood.

Yumi.

Yumi had fought for her handler. Her friend. Her companion.

She would never leave his side.

Her blood was minimal. But my mind couldn't, wouldn't, accept the possibilities.

Warm, comforting pressure enclosed me from both sides. Victoria and Maxwell. Offering what solace they could. I hugged them tight for a moment, reassuring myself they were still with me, silently swearing to them I would get vengeance on whoever had harmed Aidan and his family. A strong hand squeezed my shoulder in support. I grasped it and used Rafael's steadiness to boost my draining energy.

"Niece?" Uncle's faint voice wheezed. I wheeled to him, dropping Rafe's hand to grab his.

"Uncle," I said urgently. "Aidan. Yumi. Who did this? Do you know where they are?"

"Niece—" he began. His eyes widened. His mouth opened to say something. A familiar black mist formed over it, muffling his words.

The puzzle pieces began falling into place as I tried to wheel around to meet Rafael's sad eyes.

Instead, I fell as the last of my soul drained away.

CHAPTER TWENTY-EIGHT

I woke slowly. A mouth full of cotton greeted me. My body felt as though I had been awake for the past week, which wasn't too far off from the truth. If I didn't have my immunity to fire, I would have sworn a pack of *bulgae* had played tug-of-war with my body, charbroiling my innards through and through in the process. The quietest chirp and a nudge at my cheek let me know Pea was with me, wherever that was. However, there was a distinct emptiness to the space. A sense of knowing when loved ones weren't there.

Victoria and Maxwell were gone. Woodrow, at least, was at home with Cheuksin. I hoped.

I attempted to sit up but abruptly stopped when I felt them. Everything else, Aidan, Pea, the K9s, the Neskowin territory, *everything* was forgotten. The world around me shrank down to the sensation encircling both wrists. I couldn't *breathe.*

He shackled me.

I couldn't move. Time stopped. No. Time didn't stop. Time flashed backwards without my permission. Millennia of my worst years as a slave flooded my mind as my chest heaved with the need to get oxygen into lungs that no longer worked as well as they should.

My inability to control my shift and my masters' frustration with me.
Being forced to take the flame and losing control over and over again.

The burns throughout my body as it attempted to heal itself.

Infected with diseases repeatedly until I could manipulate the viruses so that I might cure and ward entire villages.

Taking the souls of the innocent rather than evil.

He had shackled *me.*

A brutal slap across the face forced me to take a deep inhale and chains rattled from where they were attached to the wall behind me, sending unpleasant vibrations through my arms as I startled. Pea hissed and growled at me as she waved her tail, pointing her forepaw at the chain emphatically.

I shuddered. She was right. These were manacles. Not slave bands. Not the same thing. The fact I was chained stressed that fact. A mistake on the *kariudo's* part. I wondered at his choice of restraint. It was a particularly cruel decision after our talks and yet…it was one I could break free of easily. I would need to choose my timing carefully.

I gazed around my surroundings and looked back down at Pea.

"Told you our homecoming would be via dungeon," I informed her with a shaky laugh.

The sensation of water dripping slowly down my body was unavoidable, no matter where I moved. The conditions of my prison cell had worsened considerably since the last time I had been here. At that time, I had been on the other side of opaque walls holding me in. Small cracks splintered the ceiling and wall, allowing water to seep through. I would have preferred a water cell to this incessant dripping. But, perhaps that was the point. Mildew permeated the air around me. As I lifted the blanket covering me, I wrinkled my nose at the black mold eating away a corner of the fabric. It was a small favor that I wouldn't fall ill to mold exposure. Pea chattered in disgust at the sight.

My body snapped to attention at the sound of quiet footfalls, muffled further by the wards of the prison cell. I winced as the motion pulled at the bindings around my wrists and rubbed at them. I stopped when I realized what I was doing. How the motion mimicked *him.*

My mind emptied as he appeared in front of my cell wall. He dared to look diminished somehow. I fought back the instinctive urge to shift into my *haetae* at the sight of him and the reminder of his betrayal. At the absence of my K9s at my side.

"Where are they?" I snarled.

"Safe," the *kariudo* said simply.

"As if I would trust your word ever again. Tell me what you are and where my K9s and friends are."

"You know that I am the *kariudo*, I don't think you want to know more than that, Chun-Hei."

I sucked in a breath at the name I had discarded a lifetime ago, unable to hide my reaction. Pea hissed and spat at him. The lack of effect my old name had on him was noted distantly in my mind.

"You don't know what I want or what I can handle, *Huntsman*. Clearly."

He ran both hands through his hair, pulling at the ends as he reached them, somehow managing to look even more exhausted than he already did, and dropped his glamours.

My recoil was instantaneous. An unconscious reaction that was part prehistoric brain and an enormous part trauma. I scrambled to the furthest corner of the cell my chains would allow as my mind attempted to process what it saw before me.

Rafael Sugiyama's countenance had transformed to that of an *oni's*. As if that wasn't traumatic enough with my history, his face wasn't flesh, but the skull of an *oni*; however, he had elaborate antlers rather than horns protruding from his skull. The rest of his body was incorporeal. A black mist that occasionally parted to reveal the body of different animals, but most frequently, a stag. My breath came faster and I began to sweat as my memories of the Night Parade returned.

Before my mind could fully adjust and adapt to what it saw, Rafael, the male, was before my eyes again.

"You can't look at my form too long without going mad with fear," he said without emotion. "Only animals can."

"What are you?" I whispered again.

His body sagged. I watched as he mouthed an incantation, bit his thumb to spread some blood, marring the wall in front of me, before he stepped through the ward. He sat on the bed opposite of me, like his body could no longer hold his own weight, and stared up at the leaky ceiling. A droplet fell and hit him directly in the eye, but he didn't bother to blink. The remnants of the drop fell over the edge of his eyelid and ran down his face, like a lone tear. I leaned away from him, attempting to create more distance.

"You know that I am *hafu*." The last word oozed from his tongue with so much self-disgust. That single word told me more about the *kariudo* than the entire time we had spent together. I recalled how he had said it when we first met. There had been no discernable affect in his expression that I would have found notable. His tone had been lacking in emotion. Now, I could practically taste the internalized stigma he held toward himself.

"As we've briefly discussed, I am from Brazil. Back when the Japanese began first immigrating to the country in the early 1900s, Ryūj—, the *kami*," Rafael quickly corrected himself. His tone went dead as he continued. "He sent the *kariudo* of the time to hunt down the *yōkai* who had taken advantage of the boats taking the Japanese immigrants to Brazil to seek asylum in South America. While on his hunts, the *kariudo* spotted a young Tupí woman he coveted and raped her. I was conceived. Because of the circumstances of my conception and unusual birth, my mother's mind was never the same; she became a lone soul. As such, I am not half-Quote, but half-Perigean and *oni*."

Unusual birth? I held back my question. I didn't need to know.

I could do the math. The *kariudo* he spoke of. He was the same one who came for Oliver's mother. The same one I consumed once upon a time. I felt ill, recalling the memories I had absorbed. The cruelties he had committed and the joy he had found in them.

The *kariudo* had said all this while staring up at the ceiling. His head dropped then, and he stared at his hands, turning and studying them. "Turned out, the ancestral Abstruse blood that ran through my mother was none other than Anhangá's."

There was a long pause as he seemed to collect himself. I searched through the knowledge I had acquired over my long life, but most of my years had been spent in the East. Only a fraction of it had been in the West.

"Who is Anhangá?" I asked hesitantly.

"He is many things—a protector of the forests, and a guide to Guajupiá, the Land Without Evils."

He was right, I was better off not knowing. The gods had interfered enough in my life, and I had the bloodline of yet another one here.

"Once he felt my power come into the world, he came looking for me. Once found, he activated the full potential of my *ki* and took me under his tutelage until he felt I could manage on my own. Unfortunately, after he left, my father had learned of my existence and came for me."

His head lifted then and I was startled by the fierce look in his eyes. "I can never repay you enough for killing him."

If betrayal was his method of repayment, I'd forgive him his debt.

"This assignment was going to be my last hunt. Regardless of what my orders were going to be, I was planning to leave and let disobedience take my life. Fuck, I don't even know if it would kill me. I just knew that I couldn't continue this existence anymore. Receiving the task of returning the Thread to that *kami* was the confirmation I needed for my decision."

"What changed your mind then?" My anger was starting to simmer again.

"You."

What the hell kind of simple answer was that? Before I could go off, he continued.

"Your continued existence, Chun-Hei, as the last *haetae* is not a well-kept secret. Not to those of us who have access to the dead. I have always known about you. The dead who have passed through you worship you, Baki. You gave them peace. Something they never had in their lives. They never shut up about you. Those who lived long lives after being saved from a disaster or plague sing your praises. Your mother is prouder than you could possibly know."

I shifted uncomfortably, deeply discomfited by what he had unveiled. Worship was not something I deserved after what I had done. I knew why Theo had really shown up one day proclaiming a desire to learn all things Search and Rescue. It wasn't to find the missing. He was there to monitor my karmic balance and to ensure that I did not tip too far toward evil myself. That was his true assignment. Whether he knew that I knew was another story.

"Then you have not met all my undead," I said quietly.

"As long as I never knew where you were," he brushed off my comment, as if I had never spoken, "so long as I never had that knowledge, I could get away without fulfilling the genocide. I never wanted to be responsible for one. But then I met you. And you gave me hope again."

"Hope to do what?" I snarled. "Hope to betray me? Hope to harm my friends? Hope to eradicate one of the last guardians of this Earth?"

He straightened. "Hope to overthrow the *kami*."

Pea and I stared at the *kariudo* for a hot second, then started cackling. I bent over, crossing my arms and chains over my stomach, howling while Pea chittered at my side.

"Are you *mad*? This is the *kami* who killed Ryūjin. What in Yomi makes you think we could take them? And even if we did, who would rule Ryūgū-jō then?"

The insane male just gave me a flat look.

Oh, he really *was* mad. He'd been spending too much time around this *kami*.

"Listen, you might be suicidal, but I'm not. I'm going to have to give this a hard pass and go back to feeling super betrayed by you. 'Kay, thanks, bye." I laid back down on my bed and stared up into the ceiling that was pregnant with mildewy rain, counting down the seconds until one landed in my own eye. Maybe it would be my mouth. This could be my new fucked-up game. Taking bets on what orifice of my body befouled water droplets landed in to while away my imprisonment.

"Sure. The way I see it, you have two choices left: You can die a coward's death and leave the imposter to eat your liver, seeing as how you're currently imprisoned in his dungeon. Or you could at least try. But go ahead and give up."

Before I could even begin to conceive of a thought to give the *kariudo,* a piece of my mind, he had disappeared. The smear on the wall vanished. Every trace of him gone. Not even the sound of footfalls to announce his departure.

I should have taken the time to question his vanishing act that first day on the mountain. It might have saved me a lot of pain and heartache. But then, I could have never predicted, on this realm, or the Quote's, that the male was the descendent of a death god.

"What do you think, Pea? Do we do it?" He still hadn't even told me where anyone was. Nothing other than *safe*. Clearly his idea of *safe* and mine were on extreme opposite ends of the spectrum.

Pea's nose wrinkled.

"I know. This wasn't on our timetable. But let's be honest, were we ever going to be ready?"

She huffed at me as a lilac glow settled over me. I smiled.

"I love you too, but you can't protect me forever. I can't live like this forever. I'm going to shift for my last time someday, and if I don't at least try, we'll both regret it, and you know it. That male can go walk off a long plank, for all I care; we have each other."

I sighed. Much as I hated to admit it, I was a little glad my K9s and friends weren't here. So long as the *kariudo* was telling the truth and they were safe, then I didn't want them anywhere near this realm when shit went down.

A FEW HOURS or days passed, perhaps months. Each cell of this dungeon was contained in a temporal snare. Whether time passed more quickly or slowly than the rest of the world depended on your so-called accommodations. It had honestly been too long for me to recall which type I was in. Not to mention the passage of time was difficult to measure when you were deep under a sea and held in a prison cell, regardless of whether or not the walls were solid, opaque, or bars. Boredom was boredom. Pea was good company, but there was only so much entertainment a *haetae* and a *shikigami* could come up with when all they had to work with was dank water and fire. I did manage to come up with at least thirty retorts that were absolute fire for the huntsman's *coward* comment.

I recognized the footfalls this time and realized every time I heard the *kariudo's* approach, he had been giving me the courtesy of announcing his arrival. He obviously didn't need to bother, and it was a fact about him that I had let slip as I'd relaxed around him over the week I'd spent in his company. Something I wouldn't allow myself to do again.

The *kariudo* mouthed a different incantation this time and the wall in front of me dropped completely. He frowned at the elaborate games of tic-tac-toe carved into the mold in the back left corner.

I shrugged. "Girls gotta do what girls gotta do to pass the time."

Thank the Quotes these girls were immortal, seeing as how no honey buckets were provided to us. On the other hand, maybe we really could have had some fun with that. Like summon a certain Outhouse Goddess to get us the fuck out of here.

He shook his head. "It will be time soon. What is your decision?"

I patted my numerous pockets. "Oh damn. My wallet's missing. Sorry. I can't show you whether or not I have 'Organ Donor' marked on my driver's license. Darn. Guess you'll just have to wait to find out like everyone else."

Something stabbed me somewhere, probably my conscience, but I refused to acknowledge it. This male had taken me away from nearly everything I loved for his own agenda.

That's not exactly true. That stupid annoying bitch in the back of my mind prickled. *He's trying to save his people. And Ryūjin's. Yours. It's not only his agenda.*

I ignored her.

His dark gaze studied me at length before he gave a stiff nod. A flash blinded me. As my eyes cleared, I noticed a large black fog had formed just behind him. The fog slowly dissipated and my breath caught in my throat.

CHAPTER TWENTY-NINE

Funny how one moment you think your body is numb and unable to take any more hits. Then some new revelation drags you down the highway like roadkill and you realize you never even knew what the definition of the word numb meant to begin with. Or the word betrayed for that matter.

On the other hand, the silver lining to being numb is that you don't feel. Your nerve endings are ruined. Your ability to react is null and void. So when my gaze shifted from Dr. Aoki to the *kariudo,* I simply lifted an eyebrow.

"When?" I asked quietly.

The regret shone through on his face. One of the few moments he had allowed his mask to drop and his vulnerability to be featured. He needn't have bothered.

I had no capacity left to care.

"When I arrived in America," he said, his volume matching mine. His eyes tracked me warily.

Something in me cracked. Pain flared through me. I ignored it. If there was one goddamned fact in these worlds I was used to, it was that the males in my life went behind my back and shattered me. Pain was welcome, it was familiar. I could deal with physical pain. It was the emotional pain that killed me slowly.

His eyes went wide at the same time, looking all over me. I didn't want to know, shoving his words about the state of my soul deep in me. A little bit of horror bled into his eyes, sitting next to the regret. A sick sense of satisfaction filled me at the sight of it.

"That was two days before you ever even came to me." Every word of mine came out slower, snapping with more force.

The disoriented woman standing next to the *kariudo* finally seemed to notice where she was and started at my voice, darting behind the huntsman. Poor choice of rescuers. Her first inclination to run from him when I had seen her in the woods had been wiser.

He sighed heavily and led Aoki to the other bed, sitting her on it, then attempted to take a step toward us.

Sighed.

Quotes have mercy, the male had the audacity to sigh.

Everything that had happened. His small actions. All of the little details became vividly clear in the forefront of my mind. They were all I could see now, like a sudden brick wall obscuring my sight.

The black foggy mist that wrapped around Dr. Aoki that first time Woody alerted and I spotted her in the woods. Which happened to coincide with my first interaction with the *kariudo*.

The flash of light as she vanished, like the flashes of light every time a soul died in his presence.

That flash of desire in his eyes. The light touches. The insidious methods he had used to slowly gain my trust.

No. Not only my trust. But my *admiration.* My *affection.*

Pieces of my shattered heart.

All lies. Only for him to drain my soul to use me for his own gains.

Without conscious thought, I shifted as my rage reached its pinnacle. Shifted in the split second when he began taking that step toward myself and Pea. My *ki* may have been depleted, but my abilities to shift and consume souls were simply a part of my being. As natural as eating or breathing.

Distantly, I heard Pea give a warning shriek, but it was too late.

Rafael Sugiyama stepped into me, as I pierced his heart.

The *kariudo* was not evil.

But he had never anticipated that *I* was not good.

"Was she ever missing?" I snapped, losing my temper at last after his *kamis' damned sigh.*

He held my gaze steadily, my height now above his as he sagged from my horn. A dark shadow enveloped the room as a large creature swam by. Instead of answering my question, he reached to touch my face as the shadow passed and the cell brightened again. It was a face he hadn't seen before. His hand dropped when he was unable to reach me, and he smiled sadly.

"Look at you, Camellia Kimoto. Absolutely stunning. You should never have to hide who you are."

If I could, I would have shook my head at his commentary, but his life overwhelmed me as he began to fade. I sank with him, my knees buckling, images of the past overtaking the dungeon. Sank as the vertigo from the shift flooded me and I could no longer hold myself and him upright. Drowned in his memories of evil deeds and my own.

A woman in labor, no longer screaming in pain. Her eyes are glassy and her breath is shallow. A Jesuit is attending the delivery. The child is born dead. His mother follows him in death in the same breath, still attached by the umbilical cord. As the Jesuit goes to lay the still child on his mother's skin, the babe takes a breath and begins wailing. As the mother died on the same exhale, so does she return to life with her son's inhale. I see the name form on the Jesuit's lips as his eyes widen. Rafael. God has healed.

A small boy exploring the jungles with a woman. Gone. It is the only word I could use to describe the expression on the woman's face, though the barest touches of life still spark in her eyes as she watches over her boy. It is fear, overwhelmed by a sense of detachment from the world. The boy attracts Death to him, and Death fascinates him in kind. She cannot see Him, but He watches over them with interest. The boy, with his black hair that carries walnut undertones, stumbles through the rainforest, uncaring of the dangers that would lurk for most. His cherubic face charmed by the animals he meets and befriends, both alive and dead. Every time he befriends the dead, the fear rises higher in his mother and the detachment grows.

Time flashes forward a few years. The boy is older, but not by much. His mother is dying. A wasting disease. He has never been ill, he doesn't understand fully, but his mother has been sick frequently and he does his best. It's not good enough this time. He watches, frightened, as her spirit rises. A blinding flash of light appears and he ducks behind the chair in their small home. An enormous golden stag stands next to his mother and a cruel laugh rattles the shelter when the being sees where the boy is poorly hidden. I am unable to hear what is said, but the stag shakes his head as the boy talks and he beckons the boy to follow him instead. They vanish.

It is many years later. The boy is now a man. One that I recognize. Hardened. He no longer carries the cherubic innocence of the boy in the jungle. I watch as he hunts the yōkai *that have trespassed upon the rainforest and waterways and glutted themselves upon the land. He is an uncommonly good hunter as he slaughters* yōkai *one after another, his expression flat. A flash of light blinds me every time a soul untethers from its body and passes to the next realm. Death watches from afar, approvingly.*

More years pass by. My guts wrench as a familiar face enters the scene and memories from a past soul superimpose themselves with this scene. The former kariudo. *He coerces a* kuro bōzu *to ensnare Death's bloodline. I can only watch as the shadowy figure creeps its way into his home as the male sleeps, and slides its rotting tongue into his mouth, so that it may siphon the male's breath from his lungs, sending him from sleep to full unconsciousness. The* yōkai *further ensures the former* kariudo's *success by sliding his decaying tongue over the male's face, over his eyes, into his ears, probing deep into his nostrils, spreading disease of all manners. I know that in a few short hours, this male will be deathly ill when he wakes from his unnatural sleep. Once the male is incapacitated, the former* kariudo *slides the slave bands on and whispers the incantation to activate them. I can feel the deep satisfaction of the former* kariudo, *the cloying evil from his memories still clinging to me despite the decades that have passed since I absorbed his soul.*

I stared at the light dying in Rafael's eyes. It had never crossed my mind to question his name after he had said he was Tupí. I wondered if he knew the origins of his name. The Jesuit certainly hadn't known that it had not been the Christian God who had healed them. I withdrew my horn and watched the huntsman's body dispassionately as it began to break apart before me. Images of his past danced before me. No, this *kariudo* had not been evil.

In the absence of my natural *ki*, the foreign magic swamped me all the faster and my vision tunneled. I barely heard the screaming behind me as the violence of his life and the slaughter of his own kind triggered memories of my own past.

I am sobbing. Screaming. Begging the males holding my family to let them go. Pleading to any Creator willing to listen to save us. The noon sun shines brightly down on us and sweat reeking of fear soaks my neckline.

"Shift," the mukwa *official commands me. But my* ki *is wild and uncontrolled. Though I am an adult, under times of stress it is unpredictable. When I don't, an arrow sticky with sap from the hemlock joins the men holding my mother. She does not falter though. Instead, she looks at me steadily in the eyes and begins to sing softly, calmly, and nods. The sun catches the tears falling from her eyes.*

I shift. And I do as the mukwa *orders. To save one parent, I kill another. The world cannot afford to lose its guardians. Its what I have always been taught.*

When I finally recover from the replay that is my father's lifespan, I look up to see my mother fall. The arrow laced with hemlock sap speared into her liver.

I save no one but myself.

QUOTES DAMN IT all. She was beautiful. Rafael took in Camellia's form before him, ignoring the body and the chaos below, as he floated above them all, an incorporeal mist. She had alluded to her age, but he had underestimated her. He had done so repeatedly to his own fault. Chun-Hei was one of the first *haetae* of Gojoseon. She wasn't just centuries old, she was millennia.

Unlike the *haetae* tattooed on the body laid out on the floor, she had a stunning dragon's head which flowed seamlessly into a strong leonine body. Feathers that were burnished gold with hints of burgundy lined the back of her limbs, and a pair of small wings with the same coloration sat folded in at her withers. A tail with a vicious spade at its end whipped in distress. Also unlike any *haetae* he had heard tales of, she was a gleaming onyx black with hints of cobalt. To complete her was an elaborate jade thorax, protecting her heart and vital organs. He wondered if those too were as fragmented as her soul. He cringed. The damage he had done to her soul, draining her so that she wouldn't be able to fight, then bringing her to this place, had caused extensive damage to the splintered pieces. Something he was incapable of repairing.

And finally. The spiraled golden horn jutting from her head siphoning the evil he had done throughout his lifetimes from him. He could feel nothing but relief for it. Perhaps he would know some peace now, as all the dead he had met had allegedly experienced after meeting their end through this female.

She was singing a nursery rhyme in Korean under her breath. Based on the dissociated look in her eyes, Rafael wasn't sure she was even aware of it. He translated as she sang softly.

> Mountain bunny, bunny,
> Where are you going?
> Hopping, hopping as you run,
> Where are you going?

The low, slow tones in which she chanted the tune while killing him gave the old folksong a haunted quality.

"This is the creature you are so fond of?" The voice somehow took up the entire space around them, despite its current lack of form.

"Her name is Camellia." Something about whittling her down to *creature* felt wrong, although in the end, that's what they all were. And to be viewed as a creature by this being was not an insult, but a compliment.

He sensed the amusement mingling in the space around him. "Am I to assume this Camellia is the reason why you changed your mind about coming back? It wasn't so long ago you told me you were done with this realm. That I was to stop tethering your soul back to your body so you could continue with your task in protecting the innocents from the hunt. You had told me you were tired. That you were tired of protecting *this one* from those who are hunting her."

His Grandfather motioned to the *haetae* before him. "You have been at this mission for little more than a century. This guardian has been doing this task for thousands upon thousands of years. She has done evil. She has done unaccountable good. She has taken it upon herself to kill her own loved ones in the name of justice. She has been forged in the brutal fires of unspeakable horrors to become the guardian she is today.

"And you say that you are *tired*," the voice boomed around them in disappointment.

If Rafael had a form, he would have cringed in shame. As it was, his mist pulled together into a dense cloud of black.

"That I am tired has merit," he retorted. "The fact I am tired of what I do shows that I, at the very least, still possess *empathy*, even after all these years. You should be grateful, *Grandfather*, that I am tired, because my fatigue means I still care. I needed something, anything, to show me I was still making a difference. Was this female one of these reasons? Yes. But beyond Camellia Kimoto were the beings she surrounds herself with. The brave *shikigami* who survived a severance from her master and put her master's Thread back together piece by piece. The abandoned and abused dogs who have found new purpose in the homes of this female and her family. Likewise, the abandoned and abused *people* who have found new purpose in her very presence and have become her family. What do I know of family? You and I certainly have not been one.

"The difference is that all of these people and animals allowed me to feel as if I belonged. And I betrayed them because I saw the smallest sliver of hope that I might enact greater change than I have been able to accomplish on my own. No, Grandfather. I *must* go back this time, so I might have the opportunity to redeem myself after all is said and done."

The presence coalesced into the form of a large golden stag before him. Rafael wasn't sure how it was possible for a deer to look skeptical, but Anhangá managed it often enough in this form.

"Do you think it's even possible to do so at this point? You shackled this female. I am not certain you truly understand what that did to her. What memories that brought forward. She killed you before she even gave you the opportunity to take them off, that's how angry she is with you about them. Not a single interaction you have had with her has been genuine."

That wasn't the case. That wasn't the case at all. Rafael thought back to all the small gestures between them. The first time she touched him. How his heart had pounded. A reaction he had never had to another being before. The way she had made him felt understood. Accepted. Still, he kept his thoughts to himself, they would have no value here.

"It doesn't matter if it's possible. What matters is that I make the effort to *try.*"

His Grandfather tsked. "And look at what you did to her soul. It is a tragedy. What good is she to us if she breaks apart with the next shift. I taught you more finesse than this mess here." He waved at the *haetae* whose eyes were empty, then he waved to Rafael's body.

"Mmmm. Not much body left for you to try with though." The stag squinted. "Looks like you have a pair of feet left."

Rafael sighed, sending his cloud of mist scattering throughout the space. "Grandfather. Just tether my soul already and be done with it."

CHAPTER THIRTY

Before Rafael's body disintegrated completely, the world froze. The first indication of this fact was the absolute silence. The second was the ashes of his body becoming suspended in the air. I looked around suspiciously. Dr. Aoki was midscream, Pea had frozen with her tail wrapped around my left forelimb, uselessly tugging at it to pull me out of this headspace. The shock of the utter stillness knocked me fully from my past.

"Before my favored grandson withers away completely, I thought you and I might have a word, Chun-Hei." The voice, like the silence, was absolute. But there was no evidence of anyone else in this dungeon.

I had gone over a century without hearing my former name once, at least without witnessing someone die horribly. Now, since I had been kidnapped, I had heard it multiple times.

"Who are you? And *where* are you?" I asked cautiously, still dazed from the whiplash I had experienced.

"You are no idiot. You saw my grandson's deeds and misdeeds just now; you know exactly who I am."

Contrary to popular opinion. I *was* an idiot. I hadn't considered the consequences of killing off a death god's favorite ancestor.

"Now. This…" What remained of the *kariudo* shifted, as if kicked. A foot, the left one I thought, went flying and bounced off the wall. "This one is a bit of an idiot."

I noted he was referring to Rafael in present tense. I supposed that made sense, if the dead continued their lives in one's realm. I shifted uncomfortably.

"Because my grandson is an idiot and has no idea how to gain a female's trust, I find myself doing the work for him. You need to know your loved ones are safe. The half-wit, despite his rebellious ways, keeps the secret of Guajupiá unless I or the others decree otherwise. I hadn't realized how dire you had become to his cause, otherwise I would have authorized it, as I had our other visitors. So. Come along now, little *haetae.*"

My mind was reeling. Guajupiá? Visitors? Dire to Rafael's cause? What cause? To overthrow the *kami?* I wasn't sure why this god would care about that. Not to mention I was still talking to an invisible voice in the room, so I also wasn't sure how I was supposed to *come along*, as he called it. Did that mean I had to die?

Laughter filled the room. "No, little guardian. You will not die. Think of it as similar to carrying a visitor's pass that grants you access to a high-security facility."

Fantastic. The god I was assuming was Anhangá could read my thoughts. My situation just kept improving.

"You keep referring to me as a god, and I understand that is your frame of reference, but that is not what I am. That is simply the assignation given to me by the Christians that came onto our land and forced us into a mold of their understanding. *Entity* or *being* would be a more apt description. I am no god."

I still couldn't see anything. I couldn't even hear anything outside of this apparent *entity's* voice. But I could sense the amusement in the air at my thoughts. It was deeply unsettling. Before I could react further, one of those blasted blinding flashes filled the room.

I had thought myself unsettled a moment before. That had clearly been an illusion of comfort. The fragments that Pea had so carefully collected exploded into particles as my consciousness drifted into the ether for a split second. Then, as quickly as they had separated, they recoiled back into me, the reverberations echoing through my entire being, causing my fragments to rattle and ram into one another. I fell hard, landing on my back with a thud, the back of my skull rebounding off the ground, my wings crunching under my weight.

I laid there, winded, attempting to get my breath back, as well as my senses. As they slowly came back online, the sounds of gentle waves and the calls of birds were the first thing I noticed. I fell to my side and wiggled my four limbs, feeling the sand beneath my body and the tepid water lapping at my feet, soaking my fur and feathers. I felt naked without Pea's tail wrapped around some part of me. Vulnerable. When I opened my eyes, I had to squint against the brightness of the sun and the brilliance of the blue sky.

I turned my head to find a massive glowing canid panting in my face above me. The canine looked like a fox and a hyena had a baby and then someone gave that baby steroids. It had a fox's general coloring, but long lanky legs, and a thick hunched neck, complete with a roached mane, and stood around six feet tall. And a glow, a blinding glow surrounding all of it.

"Chrysocyon brachyurus. Maned wolf," Anhangá said, his foxy mouth wide in a manic grin. "I thought to take a canid form to endear myself to you. Do you like it?" He waved a paw down his body in a movement no foreleg should have been capable of. "Now, follow me, and stay exactly on my path. While I have permitted you to be here, we wouldn't want to anger Nhanderuvuçú with your presence, though he does not generally leave his hut these days."

I rolled to my feet and shook the sand from my fur and wings. My body was numb—the toll of the adrenaline dump, shift, teleportation, and fall too much for it. I couldn't remember the last time I had remained in this form for this long. The vertigo was present, but more manageable than it had been in years. Decades. I wondered if it was because of our location.

"You only had one, possibly two, shifts left in you before your soul would have permanently fractured," Anhangá tossed over his maned withers with far too much casual ease as I followed behind him. "When my grandson drained your soul to bring you to Ryūgū-jō, he did some irreparable damage to it, I'm afraid. I did what I could to tether as much of your soul back to your body when I brought you here, but it was a one-time fix. I was able to tether the individual pieces of your soul to your body. I was unable to knit your soul back together. You might have four or five shifts left in you now if you're careful. Especially if my grandson does not drain your soul again. That was particularly foolish of him."

I stumbled in the sand at his words. I hadn't realized I was that close.

Death continued as if he hadn't just rocked my world yet again. "As I was saying, my grandson is an idiot. I do not expect you to forgive him. However, you did just experience his life, and I wanted to provide some context. Rafael does not know how to experience or reciprocate relationships—of any kind—beyond master or trainer. He has never had one. Although he loved his mother dearly, she was lost to her trauma and was not present in mind. By the age of three, he was her caregiver. He is a huntsman and a protector by nature. That is what his bloodline dictates. Rafael particularly excels at killing to protect. What he fails at is recognizing emotions. I apologize for that. That is my failing."

"You say all this as if he is alive and I will have to continue to deal with him," I commented while attempting to stretch out my wings that had folded in terrible angles during the fall. I rolled my neck as I did so, taking in my surroundings. The sand was pleasantly warm under my feet, not cool, nor broiling hot from the sun. Lush tropical greenery surrounded us with brilliantly vivid colors while what I assumed were birds called out to each other in the dense vegetation to my right.

An odd sound erupted from the maned wolf; a half roar, half bark. "Of course he is alive, Chun-Hei. You cannot possibly think it is that easy to kill the ancestor of one such as myself, can you?"

Well fuck a duck. I really really had. I closed my eyes. I wondered if the *kami* knew about the *kariudo's* true heritage. If he did, it would make the huntsman so much more valuable. A *kariudo* who was nearly eternal as opposed to immortal? A slave he wouldn't have to replace and train? No wonder he had been willing to risk the consequences of telling me his mission and didn't undergo fatal side effects when he said my former name.

The sense of betrayal I felt grew even stronger as I recalled the fear I had felt on his behalf when he had seized on my back porch. He had known regardless of if he had lived or died, he would simply return to his body. While everyone else around him panicked and fought to save his life, using up valuable resources. What's more, the act had further pushed me toward his side, believing I could trust him if he was willing to put himself at that kind of risk.

On the bright side, I could just repeatedly kill the male every time he got on my nerves without repercussions. Silver linings.

"I know the temptation to murder him is strong—I have done so many times myself—but please, for my sake, do not do so. He gets rather morose and whiny when he is killed and then I have to listen to him as I tie his soul back to his body, it is rather tiresome."

My bushy eyebrow arched. His own grandfather killed him? Repeatedly? No wonder the current *kariudo* had some socialization issues. Still. I didn't forgive that easily.

"I don't expect you to. You will probably want to shift back now; we will be encountering some people you recognize soon," he continued.

I didn't want to, despite the mixed feelings I had about being in this form. Being a *haetae* was so deeply entrenched in trauma that I could no longer separate the emotions from the freedom of being in my natural form. And now, being in this form was tainted by the foreign *ki* that fought for control. I couldn't remember the last time I had spent this much time as a *haetae*. Whether it was this place or whatever Anhangá had done to tie my soul back together, everything was simply...calmer in my body. Even so, one simply did not disregard an entity of death. I transformed back into my human form.

I had forgotten about the gore and general filth that had covered my clothing before I had shifted. I was anything but stealthy as I crunched behind Anhangá, soot and flakes of dried blood falling off of me to taint the paradise we were in. The *kariudo* had called this the Land Without Evils and here I was just shedding evil all over it.

Good thing I wasn't going to Hell, Yomi, or any of the underworlds when I died, thanks to Ryujin and what he had done to my soul. More silver linings.

"You might actually be a good match for my grandson," Anhangá commented idly as we summited a small hill. "Your inner commentary is just as morose and whiny as his. No wonder he likes you. Ah, here we are."

Before I could process his statement, a sharp yip and a duet of long howl-rumbles whipped my head from the entity down to the clearing at the bottom of the hill where Maxwell, Woodrow, and Victoria were sprinting to greet us. Where Aidan, Yumi, and the Uncles sat near a hut. Cheuksin, Oliver, Theo, and Kenichi sat on a fallen tree across from them.

"They're *dead?*" I whispered in horror. How did Kenichi even get involved? What was happening in Skamania? I would figure out how to murder the *kariudo* for good after spending months in a temporal snare torturing him. He had assured me they were safe. Dead did not equal safe.

"You have a fascinating brain, the way you jump to conclusions. Why would full-blooded *tanukis* and a *kamikiri* be in Guajupiá, little *haetae?* Or even a *tanuki*-gean cannagh hybrid? They don't come from my lands. They would be with Izanami in Yomi. And a Korean deity?" He bopped my nose with a paw the size of my face, basically face-palming me, and shook his maned head. "They are alive, much like you, just visiting, but will give the appearance of death to everyone else where their bodies lay, including the *kami*, most importantly. Holding their souls here keeps them safe for the time being."

I didn't have time for relief. As I processed the information, Max, Woody, and Vicky reached us. They were translucent and gave off a soft shimmer that radiated peace. My arms opened wide automatically and we all went down in a tangle of arms and legs and frantic puppy kisses, their forms solid despite their lack of bodies. I didn't care about relief. My K9s were here. They were alive; that was all I needed. Aidan and Yumi were okay. The Uncles were okay. Cheuksin and Olly were still breathing. Kenichi was with us. Everyone here was okay. I couldn't let myself think of the others who weren't here and why they were missing from this group.

"Sheriff Danly and his wife still breathe. Leaving a Quotidian law enforcement officer dead would have created far too many complications. Come, lets meet up with the rest."

The K9s raced ahead of the two of us, meeting up with Yumi and darted off for a game of chase in the surf. I stared at Aidan's K9, blinking hard as she shifted between appearing healthy and whole, to injured with savage gouges tearing down her side.

Aidan and the Uncles stood upon our arrival in the clearing. Not a wound upon Aidan or his jovial Uncle at first. Then they flickered. I already knew of Uncle's injuries. But Aidan.

His face laid open, flayed from his left ear to the point of his chin, bone exposed, half of his ear missing. The tears in his clothing revealed his ribs beneath and the damage to his abdomen. I didn't get further than that before his image flickered back to the Aidan I knew and loved. His skin smooth and freckled, unmarred once again by attack he had endured.

I stared at my friend silently. No one knew what I had gone through, but it was clear to everyone on our team that their director had PTSD. Aidan nodded quietly and spread his arms wide.

"I'm okay, Cam. I promise. I haven't left you. Not like others in the past. I'm right here." He stepped forward and wrapped me in a hug. "I'm right here," he murmured into my hair as he rubbed my back. "I'm not going anywhere. Despite the *kami's* best efforts."

"*Mates*," the Uncles whispered together. Aidan and I simultaneously gave them the finger. I was dimly aware of Cheuksin swatting them in the back of the head from where she had also stood after Aidan's embrace.

"After the vertebrae I sacrificed for you, Nephew?" Uncle grumbled. "See if I ever do that for you again."

"This is all nice and sappy and charming, but we have real issues to discuss." Anhangá sat on the fallen tree as if he were shaped like a human rather than a canid. "And it is not the *kami*, though he is part of the greater problem."

I disentangled from Aidan fully and looked at the entity before I stepped in to give my tiny friend a hug. She was here as herself, solid, with no transparency. Which allowed me to see the burns that ravaged her body. For her to still look like this without having healed meant that she had endured far worse. I cringed in her grasp.

"*Aigoo*. Stop that. What you did, your flames, they saved us. Far more would have died without your intervention." She swatted me too. Cheuksin could swat me all she wanted, my guilt wasn't going anywhere. I just hugged her harder before letting go and gestured to everyone in the clearing. Oliver and Kenichi remained on their log, looking exhausted.

"Why have you or the huntsman brought all these people here? And what do you mean, *greater problem*? The *kami* isn't a big enough problem to begin with?"

"Tell me, little one. How are the guardians faring in your world?"

CHAPTER THIRTY-ONE

How are the guardians faring in your world? The words kept echoing in my mind. They weren't. In the meantime, I stayed hidden, doing next to nothing as our world went to shit because of it.

I shrunk into myself. Anhangá nodded. "This *kami* may have sought out a few lineages in a genocidal rampage in a mad task to cure himself, but he is not alone and you have been aware of this. As has my grandson."

Rafael had known about the other guardian races being exterminated? It was irrational, but my sense of betrayal grew again. We had never spoken on the topic, so there was no reason for the emotion coursing through me, but I still couldn't shake the feeling that he had omitted it purposely.

The absurdly large maned wolf eyed me with amusement before he continued, "Yes, my grandson knew. He has been on a task to find out who has been pulling the *kami's* strings. It is why he allowed himself to be captured by the *kuro bōzu* and his father."

I had a sickening feeling that was beginning to develop alongside the betrayal and I was nearly certain my suspicions were correct as I recalled the images that had played through my mind.

"Did he allow himself to be captured by the *kuro bōzu* and his sperm donor for this so-called mission for the greater good? Or was he simply a young man desperate to make the only father figure in his life proud? And for what? A century of slavery, pain, and self-hatred?"

"You have endured far more."

"*There is no yardstick for suffering.*" The way the words snapped from Cheuksin were like a whip cracking through the air with the fury powering her voice. A clatter came from Kenichi as he snapped his pincers in agreement.

The way this entity simply stated I had endured more like it was some game of one-upmanship. I couldn't even. I was flat broke, out of *evens* or *fucks*. "Pain is immeasurable, you egregious jackass. It is incomparable. You cannot take one person's experience and set it next to someone else's and just say, 'Oh, well, this person lived longer, therefore they had it worse.' Are you kidding me? How *dare you*. How are you this naive? One would hope that the gods, or entity, or whatever the hell you are, had a single drop of wisdom among them. Apparently that was too much to ask for."

Everyone except the goddess and the jackass had gone stiff with my rant. Anhangá was tense, but with anger as opposed to wariness. Cheuksin simply glared at the entity alongside me.

"You're questioning my techniques?"

"Of fucking course I am questioning your techniques. Look at how screwed up your grandson is now. You call him an idiot? He is an idiot... Because. Of. You." I threw my hands up in the air. "Who do you think he learned from?"

I felt a gentle nudge from behind and sighed, dropping onto a rock next to Aidan, giving Vicky, the defuser of conflicts, a hug as I did so. Cheuky sat on my other side, as my other two wet K9s settled themselves in front of me.

I pointed at the entity, my other arm still wrapped around the sea-soaked Vicky. "I might be a lowly Abstruse, but I have been among the gods my entire life. You do not scare me. You will do your best to repair your relationship with your grandson. If it is even possible at this point."

I wasn't sure why I cared, except something deep inside of me cried at the unfairness of it all. No wonder he held so much hatred for being *hafu* if this is the path it had led him on. It didn't resolve my conflicted feelings, but it provided context for his behavior at least. Cheuksin was right. We were mirror images of one another. Where he had been encouraged to actively hate half of himself, I had been taught to hide half of myself depending on what country I was in. A message clearly screaming at me that I was less than.

Anhangá raised one of his auburn eyebrows. "As you declare. But if I may return to my point before we had gotten sidetracked by my parenting skills, my grandson has been trying to trace who has been ordering the deaths of the guardians for nigh on a century now without success. He advocated for your skills. I do not disagree." He looked around the clearing. "He advocated for all of you. I will withhold my judgment on the rest of you."

I do not disagree, he says. What high praise indeed.

"Why us?" Theo interjected from where he sat. He hadn't moved since I had arrived. Instead, he had been studying me closely. I refused to squirm under his perusal.

"Why not an agency experienced in finding what does not want to be magically found?"

"We do not belong to the agency. In fact, most of us don't." Aidan's more staid uncle spoke up, with a serious expression on his face.

"And we find *missing people*; we don't uncover global conspiracies," Aidan added.

"You may not. But you are well-known and well-respected in your communities." He motioned to Uncle. "You and your Thread are able to shift into many creatures and shapes for stealth, for example. Likewise, the *dokkaebi*."

Anhangá nodded to Oliver. "He is one of the last *kappas*. The fact he still lives speaks for his capabilities in and of itself. You escaped your curse, Cheuksin, and returned to being a household goddess. The *kamikiri* is as close to eternal as the gods. I trust you all to recruit who you feel is trustworthy to this cause."

His soul-searing gaze met mine then. "And you had a hand in shaping the outcomes of the last three lives."

"And I'm just chopped liver," Aidan put in with an uneasy laugh.

"I honestly have no idea why my grandson brought you here," Anhangá stated without bothering to look at Aidan. "He defeated you easily enough. You refuse to use your *ki*. You take nothing seriously. The only thing you have of worth is your four-legged companion."

High-pitched yelps of indignation escaped the Uncles. Aidan sat next to me, frozen, as his form flickered again, revealing his injuries once more.

Before I had a moment to collect my thoughts, scattered with rage, Oliver spoke, his voice all the more powerful with its quiet tone. "You and your ilk have spent too long valuing violence, resilience, and survival. You have lost perspective. Balance is always needed. Aidan is that balance. He reminds us of the good that is in the world. Of the restraint we need to maintain. He brings light in times of darkness. The fact that Rafael recognizes this and you do not speaks volumes to what he has learned outside of your influence."

"Great," Aidan muttered under his breath. "So I'm the clown."

"Fuck you, Aidan. Olly's right. Don't devalue yourself because this so-called *higher being* can't recognize it." I glared at him while hugging him in the same breath.

A long-suffering sigh left the maned wolf. "I will leave you for now; you have much to discuss."

Without further thought, he vanished from sight. I hated how he and the *kariudo* did that. I turned back to my friends and took a deep breath.

"Before we start with that bomb, I think I need to start with the truth."

I HAD THREE wide-eyed males staring at me after I divulged my secrets and I felt incredibly uncomfortable. Cheuksin and Theo were unsurprised. Kenichi and Oliver exchanged looks, something like pride on their faces. I hated it.

"Could one of you, maybe, say something please?"

"You were Ryūjin's Thread?" Aidan asked in disbelief, thoroughly distracted from being devalued by Anhangá.

"You're a *haetae?*" the Uncles cried.

I shrugged, not knowing what else to do.

"I had sex with a *kami's* Thread," Aidan whispered. "How was I not struck dead upon orgasm?"

I punched him in the gut. "Really? That was your first thought? I unload my trauma and that's it?"

He waved me off, coughing. "I already gave you a trauma hug. That's my quota for the year."

"*Maybe not mates*," the Uncles whispered to one another. We gave them the finger again.

I rubbed my wrist. Damn it. I was doing it again. I shook out my hands. "Anyway, I thought you should know the whole story regardless of what we decided, given that we've all been sucked into this now. It only seemed fair. I'm one of the guardians that Anhangá was talking about."

"You finally did it. You let go of your secrets," Oliver's voice was filled with compassion that made my intestines squirm.

I wheezed as I was swallowed by Uncle's beefy arms. "It's an honor, Niece. And we will guard your secret fiercely." I could sense his glare in the way Aidan suddenly shrank in stature.

"Since when have I ever told anyone's secrets?" he protested.

This time *I* cringed. Uncle could put off one hell of a glare, even if I couldn't see it.

"Okay, so maybe I was why we had to leave Hawaii, but I was a *child*. You can't blame me for that."

The glare intensified.

"What even happened to you two in the forest?" I asked to save Aidan.

"*Kotengu*." He sighed with disgust as I inhaled sharply. Aidan and Uncle nodded. "It took us by surprise; we had no idea one was in the area. It was mad from starvation. I don't know if we would have survived if Sugiyama hadn't shown up. He brought us here instead. Did you know he could inflict fear so effectively?"

I frowned, wondering when the huntsman would have been able to manage that.

"After he took care of the *kotengu*, he apologized and told me he was leaving me in the forest so you could find me. So I know where *my* body is, but we aren't sure where Aidan's went," Uncle added.

"You were bait." I grimaced. "He took me prisoner. I'm in one of Ryūgū-jō's dungeon cells right now. A chorus of indignation overtook the clearing. "I'm fine, I have Pea with me. I just don't know what our next steps will be."

I paused and took in the group around me. The huntsman's bastard of a grandfather wasn't wrong. For the most part. Each and every person in front of me had valuable skills to bring to the table. Including Aidan.

"What do we want to do?" I asked them all. I couldn't make this decision for them.

"Isn't it obvious?" Theo snorted. "We're not letting anyone kill you off, Cam. We're all in."

"Excellent." We all startled as the death entity materialized in a black cloud of particles. "That was all I needed. On that note, time to go, Camellia."

Before any of us could make a sound of protest, my entire being evaporated once more.

"I MIGHT ACTUALLY hate you. Your grandson I despise, but I understand the reason why he is the way he is. You? You're just truly an arrogant asshole." I gasped as soon as I recovered my breath from falling on my back once more, this time in my human form. We had returned to the mildewy, moldy dungeon cell where Pea and Dr. Aoki were still frozen in time. Back in shackles. The huntsman's body was now no longer just feet but a pair of legs and most of a torso. I raised an eyebrow at the unsettling sight.

"So long as his soul remains tethered to his body, he will heal." Anhangá waved a paw at the body in that disconcerting way of his. "It was never necessary for your *shikigami* or *dokkaebi* to heal him. Though it did help hurry the process along."

I gritted my teeth then forced myself to relax my jaw enough to reply, "They are not mine. They are their own selves."

"Semantics. They are yours because they choose to be. You seem to be hung up on the concept that belonging is equivalent to possession. It is not—that is but one possible take on the word. I encourage you to branch out and expand your worldview a bit more. It might decrease your stress a bit. Now, we have matters to address."

I might actually kill this entity if only I knew how.

"I might actually welcome it. It is tiring being who I am. But alas, I cannot die."

"It would have been helpful if you had given us time to actually plan." I could feel a tension headache beginning from all the jaw-clenching I was doing around this asshole.

"You have your role and they will have theirs. You do not want them here in this palace. I will send them back to your territories when the time is right. It was unnecessary and wasteful for you to collaborate."

"And what gives you the authority to decide that when it's my territories, my life, and my friends?"

"*Now* she's willing to claim them. Because I am what I am, Camellia Kimoto, and you are a mere speck of dust in my universe when it comes to the particular order of the world. Perhaps not a speck of dust. *A tiny pebble in a cracked dam that is the only thing keeping the river from flooding the plains* may be more apt. My grandson placed you in my sights and I will use you as I see fit."

A hoarse fit of hacking that may have been laughter came from the ground. The sight that greeted me was horrifying. The bone and muscles of the *kariudo's* jaw, mouth, and lower portion of his nose had knitted together, but the rest had yet to return. I watched in sick fascination as he cracked his jaw wide and began to speak, the movements of his tongue easily visible with the lack of lips.

"You do not know Baki well yet, Grandfather, if you think that argument will convince her to your side."

I cocked my head. "You have no ears. How could you possibly know what we are talking about?"

His body suddenly vanished into black mist which danced around me, before that too disappeared.

"I never needed a physical form to be in your presence, Baki. I just kept one for your comfort," the *kariudo's* deep voice whispered in my ear. I shuddered with unease, the chains on my body clattering with the motion, as I questioned everything I had ever done or said outside of his presence since meeting him.

He reformed next to me, just out of my reach, facing his ancestral grandfather. Whole. Healed. Complete. The huntsman took a moment to crack his neck. Once to the left. Then to the right. The sounds of the newly created vertebrae popping were as out of place as the sounds of the chains while Pea and Dr. Aoki were still frozen in time.

"I see Grandfather has been doing quite well at endearing himself to you. Almost as good of a job as I did when I first met you."

"Oh, but you have set the bar so much higher since I've arrived here." I picked up my chains and shuffled as far from the *kariudo* as they would allow. It wasn't nearly far enough for my comfort. "I don't know if it's possible for anyone to reach it now."

He ignored me, acknowledging his grandfather instead. "Everyone is safe?"

The atmosphere in the room somehow darkened, though the light did not change. I could feel the hairs on the nape of my neck rise, and I attempted to pick up Pea to protect her from the unseen danger in the room out of habit. Except I found that I was unable to move her frozen body in any way.

Before I had the opportunity to panic about what that meant for Pea, an explosion of power rocketed through the room and blanketed us in an unfathomable void. All sense of tactile sensation vanished, leaving me feeling as though I was floating out of space. Alone. My spark of burgeoning panic flamed into outright terror, something wildly outside of my experience, despite my long and sordid history. Nightmarish images of my past, possibilities foretelling my bleak future danced through my mind.

"Control yourself, Grandfather," a sharp voice cut through the fear. I clung to the sound, silently begging the voice to continue talking as I anchored myself to it. I dropped to the ground, curling into a tight ball and hugging my knees.

A gentle touch settled on the back of my head.

The voice. "Baki. You are safe. I would not allow him to harm you."

"You think you could stop me if I so chose?"

"With everything in my being, Grandfather." The calm, sure voice slowed the nightmares slightly.

Safe? I wasn't sure if I had ever truly understood the meaning of the word throughout my lifetime. I remained tucked within my tight ball, rocking back and forth. Death. Death was all I could see in front of me. Screams of dying ringing through my head. So many screams.

"Release the opossum. She needs Pea. You never should have separated them."

A small whiskered snout shoved her way between my shins, then my thighs. Admonishing chatters cut through the screams, like the voice had. It forced its way between the arms covering my face and began to slub against the tears on my cheeks. I choked on a sob as Pea's full face came into view and my body unwound itself from my knees and I threw myself around Pea instead, before curling back up as best I could. The past few days had broken me. I wasn't even trying to hide when I fell apart anymore.

"There she is." I looked up. The darkness had receded, allowing me to find Rafael crouched in front of me. The terror had also receded, remaining at the edges of my mind. Leaving its echoes thrumming through my body. His eyes were dark with concern—a deep brown again, no longer fiery pits, but brimming with concern. The voice that had anchored me through the fear. He smiled at Pea. "You did good, girl. You always do."

He stood, positioning himself in front of me and Pea. Where the maned wolf once was, a massive glowing stag now stood. One that was seething with rage, evidenced by the black tendrils whipping around his form. I didn't lean away from the *kariudo* this time.

"I don't give a flying *fuck* how angry you are, Grandfather. You control yourself and your power around the undeserving. We are meant to protect. That is what you taught me." Rafael flung his arm in my direction. "Did any of that look like protection? Or were you doing your best to give Camellia every reason in all the realms to distrust you? I thought we were trying to get her to work *with* us, not against us."

"We lost the *Curupira*." As if this was explanation enough. Perhaps it was. I didn't know. I didn't know all of the guardians around the world. But the fury in the entity's voice at the memory rang through my bones.

"And I am sorry to hear that. We will grieve. But anger is controlled. Not an emotion to be thrown about and used so recklessly that it damages those around you without care or thought about it." Rafael's conviction was equal to Anhangá's anger. There was an undertone to it though. Something ephemeral and difficult to grasp.

Something like wistfulness.

I shook it off and stood from behind him, gripping Pea tightly. "Who is the Curupira?" I asked carefully.

"He was one of the guardians of Brazil. Another one who protected the forest denizens, something that has been much more difficult in this latest century," Rafael answered me. The tension bled out of him slightly as the black tendrils drew back into Anhangá's glowing body. The rage in the room dampened and it became easier to breathe.

"Sansin has disappeared as well. The gods do not know if he is lost to us or simply been taken." Anhangá words rang out with a staccato beat, at the same pace I imagined my heart would have at the news he just delivered.

"Sansin is gone?" Any air I had just regained was lost to those words. "How could the Mountain God possibly be lost?"

"That is what we need you and your cohort to find out, little *haetae*. Because you were one of the few directly connected to the events that started all of this nearly a century ago. Now, you may not trust my grandson. You may not trust *me*. But do you understand the import of what we are trying to accomplish?"

I stumbled back to the bed and sat heavily. Pea scrambled to my shoulders and situated herself around my neck. I took comfort in her weight, though she wouldn't truly understand the significance of what I was just told. Not only were there no *haetae* left in Korea, but the deity that protected the land as a whole was gone. Possibly lost to us forever. I wondered if Cheuksin and Theo were aware of that fact yet. I wondered what Aidan, the Uncles, and Oliver would do. I was unconcerned with whether or not they would care about a Korean deity. That's not who they were. I wondered so many things that were useless right now.

I nodded grimly. "I had already accepted the task, as you knew. But this just settles it further." I threw them a look. "I don't like either of you, but that doesn't mean I don't understand the severity of the situation."

"Excellent." The stag carefully stepped around the frozen female in the dungeon cell. "Let's begin to discuss our plan then."

CHAPTER THIRTY-TWO

Before Anhangá vanished yet again, I glared at him. "This is the worst plan in all of the realms; I just want you to know that."

"You will be fine, little one."

I snorted. "Famous last words."

"You will do what needs must."

I shivered as the last of the death entity's words echoed the words of a sea *kami's* long since passed.

"I will make sure you stay intact," Rafael said quietly. "Whatever it takes."

And I put exactly none of my faith in that. Rafael had already proven to me once that he placed his mission above my well-being. As he well should.

I turned away and faced Dr. Aoki. She was frozen in an awkward position, half seated on the bed, half leaping off it, her face contorted in a grimace of terror. One hand reaching for where Rafael's body had been, the other covering her mouth.

"Why are you so important?" I muttered. "Who the hell are you?" I had a difficult time believing this unobtrusive, though attractive, female, in her torn beige clothing, black framed glasses, and disheveled bun was the Thread of the false *kami*. Although, I wasn't one to talk, taking a moment to glance down at myself.

Anhangá chose that moment to leave, and Aoki unfroze, stumbling into me, screaming in my face. I winced and grabbed her shoulders to stabilize her. She jumped away from me, cringing in fear, pointing at the floor wildly.

Rafael approached her as he would a frightened animal, which was apt, since that was essentially what she was in the moment. He was getting a lot of practice with terrorized females today.

"What do you think of the plan?" I asked Pea as I watched Rafael reassure Dr. Aoki. Something in me tightened as he did. I ignored it as Pea bit me and growled. "I agree. It's shit. We're definitely going to die."

"You're not going to die, Baki," Rafael called.

"You were dead!" Dr. Aoki cried hysterically.

"I'm clearly not dead," he said soothingly, holding out his hands to her. "See? I am here in the flesh and blood."

That beast inside me raised its head up and snarled as Dr. Aoki touched his hands to reassure herself that he was, in fact, alive. Rafael glanced at me as the sound erupted out of me beyond my control. I shrugged. "Gaslighting females hits a certain button of mine."

Pea chittered in my hair as Dr. Aoki cautiously looked toward me. Well. Pea was never going to fall for that lie.

"Listen. You caught me on a very bad, terrible, awful kind of day. While he might be telling the truth that he's not dead right *now,* I'm not going to give you all rays of sunshine. You're right. You did see me turn into a beast. You did watch me kill him. Turns out this one," I jerked a thumb at the *kariudo,* "is apparently unkillable. So, bonus. If he irritates you. Feel free to kill him. He'll come back."

"Baki," Rafael gritted out.

I ignored him. "Anyway. You probably won't recognize me, because it was moments in the dark, during a rainy night, and I had a swamp monster next to me, but I have been searching for you for days. I don't intend to hurt you. In fact, I had intended to keep you far away from here, but best-laid plans apparently get waylaid to hell and back, literally."

While Dr. Aoki looked overwhelmed, she also appeared to be distracted, as if she was listening intently to something no one else in the cell could hear. Whatever it was, she relaxed as I spoke. I couldn't shake the feeling of familiarity at the way she cocked her head, though I was certain I had never met Dr. Aoki before this SAR.

"There is going to be an…incident soon. I don't expect to survive. I don't regenerate like that one does. I don't imagine you do either. So, although his plan involves you being present at the grand finale, I am going to ask you…do you want to be involved?"

"You. Are. Not. Going. To. Die," Rafael forced out through his teeth. His jaw was rather attractive when that muscle clenched. It really brought out how defined it was.

"Um, ma'am?"

I turned my attention back to Dr. Aoki. "Yes?"

"Who are you? Can we begin there? And why is there an opossum around your neck?" she asked timidly. I guess mousy females did it for some *kamis*. The few I knew with Threads were bound to equally strong personalities though, most often with another *kami*. It tended to cause shockwaves through the realms when a rift happened in a relationship. A female like her would get steamrolled by a *kami*.

There was a quiet laugh from Rafael's corner of the world. "The opossum is Pea. Don't offend her and you'll do just fine," he advised her. Pea just preened. He turned to me. "We don't have a choice. She has to be involved. And she has already agreed."

As far as I was concerned, the *kariudo* didn't exist. "I'm Camellia Kimoto. You can call me Cam. Choices are the only thing that matter when the world no longer makes sense, when the world has flipped upside down and you have lost control of everything except for your ability to make a choice. However big or small that choice may be. Pea?"

Pea obliged immediately, knowing what I was asking. Her sound barrier dropped over us, but this time it thickened to an opaque silver, preventing Rafael from seeing in or us from seeing out. Dr. Aoki gave out a small cry of fright when she saw we were sealed off. Truly. A sound barrier freaked her out? *Kami*-dom was going to be a culture shock for her. Which was why I needed to do this.

"You are no more isolated than you were previously, being that we're in a prison cell. We've just excluded a member of our party. I need to know… what did he tell you about this journey and did you make an honest, informed choice? There are far more terrifying creatures in this realm than us, and we will likely encounter them soon."

Dr. Aoki sobered. "I never thought, in all my years doing research, that I would actually experience Ryūgū-jō. Something has always pulled me to this place, but I never understood it. Until I realized I wasn't aging." She opened her mouth to say something else before she cocked her head again and stopped. Was someone telling her what not to say? "I began to suspect that perhaps I was somehow connected with the *yōkai* then."

She continued bitterly, "Except that I don't fit any of the myths. There was nothing particularly special about me other than the fact that I woke up on St. Helens one day and I don't age. Which just left me with my pull to this place. My fascination grew into an obsession."

A gleam suddenly came across her eyes. "So yes, Camellia Kimoto, or whoever you claim to be. For the chance to join this world at last? I would do anything. I was informed of the risks and I don't care. I would do anything to get rid of this infernal *itch* that I have lived with for over a century now. That man outside of this bubble tells me that I'm a Thread? That I belonged to this court at one time? I need answers, Ms. Kimoto. I need answers far more than I need my life at this stage."

Okay, so she was just suicidal. Roger that. I supposed she just fit right in with the rest of us then.

I nodded. Who was I to judge what was sane or not? "Then welcome to the team." Pea dropped the sound barrier, and I gave Rafael a wild grin. "I hereby dub us the Aokigahara Squad."

He frowned. "You're naming us after the suicide forest?"

"It's catchy, right?"

"It really isn't," Dr. Aoki and Rafael chorused.

"No one appreciates our black humor, Pea." She hissed at them in agreement. "The only perk of my PTSD is my sense of humor."

"If you can call it that," the *kariudo* muttered under his breath. Before I could retort, he dropped the wards of the cell and removed my chains from the wall, leaving the shackles on my wrists. Finally, he motioned the way out. "Shall we?"

I eyed the dank corridor before him. "We shall."

CHAPTER THIRTY-THREE

B y the time we had made it out of the dungeons and to the ground
level of Ryūgū-jō, Pea was wrought with anxiety and tremors ran
through her small body. I didn't think she was aware of it, but quiet,
scared squeaks came out of her with every breath. Rafael looked back at
her distressed cries. I spied a flash of concern that resonated in the way
his hand flexed at his side, as if trying to prevent himself from reaching
out, and the slight line in the furrow of his brow, before he resumed his
stoicism. I couldn't allow myself to contemplate what it might mean.
Instead, I studiously redirected all of my attention to Pea as I removed her
from my neck and tucked her in my shirt, wishing I still had a heartbeat
to soothe her with. She immediately curled into a tight ball, her remaining
paw clinging to the strap of my sports bra.

I wasn't faring much better. Ryūgū-jō looked much different and somehow exactly the same as my memories. In some ways it had been modern-
ized, yet it still retained landmarks that would never fade with time. I drew
in a deep breath and dread washed over me as I realized the temporal snare
we had been in. The air was warm, humid with the heat of summer. It had
been early May when Rafael had abducted me. Now it had to be mid-June
at the earliest. Possibly July. Pea and I had lost *weeks* to the huntsman's plot.
Weeks we wouldn't be unable to get back. Weeks during which most of the
people who knew me would believe me missing.

I ran my hands along the bright red coral walls as we approached the gardens, focusing on the rough sensation of the coral as I went, the *ki* of this realm leaving the coral unaffected by the touch of others. A warmth coursed through me as the palace welcomed me home after my long absence away. It was the feeling of home, laughing with loved ones, a hug. The sensation was followed by a period of damp coldness, and I shivered at what it implied. The palace was deeply scarred, far more than it had been when I left. Some of the damage was from *Hyakki Yagyō*, to be sure, but the expansive washes of bleached corals that marred the crimson were far more extensive than what could be explained by a single night. I poured my grief and guilt into my touch, telling the corals how terribly sorry I was.

Rafael and Dr. Aoki stood on the other side of the once-red gates to the gardens, waiting. Dr. Aoki taking the opportunity to take in everything around her with an academic's interest. Rafael was simply a blank slate. Pea clicked and chirped with increasing anguish and dove further into my jacket, squeezing herself around my waist. The bleached white *torii*, with only thin streaks of red to signify any life left in the coral, felt like one last fragile barrier saving me from myself.

My eyes squeezed shut and I tilted my head. When my neck reached the point where it could bend no further, I opened my eyes and stared at the expanse above.

There was no sky in Ryūgū-jō. Only the vast expanse of the sea. Instead of stars, I watched as a pod of humpback whales glided through the waters, cutting through the unprecedented number of *habu kurage* that dotted the dark.

"Take my hand, Baki." The voice redirected my attention.

I stared at the hand reaching out to me. It was a beautifully masculine hand. Not too soft, not too rough. I remembered what his mother looked like and silently thanked Quotes that he was a beautiful blend of both his parental DNA and didn't favor the former *kariudo*. Instead, he was entirely his own person. "You don't need to pass through this *torii* alone."

I shook my head silently and felt a frisson of anticipation pass between us—of what could have been before Rafael's betrayal—before he accepted my decision and dropped his hand. The chain connected to my shackles rattled with my movement, the serpentine movements following the line into the hand that remained at his side, leashing me. Creating an undisputable reminder of our circumstances. Despite his acceptance, his body held a new degree of stiffness that hadn't been there a moment prior.

"It's not my lack of trust in you." The need to explain burbled out of me, despite my brain screaming that he didn't deserve an explanation.

"This is something I need to do on my own. Or—" I corrected myself, "Or with Pea. Someone who was there with me for every moment and knew me as I was then. I was not the same person I am now."

Rafael nodded in understanding, the last of the tension between us bleeding out from him. "I hope you won't mind if I accompany you through the gates? Just as a means to get to the other side. Much like the chicken and the road."

My lips quirked to one side. I knew what he was doing. It was so incredibly risky, not knowing what eyes may be upon us. But somehow walking through together, bound by a chain, yet still separate, felt okay. It was miles different than holding hands with a male who was not my Thread in the realm where I had begun and ended my love story.

"Shall we then?" Dr. Aoki had wandered through the gates ahead and we needed to catch up.

We left the comforting hug of the sea and passed under the *torii*. Again, the warmth flushed through my body as the gates greeted me, but this time it was weak, close to tepid. I halted as we came into view of the gardens set on the steps below us. I blinked hard as if to try to reset the sight in front of me.

This was a special realm, one that adjusted itself to suit each and every individual that had been granted its magic, as I had once been given. It allowed marine and land *yōkai* to coexist comfortably regardless of whether they were in an air-locked sector or a water division—provided they had been gifted with Ryūgū-jō's magic. If someone had somehow managed to find this realm on their own without being blessed, they would suffocate.

Where we now stood was a massive air-locked sector that took up far more real estate than the palace itself. The gardens were divided into the four seasons, allowing one to experience any season at any given time. The immense *ume* tree just ahead to our right, in the first of the gardens we would pass, the one signifying spring, stood tall, yet brittle and blackened with death. No petals made of shimmering gemstones hung from the branches.

I smile demurely, my facial expression not betraying the happiness blooming within me, like the branches heavy with brilliant pink blossoms. Ryūjin declares his love for me under the plum tree, describing his dreams for us. For the first time in as long as I can remember I feel hope.

This time, it was my hand that trembled as I stroked Pea's head to soothe myself as much as her. Nearly all of the vegetation around us was dead, regardless of the season each garden represented, even the flora meant to endure autumn and winter. The *sakura* trees were not rife with flowers made of pink diamonds. The *ume* trees did not twinkle with pink spinels.

"What happened?" I whispered.

"Famine. Drought," Rafael said. The simplicity of his description gave more weight to his words.

I took my first deep breath since we came out into the open. The air was distinctly different in Ryūgū-jō than it was in the Quotidian realm. Or even any other region of the Abstruse realms. It blew with a salty, fishy tang to it, similar to an ocean breeze, but it also should have been vitally alive with hints of cherry, plum, and the mix of the *ki* from the living beings within it. Except the air no longer carried those aromatics on its currents and had a noxious quality instead. The hints of cherry and plum had vanished with the deaths of the *sakura* and *ume* trees, only to be replaced with the cloying scent of decomposing matter. And one bouquet that I would always been familiar with.

Fire. Smoke. Charred flesh.

Rafael's step became lighter, quieter. His posture straighter. His head slightly bowed. The reason for it became apparent as we rounded the next corner, making our way through the extensive gardens toward the palace buildings to the north of us. To the east and west, nothing obscured our vision as we climbed and navigated turns. We caught up to Dr. Aoki, who stood still, one hand lifted to her mouth in shock. Protecting her nose from the smell. Off in the distance, smoke rose toward the hills. A white pile laid before a pit where smoke and flames licked upwards, trying to climb higher. My vision was enhanced enough to identify what the pile was composed of. I wished for a Quote's vision in that moment. I wasn't sure if Dr. Aoki could make out the sight in detail or had drawn her own conclusions from the smell and the pale gray ashes that floated gently around us.

Bodies. Large and small. Young and old. Wrapped in white, their bodies positioned so their heads pointed north. A mass cremation of *yōkai*. I realized now what was so discordant about walking through the gardens. It wasn't just the death of the landscape surrounding us, but the lack of life. No one was out on the pathways. There were no gangs of small giggling children running around playing harmless tricks on the elderly. No groups of adults sipping tea outdoors. No jellyfish floating through the air carrying out orders. It was just the four of us, Rafael and Dr. Aoki in front, me trailing behind in chains, Pea in my shirt. And a pile of burning bodies to our left.

"Mass graves," Rafael spoke quietly to us. "There has been too much death due to the famines and unrest to give individual rites to everyone who passes."

I had heard the firsthand accounts from the refugees. I had seen the footage Rafael had brought with him. The evidence in the bodies of those who attacked us. But seeing it myself was the equivalent of being kicked in the gut while your hand was slammed down on a bed of nails.

The longer I watched, the more my rage grew.

I turned back on the path. "Let's go. We have a Thread to hand over, a liver to give up, and a *kami* to take down."

I was holding on desperately to the fumes of rage as its flashfire threatened to be dampened by the anxiety I felt staring up at the massive doors we were approaching. They remained unchanged by time, as obscenely ornate as they had been a hundred years ago.

"We never discussed something. Since you were listening in and are apparently the mastermind of this whole operation, what exactly are the roles of Aidan, the Uncles, Kenichi, and Cheuksin?" I murmured.

"They're putting together a plan and working on recruiting those they believe are trustworthy. I was able to delegate once you explained my orders and our circumstances, since I am unable to do so without dying repeatedly. Made my life much easier. They don't realize it, but they're essentially Plan *B*," Rafael murmured back, his words decidedly not as soothing as his tone.

"Told you we were going to die. Aokigahara Squad was an apt name for us," I said wryly.

"Why does all this feel so familiar..." Dr. Aoki whispered before he could come up with a retort, as she traced the intricate details of the heavy doors when we arrived.

Rafael and I exchanged a glance. She hadn't spoken a word to us since leaving the cell; instead, she had been whispering quietly to herself, so softly I hadn't been able to catch most of her words. What I had been able to hear made it sound as though she was talking to something we couldn't see. The chances of that were highly unlikely between the gifts of myself and the *kariudo*, given what he was. It reminded me of another in my past, but she, too, had died during *Hyakki Yagyō*. I had seen her body myself. I shook off the nostalgia and motioned to the doors. "There's no time like the present."

He took one last moment to look me over, as if he was committing my image to memory. The idea was deeply unsettling. Then the Rafael I had known during the past week left abruptly. In his place was a cold, calculating monster. The life in his eyes fled, leaving behind a soulless depth. I hadn't previously realized exactly how much he had softened from that first day, until all his edges became sharp again. The atmosphere surrounding him was unwelcoming at best and frigid at worst. Dr. Aoki and I sidled away from him discreetly, but it was to no avail for me. He roughly gathered my chains and jerked me forward, causing me to stumble as he slammed the doors of the throne room open.

CHAPTER THIRTY-FOUR

Rafael deftly stepped aside, causing me to hit the end of my chains and fall to my knees. A boot landed in the center of my back, forcing me to prostrate myself before the crowd. The chains bit into the skin of my wrists, but I hardly noticed as the fragments of my body jarred together from the impact, distracting me with a different type of pain.

"The *haetae*," he announced to the cavernous expanse, his words loud in the silence.

An enormous Ulleungdo hemlock growing from the center of the space immediately filled my gaze when I lifted my head. My thoughts grew still at the sight. Murry had left out significant details about the tree. Its growth had obviously been magically enhanced and the hemlock was littered with scars. The bottom third of the tree was bare, exposing the round cuts from where the *onmyōji* had taken its branches. Scabs encircled the trunk from where they tapped it for sap. Strips of bark just…gone. All in the name of restraining and killing the *haetae*.

I averted my gaze, not wanting the hemlock and its violent history to fill my mind, and found the missing *yōkai* I had wondered about in the gardens. This was a mandated gathering to witness a trial. No gleam of familiarity was found in their stares. Only empty expressions. I had no fear of being recognized here. The glamour I wore now was of my true self, simply with less scars. The first time in my lifetime I had felt free to do so. I wasn't glamoured to be wholly Japanese, nor wholly Korean, as my mother and father had taught me to do once upon a time for my own protection. None of Ryūjin's subjects had ever seen me for who I truly was. It was both a blessing and a curse.

The bodies before me were weary. Dead stares and gaunt bodies. I spotted a few *yōkai* in the crowd with irreversibly twisted bodies. Above them, a wall of carapaces and *saras* that had not existed before vibrated faintly with the *ki* of their deceased. I choked down the taste of bile in my mouth.

The small *sara* there, near to the bottom left, with the small chip in it. Oliver's father. The carapace near the center. His ocean-faring cousin. One who had aided us in our escape from this place. Scars marred the shell, evidence of the fight he had given the former *kariudo*.

A low, dark laugh rang through the room, accompanied by a slow clap. I gathered my courage and looked toward the sound.

Ryūjin, in the flesh. Standing from his throne, applauding.

I hadn't realized how many details of his appearance I had forgotten over this long century. The Abstruse avoided photos as much as they could, so I had nothing to reference. His pale beauty. The full lips in contradiction with a harsh brow and black eyes that gave him a look that could scald you in seconds. The way the vibrant silk draped around his lean frame as if it too wanted to be as close to him as possible. The length of his fingers and the strength of his hands as they met together in his sardonic applause. I hungrily took him in, the voice in the back of my mind screaming at me.

It isn't him. *This is an imposter. Your Thread left you. Broke you. Infected you with his magic for safekeeping when he snapped our thread, and granted you an interminably slow, painful death. And this one…*

The tendrils of power, caressing my face, seeking, reaching.

The imposter may have Ryūjin's image, but he lacked his presence. The power surrounding him was *wrong*. It baffled me how no one else could sense it. Ryūjin's *ki* had felt like the sea settling after a violent storm. His *ki* had felt safe. It had been like being wrapped in arms capable of untold violence, while secure in the knowledge they would never lash out against you, but *for* you.

How wrong I had been.

This *ki* was his antithesis. It raged and seethed like an inferno out of control. Where the seas intuitively knew to calm after a storm, fires knew one thing and I was more familiar with them than any other element. How to ignite and consume everything in their path, fading only when there was nothing left to fuel them or they had been suffocated. My skin blistered and broke open beneath the touch of the *kami's* power, though I knew it was only in my mind.

The foreign *ki* abruptly left my face, its attention newly focused elsewhere. Sound returned to me, the volume turned to max, in the wake of its absence.

"—your Thread." The crowd inhaled and murmured in shock to one another, finally coming to life.

Dr. Aoki was roughly grabbed from where she had remained hidden behind the doors and brought to stand next to me. Not kneel. No. A *kami's* Thread would never be caught kneeling. Words drifted to me, singled out from the collective. Words wondering at Aoki's appearance. She and my former countenance looked nothing alike.

"—must be a glamour."

"—certain that she is his Thread?"

"Shhh." An increase in noise interrupted the *yōkai* I was hearing. "—anger the king."

The blackness in the *kami's* eyes took on a new depth as a cruel smile took over his face and he began to rise.

"You have done well, *kariudo*, completing not one but two of my tasks at once," he said, descending the steps from his throne and approaching us. His silks whispered sibilantly while he circled Dr. Aoki, inspecting her, before stopping in front of her and tilting her chin.

"I have missed your traitorous presence," he murmured, gazing down into her eyes while she remained rigid. His hand dropped, his slender fingers encircling her throat, his thumb stroking her carotid. A long swallow lifted his fingers like a rolling wave. His grip tightened and Dr. Aoki paled, only the slightest tremble gave away her fear. "Like a dog misses its abusive Quote, having known no better life."

He ripped his hand from her, as if repulsed by her flesh, though he had been the one to touch her, and faced the audience. Dr. Aoki inhaled sharply, allowing a violent shiver to rake through her body when he turned.

"You ask me, year after year, what is the cause of these famines? What is being done to change the tides? Talking among one another about how your *kami* has failed to provide." His voice boomed across the room. The uproar died down to a nervous murmur and he threw an arm behind him to single out Dr. Aoki.

"Here is your answer. This *yariman*—" Gasps sounded throughout the audience as the *kami* called his Thread, his supposed beloved, a whore. "She is the cause of your troubles."

I eyed Dr. Aoki as she withstood the verbal abuse. Who *was* this female? A slight air of bewilderment surrounded her while she stared at the *kami's* back.

"*She* stole your tide jewels, and with them, the *ki* that keeps our realm at peace as the Quotes destroy our seas." The rumblings of the crowd began to turn to anger.

It took everything within me not to raise an eyebrow at his statement. Ryūjin's control over the tides had never been reliant on *shiohiru-tama* and *shiomitsu-tama*. When Toyotama's husband at the time had presented the *kami* with the jewels, Ryūjin had infused them with his power, before returning them as a gift to the newlyweds. The *kami* of the seas wasn't reliant on two jewels to maintain the waters, he wouldn't have been much of a god if his power could be so easily parceled out. But it made sense for the imposter to claim otherwise, because he had no power over the tides.

This *kami* required them to maintain his farce.

"I hear your whispers of how the sea king has gone mad with time." The lucidity began to drain from his eyes. A tic began, a twitching in his forearm, causing his ring finger to spasm.

"I am cursed because of this female," he hissed, his voice dropping low. "Your fears, your discontent, the deaths of your loved ones. They all stem from this female. My supposed Thread who blighted this realm."

Because all that ails you will always stem from a female. The motto that every realm has ever relied upon.

"And *you*." Before I had a chance to react, the *kami* was upon me. His hand gripped my hair at the base of my skull. The strands pulled tight against my scalp as I was dragged onto my feet, and they began to give, tearing from my skin. My head bent back painfully as he forced my gaze. A gasp strangled in my throat and I stared into Ryūjin's eyes for the first time in over a century.

They were Ryūjin's eyes and yet not. There was something fractured within them. It wasn't madness.

No, the *kami's* fragmented pupils resembled the fragments of my body. Instead of tearing apart his body, whatever had happened to him had shattered his mind.

He was as utterly broken as me.

Rafael remained still behind the *kami*. A bored expression had taken over his face, his body at attention, but unconcerned. His stare not dead, but uncaring and callous. My memory flashed to his father's eyes, and I flinched as the *kami* thrust me in front of his audience by my hair, falling back down on my knees, unable to see anything but the ward above me due to the angle of my neck. I drew comfort from the slow progress of whales feeding in the sea, their shadows darkening the room. Another joined them, easing into formation right alongside the others. Their songs echoed faintly through the wards, a quiet soundtrack to the milieu. Our plan filtered through my thoughts.

"We will take back our realm through these two females and break this curse. The power of the *haetae's* liver will allow us to heal the damage caused by this Thread." Cheers rang through the space, drowning out the whales. A high cry rose above the rest. A *bakeneko* kitten, frightened by the noise and the fervor in the room.

This fucking plan.

I ripped my hair out of his grip with a vicious twist, ignoring the sharp pain as I faced the crowd before us. My knee lifted. Fists crashed down. And my shackles tore free.

My *ki* rushed back through me, freed now that the shackles had been removed. My time in the dungeon had done well in giving my power time to recuperate. Silver linings indeed.

The *kami's* power lashed out, but a shimmering dome slammed down before he could reach me. It wasn't the cool soothing touch of the sea, or the fury of a storm on the water. It was the burn of a raging forest fire pummeling the ward. I silently thanked Anhangá for the work he had done on my soul while my *ki* rose up around me, my transformation smoother and less painful than it had been in years. By the time I had settled into my full form, Pea was perched upon my head, tail wrapped around my horn for balance, facing the *kami*. Her hisses rang in my ears with my increased sensitivity, her rage at this usurper evident. A ripple ran through the air, the *yōkai* whispering at the presence of an unbonded *shikigami* with a *haetae*. Rafael's eyes widened from his position behind the *kami* as I went off-script. I didn't care. The plan had involved giving up Dr. Aoki to the imposter and I'd be damned before I ever allowed that to happen. Not one more person in my care would suffer longer.

"I must ask," I said as pleasantly as I could manage. "You have killed all of my family in the effort to harvest the *ki* within our livers. And yet, you have been unsuccessful. What makes you believe this time would be any different? After all, if you kill me and fail yet again, I am the last and you will be out of options."

Before the raging *kami* could respond, I rose my voice over the roar of the crowd and met the gazes of the older *yōkai*. "Tell me! Who here lived during Toyotama-hime's illness?"

Silence overtook the room again, no one wanting the spotlight. Even the *bakeneko* kit fell quiet.

I nodded to a group of elders. "Masamune." The *atuikakura* startled at my address. "You were alive in the old times. You are a strong believer in truth and peace. What happened when Ryūjin was made a fool?"

The massive sea cucumber shrunk into his shriveled body as best as he could, subconsciously seeking to avoid the *kami's* notice, and looked away.

A clear voice rang out. "Our king sought out a liver to cure the madness in his daughter and was tricked by the simian. And Toyotama-hime was never healed."

Dr. Aoki shifted behind the ward, muttering to herself while I grimaced at the phrasing. But I recognized the *kosodate yūrei* that rose after her death in childbirth in Rafael's videos. She inclined her head to me. "I do not fear the *kami*. I have already died. To die my final death and lose my *ki* means I will have been united with my lost child."

And that was what made the *kosodate yūrei* truly dangerous spirits. They had nothing to lose and everything to gain.

"Thank you...?"

"Akira."

I gave her a slight bow of respect. She was truly unafraid of the repercussions.

"Thank you, Akira. I turned back to the *kami*. "I am neither a monkey, nor has there been any proof in our long history that a liver would cure what ails you."

The *kami* gave a rasping chuckle, far darker than earlier. His voice deepened with amusement and I felt the fear in the space escalate to new heights. Rafael shifted his weight and widened his stance subtly, as though he were preparing himself. The *kami* stepped closer to the dome Pea had erected and a vicious talon grew from the tip of his index finger. A dragon's talon. Not the same as Ryūjin's and the *kami* wasn't afraid of showing it. He tapped the curved, serrated weapon against Pea's ward.

It fell to pieces around us, Pea letting out a low whimper of pain from the backlash, the shimmering remnants resembling my own far too closely. One small tap, that was all it had taken. He hooked the sharp tip of his talon under my chin and lifted my face, not unlike what he had done to Dr. Aoki, only this drew blood. When he smiled, a mouth full of blackened, jagged teeth matched his talon. He lifted his hand to his mouth and a glistening drop of the blood that stood stagnant in my body fell onto his tongue.

The *kami* bent forward and whispered with that raspy dark tone into my ear.

"I *know*."

Fear gripped my entire being as he pulled away. No, the rumors had had it wrong all along. This *kami* had not lost himself to madness. Madness might include brilliance, it might include empathy, it could include passion. But it would not include the level of cunning I saw in his eyes. This was something else altogether.

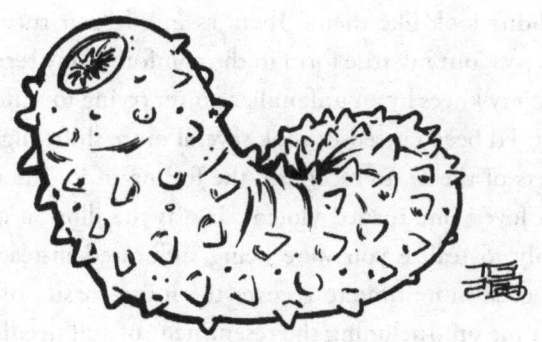

CHAPTER THIRTY-FIVE

The *kami* couldn't possibly know. Pea was the only soul who bore the knowledge. Even Murry had never caught on.

The *kami's* silks swept over my face as he spun to address each corner of the room. "The *haetae* asks how her liver might be different. Simply told, because this one here is a thief. A thief who has been living as a coward in a land far from here as her family fell one by one.

"Imagine my surprise when I came upon an *onna uo* in my attempts to locate my Thread." Confusion knitted Rafael's brow as the *kami* leaned to his audience and they eagerly mirrored him, forgetting their fear for the promises of healing their waters…and to hear gossip. I closed my eyes. *That was how he knew.*

"Imagine my surprise when this *onna uo* warned me that my power had been diminished and that a hybrid *haetae* had siphoned it from me with dark magic. A magic so foul that no one has known of it in thousands of years."

Pain riddled my body as the *kami* spun a web of lies around the crowd, passing it off for strands of gold. Rafael's shocked gaze met mine. I wanted to scream. All of these years, wasted. The foreign *ki* within my body thrashed, trying to release itself from its confines. Ryūjin's *ki*.

I didn't know what Ryū had done for the first few years after the attack. I had been too mired in my grief to contemplate shifting, remaining in my human form, doing my best to pass as a Quote in a land resistant to those who didn't look like them. Then, as my despair turned to anger, I attempted to seek out my true form in the comfort of my territory. Only to be brought to my knees by an unfamiliar power trying to suffocate my own. I had thought I'd been cursed. It took several more shifts, fighting through the side effects of the *ki,* to recognize the feeling of it. The magic was the comfort of a loved one turned violent. It was the illusion of the warmth of a hug, only to realize you were being suffocated instead of consoled. It had taken even more time to recover the roller coaster of emotions the discovery put me on. Including the resentment of still needing to hide my shift, not because of the *ki's* effect on my body, but to prevent anyone from discovering the power I harbored.

The *kami's* voice boomed, creating an echo in the throne room. "Imagine my glee when I finally came upon the yamauba who originated this magic."

A searing gust of wind cut through the air. It would make sense to the *yōkai,* for storms were within Ryūjin's purview. There were only a few suspicious faces in the crowd who noted that this gale was like a fire without the flame.

A body fell from the top of the Ulleungdo hemlock, like the world's most macabre Christmas ornament. Screams filled the hall and the *yōkai* began to crash into one another as they tried to run.

A commanding voice echoed loudly above the pandemonium. "Stop and kneel before your king." Everyone froze at the threat from the *kariudo,* the true terror that haunted their nightmares. The *kami* might sentence your death. But the *kariudo* delivered it. In a wave they all knelt, a shivering mass of fear.

"It is time for us to take our power back and set this realm to peace," the *kami* roared. The feelings of relief and triumph from the crowd had fled, only wide eyes, trembles, and a few quiet sobs were left.

The body's pendulous motion had slowed, allowing me to make out what features remained unmarred by the beating it had taken. A female. She had been tall in this life. Her hair had been shorn, her scalp bleeding in some parts. Whatever skin that remained untainted by the mass internal bleeding she had experienced was bone-white. Gaping wounds littered her limbs, a slow trickle of blood weeping from them.

Then something fell from the tree's great height.

The length of time the small round object took to fall seemed endless and instantaneous at once. It was too small for me to make out any detail. Or perhaps I just didn't want to look closer and acknowledge what I knew it would be—until it landed and rolled to a stop at my feet. My body went cold, as I stared down in horror.

It was an eye. An eye that must have been hanging by a thread, unable to resist gravity any longer. An eye that was horrifyingly familiar with its iris the color of dried blood.

Reika.

A minute motion caught my attention. Her pupil widening and shrinking. I didn't know if I was more relieved or appalled. The body strung on the tree was still *alive*. The *kami* had not found and destroyed her *deba* knife. I stared at Rafael and his shoulders sagged with shame. He was the cause of this. I could only hope his only weapons that prevented healing were in my care.

An immense pressure had been building in me while I fought against my instincts. I was unable to keep it contained as it overflowed in a wild burst of power and I shifted back to human. My present glamour melted, replaced by the Thread they knew. Only with far more scars. I would not hide them anymore. Quiet whispers rang through the crowd, unable to keep to the safety of silence.

"This *kami* with his silver words claims to be Ryūjin, the king of these seas. Yet I stand before you, as Ryūjin's Thread, and ask of you—does this male's power feel as your king's once did? According to him, you have noticed differences. Have you stopped to question—if this is Ryūjin, then where is the *shikigami* that never left his side?" I bellowed from lungs that shouldn't work but still did. The *kami* stilled at my words.

Checkmate.

The opossum's body Pea had been possessing fell limp around my neck. Rising above me was the spirit of a small, deceptively angelic girl who positively shook the palace with the force of her emotions. I knew them well. Grief, rage, resentment, loneliness, horror.

Her sweet voice ricocheted around the room, the first she had spoken in over a century. It was not wrathful. It was not fearful. It was full of disappointment and sadness.

"After all his Thread did to help forge a kinder, more compassionate king for you, you have repaid both your *kami* and his Thread with worship of an imposter. And never once—not once!—in all these years, has anybody in this room questioned where your *kami's* Beloved and his *shikigami* disappeared to, nor the strange behaviors of your king." A tremble had entered her voice at the end of her statement, and she fled back into the body of the deceased adolescent opossum, seeking refuge in silence once again.

Pieces of coral began to fall from the walls as the palace shook again, a great force ramming the ward above us. The pod of whales I had seen. The tremors had not been from Pea's fury, but from *Murry*. The *bakekujira* rammed his body against the wards again, en masse with the pod surrounding him.

The wards I had painted on him with my blood. The new moon had not yet come to pass, washing away the *ki* within them. Ryūgū-jō had taken my request when I had greeted the realm and granted my wish, weakening the wards so that they could be broken. Though I hadn't anticipated they would fall via whale.

The *yōkai* certainly didn't know this fact as they stampeded toward the doors, the fear of the death the *bakekujira* could invoke with his mere presence overshadowing all other fears in the moment. I shoved Dr. Aoki into Rafael, trusting that he would protect her despite his betrayal, and shifted back. I knew I was burning up the extra chances Anhangá had gifted me, but I didn't care. Not if it meant putting an end to this once and for all. The *kami* was making his way to the carefully hidden doors behind his throne. But I was long familiar with this palace and its secrets, and it was fond of me. The realm barred the passage from the *kami's* entrance. I bolted for the imposter, my long strides eating up the distance in two, three, five strides easily.

Then I slid to a halt as my magical sight locked onto his heart.

It was fragmented like mine. Yet...*not*. Split evenly into eight separate pieces that still beat. That wasn't what had stymied me though.

Each piece beat with a normal rhythm, unlike my heart. Some sort of magic protected each shard of the *kami's* heart. Protecting them against the onslaught of sickly green parasites that tried to eat at the magic to regain access to its original home and consume it.

Anhangá had been right. The decimation of species across the *kami's* rule wasn't because of the *kami,* but something else that controlled him for their own gains.

It didn't matter. I lunged. The *kami* weaved to the left, deftly avoiding my horn. Fire wrapped around me, the imposter no longer trying to keep his true power hidden. The heat was at once familiar and a stranger at once. It wasn't the *ki* of fire alone, but earthen in nature, the temperature of lava, cooling to rock around my body as water began to spray from the cracks in the wards.

Dead, bleached coral crashed with increasing speed, the restraints around me making it impossible to dodge their blows. The *atuikakura* cried out in pain as a large slab fell on his soft body, his form making him slow to avoid the falling debris. For once, I wished the shattered pieces of my body weren't held together by Pea's *ki.* My ability to escape the rock hardening around me would have been so much easier. Instead, I was frantically chipping away at it with the spade of my tail, trying to free myself as slab after slab of coral battered my frame, toppling me over.

I met Rafael's eyes for a brief moment. Watched as he assessed my situation. I blinked, convinced I was seeing things. Terror riddled his body, his movements betraying a sense of urgency, his body moving toward mine, seemingly unconsciously as he looked back to Dr. Aoki.

His dark *ki* rose around him, mesmerizing me as he transformed into a full *oni.* Not a hybrid, but a full-fledged demon of massive stature. A leathery, crimson skin replaced his human form as he rose to new heights. His face was a grim mask with four vicious tusks jutting from his mouth and two spiked horns rising from his head. My memories threatened to overwhelm me with visions of *oni* decimating the palace. *That was then,* I chanted to myself. Rafael hadn't been there. Rafael hadn't even been alive yet. I focused on the differences in his appearance instead. It wasn't the color of his skin, or the lethality of the brute strength backing up the tusks and horns.

It was the concern in his eyes when his gaze darted to me, tracking where I was. How he stopped to ensure Aoki was safe beneath a large table made of lava rock. The way he began moving toward the *kami* and me, delicately avoided the fallen *yōkai* who had been downed by the debris. His movements full of anger, but not bent on wild destruction, instead silent and intent. His body riddled with twitches as he fought through the compulsions that had been placed on him. My heart warred against my mind, one telling the other to trust the huntsman. The other insisting we learn from past mistakes and remember his betrayal.

A *kanobo* materialized in Rafael's hand as he neared us, then a roar shook the room as he charged after the *kami*, taking the false king by surprise and managing to avoid the erupting floor as the *kami* drew upon the molten earth deep under the seabed. My useless heart took residence in my throat and my abdomen, pinballing through my body. He had blown his cover. For me. The *kami* would never let him go now. A brilliant green glow settled over the *kariudo*, clinging to his body. Pea, giving him armor and protection against the *kami*, only able to do so through the connection they had formed on St. Helens when she had healed him.

I desperately needed to be free now. Pulling on my *ki*, I sought out the atoms of the rock and found myself rebuffed. The *kami's* power outranked mine, to no surprise, and I was unable to draw from Pea, wanting all of her effort focused on Rafael. I redoubled my efforts, bits of stone flying from my body. Blood dripped from his nose and ears and a rictus of pain marred his face.

A wail pierced through my sensitive ears. Pea. The *kami* had pierced through Rafael's shield, a spear jutting from his shoulder, the core of it still glowing red with heat. Her tiny body curled tight in pain from where she was, riding my long neck with her tail braced around my horn for stability. Rafael took his *kanobo* to the spear, smashing the thin ends, leaving the rest in his body, and charged forward once again. He ducked under the *kami's* reach, twisting, his spiked club smashing into the *kami's* knees from the back. A shimmer appeared around the false king before blinking out of sight. A burst of red light—the *kami's* shield failing. He, too, had a *shikigami* somewhere who had been protecting the worthless *kami*. My heart bled for the pain the spirit would be in now, wherever they were hidden in this place. Needles from the hemlock showered down as the power of Rafael's strike reverberated through the room.

Incandescent fury rolled through me at Pea's scream and for her fellow *shikigami*, overwhelming me and my control. My two *kis* twisted together, blending, mixing, unifying. Working together for once in my goddamned life. Without spending all my energy on tamping down the effects of having two *kis,* the power of a *kami* flooded me and I exploded from my restraints, free at last, the rock crumbling to dust beneath me.

A god against a descendent of Anhangá and a *haetae* unfamiliar with a *kami's* power suffusing her. Perhaps Rafael and I would actually have a chance. As he distracted the *kami,* I began to creep up from behind, my clawed feet dancing to stay in the *kami's* shadow while avoiding the obstacles in my path. There was no fairness, no rules, no pride in war. Only survival.

A brutal strike landed on the *kami's* chest with the full scale of Rafael's *oni* strength, sending the false king stumbling toward me. At last, the *kami* was within reach. I leapt forward, using Ryūjin's *ki* to wrap the *kami* in bands of water, restraining him in lava of his own making as it cooled rapidly around him. As he struggled, Rafael continued to pummel his body, pushing the *kami* closer toward me. I could see the huntsman weakening, each strike weakening in power. It had to be now. I pierced the *kami's* body, stabbing him through the layers of his tissue, past his ribcage, seeking what I needed, closing my eyes and refusing to acknowledge the feeling that I was stabbing *Ryūjin* instead of an imposter. I burrowed my horn deeper, deep enough to access the squirming mass of parasites. Shallow enough to avoid the magic protecting his heart.

The *kami* let out a pained bellow as I began to pull the evil from him for all I was worth, his body convulsing around my horn. Talons struck me as he scrabbled to remove himself. I ignored the tears in my neck. My organs were protected by my jade thorax. I was power drunk; I had no fear of the *kami* in this form. Not with Ryūjin's *ki* protecting me.

Until I began to fall, gravity pulling my horn free of the *kami* before I finished.

My eyes sought out the hemlock tree with its gruesome display. A set of four slash marks formed a new wound on the trunk, deep enough that the tree wept with sap.

CHAPTER THIRTY-SIX

Another haunted wail hanging in the air.

Rafael collapsing to his knees, reaching for me, a spear through his chest.

The *yōkai* slamming themselves against the barriers holding them in the room.

The ward above us breaking.

Water and whales crashing down upon us all.

The *kami* transforming, revealing himself at last.

Yamata No Orochi.

CHAPTER THIRTY-SEVEN

A massive dragon rose from where the *kami* once stood. Not one of the sea, but of the earth. He filled the room, sending the smaller *yōkai* tumbling into walls as his wings began to beat against the crash of water. Others fled for cover, attempting to avoid the swarms of *habu kurage* that spilled in with the sea and the falling whales. Murry smashed through several rows of chairs on the other side of the room, *yōkai* scattering in fear from the deadly cetacean. His corporeal state vanished, his *ki* used up, leaving the debris now *in* his body rather than under.

I blinked blearily, taking note of the *kami*. He was a lush forest green, not the midnight blues of the sea. Eight heads and tails instead of one. I knew he could be far bigger than this. He was containing himself in the relatively small space. Moss and trees covered his back. His *shikigami* was likely trapped in one of the trees, and the realization filled me with disgust. The small spirit would never have had a chance to see the world over this past century, secured away in the *kami's* human body. The dragon swept through the broken ward, plugging the sea from crashing through for a brief moment, before his body passed through. The *habu kurage* gathered behind him, following his undulating body through the waters. I didn't know what they had in mind. Orochi was of the earth and the rivers, not the seas. He was chaos, death, and disaster. The jellyfish would be unable to follow now, not like once upon a time when they had bones.

More than half of the *yōkai* remained in the room, the seas having blasted them against walls, rather than sweeping them through the now-broken doors like the rest. Which meant at least half of them witnessed Orochi's shift. Relief filled me at the knowledge as I began to fade.

Ryūgū-jō would know the truth. The minor *kami* and stronger *yōkai* could figure it out as word spread. Orochi had fled. The realm would be aware of the dangerous possibilities now.

With the last of my energy, I shoved the remainder of Ryūjin's power toward the broken ceiling, forcing the water and whales back through the gap, sealing the hole at last.

RAFAEL FOUGHT AGAINST his body dying, dragging himself by his one functioning arm, trying to make it to where Cam had fallen. The task made so much harder by the rushing current of water that remained, streaming against him through the doors and into the gardens beyond. Why were there so many Quotes' damned barriers in his way? He shoved an unconscious *nure onna* from his path, the serpent-like woman tumbling to the side, without an ounce of guilt. He had only one target in mind. He had promised her—promised *them*—they wouldn't die. Other than the familiar screams he heard behind him, all he could focus on, all he could care about, was that he had *failed* her.

Why wouldn't his fucking body *heal*?

At last, he reached Baki and the distraught *shikigami*. Colors flashed as Pea threw everything she had into trying to fix the female who lay before him.

Rafael lifted his good arm to feel for Cam's pulse, his own heart dropping when he felt nothing beneath her skin. The absence screamed at him in its silence. A sharp nip stabbed through the leathery skin of his palm. His attention turned to Pea, surprised she was bothering with anything other than Cam. A furious chatter greeted him, almost scolding in nature. When he didn't understand, Pea hissed and stood upon Cam's chest, her tail thumping against it several times, like a child stomping their foot for emphasis.

All at once he saw the slight lift as the opossum rose in the air, then fell again. The hairs on his nape rose despite the damp clinging to them.

He met Pea's gaze again, hardly daring to believe. She chattered at him once more, before dashing back to the wounds in Baki's neck. The tissue already looked necrotic, but if she still breathed, the poisonous nature of the hemlock had not yet reached her liver.

"I'm so sorry for this," he murmured to Baki's still frame.

Rafael took his massive hand and dug into Baki's body, working, prying at the edges of the scars she had exposed. His claws were well-suited for the job, having been used to rend flesh for decades. Pea bit him repeatedly in distress, but he ignored her, digging beneath the flesh and finally pulling the Ulleungdo fragment free. Rather than mangled tissue, a void of black revealed itself beneath the flesh he had pulled up. He threw the lethal fragment to the side and collapsed, his body unable to hold his weight anymore.

"Try now," he instructed the horrified *shikigami*. "You can focus on the poison remaining in her body rather than working against the sap in her wounds."

Pea regarded him for a long moment and he felt her judgment down to his soul. He could only hope he passed muster. After what seemed like an eternity, she nodded at him. The opossum fell limp, dead once more, as Pea exorcised herself from its body, and Rafael watched as the spirit dove into the void that he had exposed.

He couldn't be sure, but the unending darkness that created a snarled road map of Baki's body with pitted gaps here and there felt like Yomi-no-kuni. It was as though the land of the dead had eaten away at pieces of Baki's soul and waited its chance to consume more.

The rising of Baki's chest slowly shallowed, with longer pauses in between. Rafael grimly fought off the urge to die to speed up his healing. There was no time for that as her light exhalations stopped.

Cam's body stilled completely on a rattling gasp, a deep gurgling moan exiting her body as her last breath left her.

"No you don't," he whispered fiercely in her ear as he grasped his *ki* and forced it to rise once again. "I told you none of us would die, and I'll be fucking *damned* if you prove me wrong."

A black dome formed over the three of them, preventing her soul from leaving as pieces began to float from her body. Tendrils of his *ki* snagged the remnants as they rose and tethered them back to her body. Pea needed time to work, and he would make damn sure she would have that time.

"Orochi is still alive and I will be called back to him soon." His voice was trying to fail him, the blood drowning his lungs, making it nearly impossible to talk, but he ignored it, urgency driving him now as his *ki* started to fade, the dome over them disappearing. "You wouldn't dare leave these people unprotected. Not Chun-Hei, the guardian. Not the consort of the true *kami* of this realm. But especially not Camellia Kimoto, the rescuer of broken *yōkai*. Fucking fight, you coward!"

Cam's body heaved as she drew in an air on a gasp. Rafael laughed weakly. "Of course being called a coward would make you come back to show how wrong I am."

Pea flew back out of the gap left open, her spirit covered in a sticky sap, giving her form far more substance. A burst of light burned the poison off and she flew back into her body, crawling up to Baki's head once she did, slubbing hard, repeatedly butting her head into Baki's as her breathing began to level out.

Rafael was barely aware of whoever approached him from behind. They fought off a *kami*; whoever it was could stand in line if they wanted to harm him, Cam, or Pea. The figure dropped to their knees and he stiffened as a pale, elegant hand reached to stroke Cam's cheek.

"What happened to us?" the figure murmured. He turned to look at her. A lithe female sat next to him, her pale skin gleaming with a pearlescent shimmer. As she blinked, a nictating eyelid covered her eyes, hiding the vertical slit of her pupil. A waterfall of blue-black fell down her back, kinked and wavy from the messy bun it had fallen from. She wore ragged remains of Dr. Aoki's clothes but bore little resemblance to the professor. Then she blinked back into the guise of the professor. He recounted the familiar screams he had heard while trying to make his way to Baki. What had happened to this female?

It hadn't been Misaki Aoki at the center of this mess at all.

"Toyotama?" Rafael's gaze whipped back at the whisper that came from the *haetae*. "But how?" she murmured. "I shouldn't exist in the afterworld. Not after Ryū severed our Thread."

The female next to him went rigid. "My father did what?" she hissed.

He ignored her, he needed to get this out before it was too late, as his body grew more numb. Gently grasping her head with his good hand, he leaned his forehead to hers, careful not to bleed on her. *Oni* to *haetae*.

"Baki, I am fading. Once I'm gone, I won't return. I doubt I'll be able to with these bands unless Orochi sends me for you specifically. Call on my Grandfather if you need help; he is always watching."

A shift. Fire red and a translucent shimmer danced within his shadows while his *ki* died out and disappeared from sight. Baki's human face now looked up at him with confusion and concern. He would take it a hundred times over compared to the betrayal that had been in her eyes since the search for Aidan went south. Or her fear when she saw his *oni* form. A small hand drifted to feel the bony exterior of his countenance.

"Rafael." Her brow knitted together. "Did you die too?"

He snorted, coughing up blood with the action, his hand dropping away. "No, but I'm about to. You survived, Baki. You will always survive if I have anything to do with it. Keep fighting. Please. We need you. *I* need you. I need to know you're out there when I can't be with you."

Her gaze sharpened, looking from him to the female next to him. "What do you mean?"

He smiled sadly and dropped the glamour on his forearms. "I can't stay, Baki. I am still bound."

"But he *knows*."

"Not everything. And I will use that to my advantage."

"You can't." Her words had an undercurrent of agitation, coming out high-pitched and pressured. Her hand tightened, gripping his jaw.

"I have no choice. You know this as well as I do."

PAIN, CONFUSION, AND panic filled me. I had thought I was dying. I thought I was dead. And now this. Rafael was leaving me. I didn't know how to feel about it. I didn't know what to do about the female kneeling next to him who kept flickering between Dr. Aoki and a possibility I refused to consider right now. I transferred my grasp to his thick wrist, and gripped Rafael harder as his head fell and the muscles in his upper body grew lax. I knew I couldn't, but my heart insisted I could keep him with me using my touch. I had so many feelings about this male. I wanted him gone, yet I wanted him with me. I wanted to hate him, but I wanted the possibility of more. I wanted him to have the chance to find out who he was, with or without me. How could I possibly work through my emotions about him if he wasn't *here*? His pulse slowed, then grew still under my fingers.

"He's gone, Chun-Hei," a soft, musical voice spoke to me and a gentle touch began to pull my hand away from him. "You must let him go now. He has other work to do."

"He's not going to be able to *do* his work," I gritted out, finally facing the female. "He's going to be called back and Orochi will *torture* him for this. And when he goes too far and kills Rafael, he will find out what he is and take every advantage of having Rafael bound to him."

"I know better than anyone what Orochi will do," she said grimly. "But you have no choice."

Even as she said it, a bright light was forming over the huntsman's body. I scrabbled for his large form, pulling as much as I could into my lap, which wasn't much. I didn't care if he was *oni*. He had risked everything to save me. But it was no use. The solid feel of his shoulders and chest beneath my hands vanished as he was pulled to the *kami* through the power in the bands he wore. My arms dropped into the empty space and I stared at where he had been, a large pool of blood the only indication he had been there, washing away with the water streaming through the doors. Pea tightened her grip around my neck and let out a small growl at the sight.

Rafael was gone.

He had been in my life for such a short period of time. Mere weeks, accounting for my time in the temporal snare. And yet. The hole in my heart where he had been beginning to take residence felt enormous.

I was left with only Pea and Murry by my side in a realm that had been my home, a connection to me ripped away by this *kami* yet again. With a female I had no idea what to make of. A brutalized Reika still hanging from the Ulleungdo hemlock. And *yōkai* dying all around me. Whoever had said there was no present or future, only the past, happening over and over again, was right, and I hated them for it.

CHAPTER THIRTY-EIGHT

"Chun-Hei." That damned voice again. A gentle hand touched my shoulder.

I glared up at the female. "Who *are* you? You clearly aren't Misaki Aoki, but you can't be Toyotama. I saw her dead body myself."

She hesitated. "I don't know. My memories say I'm Toyotama, but they also say that I am Misaki Aoki."

"No. Toyo is dead to me," I hissed. I gestured to Pea. "She is dead to *her*." I pulled the trembling opossum from my neck and held her to my chest. The little *shikigami* clicked in uncertainty. I gulped, swallowing frantically, my eyes burning. "Tamayori. Died. You died protecting her and it didn't matter anyway because she *died*. Then Ryū—. Rafael." I choked on a sob, wrapping my hands around my knees, not caring who saw me. All my shields had been ripped away. My glamours, my security in anonymity, my…ally. The female dropped back down, her knees slamming against the floor and took me into her arms.

"Chun-Hei…"

"I go by Cam now," I laughed through my tears. "Chun-Hei is also dead. Dead and burned in the ashes of the past. I don't want to be her again."

"Cam then. We will find a way to get him back. Your stubbornness is your best and worst quality. But perhaps first we should fetch the *yamauba* from the tree."

I coughed. I couldn't be the one to pull a mostly dead Reika from the top of a Ulleungdo hemlock. That sounded like a fast-track to a horrible death. But it'd be worse if we left her up there for her to wake and find herself in that position. I looked around me to see who was left in the room and spotted a *hihi*. I grimaced; they would have to do.

The *hihi* approached us cautiously after I gestured to him, his large baboon-like body walking on his four limbs, dripping water from the darkened gray fur. It clung to his body, exposing his ribs and spine, defining how gaunt he had become during the famine. His large lips trembled as he tried to contain his laughter. I cringed, but the remaining *yōkai* in the room were aquatic and wouldn't be able to climb the towering hemlock.

"I need you to fetch the *yamauba* from the tree."

"H-hi-hi-hiiiii," spilled nervously from his long lips, causing them to flap.

"You *cannot* eat her. Contain your laughter if you understand." Parameters needed to be set, otherwise the opportunity for an easy meal would be too difficult for the *hihi* to pass up.

The *hihi* sat back, his body vibrating with the effort, but nothing passed his lips.

"Thank you," I said, relieved. I couldn't imagine Reika's response if a *yōkai* began eating her. It would be bad enough on a normal day for her, let alone after the ordeal she'd been through.

A shadow passed over us, and I looked up to see Murry's form swim past, no longer with the pod. I had wondered where he had gone.

"Is that Murry?" Possibly Toyotama asked.

I nodded.

"But how? I can't imagine you had the opportunity to ward the realm ahead of time and any of the old wards would have expired decades ago."

The more she spoke to me, the easier it became to adjust to the hope that this person standing before me could be Toyo. My soul cried out for it to be true while my mind violently rebelled against the thought, wanting to shield myself from more potential heartbreak.

"I've fine-tuned my wards over the past century," was my response as I watched the *hihi* crawl his way up the tree. He reached Reika and awkwardly threw her over his shoulder, then leapt down from the great height, landing with a thud that shook the floor beneath us slightly. He laid her gently in front of us and I sighed in relief.

"Thank you for this," I told him sincerely.

A small moan escaped the *yamauba* and her eyes fluttered. I wasn't sure how long she had been semiconscious, but the pain she was in had to be immense. "Pea? Could you help her?"

She scrambled off my shoulder and made her way to Reika, slowly assessing her body to determine what needed to be healed. I turned back to the *hihi*, "Spread the word that any *yōkai* who want or need to relocate are welcome in my territories. We will find a way to make space for them."

His eyes lit up. "Hi-hi-h-hi-h-hi!" This time his laughter was filled with relief and anticipation. He quickly turned from us and ran to the *yōkai* remaining in the room and began communicating with them, his titters and their chatter filling the space. I watched as they began leaving the throne room in droves, excitement filling the air.

"Do you have the space for them?" Toyo asked curiously. I couldn't look at her; the way she kept flickering between the princess I had befriended long ago and Dr. Aoki was nausea-inducing. I couldn't imagine what it felt like to her. Whatever this was, Reika had been right. The spell on her was eroding at an especially rapid pace now.

"Between the waters in Neskowin, my land there, and in Blue Bear, we'll find a way." They couldn't stay here, not until their numbers or until the realm's famines had subsided. They would only continue to become warped or die if they weren't immortal. I knelt and touched a fallen piece of coral, its color fading from its vibrant red.

"Thank you," I said softly. A dull warmth filled my hand. "You might have saved us all with your sacrifice." I eyed the female above me. "Your princess has returned," I whispered to it, wanting to give Ryūgū-jō hope, even if I didn't fully believe it myself yet. The coral vibrated with happiness before it faded out completely.

"Ah, it has finally come to pass." A weak but satisfied voice floated over to me. I turned to find Reika sitting up weakly under Pea's pink glow. Pea hissed and swatted the *yamauba* with her tail, making her disgruntlement with her patient clear. Reika ignored her and got to her feet unsteadily. "Enough with you, you pest. I can heal the rest on my own."

"You might be a little more grateful; you were lacking an eye before she got to you. Who knows how long that would have taken to regenerate," I said with an eyebrow raised as Pea made her way back to me. I lifted the little *shikigami*, cradling her to my chest, and stood. "What do you mean *it has finally come to pass.*" It was a demand, not a question.

I hated the idea that I had been manipulated into this position. The thought that I was just a pawn on a chessboard, to be used and discarded to serve someone else's purpose. Reika ignored me, stopping in front of the flickering Toyo. She reopened a wound with her nails, digging the blood from it onto her index and middle fingers, and pressed her fingers to the female, who blinked at her in bewilderment. Reika braced herself with her other arm, using my body as a crutch to steady herself. A series of sigils in *magana* appeared on Toyo's face, the old Japanese erased in some places. Reika waved a hand over them, obliterating their existence, nearly stumbling over with the movement.

A flood of *ki* took over the room, nearly suffocating in its presence. Or...rather, the deterioration of old magic. A scream wrenched out of Toyo as her shape flickered in and out. Horror subsumed me as I watched the version of Dr. Aoki literally melt off her and into a disturbing puddle on the floor. But the flickering didn't stop there. I closed my eyes against the migraine-inducing display, wishing I could tune out the screams.

When the oppressive sensation of *ki* faded, Pea began to shriek-hiss. Opening my eyes cautiously, I found myself face-to-face with a massive crocodilian-like creature. The nictating membrane of her reptilian eyes drew across her eyes briefly, before clearing again. A massive tail flailed lightly in my peripheral vision, narrowly missing an unconscious *yōkai* behind her. Her giant maw gaped open to show me rows upon rows of serrated teeth in her version of a grin. Unlike a crocodilian in the Quote realm, she had several rows of teeth. The better to rip out the entrails of enemies, she had always liked to tell me.

My breathing grew rapid and I began to sweat seeing the vision in front of me. I had been unwilling to fully accept the possibility before. Not after Orochi had fooled so many in the body of my Thread. Despite my frustration, I knew I could only tell the difference because of the connection I had had with Ryūjin. Who knew who else had access to that magic? But I was now faced with irrefutable proof. Orochi had been unable to take on Ryūjin's dragon form. No one could take on the natural shape of another.

No, this *kami* in front of me was the bona fide Toyotama-hime. The daughter of my Thread and the closest friend I'd had for thousands of years. I felt numb, the shocks that just battered me were too much all at once. The betrayal, seeing Ryūjin in the flesh again, knowing it wasn't truly him, Reika's torture, the fight, the loss of Rafael. And now this. How was someone supposed to cope with all of this?

"How?" I asked in a strained voice. Toyo simply blinked at me, dazed.

"It was the only way to protect our mutual interests," Reika responded to the question hanging in the air.

I turned to her, detached, as I recalled our conversation before I had left for Neskowin. "Define *we*."

"Ryūjin and me."

You will never truly understand what the kami has given up for his people. Reika had told me that. He had given *me* up. His Thread. What was the point of these fated bonds, if this is what came of them?

I waved at Toyo before gesturing down my own fractured body. "How was this *protection*?" The words ripped out of me in a snarl.

"You wouldn't understand," the *yamauba* sneered. "You are incapable of seeing the big picture. You have been selfishly caught up in yourself, hiding from those who needed you, refusing to fight, only thinking about what is important to *you* and not what was happening to everyone else."

My arm dropped heavily to my side as Reika's words caused more pain than any physical blow. My guilt came rushing back, every similar thought I had about myself rushing to reinforce what she had said.

"Ryūjin died so that you could continue to exist. So that his people could live."

"What made him believe that I would want to survive in a world without him? He tore my heart and soul apart." My words gained volume with every syllable. With my last sentence, I recalled what I had seen in Orochi's eyes. The way that Dr. Aoki had talked to beings not there.

"This wasn't the first time he'd severed a Thread was it," I accused. "He ruined another before us."

A swirl of *ki* wrapped around Toyo and she stepped to my side once she returned to her human form, facing Reika. "My father severed my

Thread with Orochi long before we ever met you," she directed to me. "I never understood why. He spent centuries trying to cure the damage he had wrought on my mind. He weaved a tale of lies, telling everyone I had been afflicted since my creation. But it wasn't reversible was it, *yamauba?*" Her voice dripped in disdain. "Did you even warn him about the aftermath of a severed Thread?"

Reika lifted her chin. "He knew. It was worth the consequences."

"Worth it to *who*," I spat. "*He* certainly didn't have to live with any of them. He just up and died. And you say I took the easy way out? He didn't even have to suffer."

"He came to me after the *onna uo* first visited him and gave him her prophecy. Without what he had done, this realm would have perished."

"What does it look like is happening right now?" I nudged a bleached piece of coral with my foot. "The realm is already dying, Reika. What exactly did he accomplish other than pain and suffering."

"The realm is *dying*, but it's not dead," she insisted. "We can still reverse the damage that has been done."

"To what end?" Toyotama looked down on the *yamauba*. "Who gets to determine when it has suffered enough? When our *people* have suffered enough? Is it worth it to the families who have lost their young? To the orphans who lost their mothers and fathers? To the *yōkai* who are now permanently warped and lost in their minds because of this madness? Who decides who is worth it or not."

"The future generations who get to *live* from here on out."

"And how do you propose we fix everything?" I asked, full of skepticism.

"You have his power, do you not? Find the tide jewels. You know where they are."

Find the tide jewels, she says. Like people haven't been searching for them for over a century.

"Look in your heart; the journal gave you guidance. It's up to you now."

Awesome. No pressure, Cam. Just look in the remnants of your heart. You know, the one your Thread ruined. No big deal. Then, once you succeed in that, figure out how to channel that power that's been killing you for over a century.

We were all fucked.

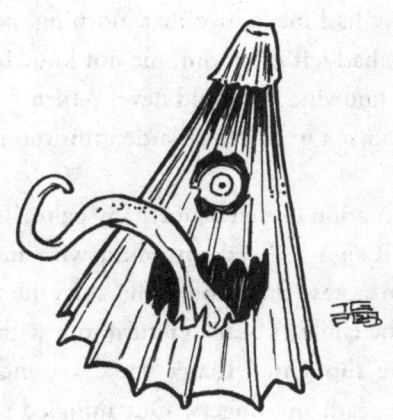

CHAPTER THIRTY-NINE

I stood before a set of doors, hesitating at yet another entrance. It was hours later. After our fruitless conversation with Reika, our attentions had turned to cleanup. Murry and his dead companions were doing rounds, keeping an eye out for any attempt to return on Orochi's part. On one positive note, the *habu kurage* had all fled with him. The downside to that was nobody knew where they went, or the havoc they would cause to the unsuspecting region.

Throughout the entire time we spent removing debris and triaging injured *yōkai*, my thoughts raced without end, speeding through nightmarish images of what would happen to Rafael, Reika and Ryūjin's manipulations, then my brain would stutter over Toyo being alive. But more than anything, my thoughts spun around the journal and what Reika had said. I scraped all corners of my memories for what they could possibly mean and the only thing I could come up with stood in front of me.

The abalone dragon inlaid in the cedar doors twinkled at me mockingly, blues, greens, and an obsidian eye staring me down. I took a deep breath and shoved past my memories and the doors and entered the room, taking care to remove my boots.

My world stood still as I took in the old bedroom I had shared with my Thread. It was as though it had been in a time capsule; nothing had changed. Even dust hadn't touched this place. The sheets were still rumpled from the last time we had made love that morning, before our argument. Before the two of us had left the room, me not knowing what would happen that night, Ryū knowing he would never return.

I laid a hand against a wall. "You warded this room from the Orochi?" I whispered.

An indignant vibration rattled beneath my palm. The energy that made up the palace and Ryūgū-jō filled my mind with images. Orochi's fury at not being able to access this room. The story he claimed in front of everyone else. That he couldn't bear to return to it with his Thread gone.

I snorted at the thought. "Thank you." I wandered to our closet, rubbing the silks beneath my fingers. Our mingled scents rose from the disrupted fabric. His spice mixed with an ocean's breeze. My fire with hints of fir and cypress.

My fingers drifted as I brushed them along the furniture, the rich *tansu* chest and drawers as polished as the day we chose them. A small nick in the corner of the top, chipped when Ryūjin had laughingly thrown me on the top and the heavy vase fell, neither of us caring as he knelt between my legs. I turned away from the memory and faced our bed again. *Tatami* mats with a thick pad laid over them taking up a third of the room, the unmade sheets covering them. My gaze rose to the intricate wall that stood behind them. Elaborately carved wood panels hung from it. Inlaid in the rich wood were gemstones, abalone, and pearls, accentuating a rich garden scene and a dragon looming over it all, watching over the scene below.

And something new glinting from the talons of the dragon.

I held my breath as I climbed over the bed, standing on it and bracing my hand against the wall for a closer look.

"You sneaky bastard," I murmured. "When did you exchange the pearls for *shiohiru-tama* and *shiomitsu-tama?* The palace wasn't just protecting your memory in this room. It was protecting *these.*"

All the effort, all the lives lost, all in the pursuit of these two jewels. And just as Murry had said, they had been in Ryūgū-jō this entire time.

The panel trembled under my touch, like an excited puppy bringing a toy to its owner. If it had a tail, it would be wagging. "Who's the best realm ever?" I patted the wall. "Can you drop them now?"

First, the forelimbs gripping the blue flow jewel opened, the large gemstone falling into my hand. Ryūjin's *ki* surged forward eagerly, unraveling from my magic, trying to rejoin the *ki* swirling within the jewel, overwhelming me with vertigo as it did. I fell backwards on the bed with it cradled to my chest, waiting for the world to stop spinning. When I felt steady, I nestled it gently in the fabric on the bed before returning to the hindlimbs gripping the green ebb jewel, disrobing a pillow of its case to catch the gemstone. The talons released their grip on it one at a time, releasing it with care. *Shiohiru-tama* fell into the cloth, Ryū's *ki* staying still this time, much to my relief. I placed both in the pillowcase with care, adding extra padding to prevent them from hitting one another.

"Well, what the hell do I do with these now," I muttered, heading for the doors I had left open. They slammed shut just as I reached them. "I know you miss him, and these jewels feel like him, but you're dying," I said gently. "You can't hold me captive in this room because the jewels and I remind you of him. You won't survive."

The doors opened again, somehow managing to do so belligerently. I crossed the threshold. "I promise to visit now that we've been freed."

The realm swung the door back and forth in distress. "I can't stay. I have responsibilities above ground." I didn't mention that I wasn't sure how much longer I'd be alive.

The doors finally shut with a soft sigh of air, Ryūgū-jō accepting my words. I gave the walls one more stroke before taking my pillowcase of misbegotten goods and heading back to where I had left Pea, Murry, Reika, and Toyo talking in the gardens, drawing their attention as I approached.

"I have them, though I'm not sure what good they will do," I said as I raised the pillowcase in the air.

Reika shook her head and sneered. "No respect. No respect at all."

"What would you have me do?" I snapped, fed up with the holier-than-thou witch and this day. "Touching them incapacitates me."

I wanted to go home and sleep for ten thousand days rather than deal with a cantankerous *yamauba*. Instead, here I was, trapped in this hellscape by circumstances. Reika ripped out a hunk of her hair and before I could react, shoved it in my mouth and slammed my jaw closed. I gagged, horrified. Not only by the gore still on the strands of hair, but the sensation of *hair in my mouth.*

I hated everything.

"Swallow," she demanded.

Thanks, but I'd rather spit. I glared at her while I did my best to choke down the hair, given that her grip on my jaw wasn't loosening. Toyotama snickered.

I raised my eyebrow once I finished, shuddering at the tactile sensation of stray hairs in my mouth. I had swallowed it all, I was pretty sure. Reika let go, satisfied. I compulsively swiped at my tongue trying to get rid of the feeling and grimaced as I pulled a long hair out, feeling it slide up and out of my throat as it went.

"What exactly was that supposed to accomplish?" I felt no different.

"Pull on your *kis* together."

Annoyed as I might be, if Reika commands you to jump, you jump. I obeyed. The world immediately spun around me as I attempted to draw on Ryūjin's *ki*. I was back to his power attempting to suffocate my own. Disappointment filled me at the realization that the moment in the bedroom hadn't been due to the jewels. Toyotama grabbed my shoulders to stabilize me when I began to tremble.

Reika's brow furrowed. "That's not right."

"What did you do to Tsubaki?" Murry demanded.

"Apparently nothing, *whale*," she threw back at him. She grabbed a crab that was scuttling through the grounds near us and dug into its underside. The *yamauba* spat into the raw flesh she had harvested, then tore off a hangnail and added it to the horrifying mix. Because that couldn't be enough, she bit the heel of her palm until her blood ran free and held it over the mess.

"Absolutely not." I eyed Reika and Pea hissed in dismay, climbing from Toyo's shoulder to mine, using her arms as a bridge. "Not without you telling me what the hell I'm doing this for."

"Do you want to live or not?"

"Not sure. Actually, no. I'm very sure I'd rather die than put that in my body."

She ignored me like a parent ignores a child protesting cough syrup, choosing to force the mixture into my mouth instead. I heaved with disgust. The texture, the taste, the smell. It was all nightmare fuel, *because I didn't have enough of that already*. I swallowed as fast as I could, not wanting it to linger in my mouth.

Toyo watched in horrified fascination. "Don't forget to brush your teeth tonight."

I threw her the finger. She should know what that gesture meant if she truly retained her memories as Dr. Aoki. The bitch just cackled.

Reika just stared me down expectantly. I sighed and tried again. And fell to my knees as my body rebelled even more strongly against the foreign *ki's* attempted takeover. I fought to keep from vomiting. The idea of the mixture coming back up and tasting even worse, along with the hair, was untenable.

"How did your father manage to fuck this up?"

"You're asking me? I'm another victim of the manipulations between you two. Do you expect that he confided in me?" Toyo scoffed.

"What does this mean for Tsubaki?" Murry asked urgently.

"She's going to die, along with the realm, if we can't find a fix."

Toyo, Murry, and Pea erupted in a chorus of protests. Ignoring them, I laid back on the ground, staring at the ocean above us.

"Why aren't you reacting to this?" Toyo demanded.

I shrugged, not bothering to look at any of them, keeping my gaze on a school of fish that had come into sight. I counted a hundred and forty-eight of them by the time Toyo noticed me. Then again, they were quick little suckers, so my count was probably far from right. "All this means is that nothing has changed. I was always expecting Death at the end of this road. To be honest, I was looking forward to it. I'm tired."

That just set off another round of protests, this time aimed at me, while the *yamauba* shook her head with irritation.

Peace would never be an option if we stayed here; it had nothing to do with the civil unrest and everything to do with this circus that was unfortunately mine.

"Listen. Those two tries didn't work and we have an entire realm of *yōkai* who need to be relocated. Can we, I don't know, regroup back in the Pacific Northwest? If nothing else, Reika will be able to access her own supplies and maybe I won't have to continue the torture she just put me through."

"I'm going to take a wild guess and say the chances of you getting out of Reika's concoctions are near zero," Murry said dryly. "That being said, we're waiting for the first group to arrive so we can take them through the linear snare."

Where temporal snares were naturally occurring, linear snares were created when a massive burst of magic tears through the sera between worlds. They were extraordinarily rare and typically created when a *shikigami* was severed from their *kami*. The one Murry referenced had been torn open the night Ryūjin died, when he not only severed his bond with Pea, but our Thread as well. The dual explosion of power accounted for the distance this snare covered. And Murry was the only one who knew of its location as he had been the only conscious member of our group when we arrived on the Oregon Coast. Letting others know of its existence was a risk we were going to have to take.

"Well, this was your big plan, Reika. What are we doing now? Obviously, we can't ask Ryūjin?" If there was some snark in my tone, I wasn't sorry about it.

"Give the jewels to Toyotama. They belonged to her once, perhaps she can be more useful than you."

Toyo let out a sound of indignation. "They were not *mine*, they were my ex's. A consolation prize from my father for Hoori marrying a broken female."

Cackles erupted out of me. Quotes, I was so tired. "He was an asshole, wasn't he?"

"The biggest." Toyo rolled her eyes. "Thank fuck you showed up when you did and Threaded with him. The entire realm might have revolted by now."

"I don't think that would be too far from our current circumstances," Murry interjected.

Still laughing, I chucked the pillowcase of jewels at Toyo, causing a grunt as they caught her in the gut. The relief I had in ridding myself of them was immense.

"Why are you giving me these?" she complained. "This feels like a spouse giving their father-in-law the dowry back after they got married and realized how awful their partner is. I don't want that kind of responsibility. I just woke up after over a century of thinking I was some frumpy, idiotic woman who gets herself kidnapped, but gives zero shits because *Oh my God! I get to visit Ryūgū-jō!* She's scared of everything, but not the possibility of being Threaded to the big bad *kami*. At least that stayed consistent." She scoffed. "And on top of that, I just found out my sister and father died? You don't want me to have that kind of responsibility, trust me."

She wasn't wrong, Toyo dealt with her emotions by shoving them down and locking them away or resorting to violence when she couldn't. She was fine until she wasn't, which I attributed to her crocodilian brain.

"How did I get saddled with two ingrates? How did we get to the place where the two people slated to save this realm don't even care." Reika threw her hands in the air.

"Maybe because we were never given any choice in the matter? Instead, we both had our bonds screwed with, I'm dying, and Toyotama was literally another person for over a hundred years with no awareness of her true self. By the way, Toyo, you probably already know this, but you're an urban legend in the Pacific Northwest. You're the big bad bogeyman to the *yōkai* in that region."

Toyo groaned. "At least I could have done something to earn the label. But no. I was a sad little professor researching Japanese mythology when I *am* Japanese mythology."

"You even researched yourself as the *bijin*. I'm never letting you live that down." I couldn't contain the snickers that erupted from me.

"I hate you. But for real, Reika. What the hell are we supposed to do with these things? My father's seed of power in Cam is—"

"Can we please never call his *ki* that again?" Murry intoned.

"Absolutely not, that's not what we're calling it." My voice chorused with Murry's in distaste.

"Your father gifted them to your husband, Toyotama. Surely he must have included some instructions with them," Murry's voice boomed in the space.

"Are you kidding me? Do you truly think my father would have bestowed his *ki* onto a Quote, of all people? Please, Murry. You're smarter than this. This was before he ever met Cam, and he was still truly a grade-A jackhole to everyone. No, he gifted them to Hoori, claiming he would be able to control the tides. When Hoori couldn't work the power within them, he beat me for it. Hoori turned obsessive, constantly waiting and watching for me to return to Ryūgū-jō so he could return and find out how to gain the power contained in the jewels. And then the bastard got me pregnant." She gazed at the pillowcase in her hand, holding the fabric by her fingertips as though she couldn't stand to be close to the memories they represented. I wouldn't want to either. She would have been vulnerable from what I knew now was a broken Thread.

"Give them here," I snagged them back amid Toyo's half-hearted protests. "Stop worrying, Toyo, they're not going to kill me wrapped up in an old pillowcase with old dirty sheets thrown in to pad them. In all seriousness, Reika—it's not that we don't care, but that we've had our hands a little full for a while now. We just got hit with so many things, we haven't even had the time to process them. For fuck's sake, Toyo has never even had a chance to grieve. And now we have to go straight into refugee coordination. Give us a minute. We're not solving anything tonight. I don't know why you're so impatient. Ryūgū-jō is ailing, but it has time left. Why do you even care so much about an undersea realm? Your home is in the mountains."

A horrifying smile of serrated teeth formed on her face. Not a kind smile; no, this one came with vicious implications you would expect from a face full of teeth. "I have my reasons, which have nothing to do with you. But fine. I want you on the mountain at least once a week until we figure out what Ryūjin did wrong." I cringed at the amount of travel I'd be doing. It wasn't because of her smile, I lied to myself. "Only if I'm not on a call-out. I do still have a job and other responsibilities." Including the work I had agreed to take on for Anhangá and Rafael. "And why do the tide jewels matter so much anyway? I understand Orochi's desire for them if he thought they could help him maintain power over the realm, but I know better. The tide jewels have no practical use."

She pointed a razor-sharp nail at me. "You know next to nothing, *haetae*. The alleged power of the jewels was not what anyone was after. No, not when Orochi was hunting them *and* you. The power must be drawn out of the jewels so they can be reunited with the *ki* residing within you. The power of the sea *kami* made whole again. *That* is what makes the jewels important."

Reika pointed at Toyo next. "And you, you will come with Cam, or whatever she calls herself now. *Kamis* know you'll need the practice now."

"And whose fault would that be, *yamauba*?"

"Yours. How am I supposed to strengthen your *ki* for you, you lazy child."

Toyo gritted her teeth. "I am far older than you, Reika."

"And? I don't see you applying any knowledge from your years. Wisdom before age."

"Oh look, Murry! The first group of refugees has arrived!" I said hastily. "Time to figure this mess out." Preferably before Toyo killed Reika. Which she could easily do.

A ragtag group of *yōkai* had started gathering at the garden entrance, clearly hesitant to cross its threshold. I placed a hand at the small of Toyo's back and began herding her toward them, separating her from Reika, but also keeping her distracted from the shitshow her life had become. The group consisted of a small family of *bitan*, their large bodies reminiscent of a hybrid of cattle and fish. A trio of *karakasa obake* tried to stay out of their way, the small umbrellas susceptible to being knocked over from their single leg and easily trampled. A *chinouya* cringed in the back of the crowd, trembling with fear.

"So. Orochi, huh? You never told me about that," I threw out casually as we walked.

"Fate has jokes," she responded sarcastically, a world of hurt and grief behind her eyes. "It's not something I enjoy reminiscing about. Ever."

"Mmm. How are the voices now that you're back as Toyo? Because it looked like they were all over Aoki." The way she had muttered to herself, the invisible imprint of hands when I first saw her. The strangeness of her skin in Whiz's projection. The way she mysteriously appeared and disappeared even before Rafael involved himself. For the love of all things unholy, how had I not realized?

"Better," she admitted. "Aoki thought she was insane and took every prescription known to Quotes to control them. At least back in this form, I have millennia of experience. For fuck's sake, life was miserable as that woman. Did you know Quote women have to piss after they have sex, otherwise they might get a *urinary tract infection*?" She shuddered.

"I actually did know that. I'm not sad that I'm Abstruse." I snickered as we neared the group. "You get the others," I told Toyo, assessing the *yōkai*. "I'll talk to the *chinouya*."

She gave me a thumbs up and broke off to talk to the others while I slowly made my way to the *chīnouya*, careful to make my movements obvious and methodical to avoid frightening the female further.

Lowering myself to sit on a large rock near her, I regarded the spirit. She kept her gaze on the ground, her arms wrapped tightly around her naked torso. Instead of looking at her, I stared at the gates. "I can't say that I remember much about arriving in America. It was a long time ago and too much happened to my mind and body for me to want to stay present," I began in a low voice, pulling Pea from my shoulders to my lap with the hidden gemstones, so I could stroke her back.

"Arriving in a brand-new world, its language largely unfamiliar, their customs foreign to me, was hard. It wasn't the adjustment to America. That certainly wasn't harder than many things that have happened in my life. It was dealing with what America symbolized to me. Fear. Death. Freedom. Loss." A sad chirp from Pea emphasized my words. I saw the *chīnouya* lift her gaze hesitantly as she listened. I continued on, "America itself was easy, the new land represented a second chance once I accepted the idea.

"No, the challenge was leaving everything I knew and loved behind, not knowing if I would ever be back here." I faced her then. Her tremors had lessened and her fearful eyes had taken on a tinge of curiosity. "The children you nurse will survive without you for a time. But if you don't survive, how will you care for the children? The trees in Ryūgū-jō have died. Without a link to a tree, your *ki* will fade and you with it. And you will need to be ever so much stronger for all the young who have died in these famines.

"No one will judge you on your decision, but I do hope you'll join us. I think we have some trees you would like along the river in my territory. And I know the *yōkai* under my *boho* would be pleased to know that you were watching over their lost young for as long as you chose to." I stood then, "We'll be making many trips from here to America in the next few days. There's no need for you to make a decision now."

I inclined my head to her, leaving her at the *torii* and trailed back to Murry and Toyo. Reika had vanished somewhere, which was probably for the best. Murry had called down the humpbacks from earlier and Toyo was helping the *yōkai* get on their backs, using *ki* to secure them and their few belongings. She raised an eyebrow, questioningly.

"I did my best, but it'll be her choice. Especially after I've been made aware of how few choices we truly had ourselves over the years." A pit of rage was growing within me, but there was nothing I could do about it now. The one my rage should be directed toward was gone.

"Are you staying here, or do you want to help organize from the other side?"

Pain bled through Toyo's gaze. "I think…I think I'm going to stay and help coordinate from this side for a bit. There are people I need to say goodbye to."

Tamayori. I nodded, I had expected as much. I gripped her tightly in a hug. "Tell her I said that she missed one hell of a shitshow and that we have some asses to kick now." Toyo laughed, her eyes glistening with unshed tears.

"She'll be so mad that she's missing out."

"Don't kill Reika in the meantime, if she's still here. Apparently, we need her," I called out as I headed toward Murry, the pillowcase thrown over my shoulder.

"I give you no promises there." Then she subtly gestured to the ghostly figure making her way toward us. "Looks like it'll be new adventures all around."

A grin broke out over my face as I held out a hand for the *chīnouya*.

Maybe I couldn't save Rafael today, but I could help these souls.

New adventures indeed.

And new beginnings.

The end…for now.

GLOSSARY

K - Korean, J - Japanese, P - Portuguese, T - Tupí

Aigoo (K), Terminology: Conveys sympathy or pity.

Aish (K), Terminology: Conveys annoyance, frustration, and/or anger.

Akaname (J), Being: A *yōkai* that licks the scum that accumulates in a bathroom.

Anhangá (T), Being: A Tupínamba entity, guardian of the forests and the creatures within them. It either guides souls to *Guajupiá* or torments them. His usual appearance is a massive golden stag.

Aoki (J), Terminology: Green tree.

Aokigahara (J), Place: The Sea of Trees. A forest in Japan dubbed The Suicide Forest due to the deaths associated with it.

Atuikakura (J), Being: An enormous sea cucumber *yōkai* known for wrecking ships.

Bakekujira (J), Being: The spirit of a baleen whale in the form of a skeleton. It is commonly seen with strange fish and birds. Known for destroying ships, bringing plagues, or natural disasters.

Bakeneko (J), Being: A feline *yōkai* associated with omens. Also able to shape-shift.

Baki (J), Terminology: The sound of a branch breaking. Camellia's nickname given to her by Rafael.

Banchan (K), Food: Small side dishes that accompany a Korean meal.

Bibimbap (K), Food: A rice dish mixed with marinated vegetables, meat, *gochujang*, and served with an egg. Most often cooked in a *dolsot* for a crispy bottom.

Bijin (J), Being: Beautiful person, but generally directed toward women. The Pacific Northwest *yōkai* use this word to refer to a mysterious woman found on Mount St. Helens.

Bitan (J), Being: A large *yōkai* appearing as a hybrid of a steer with a fish-like body.

Bulgae (K), Being: Firedogs from Korea. Known for chasing the Sun and the Moon.

Bulgogi (K), Food: A marinated beef dish.

Chabudai (J), Object: A low-set table, generally with folding legs, used for dining.

Cheuksingaksi (K), Person: Outhouse Deity Maiden. She was cursed to dwell in outhouses by her family.

Chīnouya (J), Being: The spirit of a woman with large breasts who provides nourishment for the spirits of children.

Curupira (T) Being: A guardian of the rainforests known for confusing anybody trying to damage the creatures within it.

Daeji bulgogi (K), Food: A dish of spicy BBQ pork.

Deba (J), Object: A traditional Japanese knife used in the kitchen.

Dokkaebi (K), Being: A goblin. There are different types depending on whether their interactions with humans are positive or negative. Known for being associated with karma.

Donburi (J), Food: A rice dish served with a variety of toppings that may include meat, vegetables, seafood, or eggs.

Futakuchi-onna (J), Being: A female *yōkai* characterized by having two mouths—a normal mouth with her human face and a grotesque mouth split on the back of her scalp with an insatiable appetite. In some myths, her hair functions as additional prehensile parts and/or are limb-like.

Gameshirō (J), Being: Similar to the *kappa*, they are ocean-faring, clawed, and possess a *sara*.

Gochujang (K), Food: A Korean chili paste that is sweet and savory and made through fermentation.

Goguma (K), Food: A Korean sweet potato.

Guajupiá (T), Place: Land Without Evils.

Habu kurage (J), Being: Viper jellyfish (scientific name *Chironex yamaguchii*), a highly venomous and deadly box jellyfish. The *habu kurage* in Ryūgū-jō are deadlier than their Quotidian counterpart.

Haetae (K), Being: Known for their lionlike bodies that are covered in scales with a horn upon their heads. Camellia is an older version of the *haetae* and possesses a dragon's head.

Hai (J), Terminology: "Yes/I understand."

Hakama (J), Object: Traditional Japanese pants styled from the *samurai*.

Hangul (K), Terminology: The Korean alphabet system.

Hanja (K), Terminology: Korean language written in Chinese characters, predating *hangul.*

Hanzaki (J), Being: A giant salamander *yōkai* which grows far larger than its Quotidian counterpart. As they grow, they may begin eating livestock or humans.

Hihi (J), Being: A *yōkai* that resembles a baboon and has long, flappy lips. They are characterized by their distinctive laughter and are known for consuming wild animals and the occasional person.

Hyakki Yagyō (J), Event: The Night Procession of One Hundred Demons.

Ikebana (J), Terminology: Style of floral arrangement.

Jorōgumo (J), Being: A female *yōkai* that possesses arachnid traits. She is soulless and is known for preying on young, handsome men.

Kami (J), Terminology: God

Kamikiri (J), Being: A large mantid *yōkai* known for cutting hair.

Kanabō (J), Object: A spiked club.

Kanji (J), Terminology: Japanese written characters.

Kappa (J), Being: A *yōkai* known for dwelling in rivers and lakes. They are known for their *saras* and may be a deity or demonic.

Karakasa obake (J), Being: A *yōkai* spirit that takes the shape of an umbrella with a single foot.

Kariudo (J), Terminology: Huntsman.

Ki (J), Terminology: The magic that the Asian Abstruse derive their power from. May also be spelled *gi* (Korean) or *qi* (Chinese).

Kijibae (K), Terminology: An affectionate way of calling a female friend a "bitch."

Kimengani (J), Being: A crab *yōkai* that has a samurai-face on its shell due to being possessed by a *samurai's* soul.

Kimoto (J), Terminology: One who lives beneath the trees.

Kitsune (J), Being: A many-tailed vulpine *yōkai.*

Kodama (J), Being: A Japanese spirit that dwells within trees. They are benevolent unless they have been torn from their tree and cursed.

Kosodate yūrei (J), Being: A female Japanese spirit who has died in child-birth. Their afterlife is spent trying to find and ensure the well-being of their child.

Kotengu (J), Being: A large birdlike *yōkai* that possesses human traits as well. Known for their destructive and violent ways.

Kuro bōzu (J), Being: A dark, shadow-like *yōkai* that spreads disease and steals the breath of their victims.

Kuso (J), Terminology: Shit.

Maemmae (K), Object: Stick or other object used for spanking.

Magana (J), Terminology: An ancient Japanese writing system.

Misaki (J), Terminology: Beautiful bloom.

Mukwa (K), Title: Korean military office in the highest class from the Chosn era.

Namazu (J), Being: An enormous catfish *yōkai* capable of causing earthquakes.

Nhanderuvuçú (T) Being: The Tupí-Guarani creator entity.

Nukekubi (J), Being: A female *yōkai* with a head that detaches from her body. Known for drinking blood.

Nure onna (J), Being: A female *yōkai* with a snakelike body and the upper torso of a woman. They are vampiric and are found near bodies of water.

Obaasan (J), Terminology: Grandmother.

Okaasan (J) Terminology: Mother.

Oni (J), Being: A bearded demon with tusks, typically with blue or red skin.

Oni baba (J), Being: A demon witch known for looking like an elderly woman or hag-like.

Onikuma (J), Being: A demon bear known for being far larger than their Quotidian counterpart. They are typically solitary, but have been known to eat humans.

Onmyōji (J), Being: Diviners with a connection to Wood, Fire, Earth, Metal, and Water.

Onna uo (J), Being: A massive fish with the head of a woman. They are known for their prophetic abilities.

Que caralho (P) Terminology: "What the fuck?"

Rokurokubi (J), Being: A female *yōkai* with an extendable neck.

Ryūgū-jō (J), Place: The undersea realm of Ryūjin.

Ryūjin (J), Being: The Japanese God of the seas.

Sama (J), Terminology: An honorific that implies a rank higher than one-self. May also be used for deities.

San (K), Object: Mountain.

Sansin (K), Being: Mountain Deity.

Sara (J), Object: Saucer that sits on top of a *kappa's* head and holds their strength-giving water.

Shikigami (J), Being: A small spirit known for possessing small objects or animals. They are bonded against their will to *kami* for their power.

Shiohiru-tama (J), Object: Ebb-tide jewel.

Shiomitsu-tama (J), Object: Flow-tide jewel.

Shirikodama (J), Object: An outdated belief that there was a ball-like organ called a *shirikodama* at the opening of the anus that was coveted by the *kappa* and was the reason why *kappa* would snatch humans and drown them.

Shishi (J/P*), Terminology: Urine or to urinate.

**Technically a word from Hawaiian Pidgin/Creole stemming from the Japanese word shiko/shito or the Portuguese word xixi.*

Sinhwa (K) Place: Hell realm.

Ssam (K), Food: A style of eating meat wrapped in a leafy green.

Ssamjang (K), Food: A dipping sauce often used when eating *ssam.*

Sua puta (P) Terminology: "You bitch."

Suītopī (J), Terminology: Sweet pea.

Tamatebako (J), Object: A small box. When opened, it will bring Death to immortal *yōkai.*

Tansu (J), Object: Antique Japanese cabinetry.

Tanto (J) Object: A Japanese short sword.

Tanuki (J), Being: A *yōkai* that takes the form of a raccoon-dog. They derive their power from their scrotums, which they use for all manner of things, including shape-shifting.

Tatami mat (J), Object: A soft mat made from grass and straw that is used for flooring.

Toki (K), Animal: Rabbit/Bunny/Hare.

Torii (J), Objects: Traditional gates, often found at the entrance of a shrine.

Tsubaki (J), Terminology: Camellia.

Umami (J), Terminology: A delicious savory flavor.

Umibōzu (J), Being: A massive black, humanlike being found in the oceans. Known for destroying ships.

Ushi oni (J), Being: A *yōkai* with an arachnid body, though they have six legs, and an ox's head. Known for their violence.

Yamauba (J), Being: Near synonymous with *oni baba,* these witches are known for being mountain hags.

Yariman (J), Terminology: Slut/whore.

Yōkai (J), Being: Oftentimes, this word is inferred to mean monster or demon; however, in its truest sense, *yōkai* is used as a descriptor for eerie and supernatural phenomena that may range from cryptids, spirits, demons, ghosts, monsters, and sprites, to things that go bump in the night.

Yomi/Yomi-no-kuni (J), Place: The Japanese underworld realm.

Yuki onna (J), Being: A Japanese winter witch.

ACKNOWLEDGEMENTS

Well. I did it. Finally! I began writing this book in 2021. The pandemic had been going on for some time at that point—but beyond the stress of the time, I had undergone some major life changes. The most significant of these included the diagnosis of two brain aneurysms and the subsequent surgery to stent the larger of the two to manage the symptoms I had been experiencing. In the midst of all of this, I was diagnosed with a multitude of other chronic medical conditions which necessitated a huge shift in my career to accommodate my new health status. To say the least, it was a pretty scary time for my husband and me.

So, I began writing secretly as a distraction from the major stressors in my life. I didn't tell anyone what I was doing, because to be quite frank, I had no idea if it would actually go anywhere. I made it half-way through this book before I finally told my husband.

When I tell you this man was PUMPED, realize that this is a complete and utter under exaggeration. As my dedication says, he has been my ultimate cheerleader throughout *all* of this. Not just the completion of this book, but all the health issues I've had since then. He has sat by my side through the multiple surgeries and angiograms I have gone through since then. He has been there to celebrate my wins and to build me back up during the losses. I could not have possibly done this without him. And no one was more excited than him when I told him I had finally written the words *The End*.

In addition to this fabulous man:

Aria Lockley—thank you for being the best author friend and buddy writer a girl could ask for. Here's to many more writing sprints in our future!

Andreia—not only for being a fantastic friend, but also my source for Portuguese phrases.

Cheree—my amazing Beta reader and fellow trauma bonder in literature.

Nikki and Liz—Y'all know why you're in here. This past year has been even better with the two of you in my life. Future girls trip, here we come.

Rena—The COVER ART. Oh my God. I can't even express how excited I was to work with you on it and see how much more *stunning* it became with each stage.

Holly—For the wonderful editing services and catching me when I couldn't count.

And last but absolutely not least—to any readers who were willing to take the risk and picked up Book One of *Tethered Threads*, I love you for it and I promise Book 2 won't take me four years to write.

ABOUT THE AUTHOR

SM Hyun is a Korean-Japanese American author who currently lives in the great frozen north of Alaska, though she spent a great deal of time in the Pacific Northwest. She resides with her very own book boyfriend as her longtime husband with a giant floof of a dog and a void kitty, who are the greatest supporters while being the biggest distractors. She grew up on fairy-tales handed down from her Japanese grandparents and folk songs from her Korean mother. Her favorite genres are epic and urban fantasy and she loves the growing representation of diversity in literature. So she decided to reach for the stars and give it a try.

FOLLOW SM HYUN

JOIN SM HYUN'S DISCORD GROUP AND BECOME AN ABBIE

NEWSLETTER
sm-hyun.com/subscribe